1

LLOYD H. MULLER

FAMILY TALES
AND
LETTERS

www.amazon.com

Copyright 2006 by Lloyd H. Muller

Library of Congress Cataloging in Publication Data
Muller, Lloyd, 1939

ISBN: 978-1452886480

www.amazon.com

PROLOGUE

Gentle Reader,

I am Ephraim Malone, late of His Majesty's British Legion. My story tells of our family's trials from serving truly our gracious king, George III. Of particular interest are the actions of my mother, Mistress Wyanne Malone.

How many years have passed since the start of this story? It is difficult to know when her life began here in America. When did it start?

We really aren't sure. We know that she came from Ireland as a young girl. I was born here in 1759, and she was already twenty-five or so. She had already served her indenturement. Otherwise, she wouldn't have received permission to marry. That means she had lived in America for about ten years. So, let's say 1750. But Ma was never very clear on this point.

Why? That's not very clear either.

We know her brother came first. Perhaps he was the reason. Perhaps he provided some help in arranging her indenturement. Yet, she never particularly mentioned him. So, we can't assume that they were very close. But then, again, when a brother is wanted by the law, perhaps silence is better. I actually met him once which was a forgettable experience as you will later see for yourself.

Again, Ma wasn't helpful on saying why she came. She would always say that life began here in America and the Old Country was dead. It still is amazing that she felt this way considering how loyal she was to the king. But, who knows?

So, at this point, let us begin her story and have you decide. One point, dear reader. This is my mother's story and where she told us directly what happened to her or what she saw, I have inserted these remarks into this narrative. Otherwise, I have tried to record her story based on the best information t I could get. Finally, you will see my own observations and personal narratives as the story progresses. I did so to provide insights on events that affected our family's fortunes.

Ephraim Malone
Hope Town, Bahamas
1810

Drayton Hall

1750 - 1755

CHAPTER ONE

The *Singing Siren* had arrived on a November morning tide several hours ago. The sun was hardly coming up over the horizon, and dew still covered the wharf. However, the docks were already loud and full of men sweating over cargo being off loaded. Piles of cloth, nails, rope, and who knows what else were growing as more packets were being swung over the gunwale by gantries controlled by complicated blocks and tackle.

Elsewhere around the port, other sights and sounds and smells were evident. Fishermen were bringing in their early catch for sale at the local markets. Some were already crying their harvest to fishmongers. Others were transferring their catches to wagons that would go to the Fish Market. Nets only recently underwater were now being spread for drying under the new sun.

Further, a sour stink was drifting from another ship. Old timers often remarked how slavers could be smelled miles away even during light winds. This one was no exception. Also, this sad scene was accompanied by mournful groans, clanking chains and cracking whips. The cargo was being pushed impatiently to auction blocks down on a short street named Vendue Range. Certainly it was something never to be forgotten; but here, it was simply part of life's rhythms

Further beyond, dancing horses were pulling elegant carriages. Inside them were plantation growers anxiously awaiting their latest silks that had been ordered from England almost a year ago. Wives and fashions must be served. Hopefully, the fashion illustrations that came in last month were still the rage in London. Six months to find out what was happening back home is simply unbearable.

These packages were being broken apart immediately by the side of the main thoroughfare that was called East Bay. Spanish moss lay strewn around the boxes as having served its purpose of packing material for the contents that lay within the containers.

Behind the gentlemen were heavier wagons brought for hauling cargo needed for more mundane uses. Plows for the fields. Harnesses for horses and oxen. Shovels, spades, hoes, ropes, blocks and tackle. Books on the latest developments in agriculture. Here and there an elegant piece of furniture could be seen.

Elsewhere, outbound cargoes were awaiting shipment back to England. They would have wait for several more days until the ship was off loaded. Probably a week and the ship would be ready to set sail again if all went well. Typical of these goods were rice, indigo and perhaps some tobacco. Tars and resins for sealing ship hulls could be smelled. Charles Town did have some distilleries and kegs of rum could be seen; but that was a cargo more commonly seen in Boston. . More was still awaiting transfer from the port agents' warehouses that lined East Bay Street. This particular stretch of the wharf was known as Rainbow Row after the bright colors that festooned these work-a-day storage sites. Further along this same street could be seen taverns and bawdy houses where sailors spent their wages or were occasionally shanghaied onto a new crew.

Here and there, one could see customs inspectors wandering around to check these activities, stopping now and then to talk with a ship's captain or crewman. These officials were to ensure that all inbound cargoes came only from English factories and that the outbound cargoes would only go there. Of course, the ships were also expected to be English.

His Majesty's *Navigation Laws* governed these inspectors because the colonies were founded to support the home country. After all, any trade with other nations such as the French or the Dutch would be hurtful to the king's struggle for empire. Consequently, taxes and severe penalties awaited anyone who violated these laws.

In point of fact, these inspectors were not well paid and they also had families to support. Besides, they had lived in America for many years and understood how people here needed to make a profit wherever it could be found. And certainly, profits had to be divided, didn't they? Of course they were and as long as the horses weren't disturbed, who was the wiser?

Out of this chaos slipped a small, redheaded girl. Glancing about in all directions while trying to dodge cursing stevedores and impatient animals, a frightened deer comes to mind. Her gray, simple woolen dress hung limply off a thin frame that was still lank and growing. She had neither the chubbiness of a baby nor the fullness of maturity. In her hand was a simple carpetbag that was clearly not full. It hung as limply as her dress. One would guess that she was about fourteen or fifteen years old and wonder why she was here.

Shortly, her stomach would begin to add to her misery as it discovered that the ground doesn't move like the sea had for the past three months.

"What in the name of God have I done?" she asked herself for the tenth time this morning. It was a question she had asked herself many times during her ocean trip. The question was more of a prayer during the storm last week. One sailor was lost falling from a spar.

"Where am I? Kevin said for sure that he'd be here to meet me, and I don't see him. Maybe he didn't get the letter I had sent before departing. I was very clear about which ship I was coming in on."

"Am I really in Charles Town...what is that awful smell? Dublin is no rose, but this is awful. It seems to be coming from that ship over there."

"Excuse me. I'm sorry. I'll try to be more careful," she mumbled to another swearing stevedore.

"People here are very rude. After all, I just got here and what'm I supposed to know?"

"Oh God, Ma. Whatever made me think that I wanted to come here? Our soddy was cold and food was scarce, but at least I knew where I was."

"Oh Ma...what wouldn't I give to be home with ye."

"Now what? That man seems to be looking at me. My God, he's a black man...oh no, he's coming to me...now what? Where can I go to dodge him? Oh Ma...why ain't I at home with ye? And now, me stomach's startin' to hurt."

"Excuse me Missy...Is you Wyanne?"

"Yes. But who're you and why do ye know me?"

"I's Sam, and I come to pick you up."

"And take me where?"

"What?" Sam asked chuckling. "You don' know where you's goin'? After coming all this way? No really, Massah Drayton been waiting a long time fo you."

"Umm....you mean, the John Drayton family?"

"Yes 'm. That be them."

"Then where's me brother, Kevin?"

Taking her bag from her, Sam led a path through the wharf to a wagon pulled by a mule. Throwing the satchel in the back, he lifted Wyanne lightly onto a bench seat. Then, getting in himself, Sam clucked the mule into a slow shuffle.

9

Several minutes later, Wyanne asked again, "Where's me brother? He promised to be here."

"He gone. Been gone fo' about a month. I heerd he got run off."

"Not surprising," mumbled Wyanne.

"What dat is?" asked Sam.

"Not surprising, I said."

"What dat is?"

"He left Ireland one step ahead of the sheriff"

"What dat is?"

"He was a gamekeeper who liked to keep game for himself. And poaching the lord's pheasant is good for a hanging. So, one night after being out all hours, coming home totally soaked and out of breath, he decided it was time to leave. That was about five years ago and was the last I saw of him."

Sam urged the mule into a slightly faster shuffle, and thought that over for a while as he headed along East Bay toward Queen Street.

"Seems like he hain't changed much," Sam mused.

"What'd he do here?" asked Wyanne.

"Got caught selling the Massah's sheep to a neighbor, and again, he thought he oughtta be heading west."

"How long ago was that?"

"About a month ago or so," replied Sam.

"Just about the time I was well away on my trip...so I suppose I've seen the last of Kevin."

"Yessum, I suppose so. I don' suppose it heps you any with the Draytons neither. They certainly be wondering if you also have light fingers."

"Oh God" moaned Wyanne. "As if I don't have problems enough. Pull over fast!"

"What? Oh, I see," laughed Sam as Wyanne leaned over the wagon to throw up. "That happened ter me when I'uz pulled off the slave ship. "Course I hain't et for a couple of days then and I was feelin' poorly."

Wiping her mouth with the fringe of her skirt, Wyanne asked: "Sam, if Kevin's a thief, what should I do? I can't go back home."

"Well, the Massah's a good man as owners go. I guess you better have a good talk with him when you first meet him. Tell him you know about your brother and while he may be a thief, he ain't you and you would 'ppreciate a proper chance."

A second or two passed, and Sam continued: "Besides he done paid for yo' transportation and he might as well get somethin' back for his investment."

"I guess. I hope," replied Wyanne.

Their conversation fell into a lull and a few minutes passed while Wyanne took stock of this stranger who had picked her up. She had already seen black people among the sailors aboard her ship. So, seeing another one was not a total surprise to her. However, Sam was the first one she had ever been close to, and she was curious about what she saw.

Sam was not coal black as she generally assumed was true of Africans. Rather he had a coffee-and-cream complexion that indicated a mixed parentage. Otherwise, he was typical man being about five feet nine inches and weighing about 10 stones. His arms and hands indicated a long history of hard work. They were strong, but also calloused and covered with a variety of scars from the nicks and cuts absorbed through his life. One thing that riveted Wyanne was Sam's clear green eyes. That she had never seen before.

This man's language was also surprisingly understandable as opposed to that of the sailors aboard ship. They were just impossible to understand. But, still, Sam's accent was strangely rhythmic, which took a minute to accept and follow.

As Wyanne pondered these impressions, despite the mule's shuffle, they had already passed out of the harbor area and were now entering the center of town. Sam had turned off Queen Street and shortly turned left onto Meeting Street. The houses that appeared now were easily the finest she had ever seen.

Most of the houses tended to follow a common design. Their street faces were very narrow, usually one room wide and two stories high with a door at the south

11

corner. The building material was usually brick, but other types could also be seen. Colors varied but most often the homes were painted white. Their biggest surprise came when one peered through the wrought iron entry gates.   Beautiful gardens lay hidden like seraglios in front of long pillared porches that followed each floor. Palms, shrubs, flowers, palmettos, box woods and bricked or cobblestone walkways whispered of quiet elegance. Each garden was different but each blended into the next like a kaleidoscope of symmetry, colors, and form.

Despite her upset stomach and fears about Kevin's sudden departure, Wyanne was stirred with curiosity about this new world. At least she was still alive and going somewhere. Someone even knew who she was and he seemed to know what they were doing.

"Where're we headed?" she asked.

"Fust, to the Massah's house here in town and then out to the plantation."

"How long will that be taking?"

"Well, let's see, I figure we be an hour fo lunch here and then it be about nine or ten miles out to the plantation"

"Ten miles! Hmmm, ok. That's not too bad."

"But of course, we have to take a ferry across the Ashley river, and they schedules be a sometime thing," replied Sam.

"So, we won't be getting in before dark, it sounds like."

"Yassum" replied Sam. "It be a good thing the ship came in on the morning tide. Otherwise, we could've been stuck riding through the night."

"Where'll we eat? Not that my stomach can handle anything now."

"You be getting' hungry soon enough," said Sam. "But not to worry. We'ze goin' by the town house where we get somethin' to eat. Then, later we'll have a picnic that we be bringing along."

The wagon continued on for several more minutes down Meeting Street past various houses and churches until Old Sal turned right onto *Ladson Street* and then stopped abruptly at the first gate on her left. Sam got out and tied the mule to a hitching stone by the side of the street.

12

This particular house was larger than others Wyanne had seen.

"Well, we'ze here," sighed Sam. "We be eating here and getting a basket for along the way."

"Here" was most impressive. First, it was larger than most of the houses Wyanne had seen so far. It was easily two rooms wide. In fact, she could see three windows on its second floor and below was a large bay window that permitted light into both the ground floor and the second floor. Like many of the other houses, it was also painted white, but since it was made of wood, the entire house was white and shown forth like a beacon on the street. Even the doors bespoke of cheer with their bright red and blue colors. The grounds were also much larger. Instead of the narrow and rather dark gardens seen before, this one was spacious and open. Really, it resembled a playground for children with ample "four-o'clock" bushes for hide-and-seek. Even the surrounding wall was inviting. It was very low and surmounted with delicately wrought iron rods and gates. Passersby could easily see within.

"What a house," breathed an awestruck Wyanne. "Does it also belong to the Draytons? What else have they got?"

"Yassum. This be their town house. The main one, out in the country is where we be headed. But, as I said, we kin set a spell here, eat and then head on out to the plantation."

Heading through the gate, Sam went into to a near-by shed and returned with a feed bag. This he strapped over the mule's nose. "There you are, Old Sal, something for you, oats for lunch. Water be coming later before we take off."

Returning to Wyanne, Sam led her to the rear entrance and knocked on the door. Shortly a woman, apparently another slave thought Wyanne, answered it.

"Yes, Sam?" answered the lady.

"This here's Miss Wyanne and we be here to get a bite to eat and a picnic before we take off for the plantation. Miss Wyanne, this here's Betsy. She be takin' care of you while I go back and tend to Sal."

With that, he left leaving Wyanne standing in the door wondering what to do next. Her answer came with a short invitation to follow over to the kitchen in a separate, nearby building.

"Come this way, child, and I'ze fixin' you somethin' to eat," said Betsy. "I know you'ze hungry after comin' all dis way."

13

Amazingly enough, Wyanne was hungry, which was something she would not have expected considering her stomach earlier this morning. Betsy brought out some cold ham, cold rice and biscuits with honey and laid them on a table. Beside them were set some apples. The table was roughly worn obviously having seen a lot of work through hundreds of meals. Last, a glass of water was placed before Wyanne. And that was lunch. But, after the fare of hard tack and salted meat she had endured through her weeks at sea, it was a feast. Wyanne lit into lunch with the passion of a starving animal.

More questions came to mind, but Wyanne was too busy eating to ask them before Sam returned to say that he was ready to continue their journey. Betsy meanwhile had returned with a basket of food to eat on the way. It was basically the same as lunch.

Leaving the house, several hours passed and the sun was well past the noon hour. The ambling wagon had pretty well cleared Charles Town and was on its way toward the country. Now perhaps Wyanne could ask some more questions.

"Sam, I noticed that the kitchen was separate from the house. Why was that?"

"Why, of course. Where else would it be?"

"Where else? In the house, where else? In Ireland, we always had the kitchens inside where the stove could keep us warm."

"Well, it's November now and the weather's cooler. But Charles Town in the summers get hotter than any oven and the separate kitchen keeps the main house cooler. Also, in case of fire, we don't worry so much about losing the other buildings. You see that most everywhere around here."

"Hmm. Well... I see. That makes sense. But it sure must be hot here if the kitchen has to be separate."

"Yep, it be that," replied Sam. "Shoo, Sal. Let's get a move on. We hain't got all day to get home."

As their wagon proceeded toward the Ashley River, the elegant houses of Charles Town were disappearing and replaced with clearly a poorer people. Most of them were rather mean with no paint and meager windows that often had no panes. Doors just hung from limp hinges. The surrounding ground was invariably pounded into cement making it impossible for even a blade of grass to grow. Even the nearby trees were sad ghosts covered with dust raised from the streets. Judging from the kids running half-naked around the houses, black families generally lived in them although an occasional white family was nested in among them.

"Who are all these people living around here?" asked Wyanne. "Is this what most all houses look like around here other than those of the rich people?"

"These people be jest like you. They came over or were brought over to work here. The whites of course were all indentured, but the blacks somehow got freed."

"Indentured I understand, but freed…what's that?

"What? Lordy girl, you truly don't know nothin'," laughed Sam.

"What's the joke?"

"Many's the time when indentured people and slaves like me is in the same boat. We'ze both overworked, but at least you got a limit. Me, it's jes one sunset after the next, and I still be a slave."

"Ye mean a … slave, just like in the Bible?" asked Wyanne incredulously.

"I don't know nothin' about no Bible, but I'ze been a slave ever since I got here from home. It seems so long ago, I almost forgot what home is…" said Sam vaguely.

"Then, if ye're a slave and they're black, why aren't they slaves?

"I don't know. Maybe they massuhs jes let 'em go. Sometimes slaves kin earn 'nough money selling vegetables or work to buy themselves. I don't know…but I ain't never gonna be one of 'em. That I do know."

A while later, Sam asked: "How long'iz yo' term anyway?"
"As far as I can tell, my paper says seven years."

"What you mean, 'as far as I can tell.' Don' yo know for sure?"

"Not really, 'cause I couldn't read it when I signed it."

"Then how you sen yo letter here and read the Massah's letters to you?"

"I went to a priest who was a scriber, and he wrote and read what needed to be said. So I guess it's seven years."

Questions and answers passed back and forth until a small landing appeared. It consisted of causeway about sixteen feet wide and a foot over the surface of the water to allow easy access from the land to the boat. Looking further, a rather small sailing ferry was approaching. Wyanne was doubtful that it would hold their wagon, mule and them. But, it must have gotten them over here, so she guessed it would get them back. Besides, did she really have a choice?

"Oh, good," grunted Sam. "We won't be waiting a long time for the ferry. This'll save us some time."

Clucking Sal forward up to the causeway, Sam then got down to lead the mule and wagon aboard the ferry. The ferryman approached them with a friendly greeting.

"Hi Sam, back already? Got your new girl already? That'll be an extra one and a half pennies for her."

"Yassuh, Massah. Elliot. She come in on the morning tide wif the *Singing Siren* and we found each other without no problem. Here be yo two shillin's."

The Ashley River is perhaps a quarter of a mile wide with a lazy current going to the ocean. Mr. Elliot, however, was an expert sailor and in thirty minutes pulled the ferry up to the landing on the far side of the river. Within a couple of minutes the mooring was secured and the party was allowed to disembark on the Ashley Road which paralleled the river.

More time passed and the countryside began to appear. The trees were no longer dusty ghosts but rather looked like old men with long white beards.

"Sam?"

"Yassum?"

"These trees look spooky"

"What you mean?"

"Those long beards hanging from the branches...I'd hate to be walking alone on this road at night."

"Oh," laughed Sam. "You mean the Spanish moss. I never thought nothin' about it, but I kin see what yo mean. Don' worry, none 'bout it, they's no ghosts... leastwise, none I know of."

As time continued to pass and the sun continued to arc over the sky, Wyanne seemed to have run out of questions. Silences became longer and longer. Finally, it was Sam's turn to ask.

"What, no more questions? Yo sure 'nough asked a lot of 'em."

"Nope. I just ran out. So many things have happened in the last several months, I can hardly keep up let alone understand."

"Yes, I kin understand that. I had the same feeling...total confusion when I first come over. I 'ze just jerked from home; but why be you here?"

Wyanne thought for some time before answering. She wasn't jerked from her home, whatever Sam meant by that. But, on the other hand, she didn't really have a choice. The farm was to be left to her oldest brother Jake, so she didn't have much to look forward to there. Just get older and work as a milking maid. Take in stitching. Get married? To whom? Most of the boys were farm hands growing old before their time or leaving for England or America. Besides, what was that to mean anyway? Just being a milkmaid to a husband while taking in stitching and of course...having a raft of kids. "Growing old before my time. "

She had talked to Ma many times about what lay in store for her. Even as young as nine or ten years old. Pa told her that when Jake gets married, he would need all the rooms in their cottage for the kids that surely would be coming. Of course, Pa would want some place for himself when he slows down and depends on Jake. Otherwise, what's the purpose of having children? "Anyway, the point is, there just isn't room for you, Wyanne. You gotta figure out how to go somewhere's else." Kevin sure learned that early enough.

Kevin... Wyanne laughed at that. Kevin. He always was a wild one. Maybe it was his flaming red hair. It surely matched his temper. But, ah that boy. How we used to laugh and play as wee babes. He was always protecting me from older ones too. No, no matter what he's done...poaching...or whatever, rumors gossiped about the girls...he was always my Kevin.

But that was that. Kevin was gone and had been for several years. No one knew what became of him. Of course, he couldn't read or write, so no letters came. Maybe he was hanged after all for something he did. Wouldn't be surprising. The countryside is full of young men turned to robbery...or worse. Wouldn't he be a dashing robber though? Gallant with the ladies whose jewels he stole? Course, Kevin knows more about poaching. Maybe he would be caught doing that.

Almost like that song *Geordie*. How do those words go?

17

Ah, my Geordie will be hanged with a golden chain
Tis not the chain of many
He was born of king's royal breed
And lost to a virtuous lady

Ah, my Geordie never stole nor cow nor calf
He never hurted any
Stole sixteen of the king's royal deer
And he sold them in Behenny

This lady then goes before the judge to plead for Geordie's life.

Two pretty babies have I born,
The third lies in my body
I'd freely part with them every one
If you'd spare the life of Geordie

The judge then turns her down saying:

The judge looked over his left shoulder
He said fair maid I'm sorry
He said fair maid you must be gone
For I cannot pardon Geordie

Would I plead like that for Kevin? Of course, although naturally, no babies would be involved. Maybe though he has a wife. Would she plead like that? Who knows, though once Kevin saw a woman, she never was the same. It'd be nice to hope so, anyway.

Meanwhile, she and Pa talked more about where she was to be going. Some thought was given to improving her stitching. She seemed to have a talent for it. But, it was hard work and hard on the eyes and hands. Look at old Mrs. Grable...sixty years old or so, and near blind with crippled hands. But, at least she had had a living besides what her husband brought in farming. So, life must be just a series of trades with a price to pay with each choice.

So, with the prospect of blindness and crippled hands in front of her, Wyanne started going over to Mrs. Grable for stitching lessons. The work was hard and tedious. Even Wyanne's eyes, as young as they were, got tired after hours of work. However, her hands became nimble and strong while her fingers got as tough as shoe leather after having been stuck with needles countless times.

18

Eventually, her skills grew and she began to take in work. At first, it was simple repairs but as time passed, it became more complicated. Dresses with fancy lace for brides. Baby dresses for baptisms. Even some limited work for men's breeches and jackets although generally men would go to a tailor. But, she could do it. Throughout it all, Mrs. Grable kept pushing her toward ever-tinier stitches. Hiding stitches wherever possible. Invisible was the word she used. "Don't want to see them at all," she ordered.

The years passed.

Then, from nowhere a letter came from Kevin. He was in America! Charles Town, wherever that was. Since when he didn't say, but he did say that his master wanted someone who could do fancy sewing. Kevin knew that Wyanne had had some talent for it and probably assumed that she would take lessons from Mrs. Grable. Furthermore, the master, a certain Judge Drayton, was willing to pay for passage. He also promised to provide her work and room and board in return for a commitment of seven years work. It was called an indenture.

Anyway, without any further ado, he had proposed to his master that Wyanne be indentured as a fancy stitcher and the master agreed. That Kevin, he could talk the skin off a snake. He hadn't changed at all. Full of fire and smooth words.

Asking her neighbors, Wyanne learned that many young people, men in particular had gone to America under an indenture. Many of them went in response to just such letters as Kevin's. Others from word of mouth. Some went as an alternative to a hanging. What became of them, most people didn't really know. They just left and were never seen again. Occasionally, someone would come back, but that was really seldom.

But, again, what was her future otherwise thought Wyanne. She had learned pretty much what she could from Mrs. Grable and in fact, was good. Even Mrs. Grable said so. Jake was getting married shortly and nine months later a baby would be born. You could bet on that. And Ma and Pa, well they were getting older and looking forward to taking it easier. There wasn't anyone around who attracted her toward marriage even though she was getting old enough to start thinking about it.

No, there doesn't really seem to be any good alternative. Kevin's letter didn't say much about what an indenture meant other than a trip and room and board for work, but she might as well take it. How to get word back that she would come was her next problem since she couldn't read or write. Fortunately, her priest could do both and occasionally did letters as a scriber. Once she sent off her acceptance, the next problem was how to arrange passage which she addressed to Kevin in her acceptance letter.

19

Kevin replied that she should go to Dublin where she would be helped by a shipping agent: *John Clancy and Son.* Whatever a shipping agent was…but if it's there where I'm to go, then, that's where she'd go. This agent would be able to get her passage arranged on a ship going to Charles Town.

Since she had never been outside the outskirts of her town of Shantonaugh, Jake agreed to put off his wedding until he could take her safely into Dublin. With his help, Wyanne made preparations to go, bidding goodbye to her family, friends and Mrs. Grable. Such a fuss and tears. One would think she had died and she was attending her own wake. But, in fact, she knew she would never see them again. But, again what were her alternatives?

Reaching Dublin was a two-day journey and a third one finding Mr. Clancy. Mr. Clancy didn't know anything about Wyanne or her offer of an indenturement. But, he agreed to send off a letter to the Judge for instructions. Meanwhile, Wyanne could go home until such time as he called for her. That would probably take about six months.

"Six months? Ye mean I have to go through me departure again?" asked Wyanne. "Yep, unless you want to try and find work and lodging here," was Mr. Clancy's reply. That wasn't too tasty a dish, and she decided to return home. Needless to say, everyone was amazed to see her again.

True to his word, another letter came from Mr. Clancy saying for Wyanne to come immediately as a ship was scheduled to take her to Charles Town. Again, Wyanne attended another wake and trundled off to Dublin with Jake's help. This time Jake was less anxious to leave because his young wife was expecting their first baby. But, Jake was good for his word and helped her off.

This time Mr. Clancy was more helpful. He had arranged a booking on the *Singing Siren* and written ahead to the Drayton family of her arrival. He also asked her to sign the articles of indenture that would bind her to work for seven years. Since she couldn't read, Wyanne asked him to read the articles aloud and explain what they meant. That accomplished, she marked an X on the bottom and Mr. Clancy witnessed the mark.

The ship was expected out on the following tide, so Wyanne had to go on board immediately. Jake helped her aboard and found her a berth that was little more than a hammock in the ship's hold. Asking a crewmember, they found out where and how she was to eat and take care of her toilet matters. Then he quickly said goodbye so as to get home to his wife.

For the first of many times, Wyanne asked God what she had done. Never in all of her life had she felt so alone. In fact, she never had been so alone. She knew absolutely no one. But other than that, she never discussed the trip again to anyone. It became a complete hole in her life. Some asked her about the trip only to be told shortly that it was something that was not to be discussed. That was a secret she took to her grave.

"Missy...so why did you come?" Sam asked pulling Wyanne out of her reverie. "You been gone a thousand miles away."

"Oh, excuse me. I was wondering that same question myself. It's a long story. We've got time, so how'd you like to hear it?"

"Well, as you says, we got nothin' but time. So, sing away." And that is what Wyanne did.

By the time Wyanne had finished her story, the picnic had been eaten and the sun was clearly on the horizon. By now, Wyanne was getting anxious to finish this ride.

"How much further till we get there Sam"

"Not much further. You jes relax and be patient. After all the way you come, a few more minutes ain't gonna hurt nothin'."

In fact, it was just that. A few minutes later Sal began to pick up the pace as Sam noted: "We be gettin' close now. Ol' Sal smells home."

With those words, Sal turned unto a road that was almost invisible to Wyanne, but clearly Sal knew where she was going. By now, darkness had just about set completely in, but even through the gloom, Wyanne's breath was taken away. She was looking at the biggest house she had ever seen outside of His Lordship's castle back in Ireland. She had arrived.

CHAPTER TWO

My mother would tell the story of her first sighting of Drayton Hall for the rest of her life. It seemed to be the well spring of everything that she would do throughout all the years in front of her.

"You have to understand. Of course I had seen His Lordship's house. That had been standing there from time immemorial. But, as far as I was concerned it was just a pile of rocks. No one in my family had ever stepped foot in it, and I knew I certainly wouldn't. So, again, it was just a pile of rocks on the horizon.

"But, this…this was a house…a big one…that I knew one day I would enter it. One day, perhaps tomorrow, I would enter it and be part of a bigger life than I could have ever imagined.

"Think of it. Here I was. A scared, scrawny fifteen year old brat straight from the old country. Mind you, I wasn't always old and fat and near blind. At one time, some thought I was pretty…certainly your grandfather. Anyway, where was I? Oh yes, I was still half-seasick from a three-month trip across the ocean in a rolling old tub. Then, just as I was wondering again what I was doing here, the blackest man…a total stranger at that…picked me and took me to … I didn't know where. And along the way, poor pickininnies were playing on the dirtiest, dusty streets, Spanish moss was hanging down like ghosts…it's still impossible not to remember how strange that seemed after all these years.

"And then, before Sam and I left Charleston, we stopped off at the town house to eat. That should have been a clue, but I was so overwhelmed I didn't notice. That was the biggest house I had ever set foot in. You could have taken four of our stone houses back home and tucked them neatly into this one. And, there, as big as you please, I was eating for four people with no end in sight for food. But, again, as hungry as I was, I didn't notice.

"So, then it was back on the wagon and off to the country. Twenty miles at a slow shuffle. Sal wasn't a fast mule, but she was surely slow. *That was my mother's favorite joke.* The hours just dragged by with no home in sight. Occasionally, a house would pass by. Some of 'em were well cared for, but others were just as ratty as the pickeninnies running around almost naked in the streets. But, as you can imagine, ten miles go slower than the sun and soon darkness set in.

"Then the Spanish moss really got spooky. Those long gray beards just swaying in the wind. If one of them had said "boo" I'm sure I would've died there on the spot. Old Sam didn't seem to notice them which gave some comfort. I wonder what he thought about during his first trip to the plantation. He never made much mention, but I know he must have been as scared as I was. Meanwhile, Sal just kept clip-clopping along.

"I remember Sam and I talked a lot during that trip. Questions just kept coming to mind, but he patiently answered all of them as best as he knew. How little I knew then, and the questions I did ask didn't begin to cover all that I would be learning.

"Finally, about a mile out from the house, Sal's clip-clop shuffle actually began to get faster if such a thing were possible with her. She smelled home and getting rid of the wagon tagging along behind her was on her mind. I was so tired that I really didn't notice. Not that I had had a lot of experience with animals anyway. But, there we were on the last stretch home.

"Turning the corner to the Plantation was interesting only in that we were leaving the road. But I should have known that something big was coming up. On either side of the entryway was a fence line made up of brick pillars that supported white iron pickets. These fence lines were as tall as a man, but again, as I said, I was so tired and what would I notice in the dark. Then a hundred yards along, vague shadows began to appear on either side of the lane. The next day I learned that they were slave houses. The Master had hundreds of them to work the rice fields. But at that point, I was a bit disappointed. Where was the big house Sam had promised? Looking beyond those houses one could see the moon shimmering off the swamp water. Just like the fens back home. Overhead the branches of the cypress trees were forming an arch that looked like the longest tunnel in the world.

"But ahead through the tunnel, I could see just the faintest glimmers of lights at regular intervals. Clearly they had to be candles in the windows...but so many. In my old soddy, one candle met all our needs. Not that we could afford more, so it was good that one did the trick.

"Gradually, behind the lights a dark shadow began to grow in the gloom. It was Drayton Hall.

"The Hall was not as large as His Lordship's pile of rocks, but it was large enough with more windows than I had ever seen in my life. Everywhere were windows. On the bottom floor as well as the top. Through them were flickering lights from candles and fireplaces. They made the windows dance like a woman's eyes in love.

"In the middle of the house were two porches with one stacked on top of the other. The bottom porch was covered by the first and the second was covered by an

23

overhanging roof. Peculiar roof too. It was triangle shaped and stuck out from the main sloping roof. All of this was supported by white pillars. White pillars on the lower porch supported the porch above while the pillars above supported the roof. I had never seen anything like it before. Later, I learned that it was called a *Palladian* style house and was considered to be quite modern. In the center of the bottom porch was a large doorway painted black. I never got to use it. That was for the Masters' folks, guests, and the like. Servants like me and slaves always entered around in back if need be. You had to be someone grand because it was set up on the bottom porch about ten feet in the air. You had to go up fifteen steps just to get to the door. These steps themselves were so big that they were split so that you could walk between them into a door that led to a ground floor where there were kitchens, offices and other work rooms.

"On either side of the porch was a small building. As you faced the house, the one on the left was the office for the overseer with rooms above for servants to sleep. I lived a lot years up there before I left for Charles Town. The one on the right was a washing and sewing room and it was there that I was to spend many hours stitching dresses for the Mistress.

"But, you know what? During our wagon ride, Sam talked about the Master's family. He apparently came from an old English family that could be traced back as far as William the Conqueror and probably back further than that. Anyway, his family was older than His Lordship's and about a hundred years ago or so, during the wars in England against Cromwell --damn his eyes-- a part of the family left England and settled in the West Indies. Barbados, I think it was.

"But, the Drayton family had to keep on moving. Young sons always need new land to settle since old homesteads are given to eldest sons and this was true with the Draytons. One of these sons, Thomas came to Carolina around 1670 and married a young daughter by the name of Ann Fox. This was certainly a fortunate marriage too. You see, her father owned the land next to Drayton Hall, and it was there that he built a house that was just as grand as Drayton Hall. It is called Magnolia Plantation for all of the magnolia trees there.

"In turn, Thomas's younger son, John needed land of his own and he bought a large section right next to his father's. So, was born the house to which I came in America.

"But, I saw more than just a house. I saw success. The Draytons were surely richer than I could ever be. But, each generation of them was expected to do something with themselves and each of them had reached out for the opportunities that they saw.

"I didn't understand any of this that night, but the effect was grand. Nor did I ever expect a house like the Master's. After all I was only a woman and only men could obtain mansions. But, I learned that the prospects were there as long as I remained single. Today, of course, married women can petition the Council for help when they have been wronged, but even then, as long as I remained single, I could buy and sell and enter into contracts by myself. Men couldn't deny me that. And women needed what I could do which was sewing.

"Of course, I had a contract to serve. The Master had paid my way over and promised me room and board. I intended to serve it fair and square. Kevin might get itchy fingers, but not me. I would make the best dresses that the Mistress and her children could imagine.

"Meanwhile, I figured that if the Master had built this house here, other masters had built other houses elsewhere and there would be other servants. Through them, I could see that my name as a skilled, honest seamstress would be spread. This would lead to a business of my own after my indenturement.

"Again, I didn't think of all this as I was approaching the house. Don't be a ninny. I wasn't that smart. These ideas only came as time passed. But, the house… that house. That grand house standing there as big as you please was a testament to a single man's work. That house stands as clearly in my mind as though I had seen it yesterday. That house became a monument to my own life. It sent shivers down my spine it did. My eyes were so wide it's amazing they didn't fall out. But they didn't and even as blind as they are now, they can still see the house.

"And so it was that I knew then, even then that America was the place for me. Of course I couldn't have anticipated all that lay before me. But, looking back, I wouldn't have changed anything. Nothing serious anyway. I made my choices and lived with them and here I am today."

CHAPTER THREE

Sam drove the wagon and Old Sal around to the rear of the house. There, the overseer was standing waiting for them. He had come over from the small house reserved for overseers by Master Drayton.

"I heard you all coming in. Old Sal's sighing and grumbling about having to work can be heard a mile away."

"Well suh, we be here. No problems," replied Sam. "It jes takes time for Old Sal to shuffle over ten miles."

Ma sat there like a stone statue, not daring to talk. With Kevin taking off like he did, what was she to do or think? More importantly, what was this man thinking? As a result, Ma just remained frozen in place.

"And who do we have here?" asked the overseer. "You are Wyanne Malone, the sister of Kevin?"

"Yes sir," squeaked Ma. Her voice had gotten as dry as a boll of cotton and twice as large. She was really amazed that she could talk at all.

"H'mm, well you're here. Nothing we can do about that and your ship's passage has already been paid for. I got to say, however, that your brother's trying to steal stock and taking off in the middle of the night was a real disappointment. He was so likeable and so much of a disappointment."

"Sam, take Old Sal to the barn and turn in for the night."

"Yassuh, thank you suh." Sam led Sal away who was still full of grumbles and sighs.

"So, what do you have to say for yourself, young lady?"

"Well," squeaked Ma. "Excuse me," swallowing hard to get her voice down where it belonged. "H'mm. Uh, yes sir. Well, I guess I can talk now. But what's to say, I guess that's the question. After he left home, I hadn't heard from Kevin in years until he wrote about my coming here. Accordingly, after talking to me da', I decided to come. And come I did not knowing anything about what Kevin had done until Sam told me on the way here. So, I guess what I got to say is that Kevin is me brother, and for whatever else he is, I won't deny him. But, he is Kevin and I'm me. I came here only to do a good job, and I am good at what I do. So, watch me, and judge for yourself. Anything that I might say otherwise would probably sound like a bunch of blarney and you probably don't want to hear that."

"H'mm, fair enough. And I will watch you, so mind yourself. Under the terms of your indenture, we can sell you off to someone else, and that probably won't be very nice."

"No, sir. I agree, but ..."

"But what?" demanded the overseer.

"But I think I had better be keeping me mouth quiet. Less said the better."

"That's probably the best thing you've said so far. By the way, Wyanne, my name is Mr. Smith, the overseer here. My job is to run the plantation on a day-to-day basis for the Master. Since you are a seamstress, you will be working directly on the clothing of the Mistress. Occasionally for the Master or the sons when their clothes need repair. I'll introduce you to them tomorrow. Right now, you got to get settled in and I need to get to bed. Have you had anything to eat?"

"I'm not hungry sir," replied Ma.

"Good. Then, let's find a bed for you. Tomorrow starts at 5:30 sharp. But sure you're ready to go. The Master gets up a few minutes later and he wants to see everyone already for the day."

"Yes sir." Ma wondered where sleep and the bed were. A night's rest without the ship's pitching and rolling would be heaven about now.

Mr. Smith took her over to the front building on the left. Downstairs it was the overseer's office while upstairs it proved to be a dormitory. It had several rooms in it. Glancing through the crack of an open door, Ma could see beds for a number of people in each of them. Elsewhere, she could hear people rustling around in them.

Compared to my home in Ireland, this is magnificent. It was painted white and clean and each bed had sheets. Amazing. To come so far and be so lucky.

Knocking on one door, another woman, about thirty years old answered by opening it. "Yes sir?"

"This is Wyanne. She is the new seamstress for the Mistress. You have an extra bed in here don't you?"

27

"Yes sir."

"OK, good. Wyanne will be staying with you. Oh by way, Wyanne, this is Susanna, the head housekeeper. In addition to working for the Mistress, you will be working with her as well."

"Glad to meet you, Susanna"

"Likewise."

"Well, that's that," concluded Mr. Smith. "I'll leave you here to settle in. See you in the morning."

"Yes sir, good night sir," replied Ma. With that, Mr. Smith turned on his heel and departed leaving Ma to wonder what came next.

Susanna answered that question by opening the door widely as if to welcome Ma into her new home. She followed Susanna in to see that this room was just like the others except that now she could see more details. There was a small table with a lit candlestick flickering a faint light off the walls. The beds were normal single size with ropes woven back and forth to support straw tick mattresses. Over each mattress was thrown a simple white sheet. In the corner was a small chest of drawers where extra clothes could be stored. Over the table was a small window through which the moon added to the candle's light. Judging from her rumpled bed, Susanna had clearly been disturbed from her sleep.

Ma immediately felt badly about having awakened Susanna and tried to excuse herself. Susanna waved off her apology saying that she was glad to have company. She pointed out Ma's bed and said that tomorrow is another day, and that they can talk in the morning. With that, she went back to bed leaving Ma to undress and go to bed herself.

"Tomorrow can take care of my valise. It hasn't really been unpacked since I left and another night won't hurt." With that, she blew out the candle, crawled into bed and the next thing she knew it was morning.

CHAPTER FOUR

Ma really did not awaken. She was too tired for that. Rather she was disturbed by Susanna who was getting dressed. The sun was just barely climbing over the horizon and the room had a chill from the early dawn air.

"Oh, good. You're up. It's my turn to wake you this time. Now, hurry. The Mistress does not like anyone sleeping late, and I let you sleep as long as I could knowing how tired you must've been after such a long trip. My goodness, you came all the way from where? Ireland! Where's that? Over the ocean I should guess. But I don't know anything about all that. I was born and raised right here. I got my job through my mother's mistress..."

As Susanna chattered on, Ma shook the cobwebs from her head and struggled to her feet. Finding her dress lying in a rumpled heap, she put it on and searched through her bag for a comb. After a while she found it, such as it was being without several teeth. "Well, anything in a storm," she thought as she began to comb her hair. A minute later after fluffing up her tick mattress and smoothing her sheet, she was ready to face the day and whatever that would bring.

Now, having shaken sleep from her eyes, Ma could her roommate who had been so recently awakened last night.

Susanna was indeed about thirty. Her hair was a dirty blond color which she combed back into a simple bun. Ma could it also had a few grew hairs which added highlights of silver. Looking beyond her hair, Susanna showed a strong figure that had known steady work. Complementing this first impression was a rather square face seated on a firm jaw line that brooked no foolishness. Ma was careful to note that feature. However, Susannah's blue eyes were surrounded by laugh lines which softened a forbidding expression.

The first thing for it to bring was food. Ma was amazed that she could be so hungry all the time. Turning toward Susanna to indicate that she was ready to go, Susanna was finishing her monologue, "My goodness, look at the time. The sun is well up and we had better hurry if we want breakfast. Let's get over to the kitchen for some biscuits, butter milk and coffee."

Following Susanna from their room over to a side door of the main house, Ma noticed that, unlike the town house in Charleston, there was kitchen below in a cellar under a very thick ceiling. "Well, that probably should provide adequate protection," she thought. Susanna had kept on talking without stop.

"Oh yes, we're here. The kitchen fire feels so good on a chilly morning. During the winter it is absolute heaven."

Entering the kitchen, Ma saw several slave women scurrying between a table and a fireplace. The table was laden with a variety of baked goods in various stages of preparation. Breakfasts were serious business. They fed people who were facing a lot of heavy work…even if the Mistress and daughters weren't. There were breads, biscuits, tarts, and a grainy, white, tasteless mush. More similar things were being brought from the ashes in the fireplace.

Tasting the biscuits reminded her of scones; but the mush: "Yuuck, what is that?" gagged Ma. Even though that was only her first taste of grits, she never did learn to like it no matter what she used to disguise the flavor.

Using the fireplace for cooking was not unusual for Ma. Her mother had always used one at home. However, this one was huge. It was easily as tall as a young girl, about eight feet wide and three feet deep. There was a huge spit big enough to roast a pig hanging from supports fastened to each wall of the fireplace. From the walls were also several long swinging hooks that held pots bubbling with the white paste Ma had just tasted. On the floor were a number of andirons where ashen logs were shedding hot coals that baked the pies.

From the ceiling were hanging a number of hoops from which were hanging pots and pans of every conceivable sort. One or another of the girls was constantly reaching for one as others were being hung from the wash tub.

My God, this is a food factory. How many people must this kitchen feed each day? An army?

Behind in a corner room, Ma could see tapered forms that were clearly used for making candles. There must have been enough for 36 candles. This could not be believed. Ma's mother had one that was used perhaps once or twice a year.

Meat was too expensive to use for making candles. We ate everything. But I guess that if ye can own a plantation, ye can afford candles.

Following Susanna's lead, Ma helped herself to some biscuits, honey, and some buttermilk and went over to a corner where she would be out of the way. Never in all of her life had she ever seen so much food and to be able to eat as much as she wanted. "America must truly be the land of milk and honey," she thought.

I could even get fat instead of being skinny like my mother.

Susanna did not let Ma get fat that morning however. Within a minute of getting her food, she had eaten it and was preparing to leave.

"Come along girl. Remember the Mistress does not like to be kept waiting and she is very anxious to meet you."

At that point, Ma looked at her clothes and compared them to Susanna's. The comparison was God-awful. Her dress was faded, salty, and spotted with food that had slopped over whenever the ship rolled through the ocean swells. And that was the only one she had. Ma didn't look very presentable herself either. She hadn't taken a bath during the entire voyage. At best, she was able to wash on occasion by using salt water and soap. Her hair was stringy and limp from not having been shampooed. Fortunately, her teeth hadn't started to decay as so often happened, so at least she could make a presentable smile. But still, a bath became an important goal for the day followed by a chance to launder her clothing. After all, she was a seamstress and not a coal monger.

But, dirty dress and all, and not having any choice, she followed Susanna obediently up a staircase to the first floor of the Hall. From there Susanna took her through the front entrance to a side room where breakfast was being served for the day. Here the Master's family was dining on the pies, cakes, and white paste that she had seen in the kitchen. Susanna stuck her head around the door to inform the Mistress of her arrival.

"Yes, Susanna?"

"Excuse me, ma'am, but I just wanted to tell you that Ma has arrived and at your pleasure, I will be glad to introduce her to you."

"Thank you, Susanna. I'll be along directly. Meanwhile, you can start the day's activities."

"Yes ma'am. I will be showing Ma around when you want us." With that Susanna pulled her head back and motioned for Ma to follow.

"Susanna," Ma wailed quietly.

"Yes?"

"I know this isn't Saturday, nor do I expect hot water to be available, but could I have a bath and an opportunity to wash my dress? I can't meet the Mistress looking like I do. I haven't really cleaned myself since I left home three months ago."

"Three months! Oh you poor girl, that is a long time. And, yes, you're right, you do want to make your best impression. Let's go over to the washhouse where we can scrub you and your dress. Don't you have another one?"

"No ma'am. I was told to travel light and rightly so. Living in the hold of a ship for three months doesn't provide much in the way of changing clothing."

Exiting the mansion, the two ladies returned to their bedroom where Susanna gave Ma a replacement dress. It would be a bit baggy over Ma's thin body, but much better than her old dirty one. Then, carrying this new dress, they went over to a washhouse that was about 200 yards away. Slaves were already hard at work. Some cauldrons were boiling and white sheets, linens, and clothing were being stirred. Another woman was scrubbing some stubborn stains on a washboard.

Dipping some hot water into a fairly large pan, Susanna handed Ma a washcloth and bar of soap. "Here, use this. It isn't a real bath. We get one of those only every so often around here. But, you will be a lot cleaner than you are now. We'll toss your dress into the hamper for washing. Three months in the same dress? Without changing once? That is a long time. We never go longer than a week here."

"Oh, thank you. This is heavenly. Hot water and soap. I'd almost forgotten what it feels like. Yes, three months. My dress was almost caked like a second skin. I'll have to start sewing up some replacements for myself."

"Along with everything else that the Mistress and her sons will want, you'll be a busy girl. Get along now. They will all be waiting shortly for us, and we don't want them waiting."

While they were chatting, Ma had the opportunity to see Susanna again. Last night, she was so tired and the room so gloomy that she really did not notice who her roommate was. But, now Ma could see that Susanna was indeed ten or fifteen years older. Her figure was clearly that of a mature woman and her face had begun to show the effects of hard work. But, with ash blond hair combed away from her face, Susanna had an open cheerful appearance that bode of friendship.

"Ye know, I'm sorry but I didn't catch your last name last night, and so I have been using your given name. I really do know better."

"The last name is James, but since we have been calling each other by our Christian names already, why don't we just continue doing so? It seems awkward to revert to formalities now."

Oh good, I thought she would be friendly, and I do need a friend.

"How long have ye been working here?" asked Ma. "If I remember correctly from last night, ye're the head housekeeper. But certainly, ye didn't start with that job."

"I've been here for about ten years, and yes, I have been head housekeeper during that entire time. I had learned to be one from my mother who had held a similar job at another house. So, when this opportunity came up, I was recommended and here I am."

"Amazing," Ma replied. "Such a thing just wouldn't have happened back in Ireland. I've been a seamstress for five years and a good one too with a proud name. But, I could've lived to be a hundred and never been recommended to anyone and particularly His Lordship. And yet, here, on little more than my brother's say so, I've been taken in just like you…with your mother's say so."

"Well, I don't know anything about Ireland or how you got here, but welcome to Drayton Hall," bubbled Susanna. "Now let's go back to the Mistress and meet her and her children. You probably won't get to meet the Master until sometime later. He usually is out and about tending to business or being a judge."

Returning to the mansion, Susanna went over to the drawing room where she expected to see Mrs. Drayton. Sticking her head through the door, she found that the Mistress was indeed there. Hearing Susannah's knock to announce their arrival, Mrs. Drayton turned, saw who it was, and motioned for the two women to enter.

After the awful experience last night of having to deal with Mr. Smith over her brother, Ma thought that she would be able to keep her throat dry. She was only partially right; it still got dry but not as badly.

"And you are Miss Farrell?" queried the Mistress.

"Yes ma'am."

"And the sister of Kevin Farrell?"

"Yes ma'am."

"And what do you have to say about him?"

"Well, as I said to Mr. Smith last night, Kevin is me brother and I won't deny him. But, I am not him. I came here to do a good job throughout my indenturement, and that is what I will do."

33

"Hmm, well said. However, what is a good job? Is that dress an example of your work?"

"No ma'am. It belongs to Susanna, excuse me Miss James. Mine is being cleaned after having been worn throughout my journey here. If I may, I'll be glad to show ye samples of me work. All I need is some cloth, needle and thread."

"Well, that's fair enough." Turning to a servant, she ordered that these articles be brought immediately.

Ma continued by saying, "I can't make a dress in ten minutes, but I can show you samples of my stitching. Ye'll see that it is straight and fine. For a further example, such as a dress, I would ask for a day's time. And for that, I would need me scissors."

"Well, let's see. I'll be back in a half-hour. You can then show me your 'straight and fine sewing.' From there, I'll decide what's next." With that, she left the room.

Shortly thereafter, the servant arrived with some old sheeting, a needle and a spool of thread. Susanna excused herself to attend to her duties, and Ma sat down in the light to produce a sampling of her sewing techniques. She basted one side with loose stitches and from there proceeded to develop other patterns of sewing that displayed her mastery of ever-smaller stitches. Among them was an example of "hidden stitches" along a seam where her sewing was virtually invisible. In all cases, her lines were absolutely straight. Thank God for Mrs. Grable's lessons.

True to her word, the Mistress returned to inspect Ma's work. She clearly knew good work as she turned the sample over in the light. Judging from her dress, she expected to be clothed well and would not accept anything less than the best. Ma had also figured out from Sam's comments that she could be sold to another family if her work proved to be unacceptable. So, during a seeming eternity of anxiety, she held her breath and said another prayer to Mrs. Grable.

Finally, the Mistress said, "It appears that you have been well taught, and for now, you can plan on staying here. Work with Susanna. Let her show you my clothing and drawings of the new styles that have just come in on the last ship. Meanwhile, can you make a dress for my youngest son? I want to see how well you can cut and tailor."

"Would a night dress be acceptable? I can produce it quickly and allow ye to see me skills there?"

"That would be acceptable. I shall be looking for it tomorrow. Oh, by the way, Susanna is a widow. Her husband died of malaria last year. That's rather common around here."

"Oh, I'm sorry. I didn't know. But, begging your pardon, ma'am. What's malaria? I never heard of it in Ireland."

"I'm not really sure, but it seems to be prevalent in wet swampy country which certainly describes the Low Country here. Perhaps it has something to do with the night air. Now go. I'll see you tomorrow."

Searching out Susanna, Ma found her upstairs organizing a cleaning detail. She then described the interview.

"So, now I have to make a night dress for Charles. How old is he and how big is he? I'll need to measure him in order to make a good night dress."

"Oh, he's out with his tutor and can't be disturbed. But, let's go to his room and look at some dresses that he is currently wearing. That will tell you everything you need to know."

Going over to Charles's room, Susanna brought out a folded dress that had lacing around the cuffs, hem and throat. Ma asked if similar material is available for immediate use. Susanna said that it could be found in the stores by the kitchen.

Going down there, Susanna rummaged through a supply of materials and showed them to Ma. After discarding several choices, they finally settled on a simple cotton pattern and a lace similar to what Ma had seen at home in the windows of some finer shops. Small pearl buttons were selected for fastening the back of the dress.

The remaining hours of the day were spent cutting and stitching. Lunch and dinner were just quick trips to the kitchen where the food was eaten without tasting. Almost like her meals on shipboard. Throughout this process, Ma wished a hundred times that she could try the dress on Charles at least once to ensure a good fit. But, that was not to be and using the other dress as a model, Ma concentrated on making her creation a showpiece of her skills. Finally, about eight-thirty, when she knew Susanna would be getting ready for bed, Ma laid her work down. She did not want to disturb her roommate's attempt to go to sleep. "I can finish the remaining work in the morning," she thought.

The next morning saw Ma up at the first break of dawn. Without disturbing Susanna, she quickly dressed, went to the kitchen, ate, and returned to her sewing. By eight o'clock Susanna poked her head through the door and announced that the Mistress wanted to see the dress. Nothing more could be done. Ma's fate now rested on the dress.

Going back up to the study, the Mistress was waiting who took the dress from Ma with no further ado. Looking it over carefully in the sunlight both right side out and inside out, several minutes passed with no word from Mrs. Drayton. Ma's throat swallowed another boll of cotton. The Mistress then called for her son to come and try on the dress. Ma said another prayer to Mrs. Grable.

"Well, if this is typical of your work, then I'm certain we have a place for you."

Ma's knees almost buckled under the weight of this good news. Choking her boll down her throat, Ma croaked out, "Thank ye ma'am. I'm pleased me work is acceptable. Ye may be sure this sample is what ye can expect from me in the future."

"I'm sure you're right. Meanwhile, see Susanna and she will introduce the materials and patterns that have just arrived from the last ship. Then after you have had a chance to study them, come and see me. We will need to make adjustments so that proper fits can be made for me. By the way, do you read and can you do numbers?"

"No ma'am, I can't read, but I can add and subtract. I can also use measuring sticks so…"

"So that isn't good enough. Some of these patterns are rather complicated and I can't have you pestering me every few minutes reading their instructions to you. So, you will have to learn to read. We will arrange for some lessons with the children's tutor."

"My God, ma'am. What a gift! I will be the first person in my entire family who can read. Never in all my days did I ever expect that. How can I ever be thanking ye?"

"Just doing your work will be fine. Now go, see Susanna and when I need you, I will send for you."

Susanna was again organizing work for the upcoming noon meal when Ma found her.

"Well, how did it go?" asked Susanna.

"I still have a job. No, more than that. The Mistress has told me to find the tutor and learn how to read. Can you imagine? Never in me born days did I ever imagine such a thing. Absolutely no one in me family has ever been able to read."

"Why was that?"

"She said that her clothing patterns were so complicated that I needed to read in order to understand them."

"That's typical of the Draytons. They've even taught some slaves to read on occasion. They really seem to believe in taking care of their people. And of course, it does seem to help them as well. The Draytons operate one of the most prosperous plantation systems around."

"Systems?" queried Ma. "This isn't it? My God, what else is there?"

"Did you think that this was it? Of course, how could you have known otherwise since you only arrived a day ago. But this house is not the operating plantation. It's only a winter house as opposed to the summerhouse in Charles Town that you'd already seen before arriving here. The rice paddies are located elsewhere with teams of slaves associated with each of them."

"How big is this Drayton plantation system then?"

"I don't know, but a lot. Among the working plantations, I've seen rice paddies that are each about a quarter mile square. So judge for yourself. And then, of course, the Master's father at Magnolia has a similar operation."

"I can't think about this anymore," groaned Ma. "It's too much for me. So, let's get back my duties or it'll all be for naught. No work, no job as they say."

"Yes, ye're right. Let me have a few more minutes getting the noon meal set and I'll be right with ye."

"Good, can I just wander around the house during that time and learn where I am?"

"Yes, but don't go too far. I'll need to find you and get you started quickly. Running this house takes a lot of effort."

Wandering around the house proved to be relatively simple. The rooms were spacious but very little in number. Tying them together was a large entryway. Furniture was usually pushed along the walls leaving generous space in the center.

Although each room seemed to indicate a special purpose, Ma noticed that the breakfast was held in one room while the mid-day dinner was in another. Looking closer, she found that the breakfast room faced the morning sun, which provided a ray of heat through the early chill. Dinner, on the contrary, was away from the sun and where a small breeze filtered through to provide a bit of coolness to the growing heat of the day. Later, she would learn that such concerns caused meals to be served in any number of rooms.

Decorating the walls were portraits of family members. Curtains did not exist there. Windows were protected by interior shutters. When they were folded back, they blended into the window frames, such was the thickness of the walls. The ceilings were the most interesting feature of the rooms. They often were figured with garlands and medallions. Ma had never seen such figures before and she wondered how they were carved right out of the plaster. In fact, they were carved by master masons while the plaster was still wet. Lining the corners were bas-relief pillars that were capped with ionic capitals that seemed to be supporting intricate cornices. The floors to the contrary were plain pine without rugs of any sort. Rather, they were simply bleached white.

Going upstairs via a sweeping staircase made of Philippine mahogany, Ma saw that the rooms were mostly bedrooms for the children and guests. Of course, no closets existed; hangars for clothing did not exist. Rather clothes were simply folded and laid in presses for later use. Later she would learn that extra bedrooms were needed to accommodate the volume of guests who were continually staying overnight. Unlike the more populous New England, rural plantation life did not provide a lot of hotels, and consequently, travelers did not hesitate to intrude upon the hospitality of others as they passed by.

The hosts also enjoyed these visits. Rural living meant also that news of the outside world was slow in arriving. The postal system was an expensive proposition and newspapers were seldom available. So, passing travelers filled this gap by talking on the events of the world. Many discussions would be generated later in Drayton Hall by these pilgrims on the developments of America's growing divorce from the King of England.

But this was all to the future. For now, Susanna took Ma back under the house to a room in the washhouse. It was about fifteen feet square, painted white, and lots of windows. The light for sewing was excellent. The floor was a brick, and a fireplace lined one wall. Several tables and chairs were scattered about. This was to be Ma's workplace. Many hours would be spent stitching in here starting with a discussion of the dresses that the Mistress wanted done now. They also talked about sewing some replacements for the poor, faithful rag that had covered her across the ocean.

They also talked about teaching some slaves the arts of the sewing. Keeping a steady supply of dresses flowing for the Mistress's demand for being in fashion clearly exceeded Ma's ability to keep up. She could do fancy work, but the basics of hemming, and straight seams could be done by others with lesser skills. So, Ma needed to develop her teaching skills as well. What would Mrs. Grable think of her now? Learning to read and learning how to teach no less.

Susanna knew of two girls who were clever and willing to undertake the tedium of sewing because any job in the house beat the drudgery of fieldwork. These two girls were introduced as Sarah and Sadie. They were about ten or twelve years old and had been born on the plantation. They had done some field work but were really too small to do heavy labor. Yet, their small hands made them ideal candidates as apprentice seamstresses.

After giving Sarah and Sadie some simple tasks and instruction, Susanna and Ma looked for Mr. Samuel Gordon, the children's tutor. Going upstairs where he normally gave lessons, they found him in the midst of a short recess. Susanna introduced them and explained the Mistress's decision that Ma needed to learn the basics of reading and writing.

"So, you know nothing about either reading or writing," Mr. Gordon asked.

"No, not really. As I told the Mistress, I know how to measure for cutting and , but not much else."

"How old are you?"

"Fifteen, sir."

"Good, you're a little late in starting to learn, but not too late. So, I teach the boys in the morning while it's still cooler and they are fresh. We can work in the afternoon after dinner for an hour or so. When do you want to start?"

"This afternoon would be fine."

"OK, this afternoon it is. We'll start with the ABC's, then simple stories, and finish up with the reading you need for seamstressing. Hopefully, in six months, you will be far enough along to teach yourself whatever is needed."

From there, Susanna returned to her work and Ma went back to her sewing room. She checked on the work that had been done so far by Sarah and Sadie and found that they had not really grasped the ideas she had taught them. Correcting their work and giving proper examples made her realize that teaching was truly another art. A real program would be needed if these apprentices were to progress quickly. Perhaps Mr. Gordon could help her there as well.

Dinnertime came and went. As usual, it was a heavy affair in the kitchen of meat pies, potatoes, bread, beer or water, and fruit; fare that is the curse of students around the world: sleepiness in the afternoon while listening to dull teachers. Ma would learn to keep her portions skimpy to avoid this problem. Water would also be better than any beer that just made the problem worse.

After dinner, Ma gave some instructions to her girls and returned to Mr. Gordon. He had a pile of alphabet blocks on a table. Using them, he was able to show how individual letters make up words that could be read. Constructing words from blocks and setting them in a series, he was able to show how words in turn made up sentences. The key to all of this was to memorize the names and sounds of the letters.

The remainder of the lesson was spent in memory work. Mr. Gordon would flash blocks and Ma would try naming the letters. Actually, this process was not too difficult. Illiterate people often have good memories for what they hear because it is the primary way that they learn. Putting two or more letters together was another matter altogether. The word "an" became more than two sounds of "A" and "N." The long "A" sound became a wider sound that was difficult to grasp. Fortunately, the "N" sound remained rather unchanged.

More fortunately, Mr. Gordon was patient and of good humor as Ma worked to master these new concepts. Chuckling, he warned her that English sounds and spelling often were two different creatures, but that with time, the lessons would make sense. He also talked about the local accents here and offered to help her master them. Ma accepted everything gratefully.

Toward the end of the lesson, Ma asked him about her own teaching problem. "These girls seem to be intelligent and willing to learn. But really, as I think back on Mrs. Grable when she was teaching me, it seemed so easy then. But, now I understand how difficult it was for her to teach me. Can you show me some things that I could do to help Sarah and Sadie become good seamstresses quickly?"

"Hmmm. This is teaching that is outside of my normal realm. But I'll give it a go. Let me watch you do your work and ask questions about what you want them to learn. Then I'll see if I can come up with a plan that will organize your teaching better."

"Oh thank ye...I mean, you. I know that this is an imposition for you…"

"No, no, I'm quite happy to help."

"Yes sir, but none the less, I want to do well here, and your help will get me off on the right foot."

"Good. As I said, I'm glad to help. Besides I might learn something practical for a change."

"Oh thank you. That'll help me so much in getting a sewing program going for the Mistress."

"So, let's go down to your sewing room and see what's happening."

Going down, it was obvious that both Ma and the girls needed help. Ma explained to the girls one more time what was needed while Mr. Gordon watched. After a few minutes, it was obvious that too much information was being pushed onto the apprentices and they were becoming confused. With that understanding, Mr. Gordon stopped the lesson.

"You're teaching too much at once. You didn't learn sewing in one afternoon did you?"

"Heavens no," replied Ma with a laugh. "I was a real dunce. Thank God, Mrs. Grable was so patient."

"Well, that's what you need here. For example, earlier this afternoon, when I started teaching you how to read, what did I do first?"

"You showed me some blocks…"

"Exactly, and what was on the blocks?"

"Some letters…oooh, I see what you mean."

"So for seamstresses, what are letters on blocks?"

"Needle and thread and simple stitches."

"So, start with them with the idea of just learning how to use them in simple sewing. After they learn that, then come on back and see me and we can start their next lesson." With that, Mr. Gordon smiled and left the room.

41

Ma thanked him and turned back to her charges. Taking up on Mr. Gordon's suggestions, she started again and frankly, was surprised at how fast the girls learned. This activity lasted for about an hour when suppertime came. Ma excused the girls with instructions to be back right after breakfast in the morning. She then went back to the kitchen where she met Susanna.

"So, how did it go with Mr. Gordon?" asked Susanna.

"Oh very well," and Ma described her lessons on reading and speaking and Mr. Gordon's lessons on teaching sewing.

"And so, the girls are really starting to move along. Mr. Gordon said he would help me plan more lessons after these basic ones are learned?"

"Isn't Mr. Gordon a nice man?" said Susanna.

"He certainly is. And excuse me for speaking on it, but I wanted to excuse myself for thinking that you weren't married. The Mistress told me that you're a widow now for about a year. Your husband died of ma...ma...malaria? Is that right?"

"Yes, that's right, Tom has been dead for about a year. I thought I would die afterwards. Fortunately, I had my work to keep me going. But, he was always so healthy, never a problem, and then, one day, he came down with a fever. T'was during the summer, it was. I'll never forget it. The air was hot and sticky and the mosquitoes were terrible. Anyway, he didn't last very long. I guess it was God's will because certainly a lot of people die of it. But, God I still miss him. Probably always will, even if I marry again as I suppose I shall someday."

"You never had children?" asked Ma cautiously.

"No, more's the shame. Another example of God's will I guess."

"How long were you married?"

"Let's see now, it would have been fourteen years now if Tom were still alive. We knew each other as children and when the time came, it just seemed right to marry. " Susanna laughed, "I'll never forget when we first met. We were still babies, six or seven years old, when he threw a pinecone at me. I got mad and chased him down. Gave him a good lickin' I did. Ma scolded me afterwards. Said it wasn't ladylike for girls to beat up boys. But it let Tom know right off hand who was boss. Nooo, really, it wasn't like that. He was always so gentle. I don't know when I loved him, but it must have been early 'cause I can't remember not loving him."

42

"What did he do? For work, I mean?"

"Oh yes…well, he had some readin' and writin' and could figure pretty well with numbers. He had actually gotten some schooling for some years. So, he worked on the Master's books along with Mr. Smith. A really good job it was. We were planning on staying here for the rest of our lives. Now, I guess it's just me."

"Well, I'm truly sorry for you. Tom sounds like he was a wonderful man."

"Yes," replied Susanna. "But, better a few years with a good man than a lifetime with a bad one. Really, I got no complaints, and I got some wonderful memories. We'll just have to see how the Lord wants me to go now."

This conversation lasted through supper and on afterwards in their bedroom. Finally, about eight-thirty, words ran out. Their candle was put out. It had been a long day.

CHAPTER FIVE

Mother always said that the next three months were the busiest of her life. The number of stories that she would tell about this period I can hear as though they were told yesterday for the first time.

"From the first day after the Mistress had accepted my work, my days were absolutely full. Sewing, teaching, and learning…there never seemed to be enough time in the day.

"Fortunately, I had a lot of help. Susanna, of course was a Godsend. She always seemed to know what would please the Mistress. She also knew which of the slaves could do what quickly. That saved me from many a mistake. Of course, even she couldn't keep from making a ninny of myself at times.

"I remember the time once…I guess I had been at Drayton Hall for only about a day or two. I needed some cloth to finish a piece of sewing and the only suitable swatch was dirty. So, I went to the washrooms and started to scrub it. Well, I had only been there for about a minute when a tall slave came running in shouting like a fishwife. I didn't understand what the problem was, but I wasn't to be shouted at.

"Really, she was the biggest woman I had ever seen. With powerful shoulders and arms, standing almost six feet tall, she was also the most beautiful woman I had ever seen. Her face looked as though it chiseled from black granite leaving her with dark hollows for eyes, rugged ridges for cheek and jaw bones. Her eyes and teeth flashed with an arresting energy. Her name was Sally, and I learned instantly she brooked no insolence from anyone. Fortunately, neither did I, and we learned to be good friends."

"What's your problem," I asked when I could get a word in edgewise.

"Don't you know?" Sally continued to shout. "Don't you know nothin'? Ain't nobody does no washin' but me. Tha's my job and ain't nobody taken it away from me. Jes' me and my girls. No way I'm goin' back out in the fields. I worked too hard to get here and here you just waltz in here like you owned the place and try to take this job away from me."

"Come on now. I've no intention of taking anyone's job away from anyone. It's just my mother taught me to take of myself."

"Well, yo' ma ain't here and you can jes' hep yourself best by lettin' me do my work. You want somethin' washed, you ask me, heah?"

44

"Yes, I hear."

"And that was how I met Sally. She always had a hot temper, but, I just needed to understand that getting out of the fields was the ambition of every slave I ever knew.

"But, to continue. The worst part of the day was learning to read and write. Actually reading wasn't too hard. I understood basically what it involved from having learned my numbers earlier. But, writing was another chore. Even with my hands being so good at sewing, you would have thought that learning to write would have been simple. But, it was years before my writing became anything but a scrawl. Why it took so long, I'll never know.

"Fortunately, Mr. Gordon was patient as I have said before. He just would always erase my slate and have me try again.

"The Master and Mistress, actually I saw very little of them. Susanna had more contact with them and she would simply pass on to me their sewing requirements. Oh, yes, until I got used to her figure, I would have to fit a dress to the Mistress. Other times, a suit for one of the boys. The Master had his own tailor and so I rarely saw him. He was always off doing some judging or something similar. Otherwise, I pretty much stuck to my sewing and helped Sarah and Sadie learn the same lessons I had learned long ago from Mrs. Grable.

"That's not to say that the Mistress didn't do anything except order up dresses. Through Susanna, I learned that she was constantly out tending sick slaves and making inspections of work projects in behalf of the Master when he was away. Consequently, she would often be out on horseback from early morning until evening going from one problem to another.

"In fact, I never did see the Master ever take such interest in the plantation. He was always busy as I said, judging or some such. This actually wasn't uncommon amongst these gentlewomen. During the War, I heard of wives who ran their family businesses or farms or plantations for years without any help. Often times, did a good job too. Mistress Eliza Pinckney was one of these women. Brought over from Antigua at seventeen to her father's plantation, she ran it for many years while he was away soldiering. During this time she developed the growing of indigo, which is now a very profitable crop. Probably second only to rice in these parts.

"Kind of interesting how the War changed the attitudes of many of these women. At the beginning, they referred to 'my husband's farm.' Then, as the years began to pass, they talked of 'our farm.' By the war's end, it was 'my farm.'

45

"In this regard, the Judge was always fortunate in having such good wives. During his lifetime, he had four of them. Really, in these southern colonies, having a number of husbands or wives was not too uncommon. The weather just seemed to kill people off...witness Susanna's husband. Either that, or a lot of women died in childbirth. The Judge's second wife, Charlotte died giving birth to her second son, Charles. So, people didn't waste too much time living alone before getting married again. Even Susanna got married fairly shortly after I got to know her and then had a couple of kids by her second husband. Her new husband was a good man for all of that, and while Susanna felt deep affection for him she never loved him such as she felt for her Tom.. But, that was life. Being single was just too hard for many people.

"Still, I have known many women who chose not to remarry. Myself, for example. Frankly, I got to enjoying not having to ask "By your leave Master" whenever I wanted to do something. In fact, until just before I left for the Bahamas, the law allowed me to own a business, slaves and make contracts just like a man. Whereas, had I been married before getting myself established, none of these things would have been permitted.

"Then, during the War, the laws were being changed which would have prohibited me from doing these very things I had been doing for years. Apparently, men had started thinking that women were ninnies and needed to be protected from the world. But, that's another story that I'll tell later since it made me decide to strike out again thirty-five years after leaving Ireland.

"Mr. Smith, I also rarely saw him even though he was the overseer. These overseers were the second most important people for running plantations after the masters or mistresses, but most of his time was planning the growing of rice. That meant planning for seed, flooding and draining paddies, tending field hands and planning the slaves' activities from day to day. Not that he would actually set these plans in motion. Normally, he would pass orders on to the senior field hands who would in turn organize the work gangs. Consequently, he didn't see me much which was all right by me since he was always such a cold, almost rude person. He never seemed to have time for anyone or anything. Just his work, and of course everyone else's work.

"Life at the time that I arrived was still rather easy. The heavy work of rice planting wasn't to start for several more months and the Christmas holiday was yet to be enjoyed. Mostly work just consisted of repairing tools, ensuring that the paddies were properly conditioned, and not really much else. So, the slaves were able to relax for a bit.

"Christmas in particular was a welcome period of the year. The slaves were given a day or two off and the house slaves at least were presented with gifts. If the field hands got anything, it seemed to be mostly "blue drilling" cloth for making new clothes and perhaps a pair of shoes. We indentured people also got a small gift. Mine was a book of my own to read. It was a copy of a book by William Franklin. I can't remember its name any more, but he was to become famous during and after the War. So, I guess he was considered to a pretty smart man and reading his book was supposed to have helped me. I'm not sure that it did, but that was the thought.

"During the Christmas holidays, the Master and Mistress would have many friends over for parties. They would come from all over the county and often stay for days being put up in the various extra rooms in the main house or in the side houses. Susanne and I were almost forced to move out once to make room for guests. My, but were they gallant though! Of course, I was kept extremely busy sewing, but still I could peek into the parties and see handsome men and lovely ladies enjoying their finery as they ate and danced. Often the music was provided by some talented slaves who knew how to play fiddles and such. Instead of going to bed with the chickens, people stayed up late and partied the hours away.

"And food! My God, I had thought early on that the kitchen was almost like a factory. Now, I truly believed it. The cooks were constantly cooking almost around the clock. All sorts of wild game such as venison, ducks, swans, and salted fish. Lots of sweets, pies, tarts, and sweetmeats. Breads of various kinds. And rice, rice, rice. I had never tasted rice before coming to America, but lots of it was pretty good. Some of the desserts made from it were delicious. What amazed me later to learn was that many slaves had known of rice in an African place called Sierra Leone and had grown it there. They also had made up lots of the recipes that we enjoyed.

"Anyway, the table just groaned from all the food that was piled on it. Usually it was washed down with a variety of wines or teas. The men seemed to fancy a punch, but what a punch it was. Just a sip was enough to make me dizzy, and the Irish are never one to let a dram of spirits stop them. But, this was pure lightning. In fact, I have heard it called 'white lightning.'

"Even the slaves were allowed to enjoy some parties. Not at the main house you understand. But after the white folks were done with the musicians, they would come down and play around a large campfire. The music then was entirely different than the gigues and reels in the Master's house. I can't really say how it was, but it seemed to be faster with odd rhythms. And how they could huckle-buck to those rhythms! Looser, not as formal with more hooting and hollering which was never heard in the Master's parties.

47

"Some of the slaves who had wives elsewhere would be allowed to visit them. Of course, they weren't necessarily married in a church sense, but none the less married. Really, that wasn't so uncommon with the white folks as well. In the early days, they didn't need a church wedding. They just had to pronounce a marriage to one another and live as man and wife. I heard once, for example, that the famous William Franklin I just mentioned was never married by a preacher to his wife. It seemed that she had been married to a rotter who had another wife and then later ran away. By law, she was stuck. She was married until she was widowed. So, she and Mr. Franklin just declared themselves married and remained that way for the rest of their lives.

"I might add also that Mr. Franklin had had a son from another woman to whom he wasn't married. His name was William and he became the governor of New Jersey. Unfortunately, by becoming governor, he had pretty much cast his lot with the British, and he remained a loyalist throughout his days. Well, this didn't sit too well with William because of his revolutionary activities and a divide grew between the father and son that was never healed. Such is the bitterness of that war. It was called a revolutionary war, but really it seemed to be more of a civil war in the way it tore families apart.

"Anyway, getting back to my story, those slaves who wanted to visit family or friends elsewhere were often allowed to do so. They would be given a written pass that proved that they weren't runaways and then would go for their visits. I didn't know it at the time, but when Sam picked me up at the ship, he had such a pass on him. Being caught without it was considered proof of being a runaway that would fetch a fast and painful whipping.

"These whippings would usually be administered by a senior slave and perhaps supervised by the overseer. The whip itself was a nasty thing that could cut a back into ribbons and usually did since the slave's back was bared for the punishment. They would spread the slave out on "The Pony" and start the whipping. Twenty-five strokes or more were not uncommon so slaves such as Sam were very careful with their passes. Worse crimes would bring a hanging where often slaves were brought so they could see and learn the lesson of the hanging. The Master and Mistress were considered to be fairly gentle with their slaves, but when provoked they wouldn't hesitate to order a whipping. Nor did they worry too much when the Mr. Smith ordered a whipping. That authority was given to him as a normal part of his job. Only when an overseer started to damage a valuable field hand would they object. After all, they might have paid up to several hundred dollars for a prime hand and they didn't want to lose their investment.

"Personally, after I left the plantation and set up my own business, I generally owned several slaves. They were needed to do the basic stitching for ladies' dresses and they were cheaper than hiring free women. But, I never did see much need for whippings. In fact, I'm not sure I ever had need to. But, I guess the difference was the fact that we were all women trying to earn a living as opposed to running an army of field hands where a stronger military-type discipline was needed.

"Amazingly enough, there was often a strange attitude on part of white people toward their slaves. Often times they would speak of them as machines or animals without thoughts, feelings, hopes or ideas.. Just dumb animals. Yet, many slaves were allowed to raise crops and sell them at the markets for extra money. Not that they could expect to buy their freedom. That was seldom seen. But, these people still needed things that their masters couldn't or wouldn't provide, so a small business allowed them to get it. I'm sure that my slaves sold things that they made from time to time. Just so long as they didn't steal too much cloth and thread, I could live with it.

"Quite often, despite being thought of as animals, it was the policy of many masters not to sell slaves or separate them from their families without their permission. That was based, though on good behavior. Get uppity or lazy or refuse to work and a slave would be sold in a minute, never to see friends or family again. Probably the new owner would not be as nice either...particularly if they were from the Caribbean islands. I have heard stories about those places that are not to be believed. Certainly, any slaves I knew feared that possibility more than anything else they could imagine.

"Finally, during this Christmas season, the families would go to church bringing many of their slaves with them to hear the Good Word. They sat or stood in the rear of course, but off to church they went. If they were just animals, why would their owners then bring them to church as if they had souls? Actually, many of them were religious. Sam talked about people in Africa who believed in spirits living in trees or some such.

'He called it "Voodoo" or "Root," and when someone got sick, a "Root Doctor" would come out to tend them. Other times, these same men would use their magic to cast curses against disliked people. Often I would hear slaves murmur amongst themselves, 'He got a root on him.' As they went out their way to avoid the poor, accursed soul. Amazingly enough, I even know some white people who quailed at the thought of being 'stuck with the root.'

"All this was kind of spooky and I didn't really want to hear much about it. Others he claimed were Muslim who were supposed to have believed in the same god as Christians but didn't believe that Christ was the son of God. I never did understand that. Perhaps he just made it all up, but he seemed to be sincere. But, be that as it may, the masters of the many plantations had their slaves going to church.

49

"Another thing that was curious. If slaves were animals, why weren't they simply put into barns? Yet, here again is this curious two-sided attitude owners had about their slaves. Most of the slaves had houses that weren't as bad as some houses I saw in Ireland. Sometimes, they were better. Field hands often lived in a kind of one room barracks perhaps thirty feet long by about fifteen wide. At one end would be a series of double bunk beds and at the other end, a cooking fireplace. In the middle would be a table with benches.

The house slaves usually had better quarters. Theirs would be two room affairs. Their combined size would be about the same as the field hands, but having two rooms allowed them a sense of privacy and living. On one side would be the kitchen and sitting room. The other side could be for sleeping or whatever. Overhead could be lofts for the children. Dividing these rooms would be cooking fireplace that would also heat the house in the winter. Summer times were so hot that fires were kept to a minimum. These places in particular often had decorations on the walls such as animal skins or perhaps a picture. A door or at least a passageway located on one side of the fireplace connected these two rooms.

Outside these various houses were plots of ground where the slaves could tend their own personal gardens. As I mentioned before, the slaves could use what they raised to add to their larders or perhaps sell groceries for a bit of pocket change.

Still, one wonders about slaves and animals. I never saw it, but rumors about breeding slaves like animals floated about. I remember listening to Sally as she talked about this. Of course, masters were also known to keep good looking slaves as concubines. Long after I left America, I heard tell about President Jefferson having just such a girl with him. Of course he denied it, but it was a real brou-ha-ha.
"But, enough of these things. I probably have dwelled far too long about the slaves, but to a young girl from Ireland where slaves were almost never seen, these things I have been talking about what seemed new and unusual. So, my story is one of simple sights that I had seen and amazed me.

"But returning to Christmas, it was a wonderful time for most people then. For me, however my first one here in America was mixed. Life was exciting all right, but lonely. After all it hadn't been too long since I had left my family. Even if home was bare compared to Drayton Hall, my family was there and I was here and the familiar sounds, sights and smells were not to be found. So many miles and never to see them again. Frankly, I spent more than one night crying myself to sleep. Susanna really wasn't much help here either. She had never been away from home; she really was at home except for the loss of her husband. But, even here she was being courted by her future husband and that left little time for me. Quite simply, and it wasn't her fault, she just didn't know what it meant to be away from home.

"The next Christmas and the ones following got easier until finally it dawned on me that I no longer was thinking about Ireland as home. Home was here in America. When this change came over me, I can't say. It just slipped over me like a warm blanket. Leaving America later on for the Bahamas was hard because it meant another start, but not like the first time. I had family surrounding me, and I had more experience. Life would continue and I would survive. Too many years had passed for me not to know otherwise. But these are stories yet to come."

CHAPTER SIX

"Girl, you've just got to let that dress out."

"But, Susanna, I just did," wailed Ma.

"That may be, but if it gets any tighter you'll bust right out of it and bring every boy in the county lookin' at you."

"OK, you're right. I just can't believe how I have grown these last months."

"Grown isn't the word for it," snorted Susanna. "When you arrived here, you were as skinny as any bean stalk I ever saw and your hair was as limp as wet straw."

"Sea rations weren't the best eating food in the world. Wormy biscuits are the least of it, and I wasn't too fat to begin with."

"Yuk, worms?"

"Not too bad unless you see half a one. Then you know where the other half is."

"No wonder you've been eating like a trencherman since you got here. But you're not fat. Really, it just seems that you're growing up...becoming a woman. Certainly, you're gaining weight, but putting it in all the right places. Next thing you know, boys will be coming 'round like hungry hounds."

In fact, Ma was growing into a woman. Her figure was beginning to show curves that never existed when she first got off the ship. She had even begun to have her period although that was a mixed blessing. She had wondered what had happened during the ship's voyage because it had gone away as she had gotten skinnier. It didn't seem natural, and she didn't seem to know what to do about it. But, now for the past month or so, it had returned to its regular cycle.

But, Susanna had brought up a joke that could be serious. She was now sixteen having celebrated her birthday several weeks ago, and that was not too early for many girls to consider marriage.

But, what was there to consider? Her articles of indenturement were very clear on that point. No marriage until seven years passed when she was once again a free woman. Not that Ma ever considered getting married or breaking any point in her contract. She had given her word and after Kevin's behavior, nothing was going to make her go back on what she had promised.

Actually, being indentured really gave her a good excuse not to rush into marriage. Her poor ma was only fourteen when she got married and now that she was forty, she looked sixty. None of that for Ma! Whoever marries her will have to be a good man and have a lot of patience. That she promised herself.

Still in fact, a number of boys were running errands over to the Drayton house that weren't seen when she first arrived. It was kind funny actually. They would have the lamest excuses to stop and talk in their gawky way. Shy, bragging, stumbling, all at once. Just like their long legs and arms and scraggly teeth. Susanna had teased her about them on occasion.

One or two of the boys were actually kind of cute. There was John Ripley with his blond hair. He was still growing, but promised to be a big man capable of doing a lot of hard work. Whether he was willing to do it was another question. Another boy, William Jackson could have been attractive, but his filthy habit of chewing tobacco was out of the question. Smoking a pipe was all right; perhaps a cigar on occasion. Certainly the Master enjoyed his cigars. But, chewing and spitting was too much. And his breath would gag a maggot. His teeth were already becoming stained. So, he definitely was to be sent on his way.

A third one, William Malone was also from the Old Country…funny how that phrase turned up now. So soon. It had only been six months since Ma's arrival and yet, she had begun to think of Ireland as the old country. As though it were something of an ancient past time.

But, anyway, William was from Cork and not much else. He wasn't the biggest boy nor the gawkiest. Just an ordinary young man. He was learning the trade of smithing to include making farm tools from iron as well as shoes for the horses. He worked for another planter down to the road, which accounted for his coming over to the Drayton House. Occasionally, the smithy here needed an extra hand repairing tools for the upcoming rice seasons. So, he was developing a profession that would always stand him in good work. And, without being obnoxious, he did indicate an interest in Ma.

Even Susanna noticed him. "I haven't seen that William Malone lately. What'd you do, shoo him away with a pitchfork?"

"Hush, I've done no such thing. He just hasn't had any work to bring him over here. But, he is rather nice. Not loud and pushy as some of the others are."

"Well, don't get ideas, young lady," warned Susanna. "You have a long seven years in front of you."

"Thank God for that," exclaimed Ma. "The last thing my life needs right now is a man. The only thing they bring is babies. Oh excuse me, Susanna. I know you had wanted children, but I hope you understand. You loved and knew Tom and married him expecting a long a settled life together. Children were simply a natural fit. But…"

"Don't worry about it. I know what you mean. Yes, Tom and I were looking toward a long life here at Drayton Hall and children to raise. But, with you, you're right. Nothing is settled and won't be for a long time. But, when the time comes along with the right man, don't hesitate to grab him. They don't appear too often."

"You mean loving?"

"Well, that too. God knows I loved Tom. But, if you're going to settle a business or a farm out west in the frontier, love's not all of it. Probably not much of it. Can he work with you? Can you with him? Can you see yourself being together for hours at a time just trying to make ends meet?"

"That sounds an awful lot like a business partnership."

"Yeah, it suppose it does. But that's the way things were with my ma and pa. I can't ever say they ever loved each other like Tom and me, but they managed to work things out. They had me and several other kids. They carved their farm out of nothing with only the brute labor of their backs. I remember those days. Up at dawn with slave labor till dark. Often Pa was so tired, he fell asleep at the dinner table. Ma only held on because of the kids. Otherwise she would have been asleep herself. But, still, when Pa died, Ma was real sorrowful. She looked back on a hard life, but it was hers and she didn't complain. Pa never complained neither. The two of them just did what they had to do. So, if you get a man like Pa, probably consider yourself as lucky as you can expect."

Ma thought about what Susanna said for a long time. Her ma and pa worked like that throughout her life as well. Once in a while, Pa would get into his bottle and start waking up the house. Ma would put him to bed while trying to shush him. "Hush up Pa, you'll wake up the kids" to which he would reply: "you want me to sing 'em to sleep?" before he passed out.

"I guess they didn't love each other either, but they were good to each other. At least, they didn't fight."

"Who's that," asked Susanna.

"Me ma and da. I just got to thinkin' about them as you were talking about your parents. Life was hard for them what with all the kids they had and trying to pay His Lordship's rent. But, they made do. Of course, it meant I had to get out as soon as I could cause the farm couldn't support all of us. My older brother got it. Kevin, my other brother really found it healthier to leave when he did. Not fancying a long neck from a rope. I wonder where he is now. Probably charming some colleen I imagine."

More time passed. The two women continued with their sewing. Susanna had also begun to study her sewing with more care under Ma's instruction. Conversation came and went as they sewed and cut. Of course, one or the other would often be interrupted by one thing or another. Ma would have to instruct either Sara or Sadie. Another time, Susanna would have to attend errand for the Mistress. But, for now the conversation just fell into a lull with everyone wrapped in their thoughts.

"Wyanne, could you pass that thread to me?"

"Sure. Here you are … Susanna, you left your home to become apprenticed under your mother's care. Your father was dead by that time? I need that swatch of cloth if I could please."

"Yes, and so Ma learned late in life how to become manage a home for a mistress. Meanwhile, my eldest brothers took over the farm by splitting it."

Ma was credulous. "Split it? How big was it?"

"Oh not too large. Probably a couple hundred acres. Certainly more than we could farm by ourselves. To do it all would have required slaves that my parents couldn't yet afford to buy when Pa died. Now each of my brothers have got about three or four. Here does this line of sewing look straight?"

"Yes, it's pretty good. Next time, as you sew, try looking where you want to go and not just at the next stitch. That'll keep your line straighter. But didn't you say you had three brothers?"

"Yes, that's right. Jeb is the third."

"Well, what happened to him?"

55

"He just headed out west. I haven't heard from him in several years. Course, he doesn't know how to read or write."

Ma murmured, "Just like me."

"What?"

"Oh nothing. Just thinking. Just thinking about this country. It's so big, farms can be split up with enough land for both brothers. Such a thing would be impossible in Ireland. And then, if more land is needed, people just move west and take it. Just like I had to come west from Ireland to find my space."

"Yes, that's about the size of it."

"So large. That's the size of it."

Thus, would work between the two women pass by the hour as they mended and cut and sewed clothes. Susanna had other duties that she tended, and Ma still was learning her letters while teaching her slaves how to sew. But, their days settled into a routine that included a lot of time to talk as they worked.

"So, what's the latest between you and Mr. Killibrew?"

Susanna laughed. "Always curious aren't you? What do they say about curiosity killing the cat?"

"Go on." Ma laughed in return. "But you have to admit that Mr. Killibrew is paying court and you haven't been discouraging him."

Yes, that's right. You do have sharp eyes. Well, he lost his wife last summer ago from the same illness that killed Tom, and he's lonesome. He's not much to look at, but he can read and write, do numbers; he's honest and he's quiet and gentle. So, yeah, I suppose I haven't been chasing him away. I suspect that when he asks me I will marry him. Work is fine and the Mistress is nice, but I can't take either of them to bed nor have children by them. I've been a widow long enough. Some people I know have gotten married within weeks after being widowed which is really too fast, I think. But, the time is coming when it will be right to marry again. Could you check this sewing please and tell me if I'm getting better?

Looking at the sewing, Ma gave some thought to Susanna's answer. *I don't know if I could ever marry again if I had found a real love...or a stinker for that matter. One couldn't be replaced, and I wouldn't want to chance a bad one again."*
"Yes, that is much better. Your line is much straighter and your stitches are becoming

much smaller. Of course, you understand you do fine stitches only for fancy work. Sewing for a workingman needs strong stitching, but not so fine. Rough, but strong is good enough."

"Oh, good. I'm glad you see improvement, 'cause I've really been trying. You know, the Mistress is really not a bad seamstress. I was really surprised to see her work."

"Well, I'm not. One day or so ago, she and I got to talking while I was fitting her and she was saying that sewing was an important part of her schooling. Almost as important as reading she said. Of course, she was only taught fancy stitching. More like an art she said. Frankly, that seems like a waste to me. If you're not going to use something, why learn it? Talking about using something, do you think Mr. Killibrew would teach me more about numbers? I know he keeps track of accounts for the Mistress and I think that would be something useful to know."

"What on earth for?" exclaimed Susanna. "Women don't run businesses. That's men's work."

"You think so? What about the Mistress? She is constantly going here and there on plantation work. You've seen it a lot."

"Well, yes."

"Well, yes, nothing. The more I know about these things, the better off I expect to become. And numbers and reading will help me."

"What kind of business do you plan to run Missy?"

"I don't know, perhaps a seamstress shop after my indenturement is done. Certainly I expect to help my husband."

"Oh, you're married already?" teased Susanna.

"Not yet, but I don't expect to live in a tree."

"You're always thinking ahead. It just amazes me. Only sixteen, but already thinking on down the road."

"One thing that having to move out of the house taught me and come this far to a new country. Depend on yourself. My family where are they? Most of them just starving in Ireland, and Kevin one step ahead of the law. So, who's left but me?"

"H'mm, never thought of it that way. I've always had family around and we've always depended on each other."

"Susanna, can you look at this picture the Mistress gave to me? I can't make heads nor tails from it and she expects me to make a dress from it."

Work just flowed from hopes to dreams to the reality of sewing. Susanna also talked a lot about her job running the house. There were cooking schedules to maintain which was always hard because of the entertaining the family did. Cleaning schedules weren't a daily affair, but planning was needed. Food supplies had to be estimated to keep the food factories going. Bailing the wash was always a heavy workload. Sally was sure to complain when it got too heavy. Of course, the suggestion of returning to fields usually quieted her bellyaching.

Special occasions like the start of the rice planting brought special problems. Even more food was needed to feed the slaves while in the fields. The Master's clothes became filthy during this period. Even the Mistress changed her clothing constantly as she was working along side of either her husband or Mr. Smith. Horses needed to be fed and tended because of the work they were doing pulling wagons or carrying riders. Tools constantly broke down and needed repair despite every effort during the off season to get them ready for work.

Because this was Ma's first experience with the rice-growing season, she was very sensitive to the changes she saw. Consequently, it too became a topic of long conversations with Susanna, but perhaps more with Sally, Sara and Sade. After all, they had worked the fields as very young children, and neither had any desire to return.

CHAPTER SEVEN

It was only a couple of weeks after her arrival in America when Ma had her first experience with rice planting. Known as "Carolina Gold," it was really the basis of the economy in the Carolina and Georgia Low Country. Much of what is discussed here came from conversations she remembered from the years she worked for the Draytons. She had learned from her first day that rice was an important food in those regions, but what it meant to the people there went far beyond a table's food.

Obviously, rice fed people first, but after that it was used for feeding cattle. It was brewed and distilled, made into starch, paper and paste. But mostly, it was a staple of trade with England that was rivaled only by tobacco and indigo. Of course, down in the Low Country near swamps such as was true with the Draytons, Carolina Gold was king. Not only were the swamps too wet for wheat, they were perfect for the flooding of fields needed by rice.

Because of its importance to both the Draytons and to her personally, Ma's stories have been recorded here. The Draytons of course based their lives on this crop. It brought in the money needed to support them in their splendid fashion. But, it also meant they could afford Ma as a seamstress that provided the opportunity for her to come to America. It also created a strong reason for the Revolution that sent all of us to the Bahamas.

Going to the Bahamas is another story that will be told later, but to understand why she had to go is found here in Ma's earliest taste of rice. Here she talks some more about her early days.

"I hadn't been at the plantation for but two weeks and as you know, these were the busiest times of my life. But I hadn't seen Sally for a day or two so when I next saw her and asked: 'Where you have been lately? I haven't been seeing you or any of your girls for the last day or two.'"

"Susanna didn't tell you?" replied Sally looking up from her wash.

"No, and really to tell the truth, I've been busy with Christmas dresses for the Mistress and I guess I just didn't notice."

"Well, I've been out to the fields…"

"Fields! That's the last place where I would have expected you considering…"

"Uuuuhm, yes. I guess I did scold you pretty hard, and no, I don't like to be there normally. But, this is different. It's really kind of fun."

"So, what's fun about the fields this time?"

"Well, every year 'bout this time, the Master gets all of us women slaves and takes 'em out for burning the fields. It only lasts for a two or three days, and here I am, back again."

"I remember how Pa would go out to burn fields, but I didn't think of those times in terms of fun. So, what's fun about it?"

"All of us gals have the opportunity to see one another. Sometimes it's the only time we get during the entire year. This work needs to be done in a hurry to prepare the rice fields for planting. So, they bring us together from the various plantations and set us to work. Ain't really too hard. We jes' hitch our skirts up round our knees, tend the fire to keep it from running away from us and then jes' talk and catch up with gossip. We gotta keep alert though; with the dry grasses, fires can move awfully fast…particularly when the wind's blowin'."

"I remember the men tending to fires as a young girl. Me used to do it with neighbors. Did it to burn off the old seed."

"Yep, just like for us. Anyway, that's that. A day or two of fun seeing old friends. But we done now and it's almost time for Christmas. Really this be the best time of the year. Work's easy and we allowed a day or so for the holiday. My momma don't remember this holiday as a girl in Africa, but she always took it here."

"And that was my introduction to rice planting. If it were only as easy as tending a fire. But, as I learned later it's back breaking work with no two ways about it.

"First, of course new land has to be cleared and drained. That involves cutting trees, often in swamp water that is still infested with snakes. Cottonmouths and copperheads. I never did get over being afraid of them. Actually, not too many people died of bites if they were treated quickly. You had to make a good-sized cut over each bite mark and suck the blood out. But even so, being bit meant getting awfully sick. Occasionally in Georgia alligators could be found which was entirely something else. Being bitten by them meant losing an arm or leg. The turtles in these swamps were very common, and while they generally don't want anything to do with humans, get one mad or catch them unawares, they can take big bite out of you

"But, still in the Low Country, the best land was that which drained straight into the rivers going to the ocean. That meant that water could be easily drained into and out of the fields during the various times of the seasons.

"But, I'm getting ahead of myself. After enough trees had been cleared to work a field, a large dam would be thrown up along the river. This started the flooding process which rice needed. Water would enter up stream where the elevation was higher. Smaller dikes would be built across the fields to control the flow of water downhill. Thus, a rice plantation would be a string of diked fields that would move water into and across the fields and then return it out to the river. Moving water around the fields was done by a series of ditches. Drains taking across the fields were known as '1/4 ditches' while the lengthwise ditches were known as 'fore ditches.

"Taken all together, these dams, dikes and ditches created a patchwork appearance to the fields and as a consequence, they were known as 'squares.' Generally, the squares were about a quarter of mile on a side, which indicates how large these plantations were.

"These floodings would be controlled by 'trunks.' Actually, these trunks were ingenious inventions that were apparently brought over from Africa. I tend to believe this story because I never saw such a thing in all the years that I lived in Ireland. And since they had to come from somewhere, Africa is as good a place as any. Anyway, those slaves certainly knew what they were doing.

"Again, to get back to my story, these trunks were essentially hollowed out logs with a door at either end. When raised, the door at the rear end would let field water drain out during low tide. The exit of this trunk was also covered with a hinged door. During low tide, the drained water could flow freely. However, when high tide returned with salty water, this hinged door would automatically close and protect the fields.

"To give you an idea as to how much labor was involved with the construction of these fields, as I had said before, I have seen them as large as a quarter mile square with a number of these squares strung together like a gigantic checker board. And again, these strings were just a small part of the Drayton plantations. Any one of these strings would have me poor old da green with envy to have that much land. And to own it himself and not be a renter just planting for His Lordship. I never had a chance to tell him about these things. Probably just as well. He either wouldn't have believed me, or it would have broken his heart to match his back.

"Anyway, just after the burnings and Christmas holidays, the work would really start. The slaves would plow the ground and then chop it with eight-inch hoes to prepare it for seeding. Then, to ensure that the water would flow properly, the ditches would be cleaned using long handled scoops. Again, this work was done by both sexes although Sally wasn't required to do that work. The laundry still had to be done which suited her just fine.

"Once the fields were prepared, the rice would be planted in trenches that were four inches wide and eleven inches apart. The planting was very shallow with just enough soil laid over to cover the seed. This planting was done by the women.

"When to plant was a very important decision and was usually done during two periods. It was either from the tenth of March to the tenth of April or during the first ten days of June. Lots of people wondered why. Well, the reason was birds. Birds were always looking for seed. After the burning, the birds would come in and eat the remaining seeds, which was all right. But, otherwise, the migrating birds could destroy a crop almost overnight. Again, in September, birds could destroy a ripe crop that was almost ready for harvesting. Farmers tried everything to stop them. Scarecrows, slaves shooing them away…nothing seemed to work.

"You've all heard how rice needs to be flooded. Well, here the good Lord amply provided with the rivers and swamps. Water could be drained in and out with the trunks. And again, when to flood was an important process. The first flooding occurred as soon as the seed was sown. This was called the 'Sprout Flow.' It also protected the newly sown seed from the birds. Of course, this flooding brought a lot of trash that had to be constantly collected and burned.

"When the seed sprouted, the fields were dried in order to let the seedlings take root. Then when the blades of rice appeared, the fields were again flooded. This was known as the 'Stretch Flow' and its purpose was to kill the grasses that had grown up after the Sprout Flow was withdrawn. The Stretch Flow was first very deep to really kill the grass, but then it was drained to the point where the higher field hills were just barely exposed. This was tricky, because while the rice needed the water, too much could drown it. The deep flooding lasted about a week and the shallow flooding about ten days. Then the fields were completely drained to commence the 'Dry Growth.'

"Dry Growth lasted forty days to let the rice mature. If rains came, then no more flooding occurred; otherwise, an occasional flooding was done to water the young rice. Throughout this period, hoeing to kill grass was continually done. The hoeing was done in half-acre sections, which was considered to be a day's work for a prime field hand.

"Finally in September when the rice became a golden grain, it was harvested. This of course was a time of considerable danger from birds that also came to enjoy the rice.

"But harvesting rice was very tedious. A slave would grasp three rows of stalks with his left hand and cut it with a scythe that was held in the right hand. The stalks were laid flat to dry in the sun. A half- acre plot of land could be cut this way in about two hours. The stalks were stacked in bundles the next day with about four to five stacks in each half-acre.

"When completely dried, the rice would be hauled from the fields to the miller by wagon. Actually the mill consisted of a 'conveyor house' where the rice would be poured to await milling. Then, in a second house, the milling itself would take place. From the mill, the rice would continue on to the 'Rice House' to await onward shipment.

"Altogether, plantation owners expected to get about forty bushels of rice from the acre and if successful, could make a handsome profit. Of course, whether a profit could be made was also dependent on prices during any given year, but generally planters reckoned about nine shillings per hundred pounds.

"But the labor for this profit was enormous. Daniel Hayward, who was from another famous family, needed a thousand slaves to clear his land. I never did know how many slaves the Draytons had, but it was a lot. Believe me. But, if the rice was to grown and harvested, slaves were an absolute necessity. No freeman would do that work unless it was for his direct benefit and alone, he couldn't live long enough to do enough all the work by himself. So, slaves were the only answer.

"Interestingly though, a lot of negotiation about this work went on between slave and master. Tasks were assigned to slaves and agreements were made as to how much work was done and of what quality. Once the daily work was done, the slaves were free to return home to tend their personal business. This personal business often included small vegetable gardens that could be sold in town at the markets.

"Still, the work was god-awful. Some slaves died in the snake infested waters. Being in water so much also created problems with their feet. Pregnant women were expected to continue working until the latest stages before birth. As a consequence, many died.

"I'm not saying this slave labor was right or wrong, but rather just trying to show it for what it was.

"And so went my first year. I didn't see or understand all that I'm telling you now, but basically, that was a typical year.

63

"It really wasn't until about the end of my second year at Drayton Hall that I got outside of this cycle and got to thinking about what lay behind it all. For the Master and his family, the various people who worked for them, and of course the slaves.

"I guess it was a conversation that I overheard…or really it was just a snatch…the Master was really upset. About what, I couldn't imagine. After all, this plantation was as big as the world, and the Draytons were as rich as kings. What's to be upset about?"

But upset the Master was as he exclaimed: "He knows I don't have that kind of money. God knows there's little enough cash on hand, and the Carolina money isn't accepted anywhere but here. What in the name of God is he thinking about?"

"What was he thinking about?" I wondered. "He doesn't have any money? Then how does he pay for everything?"

"I asked Susanna but she really didn't know. 'Oh well, you know the Judge. He's always had a hot temper.' In truth of fact, she really didn't care either. The Judge was so much richer than her family that even after all the years she had lived with them, she really couldn't imagine their having problems. They just were there, and she intended to stay with them for the rest of her live.

"Certainly, the slaves wouldn't have known what had upset the Master so there wasn't any point of asking them. Finally, I went to Mr. Smith, the overseer to see what he could make of the Master's conniption fit. As you know, I hadn't really liked him because he was so cold and wrapped in his work. But, that was due to change.

"Anyway, to Mr. Smith."

"Mr. Smith, have you got a minute or two? I've got a question to ask you about something that I don't understand."

"Yes, be quick. What is it?"

"Well, a couple of days ago, I was passing through the house, and I wasn't eavesdropping mind you, but the Master was talking so loudly that everyone could hear…"

"And what was that that you weren't snooping to hear?"

"Well, he was talking about not having enough money which is very confusing. Of course, the Draytons have a lot of money."

Mr. Smith looked a long time at me and finally asked: "Why do you want to know? What's it your business anyway?"

"Well, now I was irritated. For two years, I hadn't said boo to him and when I ask him a question, he starts almost accusing me of something. Angry. That's what was coming up, and I knew it. But, I bit my tongue before replying, and when I did, I knew I was rounding a corner of my life even without understanding why."

"Mr. Smith, I know that I'm just a seamstress here and a poor girl from Ireland. But I'm good at what I do. Just ask the Mistress. So, I'll not be apologizing for my skill. However, I'm not always going to be a poor seamstress from Ireland. My time will pass and I'll be free to start my own business."

"And what business might that be, Missy?"

"Seamstressing of course."

"Just what you're doing now."

"No, you're wrong. Free to do what I want, such as turn your business down if I've a mind."

"Not that you've gotten any."

"But, the choice will be mine to make."

"There, I can't argue. Your choice to make." Relenting with a flicker of a smile, "So what do you want to know?"

"Just my original question. What did the Master mean when he said that he didn't have money? Of course he has money. Otherwise, how could he afford this place? This is important to me if I am to do work as a free woman getting paid."

"Oh well," chuckled Mr. Smith. "He's got money for some stitching. That's just pocket money. But really, he doesn't have as much cash as you might think. In fact, he doesn't really need it."

"Doesn't need it? Now that's daft. Of course he needs it. How else can he pay for things?"

By this time, Mr. Smith was laughing more than anything imaginable. He hardly ever smiled, but here he was laughing out loud. Even a nearby slave or two were listening in disbelief. He didn't seem to be nearly so fierce now.

"Well, I'll tell you what, Missy. I gotta get some work done now, but I'll see you tonight after dinner in the kitchen and will explain some things to you. If you're going to be a tycoon as a seamstress, you need to know how the world works.

"With that, I made a claim to my future by learning about how the rich folks do business. It also showed me that you can't tell what a person is like inside by judging him from the outside. In fact, it showed me a whole lot more."

After the day's work was done and true to his word, Mr. Smith showed up at the kitchen. "H'mmm, now where do I start? Do you know what credit is?"

"I guess so. Does that have to do with borrowing? If so, then the Master must be a fool. Me da, he never wanted to borrow. 'If you can't pay cash, then don't pay at all,' was what he always said. At least, he meant that if you don't have what you want, then at least you're not in debtor's prison."

"Your pa was pretty poor wasn't he?" asked Mr. Smith gently.

"Yes, he was. But he never stole, and we always had food on the table. He and Ma were also old before their times in order to support us. His Lordship was punctual, he was, for the rent and he didn't care about good crops or bad. It was all the same to him. Only the rent mattered. That's the reason I'm here. The land couldn't support the lot of my parents' children. Only my brother's family. So, here I am"

"Your family doesn't have a lock on poverty. Mine came over from London where there wasn't land to be had. None of them could read or write nor did they have any sort of profession or skill. The best of their choices was either to work in the new mills that were beginning to grow up or turn to thievery."
"Did any of them meet Kevin? They would've had a lot in common...like a sudden trip to America."

Chuckling, "Nooo, I don't think so as they arrived about twenty-five years ago. I was only a tyke, but I can still remember being seasick and not knowing why."

"I knew why I was seasick. What I didn't know was whether I was going to survive. Nothing stayed down...not that the food was edible in the first place."

"You were pretty scrawny that first night..."

"God, I thought I would never eat again or get clean. It must have marked me because I still eat like a horse and take so many baths. I must wash up at least every day or so and wear my clothes no more than three or four days. Sally must think I'm trying to work her to death."

"Don't worry about Sally. She can take care of herself. Besides scrubbing clothes is easier than hoeing rice fields. Besides, as a seamstress, you need to present a good appearance. You can't look like a tramp, particularly if you intend to make a living at being a seamstress."

"But how did you learn to read and do numbers? Certainly, without them, you couldn't become an overseer."

"I was fortunate. My parents came to Massachusetts where they immediately found work. Also, there is a law there requiring every child to attend school. People are really particular about that. This law has been on the books since the 1640's or so. Called 'Old Satan's Law,' children are supposed to read the Bible everyday and learn about the good life, and you can't do that if you can't read. So, whether I wanted to or not, I learned how to read and do numbers."

"But, then from Massachusetts to here. What brought you here? Why not just stay in Massachusetts where there was lots of work?"

Mr. Smith sat back and thought a long time as if recalling half forgotten days in his life. Finally, he started talking, maybe just rambling. "Yeah, lots of work was still available, but not like when my parents were starting out. Boston was becoming more like London every day. Them that has money are rich and them that don't, ain't. It was becoming obvious that the Smiths were working well each day, but we weren't getting rich quick. Days without work were coming more often and lasting longer. Farming was out in New England since good land had long since been taken up. But elsewhere…maybe I could strike out and so something with myself. So, I just up and left…working here and there…trying to learn what I could. Did lots of things. Worked as a farm hand. Shod horses and did some metal work. Even worked as a printer's devil…Watched people trying to figure out what made them tick…Kept drifting south until eventually I wound up here in Carolina. Don't really know how I got here…Just did until I found a job with the Draytons in Charleston. One thing led to another and the Master learned that I could read, write and reckon. This isn't as common down here since they don't have "Old Satan's Law." People are a little more relaxed about churchgoing down here and reading scriptures isn't as important. Anyway, the Judge, one day he offered me the job of overseer at a smaller operation. What a break! Now I was somebody! I was no longer bending my back for someone else. From there, I have just kept on pushing…working harder and harder. The Judge gave me an opportunity, and I wasn't then and I am not now, ever going to lose it.

Every day I learn more about operating a large plantation. I also am saving money and one day, I'm gonna get me my own land and become someone."

"By now, the kitchen maids had cleaned up and gone home. The place was as quiet as a church. A couple of candles were flickering. The coals in the fireplace were slowly dying and a chill was beginning to settle in for the night. Mr. Smith just sat there in this shadowy darkness. Just sitting there in the shadows of his life. The shadows of life gone by and shadows of life to come."

We sat there for a long time, my heart was beating slowly like a clock. Finally, almost with a shake, Mr. Smith turned to me and said, "Oh my, it's been a long time. Don't know when I talked so long, particularly about myself. But, there you have it. My story. But, what about yours? I know you came from Ireland, but not much else."

"I don't need to repeat myself about how I came to live in America, but it was a long time since I had talked about it. Even Susanna, bless her heart, didn't know the half of it. But, somehow sitting there with Mr. Smith, it seemed to be the most natural thing in the world. He just sat there, occasionally lighting up his pipe.

"Again, a long silence. The chill had really settled in now. The tapers had become just stumps. One had already fizzled out."

Mr. Smith looked up at the clock and exclaimed, "Oh my, where has the time passed? I expect that it's almost ten-thirty, maybe eleven. We had better break this 'cause tomorrow comes early."

"I hope this isn't the last lesson about how the Draytons pay for things. Mind you, I've enjoyed this evening so much. It's been a long time since I…but, really I hope…well, I've got so much to learn."

"Susanna once mentioned that to me. That you're one driven woman. You hadn't been here a week when you were already planning what your life would be…where you would be going." Laughing, "I sure learned one thing today, that when you sink your teeth into something, you don't let go. So, I expect that I'll be teaching you a thing or two before you let me go."

"Well, children, it was some time before we got a chance to talk again. Mr. Smith might have relaxed for a bit that evening, but he still had to get the rice gathered. Finally, September passed and the rice was dried and milled. Work had slowed down a bit when I asked him if he had forgotten his promise."

"Mr. Smith, I'm ready for lesson two, if you please."

68

"What? Oh yes, I had almost forgotten...not the evening...but my promise to tell you how the rich people earn and spend their money. Do you want to meet again in the kitchen?"

"That'd be fine, thank you.

"And so it was that we met that evening and for many evenings thereafter.

"Rice, tobacco, indigo, pine tars, whatever was grown or made here in the colonies was bound for England. The Navigation Laws and a lot of other laws decreed that we would send all of our goods there and they would return their manufactured goods to us. No one else was allowed into this trade; sometimes we couldn't even trade with other colonies. Of course, that never let a smart ship captain from doing a little smuggling. Really, lots of smuggling. After all, money had to be made didn't it?

"But, all in all, this system really worked fairly well as long as the King didn't press things too hard. The Americas were becoming the richest land in the world. Certainly, people could earn a lot more here than they could even in England. Taxes here were pretty light which really raised the hackles of the people back home. They always complained about that. Wasn't America for their benefit? Then why were they paying such high taxes? But, again, I'm getting ahead of my story. So, let's stay with when I was just a miss.

"However, as Mr. Smith pointed out, none of this would have been possible if barrels of money had to be passed back and forth. First, there wasn't enough money in the world to fill these barrels, but more importantly, it was too slow. It was ok for Ma to pay for what he needed in town a couple of miles down the road. But, across the ocean thousands of miles away? It just wouldn't work.

"So, what was there in place of barrels of money? Credit. The planters, even the Draytons, were always in debt to their agents that were known as 'factors.' These agents would offer advance credit to their planter clients while buying and shipping anything for them that was requested. Then, the annual rice crops just paid off debts that were accumulated the previous year's buying spree. Hopefully, a bit was left over was left in the way of profits. These profits in turn were then applied toward more land.

"These planters never had enough land. George Washington, for example owned around 8,000 acres near Alexandria that were organized into five farms. Through his wife Martha, who came from the Custis family, he controlled assets valued in the thousands of pounds. In fact, to tell the truth, if Mr. Washington hadn't married Martha or someone like her, he probably would have remained a rather modest farmer. Then to top it off he speculated heavily in the Ohio Valley after he had taken a long trip there. Some say that he owned up to 30,000 acres in that wild country. Yet, despite all this land, he was constantly in debt. In fact, one year shortly before the war, he noted that he was 'only' £1000 in debt.

"Credit, I guess was the grease that made this trading machine work. Yet, it could get away from you because it was expensive. Factors charging about five per cent was not unusual. Also, when they made their sales and purchases, they would take a profit on each transaction. As a consequence, profits were often very slim and many planters could never get ahead. Thomas Jefferson, for example, had even less money than George Washington. Like Mr. Washington, his wife's dowry had vastly expanded his land holdings but he had incurred some debts from her and was never able to catch up with them. Course, I heard he was so busy writing declarations, politicking, and living in Paris, he never had time to pay attention to farming that paid money which just proves my point."

"So, Mr. Smith, what does this mean to me?"

"Wyanne, it means that you need to be careful who you're dealing with. Most of the planters here will be wanting to deal with credit if they give you a large order. And with your skills, you should expect large orders. So, when the rice crops are in, you need to be quick with your bills if you expect to be paid. Then, keep your ears to the ground. If you hear that someone is having trouble paying their bills, then your problems will start. How to decline their business while not offending them will be a big problem. But better declining their business than looking for lost money."

"From there, he taught me how to keep accounts, figure expenses, deal with banks, buy and sell property and on and on. He even taught me a bit about law. Nothing complicated, mind you. But I did learn what my rights would be as a free woman...meaning neither indentured nor married. As an indentured servant, I was totally obligated to the Draytons for the next five years. My labor belonged to them in exchange for my transportation and room and board. Afterwards, if I were to marry, then I pretty much lost my right to manage my own business affairs. Of course, lots of wives still did so, but only by the grace of their husbands. So, I learned then that any husband of mine would have to be something special.

"Of course, he didn't teach me every night. Mr. Smith would be gone for days at a time overseeing operations at any number of different locations. Meanwhile, I had started to send letters home. My writing had improved enough to be readable, and Mr. Gordon thought it would be good practice for me to write my family.

"You know, it felt funny at first. I had been away for so long. Almost two years without a bit of contact. They were almost fading away. My crying spells, particularly at Christmas, were almost a thing of the past. But, really, Mr. Gordon was right. I should write."

DEAR MA AND PA,   SEPTEMBER, 1752

HOW ARE YOU? I AM FINE. AS YOU CAN SEE, I HAVE LEARNED HOW TO READ AND WRITE. SO MANY THINGS HAVE HAPPENED TO ME THAT I HARDLY KNOW WHERE TO START. OF COURSE, THE BEST THING IS BEING ABLE TO WRITE SO THAT I CAN TELL YOU. THE MISTRESS HERE INSISTED THAT I LEARN SO THAT I COULD MAKE FANCY DRESSES FOR HER.

KEVIN IS GONE. I DON'T KNOW WHERE HE IS. IN FACT, I NEVER SAW HIM. IT SEEMS THAT HE FELL BACK TO POACHING SHORTLY BEFORE I ARRIVED. FURTHERMORE, HE WASN'T ANY BETTER HERE AT IT THAN HE WAS IN IRELAND. SO, HE GOT CAUGHT AND LIT OUT. HAS HE SENT ANY LETTERS TO YOU?

WELL, I HAVE BEEN HERE AT THE DRAYTON PLANTATION FOR TWO YEARS. TIME SEEMS TO FLY BY. BUT YOU WOULD HARDLY RECOGNIZE ME NOW. I HAVE GAINED A LOT OF WEIGHT AND BECOME A REGULAR WOMAN. THAT'S ONE GOOD THING ABOUT WORKING HERE. YOU GET LOTS TO EAT EVERYDAY.

I HOPE ALL IS WELL WITH YOU. IF YOU CAN, GO TO THE PRIEST AND ASK HIM TO SEND A LETTER BACK. MY ADDRESS HERE IS THE DRAYTON HALL, CHARLESTON, CAROLINA.

YOUR DAUGHTER,

WYANNE

Amazingly enough, I got a reply in six months scribed by the town priest.

Dear Wyanne,   March 16th, 1753

It is with great sadness that I tell you that your Da has died. As you know, he had not been feeling well even before you had left. Consequently, he had hoped to leave the farm to your brother, Jake and then have a chance to rest. Well, praise be to the Lord, he got about a year. Then during a bad rainstorm, he was out helping Jake and he caught a bad case of the grippe. The local doctor did everything he could. He even bled your Da several times, but to no good.

So, now I am with Jake and his family. My health has not been too good, and I cannot get around like I used to. But, all in all, I can't complain. Your Da, he was a good man and Jake's family is lively and healthy. So, all in all, the good Lord is providing well.

No, I haven't heard from Kevin. Other than the one letter or two that he sent that brought you over to America, he seems to have dropped off the edge of the earth…or maybe down a hangman's noose. But, no, really I don't believe that. Kevin was always wild, but not bad. I say my prayers for him everyday.

Thank you for writing. Now I know you are alive and well.

Your ma

DEAR MA,   JANUARY 13, 1752

I AM REAL SORRY TO HEAR ABOUT DA. I HAD HOPED TO TELL HIM ABOUT THE FARMS HERE. THEY ARE SO BIG. EVEN BIGGER THAN HIS LORDSHIP'S. YET, UNLIKE HIS LORDSHIP, THESE PEOPLE DIDN'T INHERIT THEIR LAND BUT RATHER WORKED TO GET IT. REALLY, WANTING AND WORKING FOR SOMETHING HERE IS ALMOST A PRAYER HERE. ANYTHING IS POSSIBLE IF YOU WORK FOR IT. AND THIS LAND IS GOOD.

MR. SMITH IS AN EXAMPLE OF WHAT I AM TALKING ABOUT. HE CAME HERE TO THE CAROLINAS FROM THE MASSACHUSETTS COLONY WITHOUT A PENNY. YET, HE HAS WORKED HIMSELF UP TO HEAD OVERSEER OF THIS HUGE FARM CALLED A PLANTATION. EVEN NOW, HE IS LIVING BETTER THAN WE COULD EVEN DREAM OF DOING IN IRELAND. YET, HE IS NOT SATISFIED. HE WANTS TO OWN HIS OWN PLANTATION. IT MEANS THAT HE WILL BE LEAVING HERE SOON AND GOING WEST TO WHERE THE LAND IS FREE FOR THE TAKING.

OF COURSE, THAT WILL BE DANGEROUS. THERE ARE INDIANS OUT THERE WHO WILL WANT TO STOP HIM. BUT, HE'S BOUND TO GO. AND WHEN HE DOES, I SHALL MISS HIM. WHEN I FIRST MET HIM, I THOUGHT HE WAS SO COLD. I ALMOST FELT A CHILL WHEVEVER HE CAME NEAR. BUT NOW, I HAVE COME TO KNOW HIM AND OF HIS AMBITION AND ALL THAT HE HAS TAUGHT ME, AND I BELIEVE HIM TO BE A TRUE FRIEND.

I WILL TELL YOU MORE OF WHAT HAS HAPPENED TO ME IN MY NEXT LETTERS.

WYANNE

Then came my final letter from Ireland.

Dear Wyanne,   March 2, 1752

It is with great sorrow that I tell you that your Ma has died. She never really recovered from the death of your pa. So, now that she is buried beside him, I believe that she is happier.

As for us, life is about the same. We have three children and the house is almost too small for us. Of course, there isn't much we can do about it. His Lordship doesn't allow money for building a larger place. But, the crops have been good and we can't complain. We get the rent paid off each year without too much problem.

Oh yes,, Kevin did write. He was in New York someplace. I really don't know where that is, but at least he's alive.

Your brother,

Jake

"So, now that was that. Jake was the last of my family and he hadn't changed nor had his life. It would be spent in the service of His Lordship. At least, one good bit of news. I knew that Kevin was still alive and probably still charming the girls.

"Still, I had Mr. Smith. By now, Susanna was now married and having kids, at first a girl, which pleased her husband. So, other than at work, I really saw less of her than when we shared a room together and gossiped sometimes until late at night. So, in her stead Mr. Smith and I spent many an evening in the kitchen."

"You know, one thing I have learned is that slaves aren't free."

"You don't say, Wyanne. Whatever gave you that idea? I thought they were as free as the breeze."

"No, now you're joking and twisting my words. What I mean is that once the Master buys a slave, there's no guarantee that he will be alive for long or at least alive long enough to have children which would be a free source of labor."

"No, you're right," responded Mr. Smith. "Actually, getting enough slaves together for the year's harvest is very expensive. The Master generally figures about one in three die will be dead soon after they arrive in America. The trip over is terrible and so many die getting here. They are just jammed into the ships until they are full with no chance to move. Then, they get small pox or malaria. A few just die

73

while working from snake bite, exhaustion or sometimes I think they just give up on living."

"I've even noticed that this weather is hard on everyone. Look at Susanna. Thirty-two years old and on her second husband. "

"The Master is on his third wife already. I don't know why. But that's the rule here. Up north in Massachusetts, the weather was colder, miserable in fact, and yet people didn't die like this."

"Ughhh, this isn't fun talking. Back home, we would say that the Haunts could hear and curse you. Can we change the subject? I have the chills and it's not from the weather."

"What would warm you, little colleen?"

"Why Mr. Smith, that's the first time you've ever called me by anything other than my given name."

"That's what you are, aren't you?"

"Yes, of course, but how did you know that?"

"There's other Irish in the sea besides you, little Missy."

"Are you trying to tease me, Mr. Smith? If so, I'll have you know that I am a prim and proper young girl."

"Sure, and I see you carrying on with the young boys coming around who are pretending to be lost until you take them by the hand."

"Oh them! They couldn't find their heads with both hands. But there is one boy I don't like. He keeps hanging around chewing tobacco and bragging about himself."

"Who's that?"

"William Jackson. I just don't like him and while I have tried to be polite, one day I'll just have to let him have some Irish temper."

"That will be something to see," snorted Mr. Smith. "But, seriously, do you want me to run him off?"

"No, I don't think so. I can handle him, but thank you for the offer."

"Just yell if you need me to send him on his way. You know..."

"What?"

"Well...through these long evenings of chats...of teaching you whatever I know...I have really come to cherish these times together. Otherwise, my work makes me very lonely. I know that people think me as a cold fish. I suppose it's true...I'm not much for words normally. But...with you, hopes, jokes and dreams seem to flow...Anyway, I love you for the warmth you give to me."

"Mr. Smith...I really don't know what to say. But yes, these evenings are a treasure. Susanna was a God-send during my early times here. I don't know what I would have done without her. And cold fish, nooo, that doesn't describe you. Icicle would be a better word. You really terrified me that first night. My mouth was just full of cotton. But, she was there to melt the frost, bless her heart. However, she has another life now...and so, here we are warming a chilly kitchen."

"Well, anyway, let me know if that Jackson boy ever bothers you. Right now, I think we need to call it a day. Tomorrow sees me off to oversee some planting."

"Good night, Mr. Smith."

CHAPTER EIGHT

It was during her third year at Drayton Place that a number of changes began to occur in Ma's life. Some of them were pleasant perhaps, but others less so.

The rice had been harvested and was being milled. Mr. Smith was scarce to be found being that his attention was devoted totally to the completion of a long year's rice planting. As Ma had indicated in her stories, he had devoted some portion of his evening hours educating her on the ways of business here in the Carolinas. But these hours were definitely hit or miss, and they left little time for personal matters. But, this was all to change.

Ma had always noted with some humor about how boys would hang around. Susanna used to tease her. Several, among them William Malone, were actually enjoyable company. Over the years, Ma and they had developed friendships of a sort, usually chatting as she was working on dresses or more recently, on baby clothes. Mrs. Drayton had just had a fine baby son named Glen who would survive childhood and reach middle age before malaria cut him down. By the time this tragedy occurred, Ma had already gone on to the Bahamas. But, still she was devastated when she heard the news. Glen was always a favorite of hers probably because she had spent time with him before she left for Charles Town.

But, one boy, William Jackson was definitely not her cup of tea. She had even mentioned her dislike of him to Mr. Smith, but nothing seemed to be needed from him about this lad. It wasn't so much that he chewed tobacco. Ma had become accustomed to that habit since discovering that many men chewed or snuffed the weed. Amazingly enough, even some women were known to do it. Smoking a pipe was not at all uncommon. Not that she liked it, mind you. She still thought it repulsive. Teeth became brown and spitting just seemed to be filthy.

However, there was something else that she couldn't place. Most of the other boys would stop by in a public place and talk. Often when she was sitting outside enjoying the spring or fall temperatures as she was sewing. Space always existed between them, and she was comfortable with them. Even at the Christmas dances when they were dancing their reels closely, space was always there. Not that William ever danced. He would just hang around looking on. Perhaps that was it. He was always just looking on.

He was also unexpected. She would be rounding a corner and bump into him. Walking between buildings and he would seemingly be walking by. Always looking as he passed. None of the other boys ever gave her that feeling. Yet, to put a point on it, he hadn't done anything wrong. Still…

Ma hadn't much to go on, but she was concerned enough about it that during a sewing session with Susanna, she brought the subject up.

"Susanna, what do you know about the Jackson boy?"

"Why, are you sweet on him? He is such a catch."

"Oh God, no. With his breath! I've smelled three day old dead skunks sweeter than him."

"Like I say, you must be sweet on him to match him with a skunk. But, really, why do you ask?"

"Well, I don't know why, but he just makes my skin crawl."

"What! Has he done anything to you? Do you want me to have Jeb take after him or report him to Mr. Smith?"

"No, I don't think that'll be needed. Besides Mr. Smith already offered to run him off the land, but I said no."

"Well, you just say the word. But, to answer your question, no I really don't know much about him. He just seems to come and go. Always has an errand or some reason to be here, but nothing of any importance. I just thought he was like the other boys who come around here to see you."

"Yes, that's just the point. Lots of boys come around and most of them are kind of fun in their awkward ways. Their reasons for being here are just as silly as Jackson's if not more so. So, that doesn't bother or surprise me. It's just that they are obvious about themselves and they know their limits. But Jackson always has a reason to find me in awkward places."

"What do you mean," asked Susanna.

"Well, around behind the various buildings here. One time as I was coming out of the outhouse. Now, really, why there?"

"Even boys have to pee sometimes," said Susanna with a laugh.

"Yeah, but just as I'm coming out?" wailed Ma.

"You ought to see my husband. As soon as I start making a dash, he's just in front of me. But never mind, here comes Mr. Smith. Does he have to pee?"

Turning toward Mr. Smith, Ma hoped that tonight would be another lesson in the kitchen. But, no, something different.

"Ma, get your things together. The Mistress is in Charles Town and she needs some sewing done. All of the material she ordered from London has just arrived along with drawings of the latest styles. She's in a real tear to be the first lady in the latest fashions."

"Whaaa…? Now? Charles Town?…I'm not sure…"

Susanna piped up: "Ma, you ninny. You're going to Charles Town. A real city. With real shops. Now get moving and pack some clothes. Here, I'll help you."

Ma was stunned. For the life of her, she could not move. After living on the plantation since the day she arrived, her world had become the plantation with its slow, rolling rhythms of burning, planting, flooding and harvesting. Only the Christmas party season provided any break and that was just a flash of color. The farthest she had traveled had been to church on Sundays, and that was only a mile or two down the road. In point of fact, she hadn't even seen any of the other plantations, hearing only stories of them through Sally and other slaves. The boys who came to tease her also came from places unknown. She knew the names of their plantation homes, but had no clear idea of their location.

"Well, come on, ninny. Let's get moving!" cried Susanna. "Statues never get to see anything."

Pushing Ma toward her apartment, Susanna took charge. She picked a few underthings and a simple dress that would fit easily into a bag, her comb, a small mirror, an extra pair of shoes, and a purse, and Ma was being pushed out the door.

"Now, go. Mr. Smith is waiting for you, and he doesn't like to miss the tide."

Ma followed Susanna like a stork following the path from the main house down to the river about three or four hundred yards away. Mr. Smith was waiting impatiently there striding back and forth in front of a barge laden with rice. Several slaves were attending the vessel with an obvious intent of poling off as soon as they were given the order. Eventually, Ma gaited down the path to the gangway and was led to a seat in the rear of the barge where there was some shade from the morning sun.

This was the third water ride that she had ever taken. Considering her first one across the ocean, Ma had frankly hoped never to float on water again. Later, going to the Bahamas was a second sea trip that she vowed never to repeat. But, the river trip really wasn't too bad. With a helmsman guiding the craft into the swifter current of river's center, a bit of breeze began to pick up and a small sail was mounted for a bit of extra speed. Birds of various sorts could be heard and seen as they flew over the savanna. Eventually Ma began to come around enough to realize that she was enjoying herself and Charles Town was beckoning.

Turning to Mr. Smith, Ma commented: "Well, sir, you do give a girl lots of time to prepare."

"What's to prepare? Toss a few things into a bag and you're set," grunted Mr. Smith.

"Just like a man" mumbled Ma. "Leave a body on a farm for three years and then expect her to be set for a trip of a lifetime in a trice."

"What's that?" jibed Mr. Smith. "Do I hear the female sounds of grumbling as she is quote: 'going on the trip of a lifetime?' Unquote. What sort of thanks is that? I tell you, men are never appreciated. And after all the trouble I went to suggesting here and there that the Mistress really needs a seamstress to show off her new fashions."

"Why, Mr. Smith. You *are* a tease. Worse than those boys who hang around every day. I swear." By now, Ma was apparently in a blithering blush. Mr. Smith was chortling from minute to minute watching her changing reactions.

"Never thought I'd live to see the day. Ma flustered without a sharp word on her tongue. I'll have to do these things more often." Reaching into the river, Mr. Smith dipped his fingers and snapped water into her face. Ma sputtered like a wet hen, which made Mr. Smith laugh even more. Finally, even Ma began to see the joke of her reactions and begin to laugh.

"So, now that you have captured me, how long will I be taken to Charles Town, Sir Captor?"

"Ah now, that depends."

"On what? Prey tell."

"Whether you are a good girl or a bad girl."

"And if I'm bad?" arched Ma.

"You'll be forced to stay in Charles Town, never to plow rice fields again."

79

"Oh lord and master, anything but that!" Then pensively, "but, really, this does mean a lot. Being able to go to Charles Town, I mean."

"Why is that?" There was a note of sadness in Mr. Smith's question.

"Well, obviously. It gives me an opportunity to see for myself all the things you have been telling me and to see if my memories of the city are true. That entire day really was the grandest sight of my entire life…even if a certain Mr. Smith was so gruff with me."

"I'll have to talk to him about that. A young damsel like you being forced to deal with such an ogre as him. But, your heart is still set on setting up business in Charles Town? Nothing could change your mind?"

"No, why? Ever since I saw the Drayton Hall that first night and learned what hard work can get you, I have been on fire to set my path. A long time has passed since then with a lot of questions on how, but never what. Just like you, in fact with your dreams of a plantation. We're really a lot alike, us two. On fire."

"Well, yes. On fire. That's a good description of us. Two souls plunging into black holes looking for light beyond our own fires of ambition. Well, I wish you luck, Miss Wyanne."

The afternoon's pleasant, almost silly cruise down the river seemed to flit away with these last remarks. Long pauses broke the stream of words, the flow of banter. Birds flew over with their joyful sweeps in the air, but they weren't seen. Fish leaping and diving were ignored. Only the high grasses of the savannah sighing in time with the slow sweep of the helmsman's steer board was heard.

"Can you hear the savannah grass? It seems so sad."

"It's just the wind rustling."

"Yes, but it's so sad. I don't believe I ever heard anything like it in Ireland."

The sweet air of the morning now was becoming sticky and sour. Clothing became a prison. Buzzing bugs picked up the mournful song of the savannah grass.

Finally, Ma could stand it no more. What was this pall that had settled over such a festive occasion?

Turning to Mr. Smith, she demand, "Are you trying to tell me something, Mr. Smith? We were having a really gay afternoon until you wanted to know if my heart was still set on Charles Town. Now, out with it. What's on your mind?"

"Ummm, nothing. Just thinking, I guess."

"Now don't be telling me that. I won't stand for it. You've gotten a bee in your bonnet, so now out with it."

Mr. Smith waited a long minute. Thoughts seemed to be passing across his face, but none of them seemed to settle into anything. Ma was not to be distracted by his musings. Rather, she sat stolidly by waiting for an answer. It was one thing to be serious about something, but another to be a wet dishrag. Especially on such a hot and sticky day.

"Well, I'm waiting."

"I know you are, and I'm not sure what you want."

"Whatever's on your mind. Seems pretty simple to me."

"Well, let's just say that Charles Town will bring a lot answers."

"And what's that supposed to mean? Mr. Smith, you can be so difficult sometimes. I just don't understand you at all."

More waiting. Time hung as heavily as the limpid air. Mr. Smith groaned, "Oh lord, how did I get into this at all?" He clearly was not a happy man in these circumstances, and Ma was not helping matters any with her arched looks at him.

Finally, he asked, "There's no way you can be distracted from Charles Town?"

"What else is there? I can't stay at the Drayton place. That's all right, but you know what I think about being kept help. My family in Ireland has been kept help since time immemorial, and now the Good Lord has given me the opportunity to change that."

"I understand that. But why Charles Town? There are other opportunities you know."

"Name one," demanded Ma.

81

"Well, with me for one," blurted Mr. Smith.

"What? What are you talking about, Mr. Smith? Please be clear."

"Well, you know of my plans to start my own plantation. I've almost gotten enough money saved and during this trip, I intend to start looking for land to buy. Perhaps in a year, I'll be ready to go."

"And you want me to follow you that is? A couple of problems. One, you seem to forget that I'm still indentured for four more years. Or do you intend to buy my contract so that I will be your hired help in the middle of a forest? Then, when the hard work is done and you're set up in your kingdom like His Lordship back home, I can be let go. To go where? Are you daft? Here I have a future."

"What makes you think of being just an indentured servant?"

"What else is there? Slavery? I'm not sure that's a tasty choice."

"No, but some people have called it that on occasion," Mr. Smith laughed ruefully.

"Then what? Spit it out man!"

A deep sigh, and then a warm smile spread across Mr. Smith's face, "This is not how the storybook romances offer these scenes, but here goes. Miss Wyanne Farrell, may I have the honor of your hand in marriage?"

"Ah, ha, ha, ha." Ma giggled until she had no more breath. "Excuse me, Mr. Smith. But, it sounded just as though you had asked me to marry you."

"But, I did. There's nothing wrong with your ears."

"Well, I must admit. When I demanded that you spit it out, you certainly did do that...My...what an afternoon...And this day started off so slowly...And now I'm off to Charles Town to announce my betrothal to Mr. Bert Smith...And he does all this without so much as a moment's notice. This is the funniest day of my life."

"Well, I must also admit. This isn't the reception I had expected from a proposal. Yes or no, for sure. I don't know...perhaps. But a joke..? I didn't expect that."

"I'm sorry, Mr. Smith. But this is the funniest thing I have ever heard. Ha, Ha, Ha! Do you have a handkerchief? I'm crying from laughing!" More giggling and laughter ensured. Even the boatmen were beginning to stare.

Noticing that she was being stared at, Ma tried with great effort to pull herself together only to break up again. Finally, "you *are* sober, Mr. Smith, are you not?"

"Yes, but I'm beginning to wish I weren't," growled Mr. Smith.

"By God, I believe you mean it, Mr. Smith. And truly, I'm sorry that I have been so unkind, but ha, ha, ha, it is truly funny. If only you could see your face. Ha, ha, ha." More giggles. "But really, Mr. Smith, what brought this on? I'm flattered, but what *did* bring this on?"

"At this point, I'm not sure you would understand if I tried to explain. Let's just drop the subject."

At last, getting control of herself, and wiping off her tears, Ma laid a gentle hand on Mr. Smith's. "Dear Mr. Smith. I truly am sorry if I ruined your beautiful moment. But, for the life of me, I was absolutely surprised. I was completely unprepared for it. My life has been so wrapped up in sewing and planning for the future, I had given no thought of here and now. Certainly, the boys hanging around were nothing to dream about. And you, being so stern when we first met…it must have created a lingering image…even though you have been warm and gentle these last months. When I think about how you patiently answered all questions in the kitchen after long days in the fields…"

"What do you think made me come in from the fields? It certainly wasn't the prospect of going to bed and dreaming about work." Taking Ma's hand in turn, "Wyanne, this is clumsy, but believe me, a good heart is being given in bonded faith."

"I know. But, let me think. I won't say no, but I can't say yes either. Besides, are you willing to wait until I have finished my contract?"

"You're right about that. I would buy it out."

"No, you won't. That's flat. No, you won't. When I came here I promised you and the Draytons that I would finish my contract and nothing's going to change that?"

"And why not? Indenture contracts are bought and sold all the time. It's not as though you were leaving like your brother."

"No, and that's that. Kevin left as a thief, and I will only leave as a woman who has kept her word. Otherwise, my name will not be any better than his, and that I can't stand. It must stand for finishing something especially when there is an easier way out. So, again, are you willing to wait? Think carefully because I won't want to be hearing anything more about this matter."

"You drive a hard bargain, and honestly, I didn't really think about your indenturement. Most people do anything to cut them short. But no, I have to want someone who doesn't take shortcuts. I suppose that's what has attracted me to you and I surely don't want to lose you. So, yes, I won't like it, but yes, I'll wait."

"Good, now we're getting somewhere. My contract says I can't marry, but nothing has been said about being engaged or wanting to be married. So, let's leave it at that."

And that was that. The rest of the trip to Charles Town was really not remembered. Ma and Mr. Smith let the hours slip away. The beauty of the savanna went by unnoticed as the boat moved to the slow beat of the helmsman's sweep.

CHAPTER NINE

"Yes, ma'am. I know you have wanted to see me, but I didn't want to disturb you last night seeing as how we got in rather late. It was well after sundown."

"Very good. We couldn't have done anything last night anyway without any light. So, now we can get started right away. Here are the patterns...just in from London. The latest thing. I'm so excited about them. Hopefully, they will make the Draytons the belle of the balls during the upcoming season. Mind you, they are complicated and we don't have a lot of extra material, so be careful."

"Yes, ma'am. As long as they are well drawn, I don't expect any problems. Mr. Gordon has done a good job teaching me how to read. In fact, if I might say so, he has been pleased with my progress. He says I should start reading poetry soon."

"H'mm, well, yes. Just don't lose sight of why you learned in the first place."

"Mrs. Drayton, I won't. But, that does bring up something that I need to get clear as soon as possible."

"Yes...?"

"It's about Mr. Smith, and for me it has been pleasant and hopefully for you as well. Anyway, I think you should know."

"Know what...?"

A deep breath...and Ma started to run with her words as she spoke, "Well, he has asked me to marry him and of course, the first thing I told him was that my indenturement contract has still four years to go and I made him promise to wait because nothing was going to break my word to you and the Master for being so good to me in spite of how dreadfully Kevin let you down and all I just couldn't that to you under any circumstances and..."

"Hold on before you lose your breath and pass out," laughed Mrs. Drayton. "Actually, I have known about Mr. Smith's feelings for you for some time. He actually has made an agreement with the Judge to buy your contract. In fact, looking at the moonstruck expression on his face every time he looked at you, I was wondering how long it would take him to ask you."

"You...you knew?" asked Ma incredulously.

"But, of course silly girl."

"Well, I'll be…But ma'am, while I appreciate the Master letting me have my freedom, I can't accept it."

"And why not?"

"As I told Mr. Smith, Kevin my brother broke his contract by being a thief and I'll not be breaking mine as a bride. You and the Master took me in under bad circumstances and have given the first chance at a better life that my family has ever had. I'll not waste it by leaving early. It'll cost me four more years, but people will say that Ma keeps her word. Otherwise, how can I face them?"

"Well, that's very honorable of you, but no one has ever thought otherwise. So, you really don't need to feel that you must stay since Mr. Smith has offered to recover our expenses."

"But, there's another point that I haven't said to Mr. Smith. In truth, I don't believe I thought of it until just now. If I marry him, and I haven't said yet that I will, I want to come to him as a free woman. Mr. Smith I know is an honorable man, but I'll not be bought by anyone, honorably or not. I just won't."

"Oh well, now that's another issue. God knows we women are treated like children all too often because the men are considered the lord and master of their homes. But ok, Wyanne, I understand you and perhaps you're right. Anyway, we'll see what sort of person Mr. Smith really is. If he waits patiently for four more years, then you'll know that he's the sort of man a woman should marry."

"Thank you, ma'am. I feel better having talked to you. Now, if you don't mind, we've work to do wooing men."

"Well said! Now, here's the patterns…"

The next weeks through the Fall months was a period of intense work making the dresses that the Mistress wanted for the Christmas season. However, it was also a period of exploring. Accompanied by Betsy, the slave whom she had met during her arrival in Charles Town, Ma was often called upon to go downtown on various errands. In particular, she explored the many shops on King Street. These shops comprised the retail section of town where sundries for the home could be bought. Many of them had signs mounted on the exterior walls that indicated the trade of the various proprietors. One in particular had a hat that comically illustrated the hatter's trade.

Ma marveled at how convenient the city was. Getting something was just a matter of minutes as compared to ordering something at the farm. That would usually mean a week or more of waiting for the next barge to go down river or sending Sam and his mule, Old Sal to shuffle down the road. Often it was easier to do without or just have whatever was needed made right there on the spot. But here, the whole world was open to her.

In this situation, Ma began to imagine herself living here more each day. Of course, the plantation was a wonderful place to live. But, she knew full well that she would never be able to buy such a place, so logic told her that Charles Town was center of her future. And what a wonderful prospect that was!

Looking above the passing shops, she could see that rooms could be found where she could work until she was able to buy her own shop. Perhaps, she could strike a partnership with a tailor and establish a regular center for herself. Her biggest problem was becoming known.

Finding food, like finding sundries, was not a problem. Betsy would regularly take her down to South Market and East Bay to the Charles Town Market. This was a line of elegant, open-air brick structures with arched entryways that were perhaps a hundred or so feet long. Here, food flooded the tables as hawkers sold all sorts of fish, vegetables, and meats. Betsy was careful where she went, warning Ma about who was honest and who would try to slip bad produce onto unwary customers. Still, starving would not be a problem and for Ma, that was a concern because she never seemed able to fill the hunger in her belly.

Money would be in very short supply for her when she started out. So, a clientele that could grow rapidly was a must. Accordingly, she started to memorize the names of the families that lived in the city. Among them were the Branfords who had just recently built a charming house on Meeting Street. It was famous for having carved cypress paneling and its drawing room was considered to be the one of the grandest, if not the grandest in Charles Town. Further along, the Bull family had erected in 1720 one of the earliest homes in Charles Town. This family was certainly one to know as it was both wealthy and well established in local politics. Other houses indicated similar stories of wealth and power. Now, if the Mistress would write a letter of reference at the end of her contract.

Ma thought about religion in this town. Although raised a Catholic who attended church every Sunday in Ireland, the issue of attending Mass did not seem very important. First, there was no opportunity here. Catholic churches simply were non-existent. There were all sorts of Protestant churches, but no Catholic ones in Charles Town. So, no need to worry about what wasn't available. Furthermore, after attending church services with the Draytons for three years in the local church, the issue no longer seemed relevant. Lightening didn't dance across the skies nor did God's thunder roll a warning as she was told as a child. In fact, she was rather healthy and so was everyone else around her. So damnation didn't appear to be a problem. Finally, on a commercial level, she understood that being in Sunday proximity to her customers would be a good way to drum up business. This considered, Ma chose to continue with Protestant services.

Still, life was not all planning for the future. Ma took sentimental strolls down along East Bay Street to see the ships that had brought her here to the Americas. How long ago that seemed, and yet at the same time, it was only an instant since she first laid eyes on it atop Sam's wagon. But the colors of the warehouses there were still brightly painted upheld the rightly earned name of "Rainbow Row". The only place she couldn't abide was the slave ships. The groaning and clanking of chains accompanied by the staccato of whips was a sound she could never get used to even though she otherwise accepted slavery as a normal part of daily life.

Eventually, however, the time came for returning to the plantation. Time had just seemed to fly! Where had it gone? Ma felt a real tinge of homesickness at the thought of leaving the excitement of Charles Town. Drayton Place was wonderful, and she was anxious to see Susanna with tales of her adventures of poking through shops, seeing the beautiful single and double houses, and meeting the high and the mighty. She also just had to talk to her about Mr. Smith. What would she think? Did she have any ideas?

Like her first trip to the Drayton Place, Sam and Old Sal kept her company. Ma saw many of the same scenes along the way, although it seemed that more houses had sprouted up. But, something of real importance had been built. A bridge! Instead of having to wait for a ferry, a bridge had been erected across the Ashley river between Stony Point on the East Side to the road leading up to the plantations further to the west. The bridge was really impressive being eight feet above the water, twenty feet wide and railed on either side. Most importantly for the large trading vessels, the bridge had a draw section that would raise up and let the river traffic pass.

Of course, like the old ferries, it wasn't free. Sam had to pay two shillings. Still, that was cheaper than the bigger wagons and coaches with four or six horses. They had to pay three shillings. But, so fast! No longer having to wait for a ferry that might arrive on time. Besides, ferries floated on water, and Ma wanted nothing to do with boat rides.

Still, Sal was not to be hurried and it was almost eight o'clock before she ambled up the front drive. Ma had almost forgotten the thrill she felt the first time she saw the grand house of the Draytons. Through the years, it had almost blended into the background of life. But, now after her long absence from the plantation, its looming shadows coming through the trees and its twinkling lights of candles stabbed her heart as keenly as a knife. Now, she knew once again why her future lay here in America. Now she knew why she could not break her contract...even for the love of a man who could secure her release.

"My God, I am here again," whispered Ma.

From the shadows, almost in a replay of the scene three years ago, a dark voice asked: "And who do we have here? A scrawny, rat-tailed redhead?"

"Mr. Smith, I just can't believe it. I'm here. Without cotton in my mouth, but My God, I'm here. I had almost forgotten what it means to be here. Of all places in the world, this truly takes my breath away."

"Can you find a moment to say hello to a friend? Hopefully, perhaps let me give you a welcoming kiss home. You've been sorely missed." Reaching up and taking Ma down from the wagon, he held her in his arms for a moment and brushed her lips.

My mother stood like a statue.

"What's the matter? Are you tired? Is something wrong?" Mr. Smith was becoming more anxious by the second.

"No, nothing's wrong." Still motionless.

"Then what?"

Long moments passed. Ma stayed frozen, just staring ahead. Mr. Smith was dancing like feet on an anthill. Finally...

"Do you realize what's happened Mr. Smith?"

"No, other than you're home...finally. I've been counting the hours."

"The first time I saw this place, I knew...I don't know what I knew, but this was it. Now, this is it all over again. Except, no that's not right. You were here last time as well. As gruff as bark you were. Now, here you are again giving me a kiss like I've never had before. Never, never."

The cool autumn evening chirped of grasshoppers and croaked of frogs and toads. The trees whispered ancient secrets of things gone by long ago. Slaves rustled among the cabins. Stars twinkled overhead. Old Sal clip clopped off toward the stables complaining about her hard life. A deft breeze took their breaths away to the far reaches of nowhere. And still, Ma stood but now looking at Mr. Smith. Looking at a man she had never seen before. His face, never handsome, showed the effects of a hard life. The nose was bent, and a scar lifted an eyebrow into a permanent question. An ear was thickened from having been hit badly. His hair was thick and tied in back but mussed from not having been combed in a long time. But, his eyes. His eyes gleamed of a light, perhaps from the moon. But hadn't the moon shown that first night? So it couldn't be from the moon.

Mr. Smith came down from his anthill and walked over to take her into his arms. This time his kiss wasn't just a brush but was longer, lingering, and gentle. Ma began to relax. First, her knees bent just a bit, then her legs, up through her back, out her shoulders and down her arms. Eventually, her hands began to rise and wrap themselves around his neck. And there they stayed as Mr. Smith's lips continued to paint circles around her face.

"You know, this is the first time I have ever been kissed. Never, never before. Of course, a peck from my pa and my brother when I left for America. But, never kissed. We just never saw it done in our family."

"Well, there's always a first time. But, there'll never be a last time."

And there they stayed for the longest time. Words were few and silences were long as they gazed at the moon and dark woods. Finally, Mr. Smith asked, "I'd like to ask a favor of you."

"What's that?"

"Do you think we know each other well enough to be on a first name basis? I do have one you know?"

"And what might that be? Mr. was the only one I know."

"Try Bert."

"Bert? Bert...Bert. OK...Kind of short for such a tall man...but if you want Bert, then Bert it is."

"Well, that's what my mother liked, so I really didn't have much choice. I was very young when Bert was given to me."

"You mean you were born? At a young age? I thought you were always old and grouchy."

90

"Mind your tongue, Missy or I'll…"

"Or I'll what?"

"I'll just have to kiss your mouth to keep it quiet."

"It's still working."

"You're right, but this'll quiet it."

Again, more long silences with only choruses of frogs and crickets singing songs. Finally, Ma pulled herself away. "Mr. Smith, oops, Bert, we've got to go in. Tomorrow is coming early and it must be almost eleven o'clock."

Bert was not at all anxious to go in. But, by now, he clearly knew Ma and didn't object. Sighing, "Lady, you know how to waste a night. But, all right. Let's go in." Taking her to her quarters, he bent down and gave her one last kiss for the night.

"Good night, Mr. uhh…Bert. You surely know how to welcome a girl home."

CHAPTER TEN

The next morning found Ma almost beside herself. She could hardly believe what had happened last night. What an amazing change had come over her. With the same man yet. The one who had first terrified her; then made her laugh in amazement; then took her head completely away from her. Her heart was longing to follow as she had never felt before.

Even going to America didn't affect her as strongly as did the moonlight last night. Probably Bert's kisses had something to do with the effect as well. Certainly she had never been kissed like that ever before.

Anyway, Ma was on pins and needles to see Susanna. She certainly would know what was happening. Hadn't she talked at length about her loving Tom so much? Well then, she should surely know what was happening.

Finally, around ten o'clock, Susanna had finished her morning duties enough to talk to Ma.

"Ooooh, welcome back," squealed Susanna. "I have missed you so much. Let me look at you, now that you have been to the big city and all. Why no, you haven't changed a bit. Or…perhaps you have…" Susanna snickered knowingly.

"Nothing gets by you does it? Were you watching from a window?"

"Why, whatever are you talking about? I declare, I don't know what you're saying. Just because someone could be kissing in the moonlight…"

Ma blushed a deep red. A red barber pole or red wagon couldn't have beamed more in the bright morning light.

"You were waiting for me! You always go to bed with the chickens. How did you know?"

By now, Susanna could hardly stand up from laughter. Tears were coming down her cheeks she was laughing so hard watching Ma's confusion and flush rising like a fever.

"Oh, you Susanna, you always get me so flustered when it comes to boys and men. I never know…I just can't seem…what it is…oh …"

"Wyanne, you are such a simpleton. From the moment you left for Charles Town, everyone but you knew that Mr. Smith was going to propose to you. Every time he looks at you, his eyes go blank. But, not you. You're so busy getting on with life, you don't have time to see it when it slaps you across the face. And then to laugh when he did propose. Haven't you *ever* been with a man?"

"Well of course, my father and brother…"

"Not them, silly. I mean, haven't you ever been courted?"

"Well, if you mean the boys hanging around."

"Hummph, they don't count. I mean a serious fellow?"

"I guess not," admitted Ma ruefully. "Besides how did you know I laughed at him?"

"Who do you think was poling the barque you were on? The slaves of course. They were watching everything and of course, nothing happens but what they gossip among themselves. So, of course I heard it eventually from Sally. And when I heard you were returning last night, I was bound to stay up all night if need be to see the show."

"So, you stayed up to watch did you? Were you satisfied with the show?"

"I must admit that you had him dancing for a bit. What did you do? Put red fire ants in his shoes?"

"No, what? Fire ants? I just stood there," wailed Ma. "I was stunned when he kissed me that first time. Honestly, no one had ever kissed me like that before in my life, and I didn't know what to do. All I knew was a thrill the likes of which I had never felt before. Tell me, Susanna, was it like that with Tom?"

For a moment, just a moment, a flash of sadness flickered over Susanna's face as she remembered those years gone by. But, just as quickly, her joy for Ma came back. Her friend had always been so serious. So focused on a foggy future of shadows. Years of passing work. And now, joy, happiness, and a future that included the gift of love. How long would it last? Could it last? Who knew. But what of it? These answers lay all in the future, but for now, Susanna could see her dearest friend finally alive with the essence of life.

"My dearest Wyanne, I couldn't explain to you what Tom meant to me. You just couldn't have understood beyond knowing that he was the man of my life. Last

93

night has changed your life. It will never be the same. A joy has entered it that is impossible to describe but instantly knowable. In your case, you probably don't even realize this now. But wait until the next time you see Mr. Smith. Wait until you think you have lost him and then see him again. You will go from the depths of despair to the heights of joy.

"I must warn you though. It will happen that one day, you won't see him and then be thrown into pits of hellish pain. When Tom died, I was certain that I was to follow shortly. As time passed, I was amazed that I didn't. Finally, acceptance of passage took over. Now, I have married Mr. Killebrew and he is a wonderful man. I am content and happy to be his wife. But, frankly the wild joy is not there. That can never return.

"But, don't be afraid of this pain. It can come shortly or hopefully later, and it will hurt. But as I have always said when you find a good man, grab him. That's about all I can say in response to all of the questions that are flying through your head."

"Susanna, ever since I first arrived here, a scared waif from Ireland, I have always looked to you as my guidance through life. This is yet another lesson. About love, that I don't even understand. Hopefully, I can learn what made my poor Ma live and become old with Pa. It certainly wasn't pearls and rubies."

With this return to Drayton Hall, Ma's situation changed. It was hard to place, but the change was real. Probably it was with the boys. Not too many days passed before their bantering seemed to change. Not that Ma said anything about it. After all, she hadn't pledged herself formally, and after all, whose business was it anyway? Yet the change was there.

Of course, in the small community that comprised the plantation, Mr. Smith's position was felt everywhere and what he felt about Ma was food for gossip among everyone. So, it hadn't been long before every boy in the county knew that Ma was "spoken for." The question was now simply when. "When will the wedding day be?" was on everyone's lips. Ma had a ready answer: "wait and see."

As the days passed, only one boy didn't seem to understand and he was William Jackson. He didn't seem to do anything wrong, but ever since he had bumped into Ma at the outhouse, she just didn't trust him. Nothing that Ma did seemed to faze him. One day, she just flat told him to stop bothering her. After all, she was "spoken for." But, even that really didn't change the situation.

"Bert, I must say. Ever since I have come back, I have been missing the boys' bantering as I do my sewing."

"Are you trying to tell me something? I would hate to think of them as competition."

"No, just fooling. Really, I'm still amazed at all that you have said and done for me. The boys I know how to push off with a joke, except for one."

"Not that William Jackson boy? He just doesn't take no?"

"No, he doesn't and I've flat told him so. But, he just keeps hanging around. Not doing anything mind you, but always there."

"Well, I've had enough of him. I'll just run him off with a stick."
"No, that's not needed. I can handle him. Just, all the others were fun, but he, well... he just turns my stomach. But, if I need help, I'll call."

"You sure? I really am getting tired of hearing his name. One more time and I'll take care of him."

"No, no. As I said, I can handle him."

"You are the most stubborn woman I've ever known. As independent as a pig on ice. But, I guess that's why I love you."

Days passed and life assumed its old tempo. Ma would do her sewing during the days while teaching Sarah and Sadie how to do increasingly fancy stitches. Occasionally, she would contact Mr. Gordon whenever she didn't understand a word she was reading. Of course Susanna was always available for gossiping during the days. But, during the evenings, Susannah could be counted on to be with her family. By now in fact, she had had two children: Betsy and Jeremiah. Jeremiah had been born while Ma was in Charles Town as so she had missed the christening. This certainly kept Susanna busy. But, where she once missed Susannah in the evenings, Ma and Bert would meet after dinner in the kitchen and talk. What had started as another tutoring session for her had now become something else again.

Now these conversations had become full of the future. Bert was talking about his dreams for a plantation. Ma listened to them, but with fear and anxiety about her own future. She had planned so much about her business in Charles Town. Now it seemed to be slipping away in a direction that sounded a lot like life in Ireland. Wresting a living out of stubborn dirt and growing old and thin before one's time.

Yet, as she thought of her mother, Ma could possibly understand why she never complained. Instead, she began to recall the evenings of quiet laughter that would occasionally ring out as she lay in bed waiting for the "Sandman" to come and sprinkle sleepy dust in her eyes. The days in Ireland were always hard and generally without hope, but still, her parents never complained. Like a long practiced team of horses, they would assume their traces and do their duties. But, how they assumed their traces was something of a mystery that Ma never had understood until glimmers came to her now.

"Are you so sure that you want to head West, Bert? Charles Town is right here without the hardship of farming. God knows what it did to my parents."

"Wyanne, I lived in Boston and saw what city life does to people. It makes them old living from week to week for a wage. None of that for me. I'd rather take my chances and try to create a plantation like Drayton Hall. These people, you must admit, have something of substance. People acknowledge who they are, and that's what I want."

"What about Indians? There's talk of war with the French, and they seem to be riling up the Creeks something awful. In some ways, I can understand their point. We're taking over the land they've held for a long time."

Bert almost exploded, "To hell with them! They haven't done anything with that land, and I want it."

Taken aback, Ma flustered and then, catching her breath, mused, "Isn't it ironic? You complain about the hardships of the city and I of the farm. Instead, we each see opportunity in the opposite situation. I guess what you haven't had, you want and no one is going to stand in our way."

Life continued like this until one day, Ma was coming up from the river toward a nearby side building. That area was rather secluded and there she met William Jackson. Immediately, she began to stiffen.

"What are you doing here? Why are you following me? Don't deny it. I've told you any number of times, I don't like you or your hanging around. Now leave me be!"

William grinned slackly showing his tobacco-stained teeth. But he didn't move either, and now Ma began to move around him. Or perhaps tried to. Wherever she went, William seemed to glide in such a way as to block her path.

"Now, what have you got against me? You'd laugh with the other boys hanging around. Is it that you think you're too good for me? Particularly now that you have Mr. Smith? I'm not good enough for you, is that it?"

"Frankly, William, that's exactly it. You're not good enough for me. Never have been and never will be. Now leave me alone!" Again, she tried to pass William and again, he blocked her path except now he was becoming closer to her. Another step and Ma could smell his rancid breath.

"Now how do you know I'm not good enough for you? You've never tried me out."

"Good God, do you mean what I think you mean? Never in a million years if you were the last man on earth."

"Now that cuts it!" exclaimed William as he lunged for her. Ma had her hands full of new sewing materials from Charles Town and was a bit awkward as she tried to evade him without dropping the materials. Consequently, William easily caught her by the wrists and started to push Ma toward a hummock of soft grass.

Realizing what was coming next, Ma dropped her sewing materials. Let them get dirty, they could be cleaned later. But, this oaf was far dirtier and she couldn't clean herself of him in a million years if he touched her. With that, she really began to struggle but it was a losing battle as William applied his heavier weight. Back, back he pushed her. Ma could feel herself losing balance and her control. Trying to hold herself up, she stepped back onto the hummock of grass where her foot slipped throwing them both to the ground.

This fall also caused William to lose his grip on Ma's wrist. That was just enough time for her to grab a long needle that she had slipped into her apron. This needle then moved like a serpent's tooth straight into William's eye. He rolled off Ma like a snake had bitten him.

"My God, woman, you took my eye." Blood and eye water were streaming down his face. William smeared his dirty hand over his face to cover it with a red, runny filth. Moving his hand around while trying to focus on it with his remaining eye he dumbly looked at it unable to believe what had happened so quickly.

Ma scrambled up on top and grabbed William by the neck and stuck the needle right to his other eye. "Aye, that I have, you bloody sod. Now, do you want your other eye taken? I'll even sew them together for you. But, as God is my witness, you try this again, and I'll see you dead."

With that, Ma scrambled up and gave William a kick in the face. Then she ran on toward the house.

She had hardly gotten to the house when Bert came around almost bumping into her. Noticing how distraught and breathless Ma was, he took her by the arms to look her over. No damage, but asking what was wrong, Ma related her encounter with William. He at once turned her over to Sally who had also overheard Ma's rasping breath and came over to see what was the matter.

"Here, take Wyanne to her house and stay with her until she's recovered," ordered Bert not bothering to explain further. "I've got to see what's happened." With that he headed off to where Ma told him the rape occurred. As described, he found the pile of new material and the tramped grassy hummock. William, however was not to be found.

"Probably just as well," Bert murmured. "Otherwise, he would have lost more than an eye and most likely I would be charged with murder. Well, nothing to be done here. But, now to see the Master."

Finding Judge Drayton was simple enough. He was working over his books in the library when Bert barged in without knocking. This rudeness was almost unheard of. The Judge was very private and did not tolerate intrusions in his deliberations. Taking his glasses off his nose, he was about berate whoever it was, when he saw that it was Bert with a wildness in his eyes.

"Bert, what's the matter? Can I get a drink or something for you? Calm down man. Nothing can be so bad as to upset you so."
"Thank you sir, but indeed it is bad, and I've come to warn you about what I'm intent on doing."

The Judge's attention was now fully taken away from his books and onto Bert. "What is it? The crops are all in order. Was a slave injured…"

"No sir, but Wyanne…Wyanne was almost raped…"

"Raped? I don't understand. Who…who was it?"

"You probably don't know him. His name is William Jackson, a young boy who comes by on occasion ostensibly an errand for his father."

"The Jackson family. I don't know the boy, but I do know the father. Not worth much, but peaceable enough."

"Yessir," replied Bert. "The same family. Anyway, he first had been coming around with all of the other lads on similar errands. Most of them just wanted to tease Ma and frankly she enjoyed their company. But William was different…particularly after she had returned from Charles Town. By that time, well you know how we are getting along and all of the boys except William left her alone. But this snipe just kept hanging around. Ma kept saying that she could handle him and refused to let me run him off. She's so independent that way. Well, anyway, today as she was returning from the wharf with new sewing material, William met her on the pathway. Since you can imagine them, I won't go into details other than to say that Ma stabbed him in the eye with a needle. He's lost an eye by it."

The Judge sat for a long time taking in all that he had heard. Bert interrupted him for a moment to hand over the sewing material with a comment, "By the way sir, here's the Mistress's new dress or I should say was. It got dropped in the dirt during the fight."

The Judge looked at it and thought for a second. Then he replied, "Well, that pretty well indicates that Wyanne was accosted. I suspect that if I went back to the pathway, I would see the grass tamped down too, wouldn't I?"

"Yessir, that you would."

"Well, then I imagine that I could take young William in for trial."

"No sir. That won't be necessary. And that's what I came to tell you."

"Yes?"

"Yessir, this is a private matter. I'll not have Wyanne's character challenged in a public scene. Besides it would essentially be his word against hers as to who started what. No sir, this is a private matter, and I just came to tell you that I intend to settle it privately."

"I understand. These issues don't really concern the public and perhaps it is best that you handle it by yourself. What are you intent on doing?"

"Going to the Jacksons and calling this issue out between the two of us."

"Who, the father or the boy?"

"Whoever. They're family and they'll stick together. So it really doesn't make much difference to me."

"Probably it'll be the father. The boy will be in no shape to fight for himself."

"Yessir. That's so. But it's not much concern to me."

"How good are you at knives? That'll be what Old Man Jackson will want to use. He's used them at times in the past."

"I've also used them," was all that Bert said.

"Do you need a second? There's nothing to say that the Jacksons won't bushwhack you if you're alone."

"Hmmm. I hadn't thought of that. This has come up so fast you understand."

"I think I might better ride along. I won't help you in the fight; that's your business. But, there'll be no bushwhacking in my jurisdiction and I don't think that even the Jacksons are stupid enough to consider that if I'm along."

"I appreciate your offer, but you don't need to," replied Bert gratefully.

"No, this is what being a judge is all about. Trying to ensure justice. One last thing now. When do you plan on seeing them?"

"I'm fixing on going right now. Better to get things over now than later."

"Ok, give me a minute to get my papers wrapped up and then, let's go."

"I'll be saddling some horses while you finish your paperwork. We can meet by the front door here."

"OK, good. I'll just be a minute."

Ten minutes was all that Bert needed to select and saddle some horses. Giving them to Sam, he asked that they be taken to the front door and wait for the Judge. From there, he went to his quarters and selected both a pistol and a knife. Checking the pistol one more time, he then took his powder horn, poured a bit out onto his hand to check it for dryness. Pouring a bit more on the pan of his pistol, he cocked the hammer and pulled the trigger. The powder ignited promptly thereby satisfying Bert that it wouldn't fail him.

Satisfied that all was in order, he then strode over to the main house, mounted his horse and waited on the Judge who was just then crossing over the porch and coming down the stairs. From there, the Judge mounted his horse and indicated that it was time to leave.

The ride to the Jackson's house took almost an hour being about ten miles away. Neither man had much to say. Their conversation in the house pretty much covered everything that needed to be said. Finally, the Jackson house appeared alongside the road. Kids and farm animals were scattered randomly about. It would be hard to say which were dirtier. The house itself was a log cabin affair that was crudely chinked to keep the winter winds out. A small stream of smoke curled from the chimney that was stacked at one end of the house.

Finally, one of the children saw the two men riding up and he ran up to the house. "Paw, there's a couple of men coming up. Pretty fancy horses too."

From inside a beefy man with a three day stubble came out. He was followed by a thin, wan woman who undoubtedly had had too many babies and too much work. Mr. Jackson stood there for a minute looking at the two men on horseback.

"You be the Judge?"

"I am."

"And you be Bert, the feller who claims Wynne's hand?"

"I am."

"Well, it seems you might want to choose better women. She stuck my boy William in the eye. He'll not be seeing out it again. Then she threatened to kill him. I don't consider that very nice of her. Against just a boy I might add. He ain't but seventeen."

"He's a man grown" replied the Judge. "He can work fields like a man and is responsible for what he does."

"And what might that be?" answered Mr. Jackson.

Bert now spoke up for the first time. "That whelp of a boy tried to rape my Wyanne. That's what it might be."

"So, what's to do about that? From what I hear, she's a saucy wench and probably was asking for what William tried to give her. Then got scared when she thought about losing you. That's no reason to stick William in the eye."

Dismounting from his horse, Bert walked over to Mr. Jackson. "I'm sorry that this has to come. But there's no way I'm going to listen to these words or let

101

Wyanne's honor be challenged. So, let's get this over with. You probably been expecting me?"

"Yep, so when and where? Right now, right here good enough? Judge, you didn't need to come here. It don't concern you."

"What concerns me is my business. Let's get on with this affair."

"Well, Mr. Smith, since you came on my property and telling me what a bad boy my William is, I guess I got a choice of weapons."

"Yessir, you do."

As this conversation was ensuing, more men gathered around, clearly other sons of the Jackson family. None of them were friendly and several were armed. At this point, Judge Drayton broke in. "Now my business is starting. There has been a wrong done here and it's being settled privately. As a public judge, I can see how this is really the best way. But, mark my words. Someone is going to die in the next ten minutes or so and I intend to see that that person is limited to these two right here." With these words, he flashed back his cloak to display a brace of pistols. "Now none of you here doubt my ability to use these things. Just don't doubt my willingness to do so if I see any cheating. I know that there are more of you than there is of me, but if anyone does succeed in shooting me, that will be the last shooting he will do. Shooting a judge becomes a public matter, and I assure each and every one of you that shooting a judge will bring a trial and a hanging in that order and that fast. Am I understood?" Everyone nodded and several laid their guns aside. "Good. Now, as I said before, let's get on with this affair."

Bert and Mr. Jackson then returned to their duel. Bert said, "Sir, I believe you have choice of weapons."

"I do and I prefer using knives."

"That's your choice and that's fine with me. So, let's get with it." With that, the Jackson family spread out to form a rough circle. The Judge remained sitting on his horse almost like he was sitting on his high bench. The two men entered this circle with their knives.

Knife fights rarely last very long. This was no exception. Circling each other for several seconds with their weapons out in front of them, they resembled a snake and mongoose dancing a deadly duet. At first, both men were cautious, judging and watching for openings. Bert, being lighter took the mongoose's part while Jackson was the snake. This meant that Bert had to take the offensive if he was to succeed getting inside the powerful arms opposing him. That also meant that he would expose himself to a counterthrust. But, it also gave him some element of surprise. Still, all this was relative as Jackson thought he saw an opening and struck. Only Bert's speed saved him, but he still took a cut across the arm. Blood immediately started to flow. Bert then cut back across the flow of movement, shifted his knife from his right to left hand and cut Jackson's arm in turn. Cut and draw. With the momentum now broken, the roles reversed themselves. Bert was the snake and Jackson the mongoose. The dance continued. Knives flicked like tongues. Silence hung like hammers over the scene waiting to crash down on the anvil below. Then, Bert struck. Dodging slightly toward his left, he drew Jackson's knife out to create a small hole. And that quickly Bert danced into Jackson's ribs and plunged his blade clear to the hilt. Twisting it to enlarge the hole, Bert further ruined the organs, severed arteries, and ensured that he could withdraw his weapon to strike again. Jackson was a dead man but like any wounded animal, was still able to strike back even in death. And that brought a long, deep slashing cut across Bert's back destined to leave a scar for the rest of his life. Bert in turn struck again as he pushed further against Jackson's right arm to open up his body. This time the blow aimed high under the rib cage where the tip of his knife could pierce the heart. Again, he twisted and again he struck to slice open Jackson's bowels. With that, he stood back and let Jackson fall to the ground. The entire fight took a minute and a half.

As Bert withdrew toward his horse, Judge Drayton turned to the new widow. "Ma'am, I'm sorry that this affair had to occur. It was really needless. Fortunately, you have a number of strong sons who will care for you. But, again, mark my words. None of your family is allowed on my property. None of your family will ever talk to any of my family including slaves and servants. If I hear of anyone disobeying this order, I assure you that I will be back and my justice will make the pain of your husband's death seem like a baby's caress. Am I understood?" With these words, he looked at each Jackson in turn. The boys looked down at the ground and shuffled their feet. The wife didn't say a word; she didn't move; she didn't show any emotion other than the tired fatigue that she was born with. Likewise, she met the Judge's eye, second for second. The Judge thought, "That woman's the toughest of them all."

Turning toward Bert, he dismounted and led him toward the shade of a tree. There he applied a tight bandage over the cut on Bert's arm. That slowed the bleeding there. Then he looked at the wound on Bert's back. While open, and despite its depth, there wasn't much that could be done about it here. On the way home, they could stop off at the Smith's plantation where one of the sons was a physician. With that, he helped Bert up on his horse, mounted his own, and led the way home.

"Where's Bert?" asked Ma. By now, she had recovered enough from her attack to inquire about the last person she remembered seeing.

Susannah replied, "He's been gone for about an hour. To the Jacksons."

"What for?"

"Let's just say that William will never be coming back around this place again."

"You mean, he's going to murder him?" This was in a century of imagined sleights and duels, but in neither in Ireland nor here at Drayton Hall was violence a daily affair. It usually came in the form of an accident that left someone maimed. So, for Bert to go somewhere for the purpose of violence was as foreign to Ma as being in China.

"No, it won't be murder. But, Bert talked to the Master at some length and then the two of them went to the Jackson place. A terrible thing has been forced on you and he was bound to see justice."

"Oh no, no, no!" wailed Ma. "That wasn't necessary. I could take care of it. I did take care of it. I didn't survive my trip across the Atlantic with my honor intact by being a wallflower. The first day I was aboard, a lady taught me about men wanting things. She also taught me how to protect myself. So, I don't need him getting killed on my account."

"Young lady, hush your mouth. You're not in Ireland, and you're not on board a ship. You're here in the Carolinas and if this issue wasn't settled promptly, you won't have an occasional sailor after you. The entire Jackson clan would be wanting revenge on you for blinding their William. Your life wouldn't be worth a plugged shilling. Furthermore, other boys would figure that you're simply a trollop anyway and perhaps they should enjoy their turn. So, leave things be and pray that Bert comes home riding his horse."

"But the Master, he's a judge…couldn't he take care of it?"

"You ninny, did the Captain of your ship help you? Did he bring the sailors up for a public flogging?"

"No…"

"And they don't here either. These things are considered to be private matters. Let this rape become public knowledge through a trial and you would be

104

branded a whore. Not to your face mind you, but a whore none the less. And Bert, he would be laughed at for being associated with such a fallen woman. Is that what you want?"

"Of course not. But..."

"But, nothing. Now just shut up and start praying."

"I'm sorry, but I really don't understand. What is the Master for as a judge if not to take care of matters like this?"

Like a teacher dealing with a slow student, Susannah explained patiently, "A public trial that people accept is when something is done that upsets the public. Rob a bank, espouse Popery in public, kill the judge. These are the sort of things that people consider to be public crimes. Your problem is a private matter that is settled in the family. Like it or not, that's a fact. So, shut up and start praying."

Seeing Susannah so distraught and hearing an urgency in her voice that had never existed before began to sink into Ma's consciousness. She began to understand the danger that existed for her, for Bert, for the future they were beginning to plan together. She began to sink into the hell that Susannah promised her just a few days ago. The thought of never seeing Bert or hearing his voice choked her throat as William's attack never could do.

Crying, Ma tore herself from Susannah's clutch and ran to her room. There she tore through her belongings until she found something she hadn't used in years: her rosary. It was all right for her to go Protestant churches on Sundays when nothing else was happening and the company was jolly. But, in this new hell, Ma reached back to the depths of her mother's prayers when she was a baby suffering from the croup. Ma began to pray as she never prayed before.

Hours passed. Still, Ma would not leave her room. The rosary beads passed endlessly through her hands. Susannah came by briefly, knocked on the door of her room, but got no answer. She only heard a moaning prayer muffled by the door. Returning to the others below, Susannah just told them that Ma had best be left alone. Hell had truly settled upon her.

More hours passed through the evening and night. Susannah finally returned to her house to be with her husband. Nothing more could be done.

"So, how's Wyanne taking all of this?" asked Mr. Killibrew.

"About as well as can be expected, I guess," replied Susannah as she changed another nappie on her baby. "She really didn't seem to understand at first. She is so headstrong that she thought that she had settled issues with William by poking his eye out. Bert really seemed to her to be jumping at nothing. At best, she thought the Master would judge the issue."

"Well, he did really by going over with Bert. Knowing the Master, he wouldn't tolerate any bad business during Bert's fight. He would make sure that it was a fair fight."

"I'm not sure that Wyanne still understands that point. But, she does understand that private matters are settled privately here regardless of what they ever did in Ireland. I really had to get short with her before she finally got things through her thick head. Once she did though, she turned as white as a sheet and ran to her room. She wouldn't come out whenever I knocked. She's still there, praying I think. But God, what a prayer. It was the most soulful crying I ever heard. It reminded me of a dog being struck…no more than that. What it was I can't say, but it raised the hair on my neck. I had talked to her about love creating heaven and hell. Well, now she's in Hell crying out from the Devil's own pain."

"What do you think we ought to do? Anything we can do at this point?" replied her husband.

"No, I don't think so. Hell is Wyanne's own journey. We can only stand by in the morning. So, let's go to bed now. It's late and the children are finally asleep."

"OK, get ready for bed. I want to go in and see them one more time. At times like this, we had best take our lives as best we can and make the most of them."

With that, the Killebrews went to bed. But, faintly, keening wails could still be heard.

CHAPTER ELEVEN

The next morning saw Ma coming out of her room walking like a ghost. Her red hair was a rat's next. Her face was ashen. Tears had tracked down over her cheeks until they looked like dirty mascara. Susannah ran to her and gave her a hug, but my mother hardly noticed. Then, Susannah took her to the kitchen like a little girl. She tried to give Ma some coffee and biscuits, and while no resistance was made, nothing was drunk or eaten. Ma clearly was not in this world.

Seeing Ma's state, Susannah went to the Mistress to report on what all had happened, and a welcome report it was to the Mistress. She had not been told anything much by the slaves and the Judge had said nothing to her before departing. So, when he didn't return during the evening, she became perturbed. Being gone was nothing new to her, but usually he would give warning.

"Ma'am, have you minute? I think you need to be told what's happening."

"Yes, please. If you know anything beyond the passing comments of the slaves, please let me know. It isn't like the Judge to leave without saying anything."

"I take it then, that you haven't really heard what took the Master away. A bad story it is if I may say so." With that Susannah recited the past twenty-four hours as best she understood them. "So, at this point, Wyanne isn't going to be available until she knows what's happened to Mr. Smith. And the Master himself of course."

"Well, it isn't good news I can say that. Otherwise, the two men would have returned last night. Since they didn't, I expect that they stayed the night at the Bartrands where one of the sons is a medical doctor. Some one of them needed medical attention, that's for sure. I expect then that we won't hear until later today when some sort of message is sent to us."

"Yes ma'am. Meanwhile, I would like to stay with Wyanne until we get through all of this."

"Oh, of course. Take care of her. You know when I first met her, I thought immediately of her brother. So you can imagine what I thought of her. But that wasn't the case. You know that she refused Mr. Smith's offer to buy her contract? He really wants to marry her and he certainly has reason to want her. The Judge had even accepted it, but no, Wyanne refused it saying that she wanted to be considered a free woman who keeps her word--regardless of what people might think of her brother. Otherwise, if she had accepted Mr. Smith's offer, she would have been married by now and probably working on her first baby."

"No ma'am, I didn't know all of that. Frankly, I was wondering about it too. Wyanne and I are very close, but she hadn't mentioned any of these details. So, now, she probably is wondering the wisdom of her choice."

"I agree, but I wouldn't be surprised by any of her decisions. As you say, she is stubborn."

"That she is ma'am. Now, by your leave, I'll be going back to Wyanne."

Hours still passed, and still Ma remained like a statue in the kitchen ignoring everything that was going around her. Susannah would drop by between errands. The various kitchen slaves remained quiet around her. Although this was all white folk business, none the less Ma had always been fair and considerate with them. So, they felt some sadness toward her. After all, hadn't they also been through the loss of someone being sold down the river never to be seen again?

Finally, around noon, the Judge returned on his horse while leading a second one. When told of this, Ma began to stir. "What of Mr. Smith?"

Sally, who had seen the Master's arrival from her wash stand and come to tell Ma, replied, "I don't know Wyanne. I only just seen the Master on his horse and leading a second one. I figured you needed to know at least that much."

"Thank you Sally." With that, Ma went out to the veranda circle to await the Master. "Sir, what of Mr. Smith?"

The Master dismounted and took my mother in his arms saying "Bert is going to live. He got cut up rather badly, but he will live. He's being brought by wagon now. I came ahead to tell you. That man truly loves you. Perhaps more than any of us will understand."

With these words, Ma almost wilted in the Master's arms. She stopped short only with the greatest will of effort. "I never knew, I guess I'm only now realizing what sort of man Mr. Smith is. If I had lost him, I'm not sure what I'd do. I only know through the night that my prayers were for his life. That I love him more than I can possibly say...perhaps more than I know. But, please sweet Jesus, let him live." Ma then pulled herself away, "Thank you sir, for being with him...for coming to me...for all that you have done for us."

The Master gave her a last hug and said gently, but with a note of humor, "Wyanne, you have become very important to all of us. But, now, go. Get yourself cleaned up. You don't want your man to see you this way. He might even begin to think you were worried about him. You couldn't let him think that let alone loving him."

For the first time, Ma began to smile as relief spread through her entire body and especially her heart. Bert was alive. Saints be praised!

Ma went to the wash room and began to clean up. While there, she began to think seriously about getting married. After all, what was magic about Charles Town? If you're living alone and working through the day, who would be there to fill a room...to fill a bed? At that thought, Ma began to blush. For the first time in her life, a warm flush of desire began to creep up through her body. Of course, she knew what married people did. Living in the small house of her parents left no secrets there. But, all that was for other people. But, now, the idea of lying with Bert sent another chill through her followed by another blush. Even Sally noticed.

"What's this? The ice lady be blushing? She feeling heat now that she know a certain man be ok.? So, when's the baby due?"

"Oh Sally! There's no baby due. I'm not even married," retorted Ma while still smiling like a Cheshire cat.

"No, but I knows the look of a baby being made when I sees it. That I do know," chortled Sally.

Leaving Sally to her own thoughts, Ma set herself outside on a stool and set about with her sewing. But really, it was mostly a poor effort to keep time moving. Will that wagon ever get here? My mother was never a patient person, but this was just simply an eternity. Each stitch took just a second with a long look up the drive in between. Looking down, Ma saw sewing as bad as anything she had done as a young girl for Mrs. Grable. Even Sarah and Sadie did better work on their first day. But really, Ma just didn't care. Sewing could be done any day, but to love someone. Now that was really something.

Finally, after a thousand searching glances down the drive, a wagon creaked up the road. Dropping her sewing, Ma flew. She hardly felt the hard ground under her feet. As she approached, she launched herself through the air to land directly on Bert to cover him with kisses. A slow moan erupted and a strange slave's voice told her firmly: "Missy, if you want to kill that man, you be doin' a fine job." Ma looked down to see a small, thin stream of blood creep out from Bert's back. "Oh my God, I've killed him!" cried Ma as she looked at her bloody hands in horror. Bert groaned again with a laugh, "No, you haven't, but I agree, you're certainly trying."

109

"Oh, you, you…what were you thinking of? Of all the dumb things I ever heard of, this takes the cake. Having a knife fight. You don't know what I've been through these last million hours. My God, I don't what to do with you. To kill you with kisses for being alive or kill you for being stupid!" Sputtering, Ma bent down with care, and gave Bert more kisses. Each more gently than the other. Each with more passion than the other. "I declare, I love you so much…more than I could ever possibly imagine…Sweet Jesus, I love you…"

"Now that's what I call a homecoming. Even worth becoming a carcass by an exceedingly ugly butcher."

"Yes, as God is my witness, I love you, but for God's sake, don't ever do such a thing again or you will have to deal with me."

"Now I really am scared. No ma'am, I'll never try this again. Next time, I'll just shoot the man who ever tries to touch you again, and that's a promise." Bert's voice was weak, but stern and full of promise.

By this time, the wagon had arrived at the main house. The Mistress was standing there waiting for Bert. Wasting no words, she ordered several slaves to carry Bert's litter upstairs to an awaiting bed. However, before letting him lie down, she looked over his wounds and saw that several stitches had popped. "H'mmmph, pretty poor work. Well, let's do this again. Bert, this is going to hurt, but I don't want to hear any complaints. These duels are really stupid." Turning to Ma, she said equally sharply: "I don't ever want to see you pulling a dumb stunt like the one I just saw. I know you finally have discovered love, but killing your man is no way to show it. Now watch, I guarantee you that you will be using your sewing skills here at some time or another in your future." Ma moved meekly and watched the Mistress do her work. For the first time, she could really appreciate the skill of her artistry. She also learned to appreciate what sort of a strong woman a plantation wife had to be. Such strength she never imagined about the Mistress. So, if she was truly going to follow Bert's dream of building a plantation, then she had better learn as much as possible from this tough lady.

"Now go, let this man rest. He's not to be needing you for at least a day or two."

"Yes ma'am. I understand that. But, you're right, if I'm going to follow Mr. Smith, then I need to learn a lot more than sewing. Do you mind if I watch you minister to him? I would really appreciate it 'cause I really need to learn."

Looking at Ma's winsome, pleading face, the Mistress laughed and relented. "Ok, I'll let you stay, but only if you promise not to touch him. Otherwise, I couldn't guarantee a long life for Bert."

"Oh yes ma'am. Thank you. Thank you. "

"Now that's enough, let's leave this poor man alone. We'll come back when he needs us." With those words, she turned on her heel and led Ma out of the bedroom like a dog at heel.

Once outside of the room, the Mistress turned to my mother and took her into her arms. Ma began to weep silently. "Ma'am, I know I behaved awfully, but I was truly out of my mind. I never knew I could love a man so. I never wanted him to do this. He just took off without saying a word to me. Besides, I thought I had taken care of the Jackson boy in a good and proper manner."
"Yes, I guess you did at that. That boy will never use his eye again. I must say that. But, remember, in this country, people tend to take things in their own hands, and Bert had learned long ago to use his in fights. You only have to look at his scars and thick ears to see that. And also, whether you like it not, this is a man's country and things aren't settled until they have had their say...not that they are always so smart. Now, listen to me girl and listen well. When are you going to get off your high horse and marry that man?"

Ma looked up and pulled away from the Mistress. "I guess he really does deserve an answer to his question, doesn't he?"

"Yes he does. God knows he has tried everything possible to prove himself to you."

"Today is certainly not the day to answer his proposal, but I promise he'll get a 'yes' as soon as he is able."

"See that you do," ordered the Mistress kindly. "He is a good man and full of love for you."

"Susannah said the same thing. When you find a good man, grab on to him, and that's what I intend to do."

"I believe you there knowing you as I do. So, let's get on with things. We have a lot to do."

With that, Ma went out into a new world. No longer was she sitting on any fences. She was committed to Bert wherever he might go in pursuit of his dreams.

111

Her realization of this fact brought a cold chill down her spine. Her thoughts of going to Charles Town now seemed like a faded dream with all of the promise that it offered.

While Bert healed, Ma spent as much time as possible talking with him in between her normal duties. She also spent a lot of time watching the Mistress doing her daily business. So much she had to learn. Just when she thought that her life was in control, Ma realized how little she actually knew. But, also as she learned and as she knew that Bert was truly going to live, Ma began to think carefully about what her future life would entail.

First, she began to understand the enormity of her decision. Of course, leaving Drayton Hall would mean leaving the comforts that she now took for granted. Looking at the deep woods that still surrounded the plantation, little was left to her imagination about what sort of terrible labor would be needed to clear them. She also had had some opportunity to watch the slaves work and the prospect of that labor wasn't too appealing. She knew that Bert had been saving his money for buying slaves as well as land, but still from watching the Mistress, her life would be full of work from dawn to dusk. She wouldn't be plowing land, but caring for a raw house and overworked people would be harder than anything she had ever done.

From talking with Bert, she understood that he needed about one more year before he would be ready to strike out for new land in the western Carolinas. So, it only made sense for her not to get married before she started her new voyage in life. First, she still felt an obligation to the Draytons and her indenturement with them. But, she also understood that getting married would mean her becoming pregnant which was not at all appealing considering the work that lay in front of her. It appeared that the only way to avoid that dilemma was to postpone her marriage.

With all of the emotions that ran through her when Bert came home with his wounds, her body cried out against the hard facts that she was facing. But, a late term pregnancy or a newly born baby was just too dangerous in the hazards of the frontier. Susannah told her enough tales about her parents to understand that fact, and besides, she had seen how hard pregnancies had been on her mother.

All of these fears she passed on to Bert. Obviously, he was not at happy about this, but he did understand the logic of her fears. Still as his strength returned, the strength of his love became ever more urgent which continued to teach Ma's body of the joys that lay in store for her. In turn, her desires for Bert became ever stronger making her resolves harder to maintain with each passing day. Really, it was probably only because of Bert's wounds that Ma was able to restrain herself. What she was going to do when he was fully healthy was not easy to contemplate.

112

Fortunately, as Bert's strength did return, the two lovers had very little time together where their love could get the best of them. Bert's work started to take him away to the furthest parts of the plantation for increasingly longer periods of time. As before, he would often be gone for days at a time. Ma in turn, was occupied with her sewing duties and trying to learn as much as she possibly could from the Mistress. She also began to expand her reading about the tasks of farming. Plantation owners usually ordered books regularly from England on that topic, and if she was going to be a farmer's wife, then she decided to learn everything she could about it. Watching the Mistress taught her that such women were no strangers to such arts. From there, she started going down to the tack rooms and blacksmith shops to learn about caring for horses. Now a young man working full time on the plantation, William Malone was surprised to see her there. He had always associated her with sewing from when he had been among many boys to flirt with her. But, as Ma had noticed from before, he was serious in his work and was happy to show her his skills. Eventually, under tutelage, she actually could shoe a horse. Not as well as William, but she could do the job without crippling the animal. Finally, it must be said that when Bert was home, people were constantly about. Privacy was not a valued commodity for people at Drayton Hall. Even the Master and his wife never seemed to have much time for themselves. So, in reality, as much as Ma longed for Bert, she really was able to maintain some sort of control although there was an incident or two in the kitchen. How Ma wished that every night could repeat those moments of joy.

CHAPTER TWELVE

Ma was always fascinated by the slaves' lives. She told many stories about them as they worked and occasionally played at the Drayton plantation. Here is one of her favorites:

"It was shortly before I had left the plantation that one of the slaves had a wedding. This was actually a rare occasion but since it was Sam who wanted to get married, he was granted an exception by the Master. Of course, even when the Master would give permission, it was often hard for a man to find a woman to marry. So many men were being imported from Africa for work that they generally outnumbered females by a great number. So, really Sam was a lucky fellow both to find a woman to marry and get permission to do so.

"Later on, as the plantations became more self-sufficient, marriage was encouraged for the obvious reason of producing children. The average family would have about six to eight children. Thomas Jefferson, who always wrote about hating slavery, opined that "a woman who brings a child every two years is more valuable than the best man on the farm.

"Of course, I had known Sam from my first day in America. He had picked me up at the harbor and taken me to the plantation. I hadn't known it then, but his job as a drayer was actually a special job amongst the slaves. Instead of having to work in the fields, he was given considerable freedom to live a life more of his own choosing. Think about it. Instead of being under the constant eye of Mr. Smith or some other overseer, he could pretty much come and go as he pleased. And he did please. Whenever he had to go to Charleston or some other plantation, you be sure that he would do some trading.

"Many owners would complain about their slaves doing any trading, but generally they didn't do anything serious about it. After all, the masters expected their slaves to be pretty much self-sufficient. They were to raise their food in their gardens and do a little trapping for meat. All of the slaves worked harder on those gardens than they ever did in the fields, believe you me. The reason was obvious; they could make a surplus and sell it. Sam hauled their goods to market and brought back was they ordered. In the old days, slaves were even known to buy themselves their freedom. That wasn't possible when I knew them, but still they would get what they could to make their lives more freedom. Of course, Sam took care of himself in each of these transactions.

In many ways, Sam was different from the field hands. First, he knew English. It wasn't the King's English, but it was a sight better than many of the other slaves who had also come directly from Africa. He was also lighter skinned. Most African arrivals were coal black, but not Sam. He and I talked about this.

"Sam," I asked, "We've known each other for about a year. But, I guess I have to satisfy my curiosity."
"Missy, you know about what happened to the curious cat?"

"Yes, I know. It killed him, but I don't think you'll kill me."

"So, what you want to know?"

"Well, I asked him about why he knew English and how come he wasn't as black as other slaves from Africa. His story was both chilling and sad."

"Well, Wyanne, it be a long story. As you might 've guessed already, I ain't pure African. Thass right. A person like me be known here as a mulatto or less kindly, a 'brass knuckler.' Back home, we be all 'Creoles.' Part white and part black. My father 'uz a Portuguese trader. Actually he come to West Africa as a sailor and settled in. He married my mother who lived in a place called Goreè and had a whole bunch of kids. Goreè 'uz really a trading town and kids living there learned all sorts of different languages. I've forgotten a lot of them, and I never really did learn English, but it did prepare me for learning it here."

A long pause and a sigh slipped out. "I hain't really thought about all this for a long time. It do seem so long ago and far away."

"I certainly can understand that," I replied.

Sam looked at me shortly, and then replied, "Yes, I guess you can at that coming in as you did."

"But anyway, tell me more of your story."

"These trading towns along Western Africa I believe be a lot alike. They 'uz a small number of white traders and lots of sailors. The traders usually marry local women and had kids like me. Eventually, a lot of these mixed children started marrying amongst theyselves. I knowed some of them by sight, and believe it or not they actually came from fairly rich families. But, I never got in with them as I 'uz just a first generation Creole.

This really puzzled me. "First generation?"

"Yes, thass right. I can still remember feelin' confused and lost there. I wasn't a black African. I wasn't a white Portuguese. I was something in between…neither here nor there. I heard my mother talking about the rich Creoles as well. No one really liked them. Dealt with them, but didn't like them."

"Well, why didn't they take you in?"

"Good question and one I thought hard about. As near as I can figure, these old Creole families had made their money, got in with other families that made their money, and just stuck together with no room for a poor kid like me."

"So then what happened to you? How did you come to America?"

"Pretty simple, actually. My father wasn't smart as the other white traders and so, when he needed money, he sold me to a dealer. From there, it was a long sickening ride to America. I suspect that some of my other brothers and sisters got sold in a similar way"

"I was stunned by this simple admission until I thought about it. Pa hadn't sold me, thank God, but he certainly was sweeping me out the door. And once out the door, my terms of indenturement weren't much different from Sam's except of course I had a limit to my contract.

"Well, anyway, Sam was smart, and he worked hard to get the drayer's job that gave him the freedom he needed to make a life for himself. Now that he had it, he wanted more. Specifically, he wanted to marry, have a family and try to live a normal life. Really, I never found slaves much different from us in that regard. So, it wasn't long before he and Sally got to courting. Sam was probably about 25 and Sally about 18 or 19 or so. These were typical ages for healthy blacks to marry when they had a chance. Sally would undoubtedly be pregnant within a year and not having to work in the fields actually had a good chance of delivering a healthy babies.

"And so it was that eventually Sam went to Mr. Smith to ask for permission to marry. Later on, Mr. Smith related how the conversations went."

"Massah. Smith, may I talk for a moment?"

"Sure, Sam. What is it?"

"Well, suh. You know that I been courtin' Sally for some time now, and it ain't right not to do nothin' about it."

116

"I rather expect you have been doing something right along, but what would you like to do?"

"I want to marry Sally, but of course, I'll need the Massah's permission. So, I thought be right by I start with you and perhaps you talk to him in my favor."

"Why thank you, Sam. I appreciate your doing that. That lets me know what's happening with the people here. I really don't expect the Master will have an objection."

"There do be one thing though."

"And that is?"

"Once I get married, Sally and I be wanting to leave the Quarter and set up a house of our own."

"H'mmm. I hadn't thought of that. But, I guess you're right. Living in a bachelor's dormitory just wouldn't work. You need your privacy like anyone else. You know you'll have to build a place for yourself after your normal work hours?"

"Yassuh. That be what I expected. We do our own work after the Massah's work. But, getting the other slaves from the Quarter shouldn't take too much time to build a house. Solomon be a good carpenter and I know he be glad to set the building up right. Of course, I'll be using old Sal to haul wood, bricks, etc."

"When would you want to start this project?"

"Soons as I can. Probably after the year's rice crop harvested and the wagon won't be needed as much."

"Well, it's August now, about October then?"

"That be fine suh."

"OK, why don't you plan on that. Meanwhile, I'll talk to the Master about it."

"Thank you suh. I thought I could count on you."

"Well, we work you people hard, but then it sets order to things. Meanwhile, we have an obligation to take care of you."

117

"So, there it was. Mr. Smith did talk to the Master later that week. The Master just asked more or less the same questions that Mr. Smith had done with Sam. Actually, he even went down to Sam later on to talk to him about it. He even teased Sam about marrying a woman with Sally's temper."

"I hope you know what you're getting into, Sam. Sally's got a mean temper. Can you handle her?"

"Yassuh, I think I do," replied Sam. "Hopefully, lots of loving and children keep her so busy she won't have no time to scold me."

"I doubt that," laughed the Master. "I never saw a woman who was too busy to scold her husband. I should know. I've had three of them now and I'm always catching their temper. Why do you think I'm always away judging?"

"In that case, I guess I better keep Old Sal hitched up so I have a reason to stay out of the house. But, thank you suh."

"Don't thank me now, Sam," chuckled the Master. "Wait till you're married and then see if you still want to thank me. No really, I think it'll make a good match between you and Sally. And, by the way, plan on seeing Mr. Smith about building a house. You probably can attach it to another house along the row."

"And so it was Sam and Sally started preparing their marriage. The house was the first project. Some slaves, particularly pure Africans preferred building a curious hut made of stick frame and mud mixed with thatch for walls. Usually, they would be circular in shape and often painted white trimmed with ornamental designs of some tribal origin or meaning. Actually, these huts were fairly practical. They tended to be cooler in the summer and surprisingly warm in winter. Sam, however chose not to follow this design. Perhaps it was because of his Creole background, but regardless, his cabin was to be of a more conventional construction.

"Starting with a chimney that would have a fireplace serving two rooms for heat and cooking, it soon became a cabin with a normal wooden pole frame and slat walls. The wood was all hewn from trees cut from the Master's property during clearing operations. Getting this much wood was no mean task as it had to be hauled from swamps, dried and cut. Ole Sal was kept busy then and she continually complained to Sam. The rooms themselves were separated for two purposes. One side was for cooking and eating; the other was for sleeping. When the babies came, there would be little room or privacy. Double high trundle beds would be needed for the children with two babies often occupying one bed. The beds themselves would be ticks or 'croaker sacks' filled with Spanish moss where lice liked to live. Occasionally, these ticks could either be changed or smoked to get rid of these little pests. But otherwise, you scratched where you lived or itched. Still, compared to the barracks-like dormitories of the Quarters, this was a far step up. At least Sam's family was private.

"Of course, Sam and his family had access to some land outside where they could grow vegetables for their consumption or sale to others. Eventually, they would have a few chickens or a pig. This generosity by the Master was not charity. It meant that he didn't have provide those provisions to Sam from his own pocket. And he didn't give time off for tending the garden to either Sam or Sally. They were tend to it only after the Master's work was done. So, both of them worked hard to get them done as quickly as possible so as to leave more time for their personal affairs. In the old days, I had heard of some slaves who were so successful at farming and selling that they could actually buy their freedom. But that was never a possibility for Sam and Sally. When I last heard of them, they were both still working for the Master. Neither did any of their children. However, this work allowed them the opportunity to buy things that enriched their lives such as a mirror, better clothing and food. Finally, it assured them a proper house to retire in when they were too old to work.

"Retirement surrounded by children and grandchildren was the fondest hope of the slaves. Most of them didn't enjoy this hope. Most of them died too soon for that or were sold elsewhere. Even then, many of the sold slaves refused to accept being sold but would run away and travel many miles and then live in the woods just to be near family. Occasionally, they would be sold back in recognition that they weren't much good to the new master by being constantly running away. Even whippings couldn't stop these people. They just had to be by their people.

"Eventually, Sam got his house built and the marriage was planned. It was to be a big social event. After all Sam's job as a drayer let him get out and about developing a wide circle of friends and relatives who would want to come to the party. The wedding was to be held on Saturday night during the early spring just after the burning of the rice fields which meant that a lot of slaves were at Drayton plantations anyway. Saturday of course was chosen because it would let the merrymaking continue on into Sunday morning.

"The masters were of various minds about Sundays. Some were like the Judge who permitted and even encouraged their slaves to attend church. Others were reluctant to do so fearing that their slaves would raise false ideas about becoming free equals to whites. Consequently, one would see more slaves practicing their old pagan religions or being followers of Muhammad which I never understood. However, for this occasion, the wedding party was the occasion of the Sunday and enjoy it they did.

"First of all, invitations were to be sent out, but since they pretty much couldn't read or write, they used drums made of hollow logs. Wild rhythms went fleeting through the woods only to be picked up by neighboring drums and sent further on its way. This drumming went on all day to notify all and sundry about Sam and Sally's wedding.

"This drumming was for an innocent purpose; everyone knew about the wedding. But if you didn't know what it meant, the sound could be horrifying. It would make the fair on the back of your neck stand straight up. As a consequence, many people tried to stop this drumming. They were convinced that the wild sounds were calls for slave revolt. Laws were even passed to stop this drumming at night, but to no avail. The blacks were bound to use them to send messages.

"Once the invitations were 'sent out,' proper preparation needed to be made for the guests. Grilling and spitting hogs, catching fish, hunting game were busy activities for the hungry appetites. The Master contributed some food since he was particularly fond of Sam. The ordinary field hands never got such personal treatment. In point of fact, many of the hands he hardly knew leaving their control to the overseers such as Mr. Smith. And even he didn't know all of them preferring to leave such details to the slave foremen.

"Sleeping arrangements were simple, people slept where they could. With friends or relatives if lucky, otherwise on the ground. Besides, they wouldn't be coming to sleep. The party was an excuse to eat, dance and drink. And slaves knew how to drink. Overseers had the Devil's own time keeping many of them sober. Thomas Jefferson had a slave who was a famous drunk. Burwell Hemmings was his name. Mr. Jefferson despaired of his ever giving up the bottle. Indeed, to the day he died, Burwell was tied to his whiskey.

"The wedding party consisted mostly of the guests surrounding Sam and Sally. There was no priest as such present to lead a marriage ceremony. As I had mentioned earlier, religion was not particularly organized, so having an official lead the service wasn't really important. Besides, in the eyes of the whites, this marriage never would exist. The Master had given his permission to marry, but in effect it really only meant permission to live together. No one else outside of the plantation would recognize it. Certainly, if either Sam or Sally were to be sold, this union wouldn't bind them together in any way. In fact, slaves often told about families being separated forever. Again, many such slaves would risk whippings or worse in order to be with their loved ones. Indeed, I was always amazed how strong the family ties of slaves were. Perhaps even stronger than mine considering how easily I was invited out of the family house. Probably this closeness was due to the fact that they really didn't have anything else.

"Anyway, an elder slave merely announced to the others gathered why they were there and then asked the wedding couple if this is what they really wanted to do.

They replied 'yes' and that was that, they were pronounced married by the wisdom and honor accorded to the Elder by the slaves at large. At that point, a curious thing happened. It doesn't happen everywhere, but it did here. The Elder laid a stick on the ground whereupon Sam and Sally jumped over it to the applause of everyone. I never really learned what that meant; perhaps like our kissing at the end of our ceremonies. I don't know...I just saw it.

"The celebration afterwards went on all night. As I mentioned earlier, negroes knew how to drink. They would have done an Irishman proud to keep up. They called it 'gubbing' from the sound of liquid being swallowed. Dancing and singing of course was a big part of the festivity. Wild dancing and singing kept to the insistent beat of the drums. Of course there were fiddles and banjos, but the rhythms of the drums became almost like singing. They could almost put a spell on a person.

"Of course, no one from the Master's family attended these proceedings. They never did...that was darky business. Even Mr. Smith rarely went. Probably if truth be known, it was just as well as everyone would have uncomfortable. I was invited by having become friends of Sam and Sally. Besides, as an indentured servant, I was recognized as being something other than Master's kin. Not a slave exactly, but not free either. So, I came and enjoyed myself immensely.

"And it was at this party that I met Jenny. Almost reverse of Sam's father marrying an African woman, she was a white woman who had married an African man and by this choice become a slave. Her story is an interesting one.

"When I first saw her, I was curious as to how she came to be here. Older than me by several years, she clearly knew everyone and was familiar with many of them. Far more than I ever felt. So, I went up to her to introduce myself."

"Hello, I'm Wyanne and I thought I knew everyone here, but I don't know you."

"Probably not since I rarely get off my plantation. I never learned ricing skills and so, don't have much opportunity to burn fields."

"Excuse me, but burn fields? I'm confused. That's slave work. Aren't you an indentured servant?"

"Servant, yes; indentured, no."

"Now I'm really confused. You are a servant, but not indentured. You're also not a relative of your master's family, and free employees like Mr. Smith don't normally these parties. Besides, you clearly know these people and some of them like family."

"I should. Through marriage, most of them are kinfolk. See those kids over there? Well, they're mine."

"Peering through the gloom and the shadows of the bonfire were two little children under ten years of age. Though not coal black, they were none the less darkies. This much was obvious even through the shadows. When they were adults, they would be colored like Sam."

"Aren't they lovely kids," asked Jenny proudly?

"They certainly are," I agreed. "But being curious, tell me your story if you don't mind"

"You want to know how I came to marry a slave and become one?"

"That's it in a nutshell."

"Pretty simple actually. When I was indentured over here, my master's plantation was nearer to the frontier than it is now. There weren't many young men around then, not that I'm much to look at. Not like you. So, certainly the Master's sons wouldn't have had anything to do with me except perhaps roll in the straw. So, where was I? Anyway, Plato saw me and courted me. At first, I wouldn't anything to do with him. I certainly wasn't gonna play straw-house with a slave. But, he was persistent and gentle and I fell in love with him. It's just that simple. I love him and will live with him forever."

"Of course, it hasn't been easy. A slave's life is hard at best which was the Master promised me and my children when I asked permission to marry Plato." Laughing, "You should have seen the expression on the Master's face when he understood what I wanted. Even funnier was when I told him that I understood it meant perpetual slavery. To this day, he can't understand me. To sleep with a slave...of course. If they're pretty, even set up house. But to marry into slavery? Never! Well, here I am."

"Later on, when I was to live in Charleston, I was to find out that all sorts of people marry for lots of reasons. I married a man I didn't particularly love for my own reasons. Mind you, your father was a good man and I'll ne'er say bad about him. But love him like Jenny...nooo...that wasn't the case. So, Jenny's case was strange...but who's to say?"

CHAPTER THIRTEEN

About a year had passed since Bert's knife fight. It was a year that had passed quickly and the time was approaching for Ma's wedding. She was well along with the stitching of her dress. Simple in line, it showed her figure off beautifully. Its bodice was rather low cut in the fashion of the day, which made her blush to think of wearing. It was one thing to make something similar for other women; that was only cloth and an order. But to wear something like that for herself? Never in her life would she have considered it until both Sally and Susannah commented on the subject.

"What you doin' gal, wid a dress like that?" exclaimed Sally when she first saw a drawing of what Ma had in mind.

"What do you mean, what you doin? Don't you like it?"

"Well of course, if that's what you want to wear, it be no business of mine, but…"

"But what?" demanded Ma.

"Well, lemme put it this way. How many times you gonna get married?"

"Once, if I'm lucky."

"Right, and only once for the first time. That's for sure. And this gonna be the only time when you can wear what you want…to tell Mr. Bert what he's really getting'."

"He knows."

"Naw, he don't, not from you. Nobody gets nothin' from you 'less you wants them to. And for durn sure, he ain't getting' no straw time 'cause they ain't no baby. Now I ain't sayin' tha's bad. You controllin' your life, but like the white folks before dinner, don't they get an appetizer? Somethin' before dinner to whet their tummies? Well, that's what you gotta do gal. Give the man somethin' to think about. And, gal, you do have somethin' to offer. Why, I remember when I first saw you, you was nothin' but a scrawny chicken. But, that ain't the truth now. You got some meat an' potatoes on yo' bones now."

Laughing at Sally's frank talk, she was just about to reply, when Sally went on.

123

"My, my. I remembers my wedding day. I didn't get no fancy dress like you gonna have, but I do remember that first meal we had...and it weren't no chittlin's and corn bread. It was pure straw time. While you and everyone else was outside dancin' and eatin' we was truly havin' a banquet inside.

"You must have eaten watermelon seed that night 'cause you sure swelled up," laughed Ma.

"Yeah, that's right and just the same one you gonna eat. Mark my words"

"I hope not too soon, because I don't want to be carrying a child too early while we're still trying to get a house started ahead of winter."

"You got a point there, but after holding Massah Bert off so long, he's gonna have to tie a knot in it after you're married if you don' want no baby right off.

And so it went. The women of the plantation each giving secrets about the mysteries of marriage to Ma. Most, she heard and ignored, but Sally's advice made sense. She seemed to be happy with Sam and her baby boy of just several weeks now. Ma hoped for similar joy, but she was apprehensive and said so to Susannah.

"Susannah, I'm getting' bit confused by all this marrying."

"What's that?"

"Well, first, look at this drawing of a dress I want to make for myself. What do you think of it?"

"Fine, if you want to become a nun. I thought you were getting married."

"That's what Sally said, only she was a bit more direct about it. Said Bert needed 'an appetizer befo' dinner.' "

Susannah grinned, "Yep, that's one way to put it and coming from Sally doesn't surprise me. In fact, that's the funniest thing I've heard in a long time. And you know...she's right. Maybe, not the second time, but my first wedding to Tom. I let my bodice come down almost sinfully far. Best thing I ever did. That man couldn't keep his eyes off me during the wedding ceremony. I didn't think he'd last through it before he'd take me off to bed. Later, that night I told him, 'Tom, you like what you see? Well, if you want to continue seeing me, then you better treat me right.' And to the day he died, he did. I was lucky though. He loved me as no man could for a woman. I hope you are too. But, for heaven's sake, Wyanne, you've put Bert off for a year. Give him something in return!"

"So you think the dress needs changing?"

"Are you deaf?"

"Well, there is another thing. You know Bert is bent on going west. He's been looking for land and slaves to buy. As soon as we get married, he'll be wanting to go up in the Piedmont and starting a plantation. That's just plain hard work for several years right after a hard wagon trek getting there. The thought of being pregnant under those circumstances doesn't really appeal to me."

"Well, what can I say? Tom and me, we tried to have children, but couldn't. Now with Mr. Killebrew, I didn't go three months. What the difference was, I don't know. Best I can say is, if you're gonna be married, expect babies unless you make him quit."

"That's what Sally said. Actually, it was 'tie a knot' in it."

"But then, I gotta ask you, why get married?

"You know I want to get married," Ma wailed. "You know how much I love him, but I also saw my ma. One child after another including those that died. She was old before she was young. Frankly, I guess I'm a bit scared."

"We're all scared. With both husbands, even Mr. Killibrew."

That's one I been meaning to ask you about Mr. Killibrew. You've been married to him now almost three years and had a baby by him. Why are you still so formal with him? Don't you know him well enough to use his given name? After all, he has one. It's James, if you didn't know. Would you want me to introduce you two properly?"

Laughing, "No, I know what you mean. But Mr. Killibrew, he's a good man...but he's not Tom. Tom and me, we were just kids in love. Maybe, it's because Mr. Killibrew is older. He's almost 45 now...pretty well middle aged...about ten years older than me and he acts every one of his years. I'm not complaining mind you. He's a good man, and I love him, but in love like Tom...no, that's not the case. And you needn't introduce us. Now scat girl! I've got work to and you've a dress to make"

Time was flying by toward Ma's wedding to Bert. Although she was born a Catholic, she saw no alternative to being married by the local preacher that administered to the spiritual needs of the Draytons. For one, there was no priest in the area. Catholics were really not welcome. "Papists" they were called. Local people were very clear on this issue. "No popery here" was a common cry. And Wyanne knew that surviving here on friendly terms meant not advertising her heritage.

Bert was in fact making arrangements for starting his plantation. After the rice harvesting time, he had gone 100 miles west into the Piedmont area to look at land and learn more about raising the local cash crops. Rice of course was not possible. Some people had actually considered silk production or indigo. The neighboring colony of Georgia was founded on the concept of silk growing. But neither silk nor indigo were really profitable. Tobacco was really the cash crop in that high, dry mountain soil. Some people were beginning to experiment with corn and wheat in Virginia as a replacement to tobacco because they didn't seem to wear out the soil.

This last issue of wearing the soil was something that Ma discussed at length. She was not going west to invest years of toil in land that would wear out and force them to start over by moving further west closer to Indian country.

"Bert, I just won't have it. I love you dearly and will give up Charles Town for your dreams of a plantation. But, you've been roaming for years going from one place to another. I swear you must be half gypsy by now. But, I didn't come all this way from Ireland to wander all over America. So, listen well, Mr. Smith, I want a proper home where our kids can be properly raised,"

"Oh, it's Mr. Smith now is it? You been thinking of marryin' like Susannah?" snorted Bert.

"No, and neither are you marrying like Bell Jackson. Once, after your fight with him, I had a chance to meet his wife. I don't know whether she was lazy and got what she deserved or was just defeated by her life. I don't really care. But, she was worthless. She had as much spunk as grass. So listen well, Mr. Bert Smith. I'm willing to work for it, but we are not going to be shanty Irish. I want lace curtains and we're not going to get them by wearing out land and moving every five years."

"Whoa, wait a minute. What brought this on?"

"I guess maybe you forgot what the old country was like or were too young to know. But, my family never got anywhere. They never had a chance. Not as long as they were tied to his Lordship's manor. America changed all of that for me. I'm the first Farrell to have a real opportunity and I'm not about to waste my youth by not taking advantage of it."

"Is that all I am…an advantage?" retorted Bert.

"For the love of Mary and Jesus, how blind can ye be, man? I swear, sometimes ye can be so dense. As hard as an oak in your head. I love ye and I'm following ye anywhere ye go. And do ye know why? Because I see a man who'll not be settlin' for less than the best. But sometimes, your thinkin' just goes astray. Probably for bein' on the road so much."

By now, Bert was laughing so much he had tears. "You know darling, I never love you more than when you're angry. Your Irish brogue comes out so thick it can be cut with a knife."

"Oh, and I work so hard at correcting it. Since taking tutoring from Mr. Gordon and being around the Draytons, I know what a proper accent is and how important the difference. You might try cleaning up yours on occasion. Being around slaves so much, you almost begin to sound like them"

Then throwing herself in his arms and kissing his face, Ma never felt better in her life. "Oh Bert, I have never loved you as I do now. When you had your fight and almost died, I thought the world would end. But now, I know each day is a new beginning…a new adventure with you that I can't wait to share."

"Speaking of sharing adventures, our wedding day is coming nigh. How is your wedding dress coming?"

"Coming well, young man and no, you'll not be knowing what it looks like until we're standing in front of the preacher. It's bad luck for one thing and besides I want you to really see for sure what you're marrying."

"You can be cruel can't you?" asked Bert grinning.

"Yes, that I can be," replied Ma, "and it'll be worth it. I promise."

"And so it must be, dear heart. But now I've got to get some trees cleared for more planting."

"How long do you think you'll be gone?"

Bert replied, "Probably a couple of days. No more than a week."

"Well, be careful. You're about to be a married man with responsibilities. No lollygagging about after young girls."

"When I have a treasure here? I never go second class."

"You're right," teased Ma impishly. "And well I know it."

"No conceit in your family, I see," snorted Bert. "You've got it all."

"No, just stating facts."

"Well, anyway, love, give me a kiss to remember you by."

"I thought you'd never asked" grinned Ma as she puckered her lips.

"Now I really must tear myself away from you, you siren hussy."

"Gets harder all the time doesn't it? And you've seen nothing yet."

With that, Bert gave Ma a final kiss and then turned toward the stables. There he selected his saddle and told the groom to prepare his horse and mule for a long ride. Even though the distance wasn't far as a bird flies, his ride would still be several hours over the rough roads to the swamp lands being cleared for rice planting. Since he would be staying several days there, he had a tent loaded along with axes, saws, and shovels that would be needed for the clearing. On top of the tools were piled some provisions that would supplement the game shot for their meals.   A lunch was stowed in his saddlebags to eat along the way. With luck, he would arrive at the site about dinnertime when he could bed down his horse and mule, eat dinner prepared by a slave, and then review the work schedule with the foreman.

Giving some last instructions to Sam about picking up some extra tools, Bert set off. Loaded horses generally don't walk much faster than a soldier's march, so covering the distance gave Bert a chance to doze in his saddle and dream about marrying Ma and their new plantation. He had pretty much selected the land that he wanted after studying survey maps and making a journey there. That trip had taken about a month, and Bert felt guilty about leaving Ma so soon after his return. But, the Master had been generous to give him the time and he felt obligated to keep up his obligations. Soon his replacement would be arriving which would necessitate one last trip to show…what was his name?…well, no matter…a few weeks showing him around and then the wedding and the departure. He wanted to be out at the site early enough to get a crop in that would sustain them over the winter. Winters were mild in the Carolinas, but still cold enough. Have to get a cabin built for them and the several slaves he intended to take. A lot of work.

The miles slid by and the sun sank lower in the horizon. Bert's thoughts continued to drift until his horse snorted and began to pick up the pace. Even the mule sensed their near arrival and matched the trot of the horse. Shortly, they rounded a bend where a group of slaves under the direction of Jupiter, the foreman was awaiting them. At the sight of the little caravan, Jupiter came forward to greet Bert.

"How you be, suh? Long, hard ride?"

"No, really not bad, thank you Jupiter. How's dinner coming? My lunch was kind of skimpy so I'm kind of hungry. People all set for work?"

"Dinner be ready in a few minutes. We held off cooking it so's you'd have somethin' hot when you got in.."

"Ah, good, that was very kind of you. Let me just wash my hands. Meantime, could you have the animals unloaded, please?"

"Yassuh, Mercury'll take care of that right away."

A few minutes later, the squirrel stew was being heated and some biscuits were being baked in a covered pan. Bert finished washing and then walked over to the edge of bog to review the next day's work. He noted that the bog quickly sank into a full swamp. That meant extra work draining the water and need for more slaves and a full time overseer. Jupiter was fine for keeping things going for a day, but neither he nor the other slaves were anxious to undertake the backbreaking work that lay before them. So, he'd have to send a note back to the Master explaining the situation and ask for more field hands and to have his replacement come out here. If he were to go back himself, the crew would just sit down and sleep. So, that meant a white supervisor. With a sigh of resignation, Bert condemned himself to a full week out here. Hopefully his replacement will arrive tomorrow or the next day as scheduled. Otherwise, he'd be out here longer than the week he had promised Ma.

"Massah Smith, dinner be ready."

Turning, "Wha..? Oh, yes. Thank you Jupiter."

Dinner was uneventful and tasteless being cooked by bachelors in the woods. Afterwards, Bert wrote a note explaining his requirements to the Master and then discussed the planned activities for tomorrow with Jupiter. Mostly, it would involve surveying the land to decide where to fell the trees to enhance building dikes that would channel water into drains. With so few slaves at hand, only the easier trees could be cut safely and without the fallen trees, the draining activities could not begin. With that, Bert went to his tent and fell into a deep sleep. The slaves slept near the smoky fire where the mosquitoes weren't so thick.

129

The next day went as scheduled. It involved slogging through the swamp marking trees as cut along the river the would allow water to flow in from the upper end of the field and then channel it out at the lower end. Of course in the beginning, the upper end would be blocked so that the field could be drained entirely allowing access to the trees in the middle when they could be cut and hauled away. But that wouldn't be until next season. Bert thought about that.

"Next season. Next season I'll be cutting trees for planting tobacco and wheat. Some of the same trees will provide lumber for our house and barns."

But shaking himself away from his reverie, he returned to the work at hand. He and Jupiter talked about the direction the trees needed to fall to minimize the work needed to start the dikes. Consideration also was needed to provide working clearance as well. Finally, by nightfall a working plan was developed, but it promised to be dangerous, backbreaking work.

"Well, let's call it a day, Jupiter. Feed the hands extra rations and let them have a tot of rum. They'll need it for tomorrow. I'm going to bed."

"Yassuh, Massah. Smith. Tomorrow will start early enough, that's for sure."

Tomorrow did start early: before dawn. Daylight was too precious to waste eating. After a cold breakfast of leftover stew, Bert and the crew started off to the high end of the field. The teamsters followed behind. A half hour later, everyone was in place and the cutting commenced.

The work was slow. The cutters and the animals were working in leg deep water. The ground underneath was soft and sticky. It sucked at the feet of every man out there making every movement a clumsy dance. Bert and Jupiter constantly supervised the positioning of the crew to ensure that they wouldn't become trapped under a falling tree. With the small manpower that they had, a loss of even one person would mean a critical delay in progress. Still, by dark of the first day, a circle had been cleared and a few trees had been moved along the river. With this hole, a slice could be cut that would extend the dike.

"Jupiter we've made a start. How are the men? Any injuries?"

"No suh. Just scrapes and bruises, but nothing else."

Bert said, "Well, they're still fresh now and alert. As time passes we'll have to be extra careful as they get tired and sluggish. We can't afford to lose anyone. So keep a close eye on them. Don't let them loaf, but also don't push them so hard they start acting stupid."

"Yassuh. I un'erstand."

"Well good night, Jupiter. I'll see you in the morning." And with that Bert fell into a coma of sleep. He didn't even dream of Ma.

The second and third days repeated the first. By then, the men were becoming visibly tired. Their movements became increasingly robotic. Still the work proceeded. Bert and Jupiter redoubled their efforts to ensure safety, but they too were becoming fatigued. Still the work proceeded.

The fourth day saw the sun come early with no relief in sight. Mosquitoes, heat, humidity, water and bog. Only the relief team of fresh men and horses failed to arrive. Bert and Jupiter reminded the crew to be extra careful, but they might as well have talked to a wall as tired as they all were.

About eleven o'clock what was feared happened. A tree fell on top of a slave. He had been moving away as it was coming down, but too slowly. Fortunately, he was not killed and really not even injured. He was just pinned and needed help being cleared out. Bert went over to see what was happening and recognizing that the slave could be slid out by pulling under his armpits, reached out to do so thereby bringing his face close to the water. A water moccasin chose that moment to attack and bit Bert directly in the throat, its venom coursing directly through his veins. He was a dead man.

It was a minute before anyone recognized what happened. Even the pinioned slave didn't notice. When he felt Bert's grip slacken, he thought Bert was merely readjusting his grip. Then he saw the snake and felt a sodden weight collapse on top of him. Screaming for help, other slaves came quickly to see what happened. Actually, Bert's weight kept him from struggling and not attracting the snake's notice. However, it didn't take long for the others to see what needed to be done and soon the slave was freed. Bert was still dead. Work came to a standstill.

"Well, I guess we's gotta take Mr. Smith back to Drayton Plain. The Massah 'll be wantin' to know what happened. Who wants to go in?"

As tempting as getting out of the swamp was, no one volunteered. The master's lash was not something they wanted to risk whereas laying around the camp would be safe...almost pleasant by comparison. So, Jupiter elected himself and a teamster to carry the body and the news back.

Not far from the swamp, Jupiter met the new overseer and the extra crew. He explained what happened and what their clearing plan was. He warned the overseer

131

that his men would not be anxious to go back into the swamp. That news didn't please him. "Well, we have ways to cure that problem."

With that exchange, Jupiter bid the overseer good day and proceeded on his journey back to Drayton Hall.

CHAPTER FOURTEEN

Day broke as most days do. The sun was creeping over the eastern horizon, its rays piercing through an atmosphere that promised to be hot and muggy. Summer was truly coming upon the plantation. People were already moving slowly in dread of the discomfort that would be coming. Even getting rid of extra shifts and other clothing normally demanded of women, chaffing sores were soon to be coming. The Mistress would be leaving soon for the sea breezes of Charles Town.

Ma shook herself out of bed and ran sleepily to the kitchen. Getting her breakfast, she quickly escaped outdoors where she could find a breeze while enjoying her tea and biscuits. She was finally getting over her hunger for food. It seemed that her soul was beginning to recognize that it was never to be hungry again. She hadn't let a dress out in several years as a result.

"Today is the day that I finish my wedding dress," Ma promised to herself. "The Mistress doesn't have any rush sewing jobs. Anything that needs to be done can be done by Sarah and Sadie."

Susannah came by and sat down beside Ma. The two commenced their usual chit-chat about what was to be happening today. Ma had learned a lot from Susannah about organizing people into teams that could get things done quickly, so she listened closely to whatever plans were to be made each day.

Susannah said, "The Mistress will be leaving by barge shortly for Charles Town. This weather will be chasing her out to the cooler breezes in Charles Town. So, a lot of packing will be needed to get all of her dresses in order. The Master will be sending some things, but since he is doing his judging so much, he really keeps clothing at any of his houses so that they 're handy for him. But, what about you, Missy? You're due to get married shortly. Have you started thinking about packing for your move West?"

Ma answered, "Not really. I've just enough to think about getting married. My wedding dress has been a real chore with all of its fancy stitching. Then of course, there is the party that we will be holding. Bert is almost useless on these details. I swear! He thinks that I can handle anything."

"Well, can't you? Otherwise, you could have fooled me. Besides, how long have you known men? They're all helpless on the details of life, and Mr. Smith's no different. You'll learn that soon enough when you move west, so get used to it now."

"You're right," sighed Ma. "As usual." Ruminating, "Susannah, I don't know what I'm going to do without you. Whenever I bump into a wall you always seem to know where the door is."

"To tell the truth, I'll miss you as well. But, hey, you're not left yet and we've got lots to do here. So, I'll see you at lunch."

Taking her plate and teacup back to the kitchen, Ma then went over to her sewing room only to find Sarah and Sally not there. Grumbling about slaves being lazy, she went over to their quarters, rousted them up and sent them over to start their day's sewing. From there she went over to Mr. Gordon for her day's lessons. By now, she could read most anything given to her. Now, she was working on her writing skills. Not that she couldn't write, but now he was trying to give her a sense of style to her prose. As a practice exercise, he even had her write a bit of poetry occasionally. *Wouldn't Ma and Pa be amazed at me now? Imagine, a Farrell writing poetry.*

Besides learning to read and write, Ma had been taking lessons in bookkeeping from Mr. Killebrew. She had watched the Mistress tend the plantation's books during the Judge's absences, and decided that she had also a need to learn that skill. At first, it had been a bit confusing trying to assign everything that had been bought or sold to a special category, but eventually she began to see the system behind the process. So, while she never became as a good as Mr. Killibrew, she did learn that her head for figures was quick.

The hours passed. The day became as sugar sticky as the dawn sun had promised. Lunch was just a light affair. Really, it was simply too hot for much of anything. The kitchen slaves simply went through their errands. The field hands would have to be pushed to do anything now.

"My God, Bert must be having a terrible time in the swamps where the mosquitoes would be eating them alive."

Finally, the evening shadows began to lengthen and with them, a slight ruffle of a breeze. It was then when some slaves began to notice that Mr. Smith's wagon was coming back. That was really strange. Mr. Smith wasn't due back for at least several days. After all, more field hands had been requested as soon as possible. Someone must be hurt. That could be the only answer. But, if it was a field hand, why would they be coming back here? After all, other camps were much closer. Not that a doctor would be needed for a field hand. Mr. Smith could take care of any cuts or broken bones well enough.

One of the slaves came over to Jupiter as he drove the wagon up the pathway.

"Wha' happen Jupiter? Who be hurt?"

"It's Massah Smith. He dead. Snake bit him in the throat. He never had a chance. He be dead almost befo' he hit the ground. So, now, I'se gotta take him up to the Massah."

"I don't envy you none with this errand."

"I ain't too happy about this myself" as he continued to drive the wagon to the main house.

And slowly he proceeded up the road to the Master's house. Other slaves came out of their houses inquiring about this strange procession. Eventually, a small crowd was trailing the wagon as it pulled around the circle in front of the main entrance. At this noise, the Master came out to learn what was disturbing his morning studies. One glance at the wagon's rear told him most of the story that he needed to know.

"What happened Jupiter? How did Mr. Smith die?"

"Well suh, he be helpin' a slave get freed from a log that rolled on him when a water moccasin struck him in th' throat. You kin see the marks in his throat from here." With that, Jupiter pulled back Bert's collar to expose the twin holes of the snake. "He be dead by the time we got him back to the shore. We didn't have no time to do anything to help...not that we could've considering where he be hit."

As these words were being spoken, Ma had also become curious about the noise. Coming out of her sewing room and around the corner to see the crowd. "H'mmm, what's this? Wonder who's hurt? Probably a slave from a near-by field."

Continuing on, a flash of fear crawled up her neck. That shirt collar looked awfully, terribly familiar. At her footsteps, the Master turned with an ashen face. Her flash of fear became a flood. Continuing her steps, Ma passed everyone going straight to the wagon where the worst of news lay awaiting her. Looking closer, no doubt existed. Her Bert was dead and with him went all of their dreams. Her fear now kicked her in the stomach and she went down like a rock. Not moving, not wailing, not crying. Like a rock. Grabbing her stomach, Ma rocked silently on her knees not saying a word. The Master tried to reach for her, but she brushed his hand aside. She just kneeled there and rocked while her stomach was taking in kick after kick. The fear was gone and now, only pain flooded over her in ceaseless waves of nausea.

After a seeming eternity, Ma stood up and faced the crowd. "What happened?" The Master quickly told her the story now old in its repetition.

135

"It seems to me Master Drayton that we had better prepare for a burial. Mr. Smith has been dead for a full day and he isn't going to last long in this heat."

Taken aback by this response, the Judge gulped and nodded his assent. "Yes, you're right. We need to attend to this right away. Meanwhile, what can we do for you?"

"Thank you sir for your kind offer, but for now I just need to be alone. I guess I won't be needing to finish that wedding dress." With that, Ma went back to her room and stayed there for the remainder of the day.

Later that evening, Susannah knocked timidly on Ma's door. "Can I come in?" she asked timidly.

"What? Oh yes, please, Susannah. You're just the person I want."

Susannah took Ma in her arms and held her like a child for a long time. Then, looking a Ma, she saw that no tears had flowed. Her eyes were sad, but dry. No sign of redness could be seen.

"How are you dear? You're not crying or wailing as you did before when Mr. Smith had his fight."

"Numb. But more than that, clear. Perhaps I've only been waiting for this. When Mr. Smith went off and had his fight, I discovered love for the first time. I only then knew what I had and what I had almost thrown away. What had almost been taken away from me. As far as I was concerned it was gone and my life almost came to an end. " Laughing ruefully, Ma continued. "You were hearing a real Irish wailing. There's nothing prim and proper about it is there? There's a lot of women back home who made a regular thing about wailing a wakes and funerals. Of course, some of 'em probably had a bit of encouragement from a bottle."

Susannah asked, "And no wailing now?"

"No, I don't think so. Since then, I've learned a lot. A lot by watching you. You loved your Tom. I know that. But, you lived. You're not the same young girl you were then, but you married Mr. Killebrew and have had several kids by him. Do you love him as you loved Tom...no, but you're living on just the same."

Some time passed, the two women sat in a quiet reverie. Finally, Ma continued. "America is a great country. It's given me opportunities that my family back home can't even dream. Look at me. I can read and write and do numbers. Mr.

Killibrew is even teaching me accounting. Bert was dreaming of his plantation, of becoming another Judge Drayton."

More time passed. Susannah just waited for her friend to talk when she was ready. Finally her patience was rewarded. "Yes," Ma continued, "America is a land of dreams. But it's also cruel. Life is taken in a blink. Your Tom died of the fever. Had he done anything wrong? No. He just died of the fever and there's no accounting for it. Bert just happened to be helping a slave caught under a tree. Was he doing anything wrong? No, just helping someone. I don't even know that slave's name. I'm not even sure if Bert knew him well…if at all. But, no matter, he certainly wasn't doing anything wrong. But, a hidden snake killed him none the less. And, now he's dead and nothing's going to change that."

Again, more time passed. Ma asked, "So where am I? An indentured servant hoping to get ahead before something kills me. Susannah, as surely as you welcomed me into this strange land, you taught me to survive and that I will do."

"Well, yes, but I do wish you'd let go. It's not natural to…to at least cry. But maybe that will come later."

"Maybe so, but it's late now and time for you to get home to your family. Please thank Mr. Killibrew for lending you to me."

That night remained a long one for Ma, but when the dawn came again, the weather was unchanged. Sugar heat was promised and would be kept. Ma ate breakfast, accepting the voices of condolence and then proceeded to the Master's office.

"Yes Wyanne?"

"Sir, life has changed for me in this past day. I'm not sure where I am. I was going west with Mr. Smith, but obviously I'm not now."

"Well, clearly you have a home here for as long as you want one."

"Yessir, and I've thought about that a lot last night, and I thank you. I knew you'd be kind enough to offer it. But, really I think not. It'd be too hard going places expecting to see Mr. Smith…"

"That's right. I've had that same experience now twice. God forbid that I repeat it again."

137

"So, I'd really like to go to Charles Town where I'd wanted to go before Mr. Smith came along. But, what's my status with you? I know Mr. Smith had paid off my indenturement or at least intended to..."

"Well, Wyanne, I can understand your desires and agree it's probably the best thing for you. In fact, Mr. Smith had bought out your articles and you're really free to leave. In fact, this morning I was just reviewing his will. Being a judge and an attorney, Mr. Smith had asked me to prepare one for him about a year ago. It seems that he has left you with a fairly large sum of money. He had intended to start buying land and slaves shortly, but now... Well, it seems that only his money is left."

With these words, Ma again went down like a rock on a chair. "Only his money is left..." Again, "Only is his money is left..." Shaking herself loose, she turned to the judge again saying, "Excuse me sir. I didn't mean to presume upon you by sitting down."

"My God, woman. Would you expect to me to think otherwise?"

"But, now sir, where am I? I'm really at seas."

"It seems to me that some time will be needed to straighten out Mr. Smith's affairs. His will is in order, but he does have some debts that need payment. Then you will receive his estate. Meanwhile, here's a plan you might want to consider. After Mr. Smith's funeral, Mrs. Drayton will be going to Charles Town to catch the cool summer breezes. Why don't you go with her? There you can finish her dresses, have some time to think about where you want to go, and then proceed from there."

"Oh sir, thank you. Mind you, I'm not asking for charity or anything that you don't think I should have. But this would truly give me the help I need. And meanwhile, I can be helping the Mistress with her clothing."

"Wyanne, I've had a lot of indentured servants in my day and certainly slaves, but you've earned everything you've gotten. Most all of them have tried to give as little as possible. But, in your case, you've honored your word in every possible way. So, anything we can do in return to make your life easier is a pleasure for Mrs. Drayton and me. So, let's call this the sealing of a bargain."

"And now, sir, with your permission, I believe I need to be getting ready for the funeral."

"Yes, sadly, I think you're right."

The funeral did take place in the late afternoon when the blazing heat of mid-day had passed. The Drayton family with all of the children were there. Susannah and her family were there. Mr. Gordon stood quietly by. A few slaves that Mr. Smith knew well were there but in the back. Sally and Sam and their children were among them. A couple of field hands who had dug the gravesite were standing by to lower the casket. Mr. Drayton led a simple service reciting a short history of Bert's life and of things he had done at Drayton Hall. The Judge was very spare in his words, not offering false words of hope about the meaning of Bert's death other than to comment how he had died trying to help a fallen slave. Rather, he simply said that Bert's death was tragic in light of the plans he had been making with Ma.

"So, for the living, we should reflect on these pages of History and try to do as well as we could. "

The service lasted about thirty minutes. Ma was numb throughout the entire proceeding.

Because of Bert's death and Ma's desire to go to Charles Town, Mrs. Drayton moved her plans forward. Still several days passed before everything was in order for a move of six months duration. Ma tried to keep herself busy, but without too much success. At best, she was able to give last instructions to Sarah and Sadie on upcoming sewing projects. But, whether they really listened to her was of absolutely no interest to her. The night before her departure was spent rover at Susannah's house where they talked about old times. Laughs were shared about Ma's first night at Drayton Hall and of the cotton in her mouth as she talked to gruff Mr. Smith. Tears were shed as they thought about the absence that would be coming between these two friends.

The next morning, Ma again had her small bag packed with a few clothes and some personal articles such as a few books, paper and a pen. Susannah was there to help the Mistress and give Ma a quick hug. Then she too was gone. The barge was loaded and everyone got on board.

The trip was as calm and quiet as it was those few years ago when Ma took a similar trip down the same river. The savannah was a lush sigh of tall grass and the birds twittered the same. The heat was the same and the rhythmic sound of poles pushing the barge along was the same as the river carried them along. Conversation between Ma and the Mistress was strained and finally it just died out. What was to be said?

The hours passed and the river became a watershed exactly as it had done before. Ma hardly noticed. Life a million years ago flowed through her memory as she thought of a marriage proposal given to her. Occasionally a smile would cross her

139

face, but only a flicker before it was gone. Then she was so anxious to see Charles Town that his proposal was a joke…how she had laughed at it…flirted with it. No siree, *she* was going to Charles Town and that was that. Well, now she was going to Charles Town.

Charles Town

1755 - 1775

CHAPTER FIFTEEN

A month passed since Ma's trip down the Ashley river to Charles Town. It was a flooded wash of memories. The excitement of a marriage proposal and the new sights and rhythms of sound came back to her like piercing stab wounds. Fortunately, the Mistress kept her busy preparing her summer wardrobe. As her fingers flew, her mind was occupied with the details of her craft.

She was also kept occupied with frequent trips to stores on King Street where she could get threads and ribbons and staples of cloth. During these excursions she was able to restore acquaintances with people she had met before. Of course, they all wanted to know how she was doing and what she was doing. Explaining the past several years was both difficult in that she had to dredge up her pains and joys. Yet, at the same time, getting them out provided relief. Getting them out relieved the pressure that comes in the middle of the night's nightmares. She could also see that her experience and Susannah's were not unique. Most of the women she knew had been through it. Rare was the person of middle age who had not been married at least once before. Yet, despite their pains, they lived and laughed.

The Judge was also a big help to Ma. His advice on dealing with Bert's will, transferring his assets to her and putting them into cash that could banked was always right on the money. Going into a bank was almost terrifying to her. No one in her family had ever entered one before. Of course they had heard about banks but living in the country on the Lord's manor never offered a reason to deal with one. Furthermore, they had never had enough money at any one time to consider saving anything. But, with the Judge's support, she entered the Farmers and Mechanics Bank and shyly asked to open a savings account.

"Yes Ma'am. May I help you?"

"I'd like to open a savings account if I may."

"Yes, of course. But who will recommend you? We can't have just anyone come in and become a customer. We need to be certain that you will be a secure investment of our name."

"Yes sir, I understand that. I'm also concerned that my money will be safe so your care is appreciated. So, for a recommendation, do you know Judge John Drayton? Well, here is his letter of recommendation."

With that name, the teller became much friendlier. "Judge Drayton? Of course...well, yes...it is a pleasure to do business with you. Now, exactly how much money are we talking about? And, please, let me call my manager." With those words, he signaled his supervisor.

Showing the teller her letter of recommendation and a letter directing that Bert's money be transferred into Ma's account, she answered, "It's really about 550 pounds. Four hundred and seventy five needs to be transferred from his account and the rest is cash from his estate that I'm depositing now."

By this time, the manager had arrived, "Yes, William, do you need me?"

"Sir, I'd like to introduce Miss Wyanne Farrell, the fiancée of Mr. Bert Smith who unfortunately died recently. She has decided to continue depositing his money here and make another deposit of her own. Also, here is a letter of recommendation from Judge Drayton."

"Vell, vell, vell, Fraulein Farrell, this is indeed a pleasure to meet you. My name is Mr. Jacob Oskarmeyer and I am a vice-president here. Certainly, I hope to do business with you for a long time in the future. Is there anything in particular we can do for you besides open your account?"

"No sir. Right now, just opening an account will be enough. I'm really just getting acquainted again with Charles Town since the death of Mr. Smith. I'm also just released from my indenturement with the Draytons although I'm still working for the Mistress. Eventually, however, my ambition is to open my own shop here on King Street. Perhaps then you will be able to help me."

"But of course. You will learn dot ve offer every modern advantage. Savings accounts, letters of credit, loans. You can name it. But for now, rest assured that your money is safe with us. We have been open for 15 years and never been in default."

"Default?"

"Never been able to return a customer's money whenever it's requested."

"Judge Drayton told me to ask you how much interest your savings program paid?"

Laughing, Mr. Oskarmeyer replied, "The Judge is teaching you well isn't he? Well, it's 1.5 per cent paid out each year. That means that for every pound you put in, ve pay you one und a half pounds at the end of a year."

Ma could hardly believe her ears. "Paying me money just for leaving my savings in their bank. If Ma and Pa could only hear and see all of this."

"Miss Farrell, I'll turn you back over to Mr. James here and he'll lead you through the papers you need to sign. Then you'll be a full-fledged customer of Farmers and Mechanics Bank. Again, welcome."

The paperwork took just a few minutes and that was that. With a fluttering heart, Ma turned over her cash and given a receipt for all of the money deposited in her account. Fortunately, the accounting lessons she had had with Mr. Killebrew let her read and understand this document. With that, Ma took her departure and continued her errands.

And the days passed like this. Entering into new relationships that slowly built the foundation of a future business. Ma was still young and thus, patient. She needed to understand what a good businesswoman needed to know if she was to be a success. Above all, she needed to develop a clientele. Of course, at this point she couldn't actually solicit business; not as long as she was employed by the Mistress. But, through her, a reputation for clever work and honest dealings could be spread throughout the Charles Town community.

The nights were another question. Here Ma had to listen to ghostly voices of happy years. Sam and Sally…getting married. Christmas parties that would go through the evenings with little work the following day. Long, gossipy sessions with Susannah. How her wise voice was missed now. She always seemed to know what to do with any situation. Even the boys teasing her. She wondered occasionally about that one chap. What was his name anyway? Oh yes, William. My goodness, she hadn't seen him in a year or two. Where *did* he go anyway? What did he do? Oh yes, blacksmith apprentice. Probably, he was sent off somewhere to perfect his trade. After all, after he finished his apprenticeship, he was a journeyman who would journey to other masters to learn their secrets of metalworking.

Then finally, there was Bert. Her longing for him remained as intense as ever. The pain in her loins seemed never to weaken. As a child, she had had her bumps and bruises. Once her arm was broken, but that pain was nothing compared to the depth of the ache she felt now. Sometimes, the only salvation was a dram. Ma well understood how a dram here and another there led to bottles. That was almost a disease back home. So many young men would waste their bodies and wealth chasing the endless bottoms of bottles. But, despite this fear, its relief was real and Ma did use it on occasion to fall into a dark, dreamless sleep.

Another solace was Susannah. Letters weren't the same as chats, but into them she poured her soul.

144

My Dearest Susannah,   March the 15th of 1755

I take my pen in hand today to write you of how my days have progressed. Of course, these letters can never replace our talks, but they certainly do provide a relief. In some respects, writing does provide a different chance for me to order my thoughts. When we are together, our thoughts flit about like butterflies. Letters force me to order them like soldiers. So, perhaps now, I can see myself being reflected as I do in a mirror.

And what does the mirror show me? Many things really. On one hand, I am still young. My mother was old long before my age of twenty. She had already borne two of her six children who lived. Another several died stillborn. Otherwise, she was diverted only by the unrelenting work of milking cattle, planting and reaping, and eventually going herself into the rocky earth that comprises Ireland. She was only forty-eight when she died.

In my case, at this same age, I have a bank account, which Ma could never imagine. Actually, that was quite an experience. You should have seen the faces of those stuffy clerks change when I mentioned the Judge's name. You'd have thought the Savior himself had recommended me. I could hardly keep a straight face. But, still Mr. Osckarmeyer was very helpful leading me through the paperwork of opening my account, transferring Mr. Smith's funds, and depositing some cash of my own. I suppose this will eventually become routine, but for now, it was quite a thrill.

But, oh Susannah! How the nights are so long! When you first talked to me about Tom, my thoughts imagined what pain it was. Actually, I'm ashamed to admit it, but my imagination was very romantic. How tragic, to feel such joyous tragedy. But, now, how I laugh at those silly thoughts. There is nothing joyous or tragic. In fact, if truth be known, I really am angry many times. How senseless. A snakebite of all things. What was he doing there anyway? I know a slave values his life just like anyone else, but why Bert? Why did he have to be the hero and try to rescue him? Why could he not have directed someone one else to effect the rescue?

I know what you will be saying in reply. That life just goes that way, and if Bert hadn't been the type of person who would stoop to help a slave, he wouldn't have been the man I would love. God, he did fool me for a long time though. That first night, he was so gruff, I would have never imagined him to have a caring side. But, the fact is, I do get angry.

With fondest wishes,

Wyanne

Susannah was always faithful in her answers. And she was always faithful in telling Ma what she needed to hear.

Oh My Dear Wyanne,   April 12, 1755

How my heart goes out to you. So many memories come flooding back of Tom's death. As I have said, I thought I would die. More, I really hoped that I would. How could life continue without the man I had come to love like life itself.

I know, and really knew, that when we first met, that you didn't have a faintest idea of what I was trying to say about my suffering. Yet, you listened and I poured my heart out to you as I didn't to anyone else on the plantation. The Draytons were sympathetic of course, but they had their own lives to live. Besides the Master had been down this road already and could only go so far down it with me. After all he *was* the master and what was I? Just a simple girl. So, when you arrived, I was still feeling pain that had nowhere to go. I still thank God for his gift of you.

So, now it is my turn to listen to you. At one level, I can only repeat back what you have already written to me and what I had already said to you before. Life is for the living, and you, my dear, must live. You know that already so I shan't repeat it. What I will tell you though is that the anger you feel is real. Amazing, I still remember it and wondered how it could be? Why was I angry? I couldn't understand it, and yet there it was. I was so angry I couldn't see straight. How dare he die and leave me? It simply wasn't fair! If he loved me, how could he leave so abruptly? It wasn't fair, I tell you.

Strange that one can feel so angry. Weeping and crying on, I could understand. Everyone did that but no one ever talked about this rage that can well up. I really thought I was being sinful. I would pray to God asking for his forgiveness for this hatred of Tom who was truly a saint if I ever saw one. It was years before it passed. I really think that I forced it into the back of my mind so that I couldn't remember it. But, your letter just brought it back in a flash. Like a bolt of lightening. So, now perhaps I understand it better from having heard from you. See there? Now you're helping me again. But, really if we two have felt the same emotions, then perhaps it's just normal to lash out at that which we can't understand.

I really don't know dear, but those 're my thoughts. May God keep you in his bosom and keep you from harm.

Your loving sister (I do think of you as my dearest sister),

Susannah

146

My Dearest Sister,   May, the 23rd of 1755

How your words have thrilled me. I'm sure I would be totally bereft without the kindness of your thoughts. Really, the days are getting better now. Another three weeks have passed since my last letter to you and with each rising sun, life becomes easier to face. The nights are still horrible though. Those long, lazy evenings that I had with Bert keep coming back like a searing candlelight on a dark night.

But, anger, thank God, seems to be receding. It started almost as soon as I put my wrath down on paper. Strange, isn't it how such a perverse emotion can rise when one would normally only expect tears (they also came in abundance). But, you're right. Perhaps it is normal that one can feel such thoughts. If we two, then perhaps others.

But all is not all tears and flapdoodle. The Mistress, bless her soul, has been keeping me very busy sewing dresses. I also have a couple of slave girls to teach. Whether they will be as clever as Sarah and Sadie remains to be seen, but at least they seem to try hard. By the way, please give my best to them. Although they were just slaves, I did feel of them as friends. Certainly, we had many warm afternoons telling stories. But, back to us here in Charles Town, I have agreed to stay here until at least Christmas. By doing so, I have the opportunity to keep productive and my thoughts off of Sam. It also gives me an opportunity to repay the Mistress for all that she has done for me through the years. By repay, I mean she will have good scamstresses both here and at Drayton Plain.

Finally, I will be able to make now contacts here in Charles Town. Among them must be clients who will want to buy my sewing rather than support slaves who may not be as clever as my work. And that's God's own truth. I am good. I suppose that He will strike me down for having such a bold opinion of myself, but the fact is, Mrs. Grable was a good teacher and I did learn well. And it is important that people know of my skills so I must believe in them myself.

Another critical factor is locating a place for my business. It must be on a street that is convenient to clients. Otherwise, they won't come to find me. Fortunately, I think that I have found an area that meets this requirement. It is King Street. Of course, no particular place has been found, but generally it is full of passers-by doing their daily shopping. The rents seem to be acceptable which is important if Mr. Smith's legacy is not to be wasted. Finally, it is convenient to all other shops selling ribbons, cloth, etc. that will be needed to make clothing for the fancies in the Charles Town.

So, in sum, staying with the Mistress is good for the both of us. I thank God that He has led me to this place of plenty and opportunity. Perhaps, in time, I will see

147

that the curse of Bert's death will be a blessing in disguise. But, frankly, I don't believe it yet.

Your dearest sister,

Wyanne

In fact, Ma was beginning to recover. The business of life was beginning to move her past the gaping hole in her life. It couldn't fill it; that was impossible. But, like the scar of a tree that surrounds a hole hacked into its bark, a scar slowly began to surround her heart's wound. At the same time, she realized that a great love had passed. She wasn't looking yet for anyone else; but, judging from Susannah's experience as well as those of many other ladies surrounding her, she understood that the possibility still existed. After all, she eventually wanted children and as far as she could tell, it was extremely difficult without a man. So marriage would eventually take place, but not with the aching desire that Bert had filled her body.

As time passed, Ma's plans began to crystallize. She eventually did find a small apartment – store that offered promise on King Street. Its rent was high, but she hadn't yet finished negotiating with the owner. It also needed repairs, which Ma intended to use as a selling point in her negotiations. As it was, she couldn't expect to occupy it before the new year. So, that meant she really could accompany Mrs. Drayton back to the plantation. The thought of seeing Susannah thrilled her immensely even though she also knew it would bring back ghostly voices of love gone by.

"Mr. Thurgood, your price is simply too high. I'm not made of money you know."

"Mistress Farrell, I know that you're not made of money, but I also know you have a savings account, so don't play poor with me. "

"That may be true, perhaps not, but if it is, it'll stay there unless you make me a price that will tempt me to give some of it to you. After all, I've waited some time before I found you and I can wait a bit longer. It's no matter to me. Meanwhile, you're losing money each day it's empty."

"Madam, if you would listen to me..."

"No, I think not. Really, I know not. This place is a pigsty. Just look at it. Needs the roof to be patched, the walls haven't been painted...Have you ever painted it, my man? You really expect me to consider such a place?"

Turning on her heel, she started to leave the premises when Mr. Thurgood chased after to stop her.

"Madam, I'm sure we can work something out. If you would only bear with me for a moment."

"A moment he asks for. Holy Mother of Jesus, you've wasted my time now for these past days refusing to consider for a second my concerns about the condition of this rat's nest and the king's ransom you've demanded for a price. And you want a moment? What on earth for? You know, you really have gall even though you know you can't possibly expect to lease this place in its present condition. Do you really think I'm that stupid?"

"Well, it is a bit worn. But, tell me, what would you offer?"

"I'll give no more than a shilling a week and you have to patch the roof. That roof is such that I shan't live under it if it were the last roof on the face of God's green earth."

Wincing, Mr. Thurmond still stood his ground even though it was becoming quicksand. The place, in fact, had not been rented for far too long and he was losing money each day. The city's taxes still must be paid and they weren't getting any cheaper. Still he gamed on.

"Madam, if I were to accept that offer, I would be consigned to Hell for making a pact with the Devil. But, don't turn away. I'm not done yet."

"What Devil's pact are you offering me now? Out with it!"

"Make it a shilling and a half and I'll both fix the roof and paint the place. Your color."

"Well, why didn't you say so in the beginning? That's a deal," offering her hand to shake. "When shall we write a contract? Judge Drayton will notarize it."

"Judge Drayton, Ma'am?"

"Are you deaf?"

"No Ma'am, of course not. But, a contract? Is that necessary? I've never needed one before and I see no reason for one now."

149

"Well, I do. Just look about. Does this place look like an honest landlord has managed it? I think not. So, rather than take simply your word for things, which I'm *sure* is absolutely good, let's just keep things business-like and on paper. Would next week be fine? The Judge will be in then and I can arrange an appointment."

Later, meeting with the Judge, Ma related her bargain and asked him if he would write a contract.

"Wyanne, I always knew you were tougher than shoe leather. Thurgood, that old scoundrel. He's been fleecing tenants for years and now, he's really gotten his comeuppance. How I would have enjoyed seeing his face as he tried to deal with you." Laughing, he agreed to meet with the couple and arrange a contract that he promised "would stand up through Hell and high water."

Dear Susannah,   September, the 23rd of 1755

Much has happened since I wrote last. I have actually found a place for my shop. It won't be ready for several months yet, but that has actually been a God-send for me. First, I was able to use its deplorable condition as a way of reducing its rent. The skinflint! He actually expected me to take his opening price. But, anyway, I kept after him. I even walked out on him at one point. But, as I expected, he was quick to chase me since he knew he hadn't an another chance to lease it. Second though, since it won't be available until after the new year, I will be able to come back and see you.

Frankly, these trials couldn't have occurred to a better person. Already, despite having signed a contract, he is already trying to cheat me by doing shoddy work. Of course, when I threatened to denounce him to the city council, he relinquished. How could he face them and the charges of defrauding a "helpless orphan in the world?" He wouldn't have had a chance.

Susannah, I long to see you. People here have been courteous and willing to help, but that's all. But, friendship, deep friendship is what is missing in my life. Of course, coming home will bring me to the hole left by Bert, but truly, I guess I have to meet it if I'm ever to get my life truly on track. And here, I need you as a watch tower toward which I can guide my life.

Did I understand that you're expecting another baby? What a joy! Your babies will be such a surprise for me. They undoubtedly have grown so much they won't be recognized. What a wonderful life you are creating with Mr. Killebrew.

Your loving sister,

Wyanne

My dearest Wyanne,   1 November 1755

How I laughed to imagine you negotiating with the very Devil himself. I bless God that he has given you the strength to stand up against the evils and iniquities of the world. Mr. Thurgood needs to realize that he can either work with you the easy way, the correct way, or the hard way. Either way, he will do what you say…simply because you are you.

I too am excited about the passing time. In only a few weeks, you will be coming back to Drayton Hall. How I relish the long chats that we will have. Mr. Killebrew will just have to wait each evening until I return home to his bed. Besides, yes, I am expecting and that means that Mr. Killebrew must abide in his instincts. So, whether he is abiding beside me or whether I am elsewhere is really not really too much of a question. He will abide in either event.

Until we see one another again, I remain

Your loving sister,

Susannah

The following days were almost a drag on eternity until finally, at last, Ma could take Sam's slow wagon and repeat the long trip back to Drayton Plain that had been made years before. Wyanne could hardly contain herself in her anxious anticipation. To see Susannah! It seemed impossible, but true. The sad white beards of the Spanish moss now were welcoming her home as she passed them by. How good they seemed now. Even Sal's slow clops and grumpy groans as she meandered along were pleasing. They were taking her home. The hours passed as she and Sam reminisced about her first trip along this road.

"Yes Missy, you was certainly a sight coming off that old ship. Scrawny and pale, just like a ghost. And sick too, if I recalls correctly. Lost your stomach."

"I can hardly believe that I'm the same girl."

"You ain't and tha's a fact. You's a woman now growd for certain. Sally and I were deeply distressed by the passing of your man, Mr. Smith."

"Well, frankly, it still hurts to be truthful. But, I guess like a toothache, I'm getting used to it. And like a toothache, I've learned that I can still eat. I understand that Sally is expecting a baby?"

"Yes, M'. That's a fact. Actually, we were surprised that it took this long. But, all things in their own due time. You heard that Mistress Killebrew is also expecting? The two women 'll be delivering at 'bout the same time I reckon."

"Yes, you're right. And I'm happy for all of you: you, Sally and Susannah."

"That's right. Children do make a family don't they? They gives you hope for living. That the future be better for their lives."

Eventually, Sal's clops turned into a semi-fast shuffle. Ma knew the turn up to the plantation was just ahead. Sal could smell her stable and was impatient to get there. A couple of minutes later, the entryway was turned and standing there were Susannah, her children and Mr. Killebrew.

Wyanne squealed with delight: "Susannah! Susannah! Here I am!" Jumping off the wagon, she flew over to give everyone a big hug. Even Mr. Killibrew seemed to be pleased enough to come down off his dignity pedestal. The children hung back behind Susannah's skirt. After all eight months was a long time and memories fade quickly.

"Betsy and Jeremiah, come here," pushing them forward. "Of course you remember Mistress Farrell. She hasn't been gone that long. " Still no movement from them. "Oh well, you know children. Shy at first, then crawling all over you. OK, Sam, let's pile everyone on board and make Sal really work for her oats."

With that invitation, the children whooped with delight, Sal groaned and Sam clucked her forward. The caravan plodded forward only to stop off at the Killibrew's house. "You're staying here for the night. We have far too much to talk about for you to waste a night in your old room. Besides, it's all changed and here you will be home."

Home. Ma was home in the bosom of her family.

CHAPTER SIXTEEN

My mother never talked much about going to Charles Town from Drayton Plain, but once many years after we had moved to the Bahamas, we asked her why it didn't upset her more than it did. After all, she had lost everything. Her house, various slaves during the war, her friends all were gone. She wasn't a youngster anymore either. It's one thing as a fifteen-year old girl to leave home in search of a new dream. But as a middle aged woman to lose her dream was another thing altogether. At that point, she rummaged in the memories of her life and gave a surprising answer.

"Yes, that's right, I did lose everything. But what did I lose? My house? I can build another one and have. My slaves, well frankly if I were a slave I'd run away too if I had had a chance. I didn't leave my indenturement easily, but that was something different. I had entered it voluntarily and I was treated fairly. Furthermore, I knew it would end. So, I wasn't going to be like my brother. I had made a contract and I intended to honor it. But slavery was something different. Slaves didn't have a choice.

"Yes, yes, I know. I have owned slaves, bought and sold them as needed. I still have them. Mind you, I always tried to treat them properly. But none-the-less, I own them and can do with them as I please. If I were in that position, and I had a chance, I'd run away too if I had a chance.

"Family, well what of it? My husband is dead. Susannah died in childbirth. The Master died during the war. So, who's left? Of course, my most precious treasures are still with me, you children. And as long as you're with me, does it really make much difference where we are?

"But, I guess I had learned long before that times change and you can't look back. I learned it that time when I had returned home to Drayton Hall.

"Although I had been freed my indenturement and could come and go as I pleased, the Mistress was good enough to provide a home and work in Charles Town for the first six months that I was there. She also let me go home to Drayton Plain that first Christmas. I was sorely homesick for the old faces. Susannah's letters probably were the only things that kept me going. I still have them and enjoy reading them on occasion. She was probably the best friend I ever had. I could hardly wait to see her again.

"And when I did see her, it seemed at first like nothing had changed. The next several days just floated by catching up on news of things going on. Sally and

Sam had their baby shortly after I arrived and a strapping boy he was too. Sally still scolded me if I tried to enter her washroom and do anything for myself. She'd say, "Girl, you ain't learned nothing yet. If I told you once, I told you a hundred times, you don't do nothing in this here room. This is my work and I ain't letting no one, includin' you, touch it." Of course, by now, she was laughing, but still serious. Sally was never going to be a field hand again. She was a house nigrah and that's where she was going to stay.

"But, then things began to look differently. First, the new overseer was ok I guess. I never did really learn his name. But after having known Mr. Smith, well, it was just a shock. I know Mr. Smith was dead, but it just didn't feel right that someone else should be in charge. I really almost expected him, Mr. Smith that is, to be standing in the gloom waiting for me when I returned to the plantation. He certainly scared me that first night, but oh! how I would have loved to have seen him again. But, that wasn't to be.

"After a day or so, almost by habit, I went down to the sewing room to take up some stitching. But when I got there, Sarah and Sadie clearly didn't need me there. I had taught them too well I guess 'cause they had everything under control. Oh yes, we chatted a bit. Talked about the new fashions coming over from London. I may have even shown them a new fancy gingham pattern that I had learned in Charles Town. But, really it wasn't anything that they probably wouldn't have gotten soon enough anyway. So, that didn't amount to much.

"I went over to Mr. Gordon who had taught me how to read and do numbers. Of course he was interested in the progress I had made in the last six months and he complimented me mightily. He was especially impressed with my setting up a bank account, renting a place, negotiating contracts and all. But, it wasn't long before I knew that he had other tasks to attend. The boys, Master Glen and Thomas were growing up quickly now and their lessons took up Mr. Gordon's time to the fullest. So, again, Mr. Gordon was polite, but I could see that he needed to attend to his lessons.

"Finally, Susannah. She was so excited to see me that first night. We must have talked until dawn. I could sleep in that next morning, but she had to work. Her husband, poor Mr. Killibrew, was so tired that he could hardly attend his notes and accounts. But thereafter, their work took them away from me.

"It wasn't too many days later that I began to realize an important lesson in life and that is, it goes on. People come and go. We get swallowed up into the daily flow of work and are carried along by it. Let one of us drop out by the wayside, and the flow just closes up behind us.

154

"This lesson was confusing at first. Of course, I belonged there. Why shouldn't I? I had lived there for four, almost five years and never seemed to lack for things to do. Susannah and I had spent hours chatting and working out on the stoop of the sewing area in the sunshine. The boys would come and flirt and I would tease them. What was wrong I asked myself. Why do I feel like an outsider? I never really even felt that way during my earliest days there.

"Eventually I could see it. I was a guest there. Life had gone on. Concerns were different. Mine lay in Charles Town where I was planning a seamstress shop. I wasn't contributing anymore to the plantation. Other people were. I was a welcome guest, but still a guest none-the-less.

"Of course, the parties and celebrations tended to mute this feeling of loneliness. My, some things never change. How I loved seeing those gallant ladies and men in their dancing clothes. They were so romantic. Even today, I can see them as clearly as if it were yesterday. And the slaves' parties were so wild. If the Master's guests were stately and gallant, the slaves were raw and wild. Their rhythms of their drums could wake the dead. They would get me so excited that I couldn't sleep afterwards.

"But parties don't last all night and all day everyday. And the loneliness still awaited me at the dawn of each day. Eventually, I knew I had to go back to Charles Town. Clearly, I knew it would be impolite to return before Christmas itself. Besides that was the whole point of the visit and it was a celebration that was not to be missed. But as soon as possible thereafter, I asked the mistress for her leave to depart. I told her how much I appreciated being able to come back and enjoy the festivities, but now the time was right for me to start my business. She understood and was very gracious about it.

"When the day arrived to float back down the river, my departure from Susannah was sad. We both knew that my returns would be rare occasions. We both promised to write which was something that I faithfully did until her death. She was such a rare friend; there was nothing that I couldn't say to her. But, in point of fact, I only saw her twice more. Once I had to deliver some clothes to the Mistress and another time, she came into Charles Town on some business. That had only been the second time in her life that she had come to the city. Then I heard the news about her dying in childbirth. It was unimaginable! She had always been so healthy and seemed born to deliver babies. I couldn't go to the funeral of course. The time and distance from Charles Town to the plantation was such that she was already buried before I knew she had died.

"So, time always moves forward. It was a sad lesson to learn but one that has held me in good stead. Does this mean that I liked leaving Charles Town? Or losing

155

my business? My husband dying in a bloody war that never did make much sense? Of course not. I had a good life and was happy. But, the awful passions that swept people away into murder against family and friends created a huge hole in my life, our lives, that was only getting bigger. Therefore, it only made sense to seize the opportunity of going to the Bahamas where we could remain under the rule of the king, Mad George that he was."

Such were the words of my mother and the strength that led her through many perils of the future. But, let us now return to her life in Charles Town.

CHAPTER SEVENTEEN

So, Ma returned to a Charles Town that was changing rapidly. By the middle 1750's, its population was approaching 8,000 residents having grown by more than a quarter in the last twenty years. It was also the richest city in North America and possibly the world. Rice and indigo had made it a trading center of international importance. Perhaps it was not too much say that Charles Town had more millionaires than any city in Europe.

These millionaires were not bashful at flaunting their wealth. Their ladies had only the latest fashions. The gentlemen wore the finest silks and rode in the best carriages that Europe could produce. Carolina Gold was not a name given to rice in jest. The world's craving for it was insatiable.

In response, Ma started a business in stitchery that was sure to prosper provided she was astute about granting credit. As Bert had explained, these planters lived on credit and some of them lived more wisely than others. So, she had always had a fine line to hew as to whom she would grant credit or demand cash. Fortunately, she had listened carefully to the casual remarks made by the Master and the Mistress about their acquaintances.

Another part of her success lay in selecting a location for her business. Of course it had to serve as her living quarters as well as a place where ladies could come to select materials and receive fittings in discrete privacy. King Street provided that proper location.

Charles Town was really two cities. The east and west streets ran toward the wharves and provided easy access to the needs of the ships' captains and chandlers. Wagons wanted to go directly from the stores supporting these world traders. North and south on the other hand provided direct access to the fine mansions that lay along the ocean fronts beyond the ships' harbors. King Street lay in the exact middle of these avenues to the wealthy, and Ma quickly recognized the importance of this geographic fact. For example, her shop lay exactly ten minutes walking from the summer home of the Mistress.

Along these same streets lay many of the other trades. Blacksmiths, carpenters, brick masons and general storekeepers could also be found along these avenues. And it was among these people that Ma found a lot of support. For example, there was Jacob Schmidt who was a German printer and who printed a genteel announcement for Ma.

**Mistress Wyanne Farrell
Requests the Honor of
Your Custom for
Excellent Seamstress Work**

**Lately Serving at the House of the
Honorable John Drayton, Esq.**

These invitations were sent out to these Carolina Gold tycoons many of whom Ma had already come to know through the mistress. Among these names were the Manigaults, Rutledges, and the Pinckneys. Others of course, would come to know her by word of mouth comments amongst friends.

Still, there were other people Ma had to know. They weren't the rich and famous, but rather the humbler merchants and mechanics that populated the city. Tailors, a trade allied to Ma's stitchery, were very important as it was they who catered to the rich tycoons with their scarlet coats, silk shirts and gold buttons. If these tailors could satisfy their patrons, then their recommendations for Ma would assure her business. So, she was very careful to cultivate their attentions through informal meetings.

Ma also cultivated the merchants whose shops lined such streets as East Bay Street and Tradd street that conveniently fed into the ships' wharves. First, she needed to buy the latest styles of cloth from them and hear whispers of the latest styles in fashion. But, again, these people dealt with planters who would want skilled people sewing their ladies' finery. Nothing but the best would do for them, and Ma wanted her name counted in that list of the best.

Likewise, silversmiths and furniture makers such as James Askew and Thomas Elfe could provide indirect references to Ma. As she was going from shop to shop one day introducing herself, she glimpsed a face that seemed to register. It had been long time since she had seen it, but where was it? Ma loved the hustle and bustle of the city and developing her business, but friends were slower in coming. And a friend would be welcome if in fact, this face was a friend. Chasing to where his face was glimpsed, she found that he had disappeared in the crowd. Disappointed, she resumed her errands.

"Oh well," she muttered. "It probably was just someone I thought I knew." Laughing, she thought aloud, "wouldn't it have been embarrassing if I had tapped the shoulder of a stranger. What would I say then? Oh excuse me, but you look attractively like someone I thought I once knew. What would his reaction be then?"

But, still the face didn't leave her. She was sure she knew him. Now what was he wearing? Clearly, he was a mechanic of some kind. His rough clothes clearly indicated that fact. That meant that he would normally be located on a north-south street along with all of the other skilled tradesmen that made up the carpenter shops, silversmiths, carriage makers and so on. So, perhaps she might see him again in the future.

Otherwise, life was a daily blur of meeting with tradesmen and merchants, dealing with her growing clientele, and trying to develop some friendships. The latter was hardest. As a single woman, she always had to be very circumspect in her behavior. Charles Town may have been rich city populated by people of broad understanding about life, but it was still small enough to watch people closely and gossip about those who follow broad, crooked streets of life. Ma's business depended on the good will of these people and gossip was not something she could afford to have trailing her.

Finally, after weighing the pros and cons of voluntarily joining a local church, she decided that it was something she had to do. Of course, her parents had been Catholic since time immemorial and tales of what happened to those who lapsed into Protestantism were lurid and horrible. But, where was such a church? By law, they were simply not allowed. The colony's Church Act of 1706 had made the Church of England the official church of the land, and while some other churches did proper, Catholics were not amongst them. Further, in the back of her mind, Ma had a suspicion that God simply didn't care as long as people feared Him and obeyed His commandments. Proof of that was found by her having attended church with the Draytons where there was no thunder and lightning striking people to the ground. Furthermore, if she was to maintain the image in town that she needed, churchgoing had to be a regular activity. Finally, she wanted to meet people and church was where people were. So, it was off to church.

That settled, the question was which church. Of course, many of the prominent families went to the high Anglican one. Others also existed such as the Baptists and the Presbyterians. Ma visited them all, but finally settled on the Anglican. Its service was most similar to the one she learned as a child, and it did make sense to attend the same church as her prospective clientele. And it was there that she attended church for the next twenty years.

As life progressed and Ma lived from day to day, she never forgot the fleeting image that had floated by her face. Who was that man? He clearly didn't frequent the merchants she did. He wasn't a silversmith or furniture maker or similar artisan dealing with the rice planters. Church didn't attract him as she hadn't seen him at any service she attended. She even wrote to Susannah asked if she remembered someone who has about twenty-two or twenty-five, about five feet six or seven inches and weighing about ten stones. Unfortunately, she could not for the life of her remember any further details. Susannah in turn was stumped. She didn't know either. Nor could she remember the names of the boys who used to flirt with Ma. That probably wasn't surprising seeing as how her flirting days had passed ten years earlier and the boys coming by Ma were just faces in the breeze blowing by. Of one thing Susannah was positive; it wasn't William Jackson. He was still living with his Ma and siblings in a shiftless squalor that remained unchanged. Ma breathed a sigh of relief at that news.

But, finding friends was not the most important problem at hand. Her success was. Ma's reputation as a skilled, honest seamstress was growing quickly and she was finding herself given more work than she could handle. Orders were beginning to back up which led to a loss of business to other seamstresses. They may not have as skilled with a needle, but they could do the work. It became quickly apparent that help was needed.

Ma had a number of choices. The first and least costly would have been to find someone to hire. But, labor in this growing city was scarce. Anyone with talent would open her own shop rather than work for the wages that Ma could offer. The second was to buy a slave, but that was an expensive choice. Slave girls normally cost about £375 which was only the beginning of her new expenses. Slaves had to be fed, clothed and trained. That took time which equaled a lot of money that she didn't want to risk. This risk would also include the chance that the girl would run away. Nor, were slaves always interested in working hard. Not that they could be blamed when one considered their permanent lot in life: unmitigated labor for the gain of others. The third choice then was to repeat her own experience. Bring an indentured girl over from the old country.

And that was what Ma decided to do. So, following the path that she herself had trod, she wrote to her parish priest with hopes that he was still alive a letter outlining her requirements.

Dear Father Donovan,   September, the 15th of 1756

Time has come by so fast and brought the Lord's blessings to me in so many ways, that I can hardly express them to you. Since I left His Lordship's manor as a scrawny waif, America has given me a great family who has supported me through my indenturement and even afterwards. For example, they insisted I learn to read and write and it is I writing this letter. From there I learned my numbers enough to operate a business. Yes, that's true!

Through the kind generosity of an overseer and a man whom I truly thought I would marry, my indenturement was shortened by a year. My original intent was to complete my contract so that I could leave it with honor having fulfilled all terms. But, the Lord's Will had his way and he died of a snakebite that is unfortunately not uncommon here. Anyway, in his will he had purchased all terms of my contract with enough left over to make a new start here in Charleston. So, it is with the continued patronage of my mistress that I have started a seamstress business.

Even here, the Lord has blessed me. The skills that Mrs. Grable taught to me now support me so well. How my hands and eyes used to hurt under her tutelage; I thought it impossible ever to be able to satisfy her demands, so high that they were. But, how I wish she were with me today. This is not an idle wish, though I know by now, she must have received the Lord's blessings in Heaven, but truly I need a young girl who can help me with my seamstress duties.

So, would you please inquire about for someone who has skills with needles and wants a new opportunity here in America? Of course, she must also be of good character and there I leave the choice in your Godly hands. But, in return, I will pay for her passage and support her for seven years while continuing her training in sewing, reading and writing. I emphasize the latter because these gifts were given to me and I feel obliged to pass them on to this girl coming up behind me.

Please give my regards and God's speed to my family and perhaps they may be able to assist you in your search for this young girl. Oh yes, while I haven't seen Kevin in all these years, word has come to me that he is alive and apparently making his way. I only hope that he has seen fit to mend his ways and follow a more honorable path than that which he did while at the Draytons. Life was decidedly chilly there upon my arrival coming as I did upon his departure for stealing a sheep belong to the Master. In fact, his thievery was a great source of my determination to bring honor to the name of Farrell by adhering to the fullest terms of my indenturement contract. It is this same determination I believe that has led to my present success. People know that the name of Farrell means honest dealings. So, for this inspiration and success, I forgive the rascal and wish him only the blessings of the Lord.

With kindest regards, I remain His devoted servant,

Wyanne Farrell

Then, having acquired a habit of filing all records, Ma laboriously copied this request and sent this letter on its way.

But, this course of action also had problems. A year would most likely pass before a suitable girl could be found and greet her arrival here in America. Meanwhile, work still had to be done that she couldn't do along. This still meant seamstresses were needed now. Then, she remembered Sarah and Sadie, Why not hire them? After all, she had taught them and therefore knew the quality of their work at least for the simpler work of seaming and hemming. That would free her for the fancy work that her clients demanded. Of course, she'd have to ask the mistress for permission and they would have to do their work after hours during their free time. But, she didn't think this would present problems. Other slaves, such as Sam often did spare-time work for money, and these girls would be no different in their need for money.

The next morning, Ma went to visit the Mistress. While she wasn't nervous as such, still it was asking a lot to hire Drayton slaves for a venture that made nothing for them.

"Good morning, Wyanne. It's been a while since we seen one another. How has your new seamstress business going?"

"It's good well. In fact, thanks to your patronage, it's almost getting beyond me."

"Oh? How so?"

"I'm being swamped, frankly."

"That's a problem most people would love to have," chuckled Mrs. Drayton.

"Not that I'm complaining, mind you. But, the fact is my work is getting ahead of me and I'm losing customers who don't want to wait for their dresses. And, in fact, that's the reason I'm here."

"I hope you're not asking me to sew," teased Mrs. Drayton.

"Oh, no ma'am. But I do want to ask a huge favor and I'm not really sure how to go about it."

"Well, why don't you have it out?"

"My mouth is as dry as the night I met Mr. Smith, but here's the long and short of it. I want to hire out Sarah and Sadie to do basic work and let me be free to do the fancy stitching. Of course, I'd pay them, and I know they'd like the work. But

162

this doesn't have anything to do with you or the Master, and I'm at a loss how to deal with it."

"Well, I'll have to ask Mister Drayton and he'll probably consult with the overseer. But truthfully, when the slaves get work like this, it really means that it's easier for us. With this money, it allows them to buy things that we might otherwise be obliged to provide. Of course, they'd have to do this work on their free time…"

"Oh yes, ma'am. I wouldn't have thought anything else," responded Ma. "Have no fear of that."

"Then, for the moment, let's just go with that. How did you intend to get the clothing back and forth?"

"Actually, I thought Sam could take care of that problem. Of course, he'd probably want some money for his services."

"Oh yes, you can be sure of that," laughed the mistress. "Sally wants only the best for her family and Sam has to hustle. So, you be sure not to overpay him."

"Oh no, rest assured of that. I can't let costs run out of control if I want to quote good prices to my customers."
"Good, then I think we can proceed."

"Thank you again, ma'am, for all that you have brought to me."

"You've earned it all, young lady. Now, if you'll excuse me, I have to attend to some of the Judge's matters. I swear, that man is always in the clouds."

As sure as had been promised, Sam came around with Old Sal in a couple of weeks. And as was foreseen, he was very happy to take the clothing and generally transport them back and forth, but only at a price.

"What? A shilling a trip? Now, Sam, I expected to pay you for your services because I know you have a family to support. But, a shilling for loading your wagon's corner is more than I care to pay."

"Yes, 'm. Tha's true, I do have a family and growing as well. You know that Sally is expecting a baby again?"

"No, really? How many kids does that make for you now?"

"This be our third, Lord willing. Sally lost one a while back."

163

"Oh, I am sorry. Please give her my regards and best wishes for this one. Now, back to hauling. Let me put it to you this way. I have to meet competition from the other seamstresses in terms of price. So, when I pay you, that comes out of my profit in order to accept the extra orders. Now, of course, I want to be fair but you have to do better than a shilling."

"Well, I'll tell you what I do. Make it three quarters of a shilling," replied Sam.

"H'mmm. That's still steep. But, I'll tell you what I'll do. If you promised to have Sally wash them so that they're clean and soft and deliver them to me in that condition, then I'll do it. That way, my customers will actually be getting a better product than if I just return the dresses in the same shape as the cloth was given to me."

And so it went, but eventually Sam and Ma struck a deal thereby letting Ma actually charge a bit more to her customers because the work would be done faster and cleaner.

So, life sped on over the next year. Ma was able to attend to her customers' needs in a more satisfactory manner. Some of them went on to other shops but that was always to be expected. In return, some left their seamstresses for Ma. So, in general, things tended to work out for the best. Sam made a trip to her shop about every two weeks picking up and delivering the sewing done by Sarah and Sadie. Finally, a letter arrived from Ireland.

Dear Mistress Farrell,   February 7, 1757

It is with sad news that I inform you of the death of Father Donovan. He was called home suddenly by the Will and Grace of the Lord. At his mass, we took the liberty of including your prayers amongst those of his entire congregation. Of course, during the homily, we told everyone about the many things that you related to us in your letter. Your family, by the way, was most interested in them and of course, to know that both you and your brother, Kevin are safe in God's own hands.

Now, regarding your request for an indentured servant, I took it upon myself to act in Father Donovan's behalf and look for such a girl. In fact, I believe that a suitable person has been found. Her name is Sundru Smith, aged 13, and in good health. She comes from a family similar to yours in that there are many brothers working their family plot and she is in need of employment. I cannot judge to her sewing skills being only a man of the cloth, but I am told by others that she is knowledgeable. Whether adequately might be something you would have to decide

164

for yourself. However, as to her morals and character, your neighbors and friends unanimously assure me Mistress Smith meets the highest standards. Of that, then, I believe her virtues will fully overcome any deficiencies in skill.

Based on this recommendation, I have taken the liberty to arrange for her passage. Time moves so slowly over the oceans that a formal response from you would cause this transaction to drag on to an intolerable length. So, Mistress Smith will be taking passage on The Hind on June 24, next with an arrival time in Charleston around mid-September.

You will know her because of her age and by the fact that she has the blackest hair and pale complexion. Her height is about five feet, one or two inches and weighs about seven or eight stones. She expects to be wearing a blue woolen dress and carrying only a handbag of minimum essentials.

Please let us know of Mistress Smith's safe arrival as her family is sadly anxious about her departure and welcome in a strange new country.

Sincerely,

Father Jonathon Kerry

As Ma read this letter, memories flooded over her as she thought of her own journey into a new, unknown world. Mostly, she remembered how hungry she was. One night, she tried to take some bread that appeared to be left untouched. As she grabbed it, a sailor came from a dark corner and seized her wrist.

"And what do we have here, little Missy? Stealing food are ye? And you know what we do to thieves? " he asked with a bright leer. It was exactly the same gleam that William Jackson had. It was never to be forgotten, but then she knew better how to fend for herself. Wearing a stickpin in her clothing was not a trick her mother had taught her. Struggle as she might, with no one around, the result was foregone. The following days were a horror. No one cared as everyone was starving and hungry. A waif more or less only an extra mouth more or less to feed full as the bread was with weevils. Bleeding was only a further nuisance for others and they were quick to complain about the odor. It was a wonder that she learned to love Bert after that experience and the rough greeting he gave her that night.

"Well, I hope Sundru is smarter and tougher than I was," thought Ma grimly. "But, I'd better prepare anyway for the worst and be prepared to care for a skinny, scared and hungry girl. As God is my witness, she'll work hard, but she will be loved.

Wha? Here am I, all of twenty-two and thinking like a mother of a girl hardly younger than I am. What an old woman I've become.

"I also hope this girl knows how to cook. I'd forgotten how much time that takes when I lived at the plantation with the slaves doing that chore. I'd only to go to the kitchen whenever I was hungry and here, I've got keep the fire tended if I want something to eat. She'll also be doing the shopping for groceries as well each day. Food doesn't last long and trips to the market are the only way to keep food fresh. Winter times of course brings colder weather that stores food and keeps it fresh. But that only lasts for a couple of months. So, it'll be off to the market each day for you Missy.

"She'll also need a place to sleep, but it'll be no pallet thrown in a corner where the bedbugs bite. No, not at all. It'll be a proper bed roped up all nice and tight with proper ticking mattresses that are changed regularly. Of course, she'll also be changing her own ticking, but it will be clean and she won't be lousy. At least, not too lousy." With these thoughts, Ma indeed did find a corner where a bed could be placed without taking up too much room.

"Finally, whether she wants to or not, she'll be bathing once a week come cold weather or warm. Between times, she'll be washing regularly. I know lots of people advise against such practices as being bad for the health. But, a scrummy, foul-smelling maid does not lead people back to a store. So, it'll be clean-up time for her."

The months passed by and as the autumn weather began to take the edge off August's heat, Ma began to go to the wharves to learn of the arrival of the Hind. Each day, the answer was always the same: "Probably be in tomorrow. We'll be seeing her pennants flying in the dawn." And each day brought no pennants until finally toward the end of September, they could be seen coming up the Ashley river. The next morning's tide would be bringing in Sundru.

The next morning saw Ma down at the wharves. The same customs inspectors were there taking bribes as cargo was being off-loaded. Gentlemen's carriages were there awaiting the fancy furniture and household wares that were expected. The slave ships were off to one side reeking with their sad cargo. Here and there lines of these black wretches were being led to the slave block for auction. Stevedores were running about cursing loudly at anything and everyone in sight. And just as happened many years ago in the early dawning sunlight came a young girl. She was the spitting image of Ma herself: thin, dirty, ragged, and scared.

"I'll bet she's praying to God why He ever brought her here," thought Ma as she moved through the chaos of the harbor. "Excuse, me. Are you Mistress Sundru Smith? If so, you're home."

An obviously scared, skinny, dirty girl answered with relief, "Oh yes, and thank God. Ye must be Mistress Wyanne Farrell? If so, then I'll never have to board another ship in my life."

Laughing, Ma said, "Yes, that's right. You'll never board another ship again. I promise you that because to do so, I'd have to board one myself and that I'll never do. Come child, let's go home."

Of course, Sam and Old Sal weren't there or otherwise the scene would have been a repeat of her arrival. Instead, Ma had to answer questions as the two walked along past many of the same shops and homes that had impressed her during her first passage in the wagon. Now, of course, Ma hardly glanced at them, but Sundru's head was swiveling back and forth as she took everything in.

Ten minutes later, Ma and Sundru arrived at her shop. Taking her upstairs, Ma ordered her to get rid of her clothing. They were to be thrown away at once. Then with a towel wrapped around her thin body, Sundru was taken to the back porch were a deep tub awaited her.

"Here, take this soap and washcloth and don't come out of the tub until you're clean."

"Clean? Ye mean, wash up? In a bath? I've never had one in my life." Sundru looked upon the waiting as if it were a snake.

"Never had a bath? Never? Surely, you jest, my dear?"

"No ma'am. Ma would make us wash up on occasion such as a funeral or a baptism, but generally we was just left as we were."

"Then you don't feel dirty?"

"No, why? Should I?"

"Well, if you don't, you surely will as you stay with me. Rule One: you will wash up every day and take a bath once a week. Usually we take them on Saturday. My customers will not be offended by a dirty little Missy handing over their clean and expensive clothing."

167

"Yes, ma'am," said Sundru somewhat frightened. "But one question, how do ye take a bath?"

CHAPTER EIGHTEEN

Sundru actually was a pretty girl once she had a bath and a decent dress to wear over clean underwear. She still was a stripling however and had not yet had her first period. In many ways, she was just a girl rather than a young woman. As such, she quickly looked upon Wyanne as her mother.

Most of the time, Sundru was eager to do whatever was asked of her. Baths or just washing up were probably the exception to this rule since it was such a new custom for her. If she could, she'd try to skip her daily toilets, but Wyanne quickly learned of that habit and insisted each day.

"Young lady, I told you on the first day we met that you would be taking baths. I don't care if you eat or sleep, but you will take baths. Do you understand me?"

Grumbling and muttering, Sundru sulked.

"What did you say, Missy? I know you said something and I want to know what it was."

Grumbling and muttering, Sundru said, "Yes ma'am."

"That's better. Now let's have no more about this. And remember, I'll be checking behind your ears everyday and they'd better be clean."

"Yes, ma'am."

One thing that Sundru never missed was a chance to eat. Ship's food left an appetite that would be exceedingly slow to fill. Wyanne didn't begrudge any food as she remembered how clearly her hunger never left her. Sundru also never missed an opportunity to go to market as it offered yet another opportunity to eat while shopping. Usually, she was volunteering to go. Besides, it was exciting for her to be amid the noise and bustle of the shoppers and sellers.

Other duties had to be taught. Housekeeping was something that she more or less understood, but it was clear that the Smiths hadn't been a particularly tidy family. But, Sundru did it with cheer as Wyanne gave her direction each day. Cooking, on the other hand was something that she was actually pretty good at doing. If she wasn't too tidy, she did know how to make stews, and tarts and bread. That saved Wyanne a lot of time each day and allowed her to attend to her sewing and customers.

169

Sewing was of course the most important skill that Sundru needed and Father Kerry had actually found a girl who knew what to do with a needle and thread. She could take the material that Sarah and Sadie had basically stitched and do almost all but the fanciest of finish work. She was also very adept at learning new techniques. Production quickly improved to the pleasure of Wyanne's customers. Their orders were being quickly filled with the highest of quality. Consequently, word spread and business improved. Eventually, a bigger shop would be possible where even a couple of slave girls could be housed and taught to do sewing. Sundru would be able to manage them as she matured. But that would be for the future.

Again, to parallel her chats with Susannah, hours spent sewing lent themselves to long conversations. Occasionally, Wyanne would record them in letters to her dear friend.

My Dearest Susannah,   March 15, 1758

What a joy, but what a responsibility is Sundru. Hardly fourteen, she is more of a girl than a woman. Like little boys, she still doesn't like baths. But otherwise, she is very happy trying to please me. She is also clever in cooking and sewing. Her housekeeping isn't too bad, and she is improving as she learns what I want. Already, she is saving me so much time.

Still, the hours we spend sewing and chatting remind me so much of the hours we spent together. I still miss them and would like nothing better than to pour my heart out to you for your warm guidance. But, now I find that the shoe is on another foot: mine!

Sundru came from a family that was even poorer than ours. I never thought it possible to say that, but her Lord only provided half the acreage of our plot and they were expected to live off it. He was Scot having come over with Cromwell (Damn his eyes. I know that's a terrible thing to say, but Cromwell was never a friend of the Irish and these protestant Scots will never be a friend no matter now long they stay.) Her mother had ten children of whom only five lived and four of them were girls. What a burden to have four girls. The one son will be hard pressed to support his parents when they are too old to work, and with his having such a small plot of ground to offer, no girl would consider marrying him unless she was absolutely dirt poor.

Thus, as was true with me, Sundru really had no choice but to find a life elsewhere. And like me, America offered her an opportunity that she seems to be using.

Fortunately, her passage here was safe. She never got enough to eat, but whoever does on such ships? She also was dreadfully sick from rough seas that caused her to throw up the food that she did get. So, little food stuck to her bones, that's for sure. Being dirty all her life meant that she didn't feel unclean in the squalor of the hold where indentured passengers lived. How the Lord does provide! Stay dirty young lady so that you won't notice the stench of the ship's hold. Honestly, it took three baths over a number of days before she could really be considered clean enough to present to my customers. Finally, she was never bothered as I was if you know what I mean. To this day, I'm ashamed of what happened. It makes me feel dirtier than if I had never taken a bath my entire life. I know you've told me so many times that it wasn't my fault, but facts are facts. That ship experience made me feel dirty and I swore I'd never feel it again. William Jackson lost an eye before I would let him touch me. Bert (How I still miss him) knew me for a long time before I could let him even hug me in even the most brotherly fashion. Then, of course, later his hands were like velvet over my skin. Talking to you like this would be embarrassing if it weren't for your kindness and gentle ways. May you always be ever so for me.

Sundru has started attending school. It's a church affair where a volunteer comes to teach people to read. At first, she didn't like the thought of sitting quietly by to squint over letters and write on a slate. But, once she saw the complex patterns we use, I didn't get any more complaints out of her. Math will be the next thing for her to learn although I doubt she'll have too much trouble with it. She seems to understand measurements and how they relate to numbers. Of course, she had to learn how to read them first! Again, all of this reminds me of myself only so few short years ago. But, I was fortunate. The Draytons and you were such good models for me to copy. I know that I will eventually lose Sundru after she completes her indenturement and she will probably become my competitor. But, regardless of that thought, I know this is the right thing to do. People gave me a chance in life, and now I must give to this poor girl a similar chance. Hopefully she in turn will provide to others behind her.

Strangely, about a year ago, remember when I wrote about a face I thought I saw in the crowd that I knew. Well, I saw him again. This time, I really do believe I knew him from somewhere. If I could only remember where. Surely, it had to be one of the boys teasing me at the plantation, but I just don't remember him. If and when I do have a chance to speak with him, I'll identify this mystery man.

Your loving sister,

Wyanne

Sundru thrived on this regimen of direction and kindness. It was not long before she started gaining weight. Within months she started to let out her dresses and

171

began to take on the beginning curves of womanhood. Then, one day, she came crying.

"My goodness, girl, what's the matter to be crying like this?"

"Oh mum, I'm not sure. I must be sick or something, but why I can't say. I know I didn't hurt myself."

"Hurt yourself? How?"

"That's the mystery. I know I didn't hurt myself, but this morning there was blood on my bed. I had been feeling tired and achy…"

"A little bloated perhaps?"

Surprised, Sundru stopped crying and looked at Wyanne in amazement. "Why yes, how did you guess?"

Laughing gently, Wyanne took the young girl in her arms and just held her for a long minute. "Young lady, didn't your mother ever tell you or didn't you notice her being cranky every month?"

"Yes, of course, Ma was always snapping at us kids. But we didn't think nothing of it. We just figured that was her way. She was always tired from working and some days was worse than others. Mostly, we ignored her little snits and they went away."

"You never had older sisters did you? No, of course not, just an older brother and he wouldn't know."

"Know what mum?"

"Well, let's put it this way. Growing up means a girl has what we call a period that is a bit bloody, and her days just don't feel right. There's nothing to be done about it except try to keep clean."

Wyanne then explained how to use an old, clean cloth to absorb the menstruation and later to throw it into a bucket of cold water for soaking and washing. Knowing this, Sundru became much happier although she did complain about being bloated. Wyanne listened for a bit until her own irritation got the best of her.

"Missy, I don't need to hear any more complaints from you. My own self is not feeling well and if we're going to get through these days each month, we'd better do so in quiet. There's nothing to be done about it, so just set yourself to living with it. Do I make myself clear?"

"Yes, ma'am. I'm sorry."

Relenting, Wyanne hugged the young girl and told her to get on with things.

Several months later and about the third time that Sundru had to let out her dresses, Wyanne began to notice other things as well. The girl's breasts and hips were definitely swelling. It wouldn't be long before boys would start teasing her on the streets. She was so innocent that these approaches could be easily misunderstood. Wyanne decided that special care was needed until Sundru understood what was happening and what the boys meant. Of course, most of the boys were as innocent as Sundru was, but there would others with serious thoughts in mind and not all of them would be nice.

"Sundru, get some sewing and let's have a chat."

"Oh yes ma'am. I'd love to." Sundru was always happy to chat and listen to Wyanne.

The chitchat started as it usually did over some complicated piece of sewing, but then after Sundru understood what was needed, the talking went on to other subjects. Sundru would chat on about whatever was happening to her: school, her lessons, her teacher, shopping in the market, some funny story about a customer. Occasionally, they would talk about the war raging with the French.

"Oh yes, ma'am. That's right, I did hear about the young Schmidt boy. Too bad. He was just bound to run north and join a Colonel Washington's army up in Virginia. Why on ever for? Especially up in that strange country. So far way too. He just got himself killed for his pains. So wild, he was, and now he's dead."

These remarks were perfectly in keeping with hundreds of others that bantered between the two women. Then, innocently enough, Sundru started talking about some boys who had stopped her recently.

"Oh mum, a funny thing happened yesterday."

"Yes, other than Mrs. Smith popping her seams from the dress she took from us last month?"

"That was funny to see her come in as she did after gaining some weight as she did. But no, these boys came skipping behind me when I was coming home from school and started to jerk my hair. Not hard, mind you, but why my hair? Why now? Boys! Whatever do they ever think about that they need to pull my hair?"

"Only that?"

"Pretty much. I really think that they just want to be noticed and don't know how else to show it."

Wyanne didn't say anything and let the conversation pass on. Sundru was innocent, but she did understand that these pranks were basically harmless. But, after another thirty minutes passed, Sundru returned to these boys.

"Mum, why is it that one boy. I don't know his name, but he doesn't seem to be satisfied with pulling my hair or the other silly things they do."

Alert, but waiting, Wyanne didn't raise her voice as she replied, "Yes, what about him?"

"Well, he seems more interested in stopping me. He's actually a bit older than the others and somewhat of a leader of this whole passel."

"Stopping you? What do you mean?" Wyanne was really keyed up now. Charles Town was growing fast with lots of strangers pouring in whose background was totally unknown.

"It's hard to say exactly, and I've had no problems with him, but he does make me uneasy."

Now Wyanne dropped her pretenses and addressed Sundru directly. "I'm sorry to say this, but surely you know that there are bad people in the world?"

"Oh yes, ma'am. We've read about some of them from the Bible in school recently. You don't suppose he's one of them do you?"

"I don't know, but I want you to be careful. Be alert as well. If he continues to bother you, stay clear of him by walking in the street away from dark alleys. Also, if you can, try to learn his name. Is he an apprentice?"

"I expect so, mum. He looks like a blacksmith from the apron he's sometimes worn. You know, it has a slit up the middle."

"Yes, I should think so. So, he must be about 17 or so?"

"A bit older I would say. Dirty blond hair, about ten stones in weight, blue eyes, and strong arms such as you'd expect of a blacksmith."

"Do you know where he works?"

"No ma'am. But I'll try to find out if you wish." With these words, Sundru's eyes got wide and pensive. "I haven't done anything wrong have I?"

Grimly, Wyanne took both of her hands and, looking straight into the girl's eyes to say, "No, absolutely not. It's just that there are bad men outside who want to hurt young girls. Trust me, I know what I'm talking about, and I'll not let anyone hurt you. Just be careful and keep talking to me about anything strange that goes on out in the streets."

Promising faithfully to do so, Sundru reached out to Wyanne for a reassuring hug that was immediately given. From there, the conversation returned to its former light self.

Several weeks later, Sundru brought up the discussion again about this forward apprentice. She didn't seem to be worried about her encounter this time however. Actually, she was rather proud of herself.

"And why aren't you worried about him this time, Missy?"

"Well, the last time we talked about him, you wanted to know his name and perhaps where he works."

"And you found out?"

"Oh indeed. Remembering what you said, I stayed well in the clear, but since he wanted to talk then I figured I might as well let him."

"So…"

"His name is Barton James, but he told me I could call him Bart since I was a friend of his."

"I bet," snorted Wyanne.

"And from there, one thing led to another and he mentioned that he was apprenticed to a Mr. William Malone who is a master blacksmith working on Broad Street, near Bay Street. But, other than being somewhat stuck on himself, he really doesn't seem to be a bad sort of person."

"Well, we'll see about that. Meanwhile, while I'm happy you got this information, you must stay clear of him until I've had a chance to check him out."

Sundru seemed disappointed at this reaction but gave a firm "yes ma'am." Wyanne noted this disappointment and thought, "she's growing up isn't she? She doesn't understand what's happening to her, but she does like the attention the boys give her. Won't be long before she figures things out and it won't be long before I have to tell her the facts of life…although I really don't know much about them other than to know a lot of evil men exist out there and a girl can't be too careful."

From there, Wyanne's thoughts continued on. "William Malone. Strange I seem to remember that name. From the Draytons I expect. If he's the age I think he is, then I really do seem to recall a boy who came by to tease me on occasion. Not a bad fellow actually. Had all of his teeth and not just a nuisance when he came by. He did seem to listen a bit. Well, I'll find out tomorrow." Chuckling to herself, "Be just my luck that he's a hundred and ten years old."

That last thought brought Wyanne up with a bit of a start. Thinking over her last remark carefully, she knew that she had rounded a turn in her life. The thought of another man entering her life had now seeped into her head: "*Just my luck and he's too old to consider.*" Bert's death was now behind her. Not that Bert was behind her. The love she had for him would always be fresh. But, his death was past and Wyanne knew her life was moving on. This thought both saddened her and gladdened her. She was sad that in fact, Bert was no longer with her, but glad that the burden of grief had passed. She would have write about this to Susannah in her next letter. Susannah would probably talk about her passage from Tom to Mr. Killibrew. Wyanne wondered how her passage would go.

The next day saw Wyanne going to market early in the morning. But, before getting the daily supplies, she went by the blacksmith described by Sundru. There was to be no more waylaying of this girl on the street. For one, she was entirely too young and naïve. Secondly, a lot of money had gone into getting her over to America and training her. Even though Sundru was indentured, she effectively was an apprentice who was beginning to bring a return to Wyanne. No sir, teasing was one thing, but stopping her was entirely different and she intended to have it out with his master.

Arriving at the shop, she saw all of the familiar sights of such an enterprise. The outside looked almost like a paddock for the horses awaiting their new shoes. It had a hearth where coals were burned to a glowing red by a large billows pump operated by a small boy. Nearby by were various anvils mounted on what looked like sections of a once large log. By the anvils were buckets of water where hot metals were annealed into hard tools or shoes for horses. Rough tables lined the walls where

176

hammers, pliers, saws, and files were scattered. The air was filled with the noise of air whooshing through the billows, hammers banging iron and water boiling into steam. Men were grunting with the labors of their various tasks.

It appeared that the shop had about five or six men. Two were outside working with a horse. One was holding it or standing by to bring shoes to the senior man who was at that moment filing a hoof. Inside, another man was preparing a horseshoe while another was manufacturing some tools obviously designed for a carpenter. The other two were discussing some business and they were the men Wyanne wanted to see.

"Excuse me," going over to the men, "but are either of you Mr. William Malone?"

One turned to her and replied, "That I am, and who might you be please?"

It took just a moment for Wyanne to recognize this person as the phantom stranger she had seen on the streets these past months. Catching her breath, now she knew. Of course! This blacksmith was once the young boy who came by on occasion at the Drayton plantation. At the same time, a flicker of recognition crossed his eyes as well.

"Well, this is a surprise. I'm not sure you recognize me, but I'm Wyanne Farrell who was once an indentured seamstress with the Draytons. You used to come by on occasion to visit."

The flicker now became a broad smile as William now recalled these pleasant afternoons. Sticking out his hand to shake hers, he quickly retracted it when he remembered how black with grime it was. None-the-less, the grin remained fixed.

"My goodness, this is a surprise, and a pleasant one to boot. Could you excuse me though for just a second until I tend to problem this gentleman has? I'll be right with you."

"Of course," replied Wyanne. "I'll just stand off to one side." As she did so, she tried to identify the boy who had accosted Sundru. As her eyes accommodated the darkness of the interior, she saw that the person making a horseshoe must be the lad Sundru described. Weighing about ten stone and more or less blond, it was hard to tell with the black soot soiling his hair, he seemed to be about right for Mr. James. He seemed to work hard enough, but for his character, Mr. James had yet to prove himself as the nice boy that Sundru seemed to think he was.

Eventually, William came by wiping his hands so that he could shake a greeting properly with Wyanne.

"And what do I owe the honor of your visit?"

"Well," said Wyanne laughing, "several things. Actually, I had seen you several times on the street and while I couldn't place you, I did seem to remember you from somewhere as a friend I once knew. I've been here in Charleston for about two years and at first it was terribly lonely here not knowing anyone. So, your flashes by seemed to offer some hope of finding a friend. And here you are, not more than ten streets from my shop."

"Your shop? You were a seamstress, and now you have a shop? Very good. Where is it? I probably have passed it by any numbers of times."

"It's over on King Street and trod, right near the Manigault store. Right now, it's an upstairs flat, but I'm hoping to expand shortly. However, unless you knew it was there, which as a man, I doubt you would unless your wife sent you, you'd never see it."

"In that case, I'd never see it since I'm not yet married. Too busy making this shop a success. But I know you didn't come all this way just to see a dirty blacksmith who might just be a friend. What can I do for you?"

Knowing William as an old acquaintance made the second part of this visit a bit awkward. Sundru needed to protected and yet, Wyanne didn't want to lose the possibility of losing a possible friend. But, awkward or not, first things first and Sundru's safety was first.

"Yes, that's right. And this is a bit difficult, so could we go somewhere in private?"

Gesturing to a corner, William led Wyanne to a place somewhat quieter and away from his workers. Then, he waited for Wyanne to begin.

"As I mentioned, I do have a shop where I have an indentured girl working as a seamstress. She's a capable girl in whom I spent a fair amount of money paying for her way here and training. I don't want to lose her either. She's only fifteen and very innocent about boys."

"Boys?"

"Yes, and one in particular. Most boys tease her like you once did with me. But, I believe you have a Barton James…"

Seeing William nod, Wyanne continued, "Well, he was more aggressive than just pulling her hair or what have you. According to Sundru, my girl, he seemed anxious to corner her for more than just teasing. Of course I haven't seen anything myself and I only have Sundru's word on all this, but I'm convinced she's telling the truth, and I can't take chances with this girl. She's too valuable and too young for me to lose to an overeager stripling."

"And what would you want me to do?" asked William raising his eyebrows.

"Well, of course. Actually, when I was on my way here, I will really angry and wanted him to be sacked. But, now that I know who his master is, I want you to have a long talk with Mr. James and ensure he leaves Sundru alone. He probably doesn't mean to hurt her, but young stupidity can do just that thereby causing us both to lose valuable people."

"All right, I can do that. I agree. I don't need Bart, who's still an apprentice, getting a girl in trouble and causing me to find another. Like your Sundru, he is a clever lad and I'd have a hard time finding another who's half so good. I'll talk to him."

"Thank you. Your kindness is most appreciated. Now I know you're busy and I'll leave you alone. But, if you're ever of a mind to tease a young girl, I'd enjoy seeing you come by."

Grinning, "I may do just that ma'am. And thank you for bringing all of this to me."

Returning home, Wyanne immediately cornered Sundru to tell her what all happened at the Malone's blacksmith shop. While she listened eagerly about William having been Wyanne's mystery man and how they had known one another at the Draytons, she became a bit distant at the discussion of Barton staying away from her.

As she did so, Wyanne thought to herself, "H'mmm she really growing up and beginning to feel her oats. I'll have to talk to her about what men are like sooner than I had previously thought. That's going to be a real challenge. Being so innocent, she'll find it all hard to believe. But, it's something I've got to do. But, not today. Let's let it ride for a while." But then again, as Sundru sat there wondering, Wyanne thought twice about it, "Oh Susannah, now what do I do? This can't be delayed, but what do I say to this girl? I really don't know much more than she does, and yet…yet, I've got to protect her. So, what do I say?"

179

Screwing up her courage, Wyanne turned to Sundru and began to stammer. "Ummm, well, ah yes, well…"

"Yes, ma'am? Is there something you'd like to tell me? Have I done something bad? If I did, I'm truly sorry," flustered Sundru wide-eyed.

"Oh no, child. You've been an angel to me. And you know that I truly love you and want only the best for you."

"I do know that ma'am. Sometimes you get riled on occasion like when I try to skip a bath, but if there's one thing I know, it's that you love me. It's almost like you was my Ma, it is."

"Then just like you Ma, there's things between women we gotta talk about. But, I'm blessed if I really know how to start."

Relieved, Sundru sighed, "Oh good, I had thought I had done something to displease you and that makes me ache when I do. But, what is it that we need to talk about?"

Plunging ahead, Wyanne began to get her words together, "It's about men and how boys can tease you?"

"Like the Barton boy?"

"Exactly."

"Yes, ma'am?"

"Well, ummm, well, how do I begin? OK, here's the short of it. Do you know how babies are made?"

"They're the gift of God. That's what Ma always told me and I guess He loved us 'cause we certainly had a lot of 'em."

"Ahhh, yes. Right. But, otherwise, you don't really know."

"That's all I know."

This isn't getting any easier.

180

Ma then said, "Ummm, you lived in a small house. Did you ever hear your Ma and Pa making noises in the night? Did you ever see them together under the blankets?"

Laughing,, Sundru almost shouted, "Oh, you mean bundling? Of course, why didn't you say so Ma'am?"

Continuing, she went on to say, "Lots of times, and once I asked Ma about it, and she just smiled without saying anything. But, this is a fact, she was always happier the next morning, she was."

"Happier?"

"Oh yes, like a couple of love birds they were. My Ma and Pa were always teasing and playing on. They might get cross at us kids, but between themselves, it just seemed that they had their own secret language where they could share their own private jokes. And I know life was hard for them what with not having much land, too many kids, and a protestant Lord always demanding more of our crops. But, between them, they were never unhappy. Not with each other at least."

A flash of sadness crossed Wyanne's face as she thought of what might have been with Bert and Sundru picked up the expression immediately.

"Ma'am, did I say something wrong?"

Returning to the moment, Wyanne replied, "Oh no my dear. I was just thinking of someone long ago whom I loved very much. But, now back to what I was trying to say. Your parents truly loved each other and your Pa would never hurt your Ma. But unfortunately, not all men are like that. You talked about bundling, well, there are men who would bundle you in a very rough manner." Turning to Sundru again, she asked, "You do know the difference between men and women don't you?"

"You mean their PP's? Of course. I've always thought the men were the lucky ones. They get to pee just standing up wherever they was."

"Do you know what else it's used for?"

"If you mean bundling, I think so. Pa many times afterwards would have to go pee and he was straight as an arrow."

"Now your Ma clearly allowed him to do what he wanted to didn't she?"

181

"Yes, ma'am and if he didn't get laid off for a period of time, she'd tease him: 'getting too old are ye? I'll have to find a younger man' But, she didn't mean nothin' by it, of course. She'd have never left Pa."

Now Wyanne was surprised. Sundru wasn't as naïve as she appeared. Like all girls living in small shanties, she had a clear idea of what men and women did at night. Furthermore, her ideas were far different than the ones Wyanne had gotten from the sad resignation of her mother. So, of course, now Sundru's thoughts about the Barton boy would follow those same lines.

"Sundru, my dear, I'm happy that your Pa was so good to your Ma, but I can tell you that not all men are as gentle and nice. Some of them try to force themselves into women almost like they want to hurt them on purpose. And this is what I'm concerned about with you. Boys teasing you by pulling your hair is one thing. It bothers you and confuses you, but how would it seem if they were to try and enter you like you Pa did with your Ma, but instead of bringing smiles, it was hurtful like pulling hair is hurtful except a lot more so?"

Sundru thought long about this before replying. "I think I see what you mean, ma'am. Boys don't know no better, but a man doing what I think you mean is another thing. Like a stick going inside you and once I fell on a stick and it poked me bad, it did, and it was awful hurtful, it was. No, ma'am, I sees what you mean, and I'll be careful of them, I will. Stay away from dark streets and all."

"Sundru, my dear. This has been very hard for me to talk to you about all this. Actually, I'm not much older than you and in some ways don't know too awful much. But, you've got a lot of living to do before you think seriously about men. Right now you're an indentured apprentice with a chance for a good start in this new country. You're doing well at it too and I'm so proud of you for it. I just want your opportunities to grow as mine have done since I first came here as a scared skinny girl just like you were almost a year ago. Now, boys will continue to tease you and that's all right. They teased me too, and here and there, some will really interest you. But you've got time girl. You've got time. And if one really takes your attention, then I want you to tell me. Promise me that."

Somewhat confused by Wyanne's last outburst, Sundru stammered with very wide eyes, "Of course ma'am, whatever you say."

Wyanne caught the confusion in Sundru's voice and softened a bit, "I know all this is hard 'cause I've been your exact shoes not too many years ago. But, I truly love you and want a good man for you who will treat you kindly as your Pa did to your Ma. I also want you to be strong and able to care for yourself because I also know you can never tell about the future when you might be left alone. Do you understand me better now?"

Sundru wiped a small tear from her eye and smiled. Wyanne wasn't angry with her and really was concerned about her.

"Good, now give me a hug, and let's get on to work."

CHAPTER NINETEEN

"Hello Seth, may I speak to Mr. Manigault please? "

"Good morning, Ma. Of course, glad to have you here. It's been a long time. Coming to buy or sell?"

"Actually, neither. I just need to pick his brains is all."

"Good. Advice is always free here. Hopefully, it's better than the usual tar and rope that we sell here."

"Well, when it comes from a person like Mr. Manigault, then it's probably the most valuable thing I could get today."

"Right you are there. Anyway, let me check and see if he's free."

"Thank you. I'm most obliged to you."

After a couple of minutes, Seth returned saying that Mr. Manigault was free and happy to see Ma. With that introduction, Ma entered his office.

"And to what do I owe the pleasure of your company, Mistress Farrell?"

"Sir, unfortunately it's not profit for you, but only for me. I really need your advice. I know you're not in the business of trading much with England, but rather with the Indies and also that you don't deal in ladies finery, but none the less, you do know international business and that's what I need to learn."

"Of course I'll be glad to help anyway I can. So please, tell me what's on your mind?"

"As you know, I've been in business for about three years, and doing well, but I'm thinking I can expand my business. You see, occasionally my clients and others come in looking for fancy cloth for dresses. As you know, many plantations have their own seamstresses and they need cloth to supplement that which they order from England. So, I got to thinking, why not start a sideline of selling cloth, thread, needles, etc.? That's a whole lot easier than just sewing dresses and might make an extra profit. Besides, if I stock these goods, then more people might be attracted to my shop for new dresses which I could produce faster than others because I already have stock on hand. But, really I don't know how I would find someone who could get what I need. I certainly can't go to London each year for these shopping trips."

Mr. Manigault thought for a moment or two before replying. "As you have already said, I don't deal directly with England, but I do happen to know of a factor who could buy things in your behalf. He's fairly reliable, as honest as the best of them, and wouldn't charge you too much in service fees beyond the basic prices of the goods. His name is Mr. James Stockton and here's his address." Handing it over to Ma, he also asked, "By the way, do you have a line credit? He won't work for cash."

"Yes, I have a good line at the Farmers and Mechanics bank up to £250 and I know that's far more than I'll be needing to buy."

"Then you're in business. Good luck with your venture."

"Thank you so much, sir. This has been most kind of you to help me this way. And, oh yes, before I forget, I have your wife's dress completed."

Laughing, Mr. Manigault replied, "You come in here for free advice and then send me a bill for accepting it. Off with you now, young lady and I'll tell my wife. Also, that in the future, she'll be more able to spend money at your shop as you get your new stocks."

Ma returned home, gave directions to Sundru, inspected the goods sewn by Sarah and Sadie, and then proceeded to write a letter to Mr. Stockton listing the goods she required. Of course, six months would pass before they arrived, but this initial order would be followed by others that would generate a pipeline of material that would be flowing into her shop. As it did, she could eventually foresee needing a proper ground level store where people could come in and shop and attend their fittings in private chambers. But, that would be another day. She had to get her materials flowing in first.

To help stimulate that business, Ma began to think about having Sundru go out to the various plantations and offer to help the slaves learn how to sew. At first, when Sundru heard about this idea, she was dubious. After all, that would seem to take business away from the shop.

"Not necessarily. When I worked at the Draytons, they had wanted their own sewing staff. I was brought in to form it. And now Sadie and Sarah are working for me. But, their first duties are to the Mistress there, so really I don't have that business anyway. I figure the same will be true elsewhere, so why not teach them how to sew the basics using our material that we sell. Then, their work can be sent in to us for finishing. And instead of paying these people as we do Sarah and Sadie, they'll actually be working for us for free. So, really, I figure we can teach them for free and generate more business for us in exchange."

185

As anticipated, the first batch of material finally arrived in about six months allowing for three-month voyages from Charles Town to London and back. By this time, second and third orders had already been sent out and the pipeline of fancy silks was established. Much of this material was used directly for new dresses that were ordered from her stock on hand. The rest was sold quickly in individual orders.

Eventually, Ma decided that it was time for her to send Sundru out to the nearby plantations and teach sewing. Considering the time needed to travel even to the near-by families, she would be gone for about a month. But, it was good for business, and Sadie and Sarah would be the first people taught some fancier sewing that would result in more finished goods coming from them. Their skills had improved immensely during the years, and Ma was confident they would be up to these new tasks. So, after invitations were sent out, several families responded and Sundru was about to make her first journey.

Ma was a bit apprehensive about sending Sundru out alone, but after all, she had come alone all the way from Ireland hadn't she? Also, she seemed to be knowledgeable enough now about boys and people in general to understand how to stay out of trouble.

Still, when the day came for Sundru to leave on her trip, Ma clucked over her like an old hen asking if she had enough clothing, had she taken a bath, would she promise to bath at least once a week and wash every day, watch out for strangers. Through it all Sundru dutifully responded with "yes ma'am" to this and "no ma'am" to that. But, it was obvious that when Sam finally came by with Old Sal, she was more than ready to leave.

After their departure, Sundru said, "Sam, you know I love Mistress Wyanne like my own mother. But, she does fuss over me. After all, I'm almost sixteen now and had made a trip over the ocean when I was hardly fourteen. "

"Yes, 'm. She be that and I can remember when she was just a skinny, raggedy haired girl who threw up after we was hardly underway home." Chuckling, Sam continued, "Yes 'm, she be a fuss. But even then, I could see she was a girl who was knowin' her own mind.. So, you's smart to just let her fuss, and perhaps even try to learn from it."

My mother, on the other hand, was seized with a loneliness as she hadn't felt since she came here after Bert's death. She had become so used to Sundru's presence, the air just left when she departed in Sal's creaky wagon. But, to be truthful, Sundru needed to expand a bit. She needed to get out of Charles Town and see more of Carolina. Plantation life was far different from city life, and she needed to recognize the difference. Besides she was going directly to the Drayton's where Susannah could care for her. "I know Susannah will write about Sundru, so I won't be completely out of touch with her," she thought.

The days of that week began to pass. Fortunately, after their initial meeting, William was faithful in coming by for Sunday worship. Not that there was much time otherwise. Both of them were completely occupied with their businesses, and neither was interested in giving them up through marriage. Sundru in particular would have to be careful on that account. She was not at all interested in losing everything she had built up through a marriage that would transfer everything over to her husband. But, on Sundays, when things were quiet and when Sundru would normally have filled her apartment with noise, William helped to fill the void. For that, Ma was grateful.

Normally, they would meet at the church, attend service, and then go to a tavern operated by a friend of theirs. There, they could both have a hearty dinner and talk about what had happened during the week. From there they would often ride out along the riverside or into the country. Because William operated a smithy, he always had horses and a wagon that could be used for these excursions. Summer days in particular were often very hot and these rides along the cooler incoming ocean breezes were very comforting.

On this particular Sunday however, Ma was not in the mood for the company of the tavern. Sundru's absence had left such a hole in her life that she was feeling despondent. So, before going to church, she prepared a picnic. My goodness, already she had forgotten the effort of cooking since Sundru's assumption of that chore. But, today called for the effort. Ma wanted to go out in the countryside and enjoy the solitude there.

After church, William came out and met Ma to escort her to his wagon. Seeing the picnic hamper, he smiled and said, "Ah ho! And what do we have here young lady? Are you planning to take me off and seduce me?"

Blushing, Ma sallied, "I think not, sir, for it is a blushing virgin that I am and know not of such things."

"Well, we'll see about that then," helping Ma into the wagon. Then clucking his horse into action, he turned and asked, "Where would you really like to go then?"

"Oh just out into the country side or perhaps along the shore. Anywhere there's not a crowd. "

Noting the wistful tone in her voice, William asked, "What's the matter? Feeling a bit sad?"

"Yes. Really I am. Sundru's been gone for about a week. As you know, I sent her out to some of the plantations to teach sewing and drum up more business. But, oh my, I do miss her. Her voice, the little things she does that please me, they all add a spirit to my life. I truly do love her almost as my daughter and strange, we're not that far apart in age. But, love her I do, and I miss her terribly. I also worry about sending her anywhere near the frontier. With the Indians all excited by the French, they've made more than one raid into territories even as close as Columbia. I do wish this stupid war was over, or better yet, never started."

As Ma was talking, William headed the horse up King Street in a northerly direction. If they wished to pursue it, they could have reached Goose Creek, a town situated about ten miles from Charles Town. But, that would have meant a whole day's drive there and back and they only wanted an open space where their picnic could be enjoyed.

It wasn't long before the bustle of Charles Town lay behind the couple. The horse's clopping rhythm had dulled their conversation. The day was warm anyway, balmy was perhaps a better word for it, and their attention became diverted to the passing countryside. Eventually, William rolled up his sleeves and opened his collar.

"It's just too warm for stuffy church clothing," he murmured. "Please excuse me."

"Only if you excuse me as I want to do just the same thing. I'm beginning to sweat and I don't want to stain my clothing just for appearance's sake." With those words, Ma removed her shawl and loosened the top of her bodice. "Oh, that's so much better feeling the breeze around my neck. And now if you don't look, I'm going to remove some other underclothing as well."

Grinning, William replied, "I promise not to look…too much. For t'is such a temptation to view such loveliness as nature has given to you."

Turning her back to William with her legs extended into the bed of the wagon, she started to peel off her bloomers. As she did so, her words teased him further.

"Such an evil mind we have here. But, I don't fear it, for not even the Holy Ghost enters those regions."

Laughing, "But I'm not the Holy Ghost. My name is William Malone so I grant myself such pleasures as to view upon you."

"Slight view you'll be getting through my skirt and bodice unless your eyes are magic."

"In my mind's eye, clothing is of no consequence."

Finally, Ma turned around to face forward and thrust her face into the breeze. "Oh yes, that is so much better. Now, how far do you think of going, kind sir?"

"Not much further, perhaps a half hour, where's there's a nice spot. It's fresh with a nice view of a stream."

"Good, 'cause by that time I'll be hungry."

"You do have a healthy appetite. I've noticed that about you."

"It's better now than it used to be, but as I sailed across the ocean I thought I'd never have another meal. At the Drayton's kitchen, I tried to eat everything laid out on the tables. I couldn't of course, those places were food factories, but I made them work overtime. Of that I can assure you. I must have gained a stone that first year. Sundru almost ate me out of house and home as well. She never talked about it but I know she also starved as well coming over."

"It was really that bad?"

"Worse, the flour was maggoty and water barrels were full of green, slimy scum. We soon learned to knock our biscuits on the table to remove the awful crawly things from them. Occasionally, we'd get a lemon or lime to suck on for the prevention of scurvy, but some people still got loose teeth. Fortunately, my bones and teeth are very strong and they survived."

"Better than mine," grimaced William showing gaps in his molars. "Even now, some teeth are hurting. I'll be going to the surgeon soon to have them removed."

"Amazingly enough, the crew didn't eat much better than we did. Even the captain of the ship needed to get his water from the same barrels as we did. Of course, he could lace his with rum to kill the flavor and he could have all the limes he wanted for his grog."

Eventually, the wagon wound along the road until William found a lane rutting through the woods. Turning the horses, they plodded through the trees until they came by an open spot by Goose Creek. Here, one could see up and down the river as the sun danced over the water as it gurgled over the rocks. William pointed out a large half submerged rock and promised to return with a trout shortly for lunch.

"I know you've prepared a lovely picnic, but when was the last time you had a truly fresh fish? This won't take but a few minutes and meanwhile, if you'd prepare a fire we can grill it."

"Over what?"

"Wyanne, you underestimate me, for am I not a blacksmith?" Reaching under the seat, he found a low grill and pulled it out along with a bag containing a flint and steel. "Actually, I come out her often and find that keeping this grill is a handy way to enjoy a fine meal. So, off with you here and if you'll go over there, you'll find the remains of many old fires."

"Oh lovely!" squealed Ma. "This truly will be a fine picnic."

Jumping down, she went where William had indicated and started to gather fine twigs and powdery dry leaves. Building a cabin of twigs around a pile of leaves, she started to spark the fire. A few strokes saw the first wisps of smoke rising from the smallest of embers. Continuing to strike the flint, she started to blow gently on the embers until the first tongues of fire began to climb up through the roof of the cabin. Now, the fire was well started and Ma could feed it ever-larger twigs until some stout pieces were laid on. This fire would be built larger over the next several minutes until a roaring fire was snapping at the wood. At this point, Ma left the fire alone allowing it burn freely down to leave a bed of hot embers and smoke that would give the trout a smoky flavor. The grill could now be laid over the heat and become heated enough to sear the fish.

When these labors were done, William returned as promised with two fish. "Here we are, madam, just as promised. And yes, you have laid a lovely fire. Keep at your tasks in this manner and I shall have to marry you. Such a talented woman is not to be wasted."

"And you'll to do better than a couple of fish to attract this women into firelady duties. I'm good, but I'm expensive," teased Ma.

"Be that as it may, we do have fish, a fire, and a picnic complete with some ale in a sealed bucket. Now, let me have my way to clean and cook these fish."

"A cook no less? On a grill? Pray, what other talents do you have?"

"That you'll have to marry to learn," replied William with a grin as he cleaned the fish and laid them over the hot grill covered with wet leaves gathered by the stream. Afterwards, he laid more wet leaves so that the steaming water would mix with the smoke and heat to create a moist, delicate aroma.

"Then be prepared to wait. But, I must admit, these fish do smell delicious even now."

"Give me but a few more minutes. Meanwhile, why don't we break out the ale and enjoy a glass while we wait?"

"Excellent idea, kind sir." With that, Ma took out the bucket and some glasses and poured out a ration for each.

"Now, this is my idea of pleasure," sighed William as he leaned back against a nearby tree.

A few minutes passed as the wet leaves and the fish burbled up steam. Meanwhile, Ma spread a blanket and set out a bowl of potato salad, a loaf of bread, some knives and forks, a few tarts. Occasionally, she too drank some of the ale.

"It really is a lovely day. Thank you so much for coming out here. With Sundru being gone this last week, I had really been feeling pretty sad."

William asked, "You've lived alone a long time now, haven't you?"

Reflecting on this question, Ma looked up into the branches to see some cardinals fluttering around a nest. "Yes, I guess I have. Starting from the shock of Bert's death, and then recognizing that I can't go back to Drayton, I really had been alone for a long time. I guess that's why I kept looking for you. Charles Town is a harsh city. It's full of opportunity and certainly my parents could never have had the chances I've been given. None-the-less, strangers fill the streets jostling and rubbing each other in the most curt manner. A friend is what we all need and I had been truly missing Susannah and Bert."

"I never suffered the losses that you have, coming from Ireland, living in a new country, losing a future husband, but I agree about Charles Town."

Time passed as birds twittered above and flies buzzed around the picnic blanket. The stream continued to drone over the rocks with an occasional fish splashing in quiet eddies as they leapt for the bugs flitting around. Slowly the sweet aroma of trout began to spread out from the fire until it was wrapped about the heads of Ma and William. Draining a last dreg of beer, William sleepily rose and went over to the fire to check the progress of lunch. Ma just lazed in the warm sunlight letting her feet wiggle in barefooted delight on the picnic cloth.

"Whoa, lady. I do believe these fish are just about done."

191

"Ummm. Yes, they do smell that way. And kind sir, would you be good enough to wait on a poor working girl by offering a bit to eat? For I am sore afraid that I'm too sleepy and lazy to move."

"And what would you offer for such gentle service madam?" asked William.

"My eternal gratitude say I."

"Then so it shall be done." With that, William took the plates and gently slide a fish onto each one of them Then, running a knife along the back and belly of each fish and with a deftness surprising for one with such large, strong hands ran a knife along their rib cages to let the meat be flipped brightly onto the scaly skin.

Ma was impressed.

"Now that is what I call a gentle service. I haven't seen anything like that since I left the Draytons. Only the best of the house slaves could perform such a trick."

"That's who I learned it from. It took a while to master it, but as you practice, your movements become swifter and more confident. Kind of like shoeing a horse. The first time I tried that, my hands actually shook for fear that I would injure the horse. My master was certain that was my intention as well. But, then, your hands become confident as they learn to do things right. How does the fish taste?"

"M'mmm. Simply the best I've ever eaten. And how did you learn about steaming fish this way?"

"Again, from the slaves. Most of them supplement the food that their masters provide with food they catch or hunt in the woods and when you're away from the frying pan, you learn to use what nature provides."

"You must have learned a lot from them."

"Yes, being a poor apprentice let me mingle with them such as the masters' children never could. I spent a lot of time in the woods with them. You'd be amazed at what they know about living in the forests. Many of the them could navigate them like ships on the ocean. Occasionally, I'd meet with small colonies of blacks living in a rude freedom out on the outer edges of the forests. They'd be coming in to get some support from the plantation slaves and perhaps a bit of news about a loved one. They'd be known as maroons."

Ma said, "Maroons...maroons...maroons..., oh yes, I'd heard vague stories about them. Occasionally, I'd hear Sam and Sally talking in vague terms about them. But, wouldn't that be illegal, running away like that?"

William replied, "Of course, but runaways have to be found before they can be whipped and that's sometimes a difficult proposition. I know you've seen advertisements for runaways."

"Certainly, and on occasion, one would be found living in Charles Town as free as you could please. But, I never thought about living in the woods. Weren't their lives rather rude?"

"Yes, but not always. Sometimes, they'd have regular towns way off to the West. Not that I've ever seen one, but I have heard stories. I suppose slaves are like regular people sometimes. They'd rather live rudely in freedom than better in slavery. I know they'd talk about it on occasion with me."

Ma nodded and said, "I'd agree with that. Sam also made remarks to that effect with me as well."

With these words, Ma looked at the sun and noted how it had begun to drop over the tree tops. She said, "Unfortunately, I think we've got to be getting back. The sun's well along now and it'll be pretty dark by the time we get back."

"Why madam, didn't you know it was my dastardly intent to keep you here and ravish you so that no man would e're look at you upon your return thus leaving you only to my lustful desires?"

Laughing, Ma began to gather the picnic together into her basket. "That may be so, sir, but not today. Tomorrow I must pay accounts and unless you wish to assume them, ravishing me would force you to do so."

"Anything but that! So, now we're off."

With that, he gathered his horse and wagon and brought them near for the picnic to be stowed and Ma mounted onto the seat. Once everything was secured, he clucked the horse into motion for the return trip home.

As they exited the woods, the last of the day's sun baked onto Ma's face. She stretched, kicked off her shoes, wiggled her toes again, and leaned her head on William's shoulder. Within an instant, she was asleep. William in turn, chuckled to himself, turned his head toward Ma and gave her a kiss on the forehead.

193

"One day, madam, you'll be my wife," he murmured to himself.

The trip home lasted about an hour and as Ma predicted, the sun was well gone into deep twilight by the time they returned to the city. Nudging Ma gently, he whispered, "It's time dear lady to awaken. The town will be gossiping that I got you drunk if they see you sleeping on my shoulder."

"Oh my, I was asleep. Are we home already? I was out all this time?" rattled Ma as she put on her shoes and buttoned up her dress.

"Yes, that we are as soon as we round this corner."

With those words, the wagon creaked up to Ma's apartment. William alighted and came around to help Ma down.

"William, I have truly enjoyed this day. I was missing Sundru terribly, but now I feel that her hole has been filled. Although, I shall be glad to have her smile and tuneless humming back again. Please, though, let's do this many times again."

Climbing back into his wagon, William gathered up his reins and prepared to leave by turning to Ma and promise, "My dear, that we shall do. Many, many times, I promise."

"Then, we have a bargain to keep. Again, thank you."

CHAPTER TWENTY

My Dearest Susannah,   January 12, 1759

I really need your help now. Mr. William Malone has asked me to marry him, and I don't know what to do. So, as usual, I turn to you for guidance.

I know we have talked about marriage so many times, but it's always been from a distance for me. When Bert was alive, I was ready to marry and follow him wherever he may take me. Even the remote frontier of Carolina with its Indians wasn't too far. Even the work I knew was in store for me wasn't too much. I just knew I had no choice when I saw him coming home on a wagon all cut up from his dreadful duel. I loved him so much my insides just died at the sight of him. And when he lived, my fate was sealed.

But, now William has asked me and none of the same emotions thrill me as they did with Bert. You perhaps remember him, and I have spoken of him in letters. Of all the boys flirting with me, he was perhaps the nicest. He teased, but he wasn't clumsy as so many boys at that age can be. Since then, I have seen how he works and treats his men. He's firm but not a slave driver. When even an apprentice has a problem, he becomes concerned. With me, he can still be quite a tease.

I told you about the afternoon we spent having a picnic recently. We rode out to the nearby woods on a hot, sultry day. I just had to get rid of some under things, and I felt comfortable doing so in his presence. He turned his eyes of course, but still, it was not difficult. At most, we made a joke of it.

But, if you ask me, do I love him. No. Not in the way that Bert aroused me. Am I friends with him. Yes, that's certain. I feel a strong friendship toward him and truly enjoy his company.

So, Susannah, my dearest sister, is this enough? You have spoken about being married to Mr. Killibrew. Is this the same thing? Can I make a true life with him?

Your answer and guidance is urgently awaited.

Love,

Wyanne

Dearest Wyanne,   24 January 1759

How you think too much! You'll never change will you? You just look beyond any hill on the horizon wondering what mountains lie beyond. Not that you're afraid of climbing them. Nothings seems to daunt you. But, how you look ahead.

Of course I can't tell you what to do. Your Mr. Malone sounds fine, but frankly, I really don't remember him. If he were to bump into me, I wouldn't know him. So, from personal experience, I can't say whether he's a knight or a knave. So, you'll have to trust your instincts.

You have talked about the treatment he gives to his men. Your afternoons with him have been very proper. Of course, he should make fun with you. Marriage is hard enough without humor. Even Mr. Killebrew and I can laugh at each other and the children. And we do a lot of it.

Here are some other questions you might ask yourself. Does he attend church? Is he sober? Has he been known to attend taverns where loose women frequent? This latter question is most important as certainly he could be diseased. How does he relate to children? Finally, while he teases you, does he respect you?

Since you clearly don't love Mr. Malone as you did Bert, your head will decide this question. But, if you do choose to marry him, then work to become close to him. Your life with him should not be a business contract as that's too cold. But if you foresee such a marriage, then your answer should be "no." I made a decision to marry Mr. Killebrew and have never regretted it. He has been everything I could expect from a husband. I pray your Mr. Malone will be as fine should you decide to marry him.

Love,

Susannah

Dear Sister,   1 February 1759

Your letter arrived just today and I must take pen in hand to tell you of my decision. Yes, in fact, I have decided to marry Mr. Malone. The wedding will be in three weeks. I know you can't come; the distance is too far. But, oh how I would love to have you with me on this occasion.

Truly, your words are always so wise. I had thought many times about your early comments to me about marriage and decided that Mr. Malone, in fact, is the person I can live with. Your letter today just confirmed my own conclusions.

Now, you'll laugh, but I am not going to give up my business. I have worked too hard developing it, and I won't let some silly law tell me that I must turn it over to William. First, he doesn't understand a thing about selling buttons and bows any more than I know about shoeing a horse. So, why should we mix our businesses? Secondly, how do I know what he'll be like after we're married? No ma'am, I shan't take that chance.

To that end, I went to see the Judge and asked him what to do. When he heard what I wanted, his eyes got big and then as he understood how serious I was, he just laughed. "Wyanne," he said, "you'll never change will you?" "No sir," said I, "and if you would please help me, I'd be most appreciative."

So, he told about a part of the law that covers such matters. It's not used much, since most women just accept what marriage brings. But, have you ever heard of a prenuptial agreement? If you haven't don't be surprised as I hadn't either. But, essentially, we both sign a document that says what's mine is mine and what's yours is yours.

Now, you can well imagine how William felt about this when I presented it to him. But, ultimately, it was either sign the document or not get married. It was his choice. At first, he tried to counsel me that passing my property over to him was just for my own good. That women had no business in the daily affairs of business and law. In fact he tried to use the word "covertures" with me meaning that I needed the coverage of male protection from the evils of the world. My reply was very simple: I had protected myself well enough without his help as I crossed the ocean and founded a new life on my own. I didn't need his help now, thank you very much.

While grumbling, he ultimately signed it, but he asked me not to tell anyone. If anyone heard of what he had done, he was certain that his reputation in town would suffer greatly. So, yes, I did agree to that, and with the exception of you, I haven't told anyone.

Meanwhile, as the Judge listened to all of this, he could hardly keep from laughing. Finally, he told William that he might as well sign the document as no one has ever been able to change my mind when it's set in place. "Just sign it and get on with things."

Thank you again for being such a wonderful friend. The Lord blessed me indeed when he brought me to you.

With love,

Wyanne

My Dearest Wyanne,   February 12, 1759

My, you do make up your mind in your own fashion. Exactly as you had refused Bert's first offer of marriage: the law of contracts was foremost in mind. And now, with Mr. Malone, you're still demanding independence.

But, Wyanne, I love you so much. You're such a dear that I cannot imagine anything less than a wondrous life for you and your new husband. I know that your marriage hasn't taken place yet, but as you receive this letter, your name will change to Mrs. Malone. Learn to love it as you learn to love your man.

No, your love shouldn't be that for Bert. Mine for Mr. Killibrew is not for Tom, but as the Lord is my witness, I love my husband. If you have this same love for Mr. Malone, then I will truly be blessed.

Now go into your new life, my love.

Your happy sister,

Susannah

Dear Susannah,   February 24, 1759

Well, it's done. I'm a married woman, and to tell the truth, I'm not sure what to make of it. This is really hard to explain because I really understand what's happening. So, please be patient with me as I try to say what I mean.

William is a fine man. He has continued to be gentle and really funny. During the day, I look forward to being with him. Of course, since I still am operating my business, many hours of the day see us apart. But, during dinner and supper and our short evenings, the hours just slip by in a very pleasant haze. It's during the nighttime that I feel unsatisfied.

I recall with eagerness the emotions you described when you with Tom. I also recall the thrills I felt with Bert. I didn't really expect William to match those levels of emotion, but I do want more than what I'm getting. It's not that William is rough or hurtful, he just is so fast and then asleep! Snoring like a sawmill with me lying there wondering what happened.

To change the subject for a bit, since I have moved out of my shop, that leaves more room for business. Sundru has proven to be reliable and absolutely trustworthy except for occasionally wanting to skip her baths, and I can leave her alone to live at the shop now that I've moved into William's place. Actually, she is continuing to mature and seems to enjoy having some privacy.

I know that she will be leaving at the end of her indenturement and will most likely set up her own shop in direct competition to me. But, meanwhile, she's such a dear. I truly love her like a daughter. How I laugh at myself to say that seeing as how I am only a few years older than her. But, facts are facts.

So, dear Susannah, I can't really complain. My husband is a good man and he tries hard. My Sundru is a joy. Our businesses are doing well. The Lord has blessed us.

With love,

Wyanne

Dear Wyanne,   March 12, 1759

I well understand your disappointment. Mr. Killebrew is no comparison at all to my dear Tom. He usually is asleep before he even knows his head has hit his pillow. Actually, months can go by with no affection at night, and then when it does, I'm pregnant. So, perhaps it's a blessing for if we bundled more, I would have more kids than I would know what to do with.

Really, when I think about it, the less done about bundling the easier it is. Why people make such a fuss about it, I can't understand. Yes, with Tom, the ecstasy was there, and I know I enjoyed it. But, it was probably only because we didn't have children. Had there been babies, I'm sure the thrill would have long since passed.

So, Wyanne, don't fret yourself about anything. As long as William is gentle with you, let him have his way, and then relax for a good night's slumber.

Your sister,

Susannah

Dear Susannah,   April 1, 1759

Wonderful news. I'm expecting a baby. Whatever else William is, he can sire babies quickly. I must have conceived shortly after we were married. Perhaps that first night. Anyway, it's due in mid-December and I can hardly wait.

Have to run. Sundru is up to her neck in work and I need to help her.

Love,

Wyanne

"Well, good morning, Wyanne." With these words, Mrs. Drayton gave her a warm hug. "What's this I hear about your having a baby?"

"News doesn't let grass grow under its feet does it?," said Ma happily. "Yes, it's true. Amazing. I've hardly gotten used to the idea that in a few months now, I'll no longer be caring only for myself and William. Now that I no longer live in my shop, but over William's smithy, I really don't even have to care for Sundru. She's really a grown woman now and after her trips through the plantations, she's become wise to the ways of the world. So, it'll be a change."

After a few other pleasantries, Ma continued, "Now I know you're getting settled into your house for the summer. But I do have a question to ask of you, if you have a minute, ma'am."

"OK, be glad to help, but give me a second." Then, giving a few comments to a slave about unpacking details, the Mistress turned her attention fully to the young mother.

"And what might that be? From all I hear, you've become quite a business fixture in Charles Town...far beyond my poor skills."

"I wouldn't go so far as that ma'am. I've seen you manage the estates and they're far larger than my simple shop. But thank you for the compliment. I couldn't have done any of it without your patronage."

"So, I expect then that it isn't business then," Mrs. Drayton asked with a sly, knowing smile.

"That it isn't ma'am. You see, I'm really looking for a good mid-wife. I've done many things in my life and a lot of them alone. But, this is different, and I need advice. There's a new life growing in me, and I want him to get the best start in life that I can provide. To do this will require help that no man I know of can provide. William, well, he's proud as any man can be, and he means well, but I know he'll be totally useless if he takes after my Pa. Mind you, once the babe is on his way, he'll be a good father...gentle and caring. But what man knows a tittle about babies?"

"Well said," agreed the Mistress. "H'mmm. It's been a while since I needed a mid-wife, and most of them are now too old. But I'll look around and when I find someone reliable, I'll let you know."

"Oh thank you, ma'am. That's most kind of you. Now, changing subjects, the ships have come in with the latest fashions. The least I could do is make a dress for your summer comfort. May I leave some drawings?"

"Why, bless your heart, child. Of course. Nothing would make me more pleasure than seeing what will be worn this summer."

"Hopefully, wearing something new will bring you even more pleasure. Now, by your leave, I'll leave you to your devil's labors." With these words, Ma started toward the door as the Mistress turned again to directing her servants.

Despite her happiness at having the baby and knowing that the Mistress will be helping her find a suitable mid-wife, Ma occasionally came down with unexpected bouts of sadness. Such hit her now unexpectedly as she walked along. After having lived by herself for so many years, she still wasn't accustomed to accommodating others. Of course, when she was at the plantation, she had to blend in with the larger family of the Master and his slaves, but still, at night, after the work was done, she was alone. When she came to Charles Town after Bert's death, she felt as abandoned as a cork on the ocean. But, with work of getting her business started, even that pain departed. When William was courting her, Bert's void was partially filled, but again at the end of a day, she was still alone.

But, now her solitude was gone and so quickly. William was beside her in the darkness of every night, and he snored. My God, how that man snored. It seemed every minute Ma was punching him to roll over unto his side where he could breathe quietly. William never objected, but he didn't stop snoring either. Probably, the closeness could eventually become normal, but time wasn't allowing for that to happen easily. This intruding baby was a reality. For several weeks, nausea greeted her with the sun. Many were the times when she had to dash for the thunder mug and throw up. Of course, the odor of the mug didn't add to her comfort.

Why do men stink so when they relieve themselves? Snoring and stinking! Is that the fate of wives?

With these thoughts, Ma pulled herself up short with a guilty start.

"Now wait a minute, young lady. No one put a pistol to your head when you accepted William's offer of marriage. He is after all, a good man, and Lord knows, I saw the difference coming across the seas. You also knew what would happen when you did get married. Your mother was living proof of that with all of her babies. Besides, you know you wanted kids or otherwise you wouldn't have gotten married. So, let's just get on with things."

202

Not that she really felt better with these cross words to herself, she trudged on toward her shop. For some reason, the trip from the Mistress's house to her shop seemed more like a journey than the stroll she used to enjoy. Likewise, going to the Fish Market now just gagged her.

Thank you God for Sundru. She enjoys being there. Impossible to imagine that once I too enjoyed wandering up and down those smelly aisles. No more thank you.

With these and other thoughts, Ma arrived in time to see Sundru opening shutters and preparing for the day's business.

"Well, it is that time, isn't it Child?"

"Yes, ma'am. It is that. I tended the books last night and have the accounts ready for your review. Today's sewing needs sending to the river docks for Sam to pick up. He should be coming back with the Oskarmeyer order. We ought to charge Mr. Oskarmeyer double for all the cloth and thread that order needed. His wife is probably the fattest lady in town."

Chuckling, Ma said, "She is that. She is that. I know now how the old expression, 'The whole nine yards' came into being. It had to be for her. But, I guess we can't complain as she is a good customer."

"Indeed, ma'am, but Sarah and Sadie just groan when another dress comes to them from her."

Ma said, "Let 'em groan. They're earning more money from us than they'll ever get from the Master. But, thank you for attending to these things. I just haven't felt up to it lately."

"Yes ma'am."

With this exchange, the day's work lay before them. Roughly basted dresses had to be fitted for final sewing. Threads, ribbons, and cloth were to be sold. Offering free lessons at the plantations proved to be a good stimulus for business. The mistresses now knew to come to Wyanne Malone's shop for goods whenever they wanted new clothes to wear.

In fact, business was going very well. So much so that Ma had begun weighing the idea of buying a good woman. Sarah and Sadie did good work, but the time needed to send clothes back and forth to them was slow. Clearly, sewing jobs tended to linger as they had more direct duties for Susannah and the Mistress to attend. Her business was strictly spare-time work for them. However, if a person or two were to devote their time for her instead of others, production could go up and she could supervise their work more closely.

Finally, Sundru would most likely be leaving upon termination of her indenturement. She had about five years left on her seven-year contract, so there was no hurry with this decision, but there was no reason her to stay after her time was finished. So, buying and training a slave would ensure a lifetime of trained help for the business. But, Ma knew she alone wouldn't have time to teach a slave while caring for her business and family. That meant she needed to be trained before Sundru's departure. Also, it meant Sundru would have to take on that additional duty. Not that Ma worried about giving the girl the task.

After all, if she does start her own business, then she'll need to know how to teach the sewing craft to her own girls.

No, all in all, the shop was making plenty of money and Charles Town continued to prosper each day on the backs of slaves growing Carolina Gold rice. So, it seemed to be a wise investment. The question then, was whether to buy a second generation Creole who knew the ways of white people or buy one off the boats. The first was more expensive because of the girl's experience. Also, her background would probably be known better. All of these factors were well understood by local plantation owners who regularly sold off slaves like a crop to be harvested. She remembered what Thomas Jefferson had said about the profitability of growing slaves. Of course, a sulky girl wouldn't do, and Ma had to be careful of sellers who were ridding themselves of poor labor. On the other hand, a girl off the boat is cheaper only because she is raw. That's the only word to apply to them: raw meat. Many of them didn't have much of that either. Another factor also had to be considered. New arrivals often died quickly because of their poor treatment across the ocean, and no money-back guarantees were provided against unexpected death.

"My God, those slavers are inhuman people," thought Ma. "I need to buy a slave and she'll be my property, but must they be beaten so? I wouldn't treat a horse that way."

With these thoughts, her decision was made. A slave would be a good investment and was a project to be undertaken. However, from having lived around the Draytons and seen other families buy slaves, Ma knew that care had to be taken before her decision could be enacted.

Through the next several weeks, Ma spent time reading circulars advertising slaves. Generally, slave ships brought up to 400 humans into the Charles Town port two or three times each month. As they did, she started going to the markets and listening to the bidding while at the same time hearing conversations about what made for good stock. She watched men poke and prod, check teeth, and look for scars that indicated beatings.

There were careful decisions being made here. A prime field hand would cost up to £500 and a domestic servant would bring as much as a £1,000. A seamstress would be less at £750, but she could still be an good investment because it involved a lifetime relationship. Of course, there would be follow-on living costs. Field hands who were hired out for a season could bring up to £100 including rations and clothing. In summary, slavery was not free labor. Cheap, yes, and profitable, yes. But, free, no.

Ma also started to read newspapers advertising slaves for sale. Quite often, however, the notices were concerned with runaways. Most of them involved the same wording:

Reward Offered

For information leading to return of
Jackson

A likely man of chocolate color and above average height
who often is seen around the Charles Town ports
where he can find work as a waterman.
A scar exists on his face and stripes along his back.

If found, contact
Thurston James
through this newspaper

This was another concern to be considered. How could she be sure that her expensive investment would not run away like this Jackson fellow? Being a lone female would make a slave more dependent on her, but with a man, possibilities existed for escape. Also, Ma was well aware that her future slave would have a lot of freedom to move around town in the course of her duties. This movement provided ample opportunity for meeting a man.

Preventing this desire to escape caused many slaveholders to use various means of deterrence. Some were horribly cruel to create a sense of fear while others were most benevolent. One owner refused to whip his slaves at all. Rather the fear of being sold down river replaced beatings and paradoxically, it apparently was effective But, the desire of liberty for slaves made success was mixed in both cases.

"Well, this is another problem I'll have to deal with. But, let's take care of that later when the time comes."

Several weeks passed when a slave came to Ma's shop saying that the Mistress wanted to see her whenever it was convenient.

Thanking the slave, Ma turned to Sundru with instructions about the morning's work. while thinking, "I hope the Mistress has been able to find a mid-wife for me. My tummy is already beginning to swell and I'm anxious to get started with a good tending lady."

"I hope so, ma'am," replied Sundru. "I'll see you when you get back."

Following the slave, Ma arrived at the Drayton house hoping that in fact the Mistress was in, and not off on an errand. As luck would have it, the Mistress was just leaving the house when she saw Ma.

"Oh, good. You did make it. Come on in please? I haven't much time as I'm off to a tea, but I do have good news. I've found someone whom I believe will be good."

"Ma'am, that's wonderful news. I'm so grateful. Who might this lady be?"

"She's a slave of the Manigaults who has been with the family for many years. Somewhere along the way, she learned the art of midwifery and wet-nursing. She's delivered a lot of babies and nursed even more. Mrs. Manigault tells me that she's really good, and since her services won't be needed at the plantation, she can come into Charles Town for several months until your baby is delivered. You're how far along now?"

"I figure I'm about two and a half or three months pregnant."

Oooh? ,That means, h'mmm, you're due in December sometime?"

"As near as I can reckon, yes, ma'am."

"Well, that cuts it a bit close to the Christmas season, but if no one's pregnant elsewhere, then I doubt Mrs. Manigault will object to her staying over." That means along in September the mid-wife can come into Charles Town to start seeing you.

"And who is 'her, ma'am?" asked Ma.

Laughing, the Mistress said, "That's a good question. I haven't the slightest idea. Well, you'll find out soon enough. Meanwhile, don't worry about anything. Right now, you're healthy as a horse and you have Sundru, that's her name isn't it? She can and should be doing all your lifting for you."

"Fortunately, needles are not very heavy," replied Ma.

"Ummm, yes. Quite so. None-the-less, don't overdo things and you'll be fine."

"Well, again, Mrs. Drayton, I do want to thank you, and your dress will be finished shortly. I've taken some liberties with your original design and hope you'll enjoy them. I'll not say what they are 'cause I hope they'll be a pleasant surprise."

"Oh good. I love surprises. Wyanne, you are a dear. But, now I must run. My tea awaits me."

By the time Ma had returned to her shop, William was waiting for her. Normally, men ate lunch above their places of business, but since Sundru had doing the cooking before his marriage, it seemed natural for an extra plate to be set for him. Besides, if the truth were known, Ma did not particularly like cooking nor was she ever good at it. Evening meals were generally simple suppers of cold leftovers, bread and ale. William would joke that even Ma couldn't make more of a hash of leftovers than they already were.

"I've got good news," announced Ma.

"Oh? And what might that be?" replied William while munching on a hard crust of bread.

"Mistress Drayton has found a mid-wife. She's a slave of the Manigaults who's been doing this for years. Mistress Drayton assures me she'll be good although she doesn't know the name."

Sundru squealed in delight while William smiled quietly. While he knew that their marriage would never be a passionate affair, he loved Ma deeply and wanted only the best for her. Also, the prospect of being a father was thrilling to him. Again, his baby son would have to get the best care available, and if Mistress Drayton swore by this unknown mid-wife, then he was pleased.

Sundru wanted to know all about the mid-wife, but really Ma didn't have much more to say since really she didn't know anything more. Eventually, this topic of conversation broke down into silence as the three ate their meal.

Finally Ma broke the silence to raise an issue that had been discussed briefly without conclusion. She said, "I've made up my mind. After looking around for a number of weeks, I've decided to buy a slave as a seamstress."

Almost as one, William and Sundru grunted in surprise. "What?" "What!" "What brought this on? Since when?"

"Well, for a number of weeks now. Times are good, and my business is expanding so she'll be able to pay her way in a bit after some training."

"Ma'am, is there something I've done wrong?" asked Sundru fearfully.

"Why no, child, you've been a blessing to me and I love you so much for it. But, one day your indenturement will end and you'll be wanting to follow your own path. So, while I still have you here, now is a good time to train a slave and prepare her for sewing. That'll be your job, by the way, to teach her. You need to learn how to do that anyway, and no time like the present to start."

"Oh thank you, ma'am. I'm happy to be doing anything for you, and I can't stand the thought of leaving you."

"That day'll come, mark my words. Meanwhile, you're to stay here through your indenturement and as long as you want thereafter. Just as though you were family."

William listened through this exchange, and then laying down his fork, asked, "How much will she cost and do we have the money?"

"That's a good question, and I can't answer either question right now. But, here's what I do know." With these words, Ma related the information she had gotten about different qualities of slaves, prices, and so on. She concluded by saying that she will not be making a decision until she fully understood what it all involved. "I am convinced though, that this will be a good investment if we take our time and care."

"Well, I can't say I'm really pleased by all of this. Buying a slave is a risky proposition whereas hiring someone allows me to pay them for what they're worth. If they're no good, then I fire them and find someone new. A slave is a long-term commitment that's hard to quit if they prove to be no good. But, Missy Wyanne, I know you well enough to know that if you've got your heart set on something, then you're going to do it. Once having said all of this, then before you buy someone, let me know 'cause I've had to do dealings with people in times past and perhaps I can shed light on things that could otherwise prove to be bad."

"OK. That's fair. So, let's enjoy the rest of this meal."

The weeks continued. Ma pursued her search for a good slave and checked her finances. Cash money was always short, but the Manigaults were always available and her credit was good. Whether she could afford the interest that borrowing would demand was another issue. Consequently, she continued to review her books and prospects for continued business that would pay off a loan.

Ma's tummy continued to swell when an event occurred that Ma would never forget. Her baby moved. It felt like a stitch, or perhaps a twitch. Whatever…but then it was gone. It was gone almost before it started or before it was noticed. But, Ma was positive and for the first time, she absolutely knew that she was carrying a new life. Hardly five months along and already it was making its presence known.

Turning, she pushed William on his side of the bed. "Wake up!"

"I'll roll over. No problem. Sorry about snoring," mumbled William as he did many times before.

"No, you silly. The baby moved. I'm positive, it moved."

Still groggy, William replied, "OK, you moved and I'll move, but let's go back to sleep."

Shoving him again, Ma insisted on more attention. "Did you hear what I said?"

"Yep, move. That's what I'm trying to do but I'm about to fall out of bed."

"Then do so at once if it'll awaken you. But wake up. The baby moved!"

Finally, William reacted. "Moved? Why didn't you tell me? This is wonderful. Where did you feel it?"

Ma gently laid his work-hardened hand on her tummy. "Here. But there's nothing to feel now. It was gone almost before it started. But, I did feel it."

At this point, William was wide awake, and sleep was forgotten. The two talked then through the night as they dreamed of things to come for them and this new stranger coming into their lives. All things became possible to them as they spun their hopes for a future that could now be seen into the far years.

With this movement, Ma's energy now returned. This life was magic. It gave her direction and joy even when her back hurt. Her depressions disappeared. Even Sundru noticed a change in Ma's mood as she began to whistle and sing off-key in a distracted way.

This first movement now was followed regularly by others. Some were real kicks that actually hurt. Others were almost tickles that made Ma giggle at odd moments. Sometimes, the baby seemed to be doing somersaults. At each time, Ma said a short, unconscious prayer of thanks for this precious gift of life.

During the last week of August, when Charles Town is gasping for any breath of sea air that can be had, the Mistress called Ma to visit. When she arrived, there was Mrs. Manigault beside Mrs. Drayton. In back was a large black woman who weighed about fifteen stones. She wasn't fat, but rather big. Just big.

"Wyanne, come in please. You know Mrs. Manigault I'm sure."

"Yes ma'am. Good afternoon. You liked the dress I sent to you?"

"What a delight and your liberties were perfect. Mrs. Manigault here has kindly agreed to let Abby attend you now."

"Yes, we checked our plantation slaves, and no one is needing Abby's services anytime soon. So, the sooner she starts attending you, the better. Of course, you'll have to put her up and pay for her room and board."

"Not to worry. There's plenty of room over my shop where she'll be safe and dry. But, is there anything else that I can use her for? Or perhaps another way to put it is, will my having Abby trouble your household, ma'am?"

"No, I don't believe so. If such were to occur, I'd let you know," replied Mrs. Manigault.

"Well then, this is most kind of you. I'm deeply in your honor and debt."

"Just take care of Abby and make good dresses for me, and I'll be satisfied."

With this exchange, Ma and Abby left feeling somewhat awkward in each other's company.

Ma said to her new mid-wife, "You'll have to forgive me, Abby, but I've never had a baby before, so if I appear a bit uneasy, it's just that I really don't know what's to come of things. Of course, my mother had babies, and lots of them, but I guess from a little girl's perspective, that just seemed normal."

Abby let them walk on for a bit longer before replying as though thinking over what she in turn ought to say. On impulse, Abby took Ma's hands into her own. Despite their size they were the softest and most gentle hands that could be imagined. Ma would often remark on them in the years to come.

"Well, this here's unusual for me too. Before, I was always around friends and family where I knew everyone. Now, I'm being sent off with a strange woman and her strange house to stay for a fairly long period of time. But, I guess we'll get along fine."

Ma replied, "Hopefully, we'll do better than that. I remember when I left Ireland, and watching its hills recede in the distance, I felt very lonely and a bit scared."

Abby said in turn, "My mother said she was terrified when she was brought to America. In my case, I've always been with the Manigaults so this is a bit scary."

Looking at the size of Abby, Ma had to laugh to herself. *A woman this size could easily scare a lot of men.* But, to reassure her, Ma continued on to tell Abby where she would be living and what sort of chores she'd be doing while not attending the baby.

In fact, when the two women arrived at Ma's shop and Abby could see for herself what lay in store for her, she was much more relaxed. As Abby relaxed, so did Ma as she introduced Sundru. Sundru, in turn, just reached out and gave Abby a big hug and bade her to come in for some tea.

"Come in Abby. I've been waiting for you. Mrs. Malone, I know you're tired and in need of a nap. Let me take care of things from here."

"Thank you Sundru. In fact, an hour's nap would feel good. The baby's kicking from our walk."

Sundru and Abby went over to the pantry table by the fireplace where a pot of water was boiling. Sundru then brought out some tea and put it in a steeper for brewing. Abby watched attentively. In a moment the tea was ready for drinking.

Sundru continued talking, "I imagine that you're curious as to what sort of woman Mistress Malone is. Well, she's just married. In fact, it still sounds awkward to use her new name after knowing her for so long as a single woman."

211

"Yes, 'm. I is curious."

"My experience is that she'll leave you alone if you're quick about your business. One thing, ye're to wash every day and take a bath once a week at least. If ye've been doin' heavy work, then she'll be expecting ye to wash more often." Laughing, "I learned that the hard way. In fact, I had never heard of such a thing when I grew up in the old country. But, we are constantly meeting with the public and she wants us to present ourselves properly to the ladies as they come in. So, since you're here, ye'll have to present the same appearance."

"Yes, 'm"

"Now, let's see. Do ye have any other clothes?"

"No, mum."

"Well, that'll never do. Can you sew?"

Abby replied, "Not much, I've always been a field hand when I wasn't tending babies."

"Um, hum, we'll be changing that. Ye'll be needing more clothes then. We'll have to make a couple of dresses for you so ye'll always have a fresh change. But, that won't be hard to take care of. Come here and let me measure ye."

Abby's eyes got wide with these words. A white woman actually attending her. That had never happened in her entire life.

As Sundru started to measure Abby, she continued by saying how Ma had pushed her to learn reading and writing. "I've even started writing letters home now and can reckon all of the accounts. Mrs. Malone is very good about my improving myself. No, really, that's not right. She insists on it. Now, I'm not certain what she'll be having ye do, but she's not afraid of letting ye improve yourself. That I can tell ye."

Abby stood like a statue at hearing these words.

"How old are you? Are you married yet?

"I reckon I be about thirty. I had a husband, but he got sold several years ago. I ain't seen him in since. The same be true wi' my children." With these words, Abby's tone became cold and dark.

212

"Oh, I'm sorry to hear that. How long ago were they taken away?"

"About a year ago. My man, he be hard-headed and difficult to manage. He kept running away. My children was well grown and brought a good profit to the Manigaults. They don't have a large plantation being mostly city people and didn't really need extra slaves. So, my children just brought a good price."

Abby didn't say anything further, but Sundru could feel a cold iciness descend into the room.

Sundru said, "Abby, nothing I can say will change what has happened or what ye're feeling right now. But, neither Mrs. Malone nor I had anything to do with that, and so, I can only ask ye not be holden it against us. In turn, I can tell you that Mrs. Malone will treat ye fairly while you're here. More than that, I can offer ye nothing."

"Yes, ma'am. I understand. No, you not to blame for what happened, but tell me, you a slave?"

The bluntness of these words took Sundru back a bit, but she replied, "No, I'm indentured for another four years."

"Then you be free won't you?"

"Yes, that's right. I'll be able to lead me own life."

"That be a hope I be never having." Pausing, and slowly removing the newly cut patterns, Abby straightened herself and continued as though nothing before had been said, "Now, ma'am, what I be doing now?"

Sundru picked up on this change and explained what she thought Ma would be wanting her to do. Almost on a whim, she turned to Abby and asked, "Tell me, ye don't know much about sewing, but you can do it a bit?"

"Yes 'm. I do a bit. Enough to keep my clothes repaired."

"Let me see you do a bit of basting here" handing over the patterns. "Here's a needle."

Abby was a bit awkward, but it was obvious that she knew what a needle and thread were. Thinking aloud, as she watched Abby, Sundru said, "I really don't exactly know what Mrs. Malone had in mind for you to besides helping her have the

213

baby, but we can use some sewing help here. If you're willing to learn more, you be making yourself a lot more valuable to anyone who owns you. So, how about it?"

This was all happening too fast for Abby. Being given to a strange white woman, being hugged by another and given new dresses, and then being offered a chance to learn sewing. All this is in a single afternoon was disconcerting. But she had learned well to take quickly whatever was offered to her, and she found herself nodding her head. With that silent motion, an agreement was made.

Shortly, Ma returned from her nap and found Abby basting the last of her new dresses.

"Oh! You sew?"

"Not really. Not like you and Miz Sundru does, but I can do some things and Miz Sundru be having me do this basting here. She also said she'd teaching me...that is, if it be good with you, ma'am."

"Oh...well. Frankly, I wasn't sure what I'd be having you do, and if Sundru has uncovered a talent, then I'm all for it. Of course, I'm happy for you and happy that we've solved the problem of what's to be done with you while I'm having this baby."

Abby's previous chilliness had passed, and she then turned to Ma and asked, "Has anyone looked at you ma'am? 'Bout your baby I mean."

"No, really, no one has. I'm feeling well enough other than being tired and in need of naps more than before. But, no, no one's looked at me."

Abby's demeanor became a bit more business-like as she entered into her area of real expertise.

"Then I expect we be needin' to take a look at things if we's to be delivering a healthy baby. Where you intending on delivering the child?"

"You know, I hadn't really thought of that. Shows you what I know. What do you suggest?"

Abby started ordering the things she needed, "We be needing a comfortable place, fairly clean and near a kitchen where water can be kept hot. Things get a bit messy during birthing, and keeping things neat and orderly I find be important."

214

Ma replied, "Then we'll be doing it here. There's no real kitchen or convenient fireplace at the smithy shop, so we'll have to set things here. We do most of our eating here anyway and so, doing women's work is more natural here."

"Then it's here where the birthing will take place. They's a bed here?"

"Yes, of course. Before I got married, I lived with Sundru so beds are available."

"Clean ticking and sheets?"

"We change the ticking about once a month," answered Ma.

"We'll change both the linen and ticking more often than that now. In fact, I'd prefer both be brand clean for the birthing, ma'am."

Ma answered, "That can be arranged. Anything else?"

"Yes, let's take a look at you. Could you take off your clothes please?"

These instructions took Ma aback. She had never disrobed before a nigrah before and particularly had never taken such orders before. Of course, Sally had scolded her at Drayton Hall about doing her own washing, but that seemed much less personal than disrobing. Still, if she was to have a baby, and if she wanted expert help, then it seemed best to do as she was told. Meanwhile, Abby stood by patiently as Ma made up her mind.

Once Ma was disrobed, Abby looked her over carefully while asking a variety of questions. Had she ever broken bones before? Any illnesses? How are you feeling now? Any bleeding? Baby moving strong? Ma felt like a cow being inspected for auction. A fleeting thought passed through her that perhaps that's how slaves felt as they were being examined, but it didn't last as her concerns were for her arriving baby.

About twenty minutes later, Abby sat back and opined that Ma was a fit, strong mother.

"You shouldn't be having no problems ma'am. I's had a lot of babies come into this world, and you's about as good as any for delivering them.

Smiling broadly, Abby continued, "Yes ma'am. I think we is gonna be havin' a good time here. What you be wantin'? A boy or girl?"

"I suppose a boy for William's sake. He does so want one, but as long as it's normal."

"Yes, ma'am, it be normal. That I can promise you."

"Then welcome to our family, Abby. I feel much better knowing you're here to take care of things."

"I's pleased to be here ma'am."

Later that day, Sundru told Ma about all that had happened during her nap. Her commentary concluded with two observations.

"One ma'am, she's real bitter about losing her husband and children. Not that I can blame her. But, she did seem to warm up a bit as time went along. Second, she does know how to sew to some extent, and while she's here, I'm thinking she might as well learn something. As her skill improves, she'll be a relief to me. Look, she can already do rough basting."

Abby's work sparked a thought in Ma's mind about possibly buying her. If she really did have some talent, then she would be a solution to buying a slave. She'd have to consider Abby's bitterness and see how bad it was. If it interfered with work, then clearly she wouldn't do. Also, her talents as a seamstress would also have to watched. If any talent were there, it'd be seen shortly, and again if none were to be seen, then it's back to Mrs. Manigault. Speaking of Mrs. Manigault…Sundru almost seemed to read her mind.

"Abby told me that the Manigaults are city people and don't have need for slaves like the Draytons do. That was why her children were sold off…simply for profit. Perhaps, if an offer were made."

Ma said, "Well, before we buy out Africa, let's see what this woman can do. Meanwhile, teach her what you can and keep me informed."

"Yes ma'am."

The summer months continued to swelter and Ma became convinced she wasn't having a baby but a stove. Carolina summers were hot, but this was ridiculous. She swore she'd go naked if it would help. Abby and Sundru both laughed at the thought of Ma tending the ladies of town in her birthday nakedness.

"Miz Wyanne. You do that, and you be losing all your business and I be having to go back to Miz Manigault before you be having your baby. Then what you be doin' then?"

"If a lake were here, I'd be jumping in for a cool stretch, believe me. But, otherwise, I'm spending all my time now just letting out my dresses. I never noticed before how big tummies can get. Back home, Ma was always big and I never noticed otherwise."

Noticing Abby doing some hemming, Ma then leaned over to look at the stitches.

"Not bad, in fact they're pretty good. Very tiny. Actually, for hemming they really don't need to be that small since they're not seen. Being a bit looser also helps the hem keep its shape as it allows the material to flex a bit. They got to be tighter than basting stitches, but … ah, ok, that's it. Good work. I'm beginning to think you've got some sewing talent."

Abby beamed. She really did. As the weeks passed, her treatment here was all she could hope for besides getting her liberty and finding her family.

Abby also had met William and assured him that both his wife and arriving baby were doing well. William's relief at these words was palpable.

By October, Ma had made up her mind. Abby was to stay if it were at all possible. Ma had become comfortable with her ministrations as a mid-wife. Her talents as a seamstress were improving each day, although she probably would never be Sundru's equal. But, with Sundru's patient coaching, Abby's progress was obvious. Eventually, she'd be able to do everything but the most complex pieces of work, and that was enough. Even if Sundru did leave after her indenturement, perhaps a deal could be arranged whereby Sundru would take Ma's fancy work on consignment. That would give her sorely needed business until her own shop flourished while permitting Ma time to manage her shop without the care of tending just sewing.

The question was how to arrange the sale.

After giving the matter careful consideration, Ma decided that she had better talk to the Mistress. After all, she had arranged for Abby's loan; she should at least have the courtesy of knowing beforehand what was at hand.

"Wyanne! Let me look at you. You've just blossomed these last weeks. How long has it been?"

"A couple of months ma'am. And thank you. Abby's been a godsend by taking up a lot of duties that Sundru used to do. Now, Sundru and I can concentrate on the sewing business. That also means I can take naps that I find I really need."

Mrs. Drayton just laughed. "How I remember those naps. To get off my feet and lie down was sheer heaven. How's your back? Hurt?"

"Hurt? My Lord, it never seems to quit until I'm flat on it. Sometimes I have to have William rub me down at night. But, otherwise, Abby just laughs and says I'm doing fine. That is such a relief to the both of us. William and me, I mean."

"William's doing well then?"

"Yes, he's a dear in his attentiveness. But, I know he'll be useless during the birthing, so I'm planning to send him to the tavern for an ale where he can relax."

"Good idea. Keep men out of this business is what I say. Meanwhile, what can I do for you, Miss Mother?"

The crux of her errand was now fully on Ma, and she squirmed a bit before answering.

"Ummm, well, ah,"

"Don't fluster girl. What's on your mind?"

"OK, then. The long and short of it is that I want to buy Abby. She has a lot of talents that I can use for both my family and my shop."

In a few short words, Ma described all that had gone on with Abby during the past several weeks. Mrs. Drayton listened attentively as Ma then led to her question, "How should I approach Mrs. Manigault? Clearly, she had intended to loan her to me with every intention of getting her back. She also granted this favor because of you, and I wouldn't ever want to abuse your trust. But, I really believe Abby 'll be a tremendous help to me and my family."

Thinking things over for a few moments, Mrs. Drayton replied, "First thank you for confiding in me. Knowing your intentions beforehand keeps things up on the table where they belong. I can always face Mrs. Manigault now in society without reservation. That being said, I suggest that you just make an appointment and see if a sale can be made. As you do, you can tell her that you had told me beforehand, and I suggested you contact her. She'll hear you out I know because of your reputation for honesty and will tell you of her decision. The least she can do is say 'no.' Mind you,

218

she'll drive a hard bargain. The Manigaults are merchants and put a high price on all that they sell."

"Thank you ma'am. It's reassuring to hear these words, particularly about my public reputation. It's been something I've always tried to keep bright."

"And that you've done well, my dear. So, go along now and see if your bank account can accommodate Mrs. Manigault's price."

Ma spent the next several days reviewing her financial resources to determine whether in fact she could afford Abby. Since she was born in the colonies and had valuable assets as a mid-wife and now, as a seamstress, she would not come cheaply. Also, this would be an unplanned sale, so Mrs. Manigault would not be in a hurry to sell her. But, after looking at current market prices, and checking with Mr. Oskarmeir about a possible short-term loan, she decided that a price of £800 could be afforded. It was a bit higher than current prices, but considering everything together, it was fair to Mrs. Manigault and Abby met her needs.

With this research behind her, Ma made an appointment with Mrs. Manigault and showed up as scheduled.

Actually, Mrs. Manigault already knew about Ma's purpose for the meeting from Mrs. Drayton. The two met regularly for teas and other social engagements and Ma's desires for the slave became a topic of conversation.

"Of course, I can hardly let her go. You understand that being a mid-wife makes Abby a valuable piece of property. I have actually been able to hire her out to others. So, for you being able to borrow her was really a favor to Mrs. Drayton."
"Yes, ma'am. I understand that and am very appreciative. Believe me, I'm anxious to do right to both of you kind ladies. But, on the other hand, Abby's being with me has relieved you of maintenance costs in lieu of any mid-wife charges you've been able to make for me. So, perhaps I might want to make a counter-offer. Perhaps Abby will be able to act as mid-wife for your other slaves as the need occurs. Your home is located close to my shop and so, she always be available when you need her. Meanwhile, she's my expense."

Mrs. Manigault then asked in return, "Well, why do you want her beyond your pregnancy? What makes her so worthwhile to you?"

"As you know, I run a seamstress shop and keeping up with demand is always a problem. I have been partly able to keep up with Sundru and piecemealing the rest out to two slaves I trained at the Drayton plantation. But, still moving work back and forth to them is slow. Now, I believe that Abby will be able to relieve this delay. Mind you, she's still raw and in need of a lot of training, but the potential is still there. Besides, if William has his way, I doubt that this child will be the only one I'll carry. So, for what I have in mind, I'm willing to make a good business offer to you."

"You would, would you? And how much are you willing to pay? Also, do you have the resources to do so?"

"Whether I do or not is pretty much dependent on you ma'am. Price Abby out of my market, and I'll have to say no. But, then again, I know you occasionally sell slaves for a profit, and without a sale, where's the profit, ma'am?"

"Well said. Where's the profit? So, what's your offer?"

"I want to be fair to you and Mrs. Drayton."

"Oh you're offering a part of the price to her?"

Laughing, Ma said, "No ma'am, but it was through her that I came across Abby in the first place, and above all, I want to keep her patronage with yours. Also, I want you two to remain good friends."

"Friendship and business. That is a dangerous combination isn't it? Well, enough. What were you willing to offer?"

"Well trained seamstresses can go upwards to £700. Since Abby is yet untrained, I'm willing to offer £500."

Mrs. Manigault exclaimed, "Five hundred pounds? Surely you jest. And after your protests of patronage and friendship."

"Mrs. Drayton also said you drove a hard bargain," said Ma with a grin. "So, do you want to haggle or would you prefer a final offer?"

"Mrs. Drayton does know me doesn't she? Well, …A final offer then, and no tomfoolery young woman."

"No ma'am. Here it is. I'm willing to pay £800 for Abby which is above the going rates for a seamstress, plus you can have access to her for midwifery as you need her. More than that, I can't go a shilling further. I believe you know me well enough to know that my word is my bond."

"That's it? Well, yes, Mrs. Drayton has told me stories about your honor. So, I'll accept it at that. Before I decide, however, I'll be needing to talk to Mr. Manigault. You know how the law is, the husbands are the final arbiter of all financial transactions. He's tending business for several days and won't be available immediately. So, you'll have to await his decision."

"Thank you ma'am. That's all I can ask for."

The next week passed with some anxiety. Sundru knew what was happening, but nothing was said to Abby since she really didn't have much choice in the matter anyway. However, both Ma and Sundru believed that Abby was fairly happy being with them. She seemed to enjoy the sewing and it was better than any field work she would otherwise be doing."

Finally, as promised, a black runner came asking Ma to attend Mr. Manigault at his office in the morning at ten o'clock. Ma promised to be there.

At the appointed hour, Ma met Mr. Manigault in his store.

"Mr. Manigault, I'm pleased to be here. I presume it's about my desire to buy the slave, Abby."

"Yes, it is. Mrs. Manigault told me all about how she had loaned the girl to you and you came back wanting to buy her. I'm glad I didn't have you in my house as a guest."

Ma's heart leaped. She had the sale. "I think sir, that such a purchase would be way beyond my poor means."

"Possibly, but now to Abby. You had offered £800 for her on a final offer basis?"

"Yes sir, I checked prices for slaves with her qualifications and my financial resources, and finally considered what would be fair to you and Mrs. Manigault. £800 is the best that I can do."

After some moments of consideration, Mr. Manigault offered his hand in agreement to the sale. "Of course, I'll need your husband's permission and signature to complete the sale, but for all intents and purposes, it's a done deal."

After running her business alone for as many years as she had, these last words caught Ma by surprise and irritation. But, Mr. Manigault was only acting in accordance with the law that essentially made husbands the masters of spouse property.

"I'll be bringing William in as you request, sir; however, you might want to know that he and I have signed documents that essentially split our businesses in two. He retains control of his smithy, and I of my seamstress business. So, as far as I'm concerned, I can sign any document you might want to present. You, of course, are advised to check with Judge Drayton on this issue."

Now, it was Mr. Manigault's turn to be surprised. "My, my. This is something I've never run across in my years in business. Let me check this out before we make the transfer, but for moment, I'll accept your word. I have no doubt about what you say, but I just want to be sure that no complications will arise from this transaction."

"Yes sir, I would do the same thing if I were in your shoes. Rest assured that I'll be willing to do whatever is needed to make this sale legal and proper. Keeping things business-like is what I always want to do."

Mr. Manigault said, "I agree Wyanne, and that's one reason why I'm dealing with you now. Had any other woman been dealing with me on these matters, I probably would have cancelled it out of hand. So, let me have a couple of days and I'll send a runner over when the papers are ready."

"Thank you, sir. Till then. Meanwhile, I'll be wanting to go back and tell Abby what's happened."

Returning to her shop, she found Abby and Sundru busy with sewing. It was obvious that Sundru had been coaching Abby on some of the finer arts of the craft.

"Abby, could you lay your work down for a second, please. Sundru, you already know what's happening, but you might as well listen too."

In unison, the two women responded: "Yes, 'm."

"Abby, I've been over at Mr. Manigault's office today, and we've agreed for me to buy you. Some paperwork needs to be finished, but essentially, the sale has been made. So, for now, you're going to remain here permanently. By permanently, I hope you feel that you have a home here."

Abby's response was surprisingly muted. "Yes ma'am. I's pleased that my work has found favor in your eyes. You and Miz Sundru done treated me good and you've taught me a new trade that adds to my value."

222

"But…?"

"Nothing, ma'am."

"Yes, there is something more. There's something on your mind, and as long as we're staying together, Sundru will tell that we need to talk openly. That's the only way I work."

Some long seconds passed before Abby decided what she wanted to say. Clearly, she was trying to decide how far she should take Ma at her word. Finally, perhaps because she had nothing really to lose, she started speaking.

"Miz Wyanne, I ain't never been free. I don' expect ever to be so, but I also never expected my man and chillun ever to be sold neither. I knowed it was done, but never expected to hit me. Now, I find I been sold. Just like a head of cattle. It ain't nothin' against you 'cause as I said, you and Miz Sundru been good to me treatin' me like I was worth somethin'. But, once your family been sold out from under you, you always feel mistrusting afterwards. A little voice goes off in my mind asking if I knows when I'll be next and gone to someone who ain't good?"

Sundru sat and watched this conversation with saucer-like eyes. She had never heard a slave talk so to a white person. Ma, in turn, paused a long time before answering. Abby just sat passively awaiting whatever would happen.

"Abby, where I came from, powerful people ruled over my family. Not quite like slaves, but almost. What they could do to us was not right, and my people suffered terribly. So, I have some idea of what it means not to trust someone. Now, if I'm not careful, you'll look at me like my family looked at His Lordship trying to get away with as much as possible. Still, I bought you because I think you'll help my business, and to that extent, we'll always have that reason for being together. Your interest here is clearly not the same as mine since you'll get little profit from it. I understand all of that."

Ma paused to watch what effect her words were having on Abby. The slave just sat there waiting.

"Whether you ever learn to trust me, only time will tell. Perhaps talking to Sundru will help you make up your mind. I, like her, have also been indentured liable to be sold at any time, and she's still here learning more everyday about the seamstress business. I agree she will be freed at one time, but that's the fact of life."

Abby still listened passively.

223

"So what do I expect from you? A good day's work after which you have your time to yourself. If you want to pursue a small sewing business or do some midwifery on the side, that's your business. I'll not object as long as my work comes first. Agreed?"

"Yes ma'am."

"And what can you expect from me? I'll be honest with you and help you develop your sewing skills. I'll never sell you as long as we treat each other fairly. That's a promise, and you can ask anyone if Wyanne Malone keeps her promises."

Abby spoke slowly and quietly, "Thank you ma'am. You being honest with me now, and I appreciates it. I's sorry to be slow, but you axed me to speak my mind, and I done it. At least, now, we knows where we stand wif one another."

Several days later, and true to his word, Mr. Manigault's messenger came by asking Ma to come by alone to complete the sale. When she arrived, the papers were all laid out showing the transfer of one each slave named Abby from the Manigault estate to Mistress Wyanne Malone on October 15, 1759. This consideration was made in consideration of £800. The papers were signed and witnessed. Mr. Manigault congratulated Ma on her purchase and she in turn thanked him and his family for all the support they have given her through the years.

Following Abby's arrival, Ma's baby continued to develop. Through November, it was turning inside of Ma's tummy that was now hanging out like a barrel. Abby watched these developments carefully.

"It won't be long now before he starts lowering down getting ready to come out. This turning hopefully means that he be coming out headfirst. Coming out backwards makes things hard. It can be done, but it be terrible hard on both mama and baby."

True to her word, in December's first weeks, the baby dropped. Ma's barrel was clearly lower than even a week before.

"Next, we be watching to see if your canal be getting bigger so's to allow the baby to slide on through."

"How big should it be, Abby? My ma never talked about these things."

Abby had to laugh. "Miz Wyanne, for someone who knows so much, and who was around brothers and sisters like you was, yo sho don' know nothin' much 'bout babies. How big's a baby's head? Thas how big you canal gotta be or leastwise, close to it. Meanwhile, how you breasts doin'?

"They're bigger than melons, and I always was big."

"Thas good. Means you be havin' lots of milk which you'll be needin' to do by yourself. My not having had babies for a long time has me all dried up. It also means you won't be havin' more kids while you be nursing. Nature seems to be trying to protect mothers that way."

"William isn't getting inside of me for a long time," promised Ma.

Abby had to laugh again. "Lots of women say that and next thing they knows, they barrel housed again."

About three days later, Ma started fussing around the apartment above the smithy. First, she was putting baby things away, then cleaning and dittling on little things. It was around nine-thirty, and William was tired.

William said, "Wyanne, can't you come to bed. It's nine-thirty and I got a long day's work ahead of me tomorrow."

"Abby said the baby is due any day now, and I just want everything just perfect."

"If it ain't done by now, I reckon it'll never be done. Anyway, what's not done can wait. Let's go to bed. Quit your fussing. Please?"

William's plaintive voice spelled the difference. What's not done can wait until tomorrow. Abby didn't say the baby was due today anyway. So, she lowered herself into bed.

Still she couldn't sleep, and it wasn't just because of William's snoring. That was bothering her less and less as the months passed. Her back hurt, but no more than usual. Her feet were tired, but again, no more than usual. Well, she'd just have to go to sleep and get some rest. Tomorrow would be busy for her as well. With that thought, Ma drifted off to a troubled sleep.

Several hours later, Ma arose to relieve herself. This was a frequent task for her now that the baby had dropped down. She couldn't go more than a short while before nature called, and occasionally it meant that she had to turn a customer over to Sundru.

Sleepy, she wandered over to the thunder mug when she felt something wet flowing down her leg.

"Strange, I haven't messed since I was a child" mused Ma. "And I still feel like I have to pee. Wonder what this could be?"

Finding a match, she lit a candle to find a pool of water mixed with some blood on the floor. More was adding to its size.

"Oh my God, my water's broken. And just when William said nothing was going to happen."

Returning to bed, she pushed William with urgency.

"H'mmmph. OK, Wyanne. I'm turning over."

"No, you dummy. Mr. Know-it-all. Saying to come to bed before everything was set. Guess what? My water's broken. We got to get to my shop where Sundru and Abby are waiting." With that, Ma put on a robe and wrapped herself with a warm blanket.

William meanwhile, shook his head, rubbed his eyes, and turned his feet to the floor. When the chill of the room reached him, he realized what had been said.

"What? The baby! My God, Wyanne, why didn't you tell me? We've got to get going." He now was fully awake and throwing on his clothing.

"Stay here. Let me hitch a horse to a wagon and we'll be away in a second."

Now Ma began to laugh. William was flying in all directions talking a mile a minute. *Men, they really aren't any good for birthing.*

Ma then began to give orders. "Just go out and hitch the wagon. The baby isn't coming out yet. We have plenty of time."

A couple of minutes later, William called up saying the wagon was ready and can she come down by herself.

"I'm not sick, just having a baby. Yes, I'm coming down now."

Coming down and getting into the wagon, Ma settled in for the short ride to her shop. William clucked the horse into a fast trot.

"Slow down, William. We're not going to race."

"Oh yes, of course, we don't want an accident now," said William slowing the horse to a fast walk.

A minute or two later, the couple arrived at the shop. Ma got out and headed towards the stairs where Sundru and Abby were sleeping.

As soon as Ma entered the shop and lit a candle, both Abby and Sundru knew what was happening. They jumped out of bed and came over to help Ma. Sundru offered a chair while Abby was tightening up Sundru's bed. Meanwhile, Ma did not offer any resistance to the chair.

"When you water break, ma'am?"

Ma was surprised with the directness of the question. "How could she know without asking?" she thought. Then, with a laugh despite herself, "Of course, she's only delivered dozens of babies. What else would she ask?"

"Have any pains started yet?"

"No, just the wate……Ooooh, there was one."

"Yep, just about on time. Like I says, ma'am, this baby be coming on easy. Now you come over to the bed. Sundru, get some hot water and extra cloths. We's gonna have a mess here shortly that'll be needing cleaning." Abby was clearly in charge now and no questions came from anyone. Ma went to bed like a little girl, and Sundru jumped to stoke the fire and get some water boiling while looking for soft, clean cloths.

Turning to William, Abby said, "The best for you to do is get on back home. We be sending for you when the time comes." William turned meekly away like a little boy dismissed by a teacher.

Shortly, the second contraction came which caused a grunt from Abby, "Yep, they be coming for sure now, and a lot faster and harder. Now, when they do, I want you to blow hard and push."

Ma waited a minute later and started to puff a bit which brought a sharp order from Abby, "When I say, blow hard and push, I mean blow hard and crunch you stomach muscles as tight as you can."

"Yes ma'am. I'll try harder."

227

"See that you do, ma'am, otherwise this baby 'll think you not serious about his coming out."

The contractions continued over the next several hours at an ever faster tempo. Ma had never done anything as hard as this in her life. The pain was also tiring. There was never time for rest. If only she could get a moment to sleep. Oooooohhgg. That was a tough one. Unnnngh,....

"Push, push, push! Come on, ma'am, make it harder!"

"What the hell do you think I'm doing? Uuuuuhhgg. Uuuuuuhgg!"

"Now you is starting to push right. You's also getting bigger making room for the head."

Sundru kept cloths boiling and occasionally cooled one by the window. These she used to wipe Ma's brow. Otherwise, she kept a hold of Ma's hands to give her some resistance for pushing. Otherwise, she was quietly wide-eyed as she took in all of the activity going on around her. Abby, on the other hand, was focused entirely on the drama that was occurring between Ma's legs.

After several more hours, Abby reached gently inside of Ma. "Yep, you be having 'nough room for the baby to slide on through. I can almost feel the head now so it won't be long now.

"Uuuuuuuuhggl! Uuuuuuuuhgg.! "

"Jes' keep on pushing ma'am. I knows it ain't easy, but the harder you push now the faster it be done. Now push, damn it."

"Uuuuuuuhgg! Better now?"

"Getting there. I be feeling the top of the head now." With those words, Abby worked to spread the delivery canal a bit wider. Ma by now was between contractions and had fallen into a sound sleep. Actually, she had been sleeping between contractions for some time now.

"Sundru, get some toweling under Miz Wyanne now. The baby be coming shortly and that be bloody. No sense messing up the bed."

"Yes, ma'am." She started to gently move Ma, and Abby pushed her away to assume the duty herself.

"You can't be delicate here, Miz Sundru. Miz Wyanne be sound asleep now and don't feel nothing. So, just get it done quick-like."

A couple more contractions and Abby shouted triumphantly, "The head's comin' through, Miz Wyanne you push like you never done before."

"Uuuuuuuuhgg!"

With that last grunt, a wet, red, dark-haired body slide out into the world. I, Ephraim Malone was born at 2:34 a.m. on 23 December 1759. My mother, on the other hand, had fallen back asleep.

As Sundru began to attend Ma, Abby gave a final order, "Don' monk wit' her. We's got to clean this baby up and cut his cord. When he be ready, then we can present this boy to his mother. I knows then she be wanting to see him and he be wanting to eat. That chile done a pile of work these last hours and he be really hungry."

And so I was born. Ma always called me her Christmas gift. "A wee bit early, but none the less, my Christmas present."

Ma also said that my birth brought in her best years. In fact, the next fifteen years were good. My three siblings were born in fairly regular order about two years apart. Considering what happened to us during and after the war, my youngest brother, David was born on July 4, a day that brought our good years to a close. But, those days are another story. Meanwhile, let Ma tell the stories that she related to us many times during our years in the Bahamas.

"Yes, these years were good. Our family had started to grow and William was a wonderful father. He even learned to take part of their birthing. But, I guess if you have enough practice, then you start to learn something.

"Of course, he couldn't feed them during the early months of each child; men just don't have the equipment to do that. But, he'd get up with me, stoke the fire into flame to warm the room, and then, sit back just to watch. Often, we'd talk about whatever came to our minds. Daylight hours were often so hectic that we really didn't have a chance to chat. So, these nocturnal visits by our babies were often occasions for us to become reacquainted.

"But, to introduce you children, there was first Ephraim. He was born on December 3, 1759, and it has become his lot to gather the family letters and tales of our history.

"Next came Sarah. My, she was such a frail child. William and I had many nights together keeping her alive. First came ear problems. She went from one burst eardrum to another. Such pain she had! No one should endure it. Later, she told me that pain in her ears were her earliest memories. Then, later on, she had the croup, which meant that we would have to put a pot of water on the fire and fill the room with steam. Sometimes we would put a heavy tea of camphor that would help clear her lungs. Finally, by four years of age, she just outgrew these infections and became a strong and healthy child. Unfortunately, she had a terrible experience with William Jackson, the same man who attacked me, and while she wasn't permanently harmed physically, she grew to be a frightened and shy woman.

"Third was Vianna. In contrast to Sarah, her birth was my easiest and she never had a day's problem with her health. But, stubborn. I never saw the likes of her. Of course, I could never imagine where she would have gotten her spirit. Even from her earliest days on earth, she knew what she wanted. For example, I would often let her lie on my tummy while I was taking a nap. But, once when she was only three weeks old, I laid her in the cradle and that was not acceptable. A hard cradle was not to be substituted for my warm tummy and bosom, and I was to pull her out immediately. To this day, she clearly has the hardest head in the family.

"Fourth, Walter. He remained behind in Charles Town to become a banker. As such he represented the Malone financial interests after the rest of us moved to the Bahamas.

"Finally, David was born on July 4, 1766. Frankly, he was the brightest of you children and only the War prevented him from attending college. Of course, he has done well in his life and been a stalwart support of the family through all of the viscitudes that have befallen us. He has also become a well-educated man with perhaps the best library in the Bahamas. But, to deny a sparking mind such as his with an opportunity to attend college because of a stupid war is just a crime.

"But, to return to happier thoughts, the children came along and with them, many funny occasions. You, Ephraim, were always a climber. Up the bedstead, down the bedstead. Up the back tree, and down the tree. If I didn't know where to find you, I'd look up. The funniest example of your climbing happened when you were just a tyke of perhaps three, maybe four years old. I had taken you to Mr. Manigault's warehouse to pick up some newly arrived cloth. While there, I got talking to Mr. Manigault and lost track of you, and that was enough for you to disappear. When I finished my chat, I started looking for you, but you weren't to be found in any of aisles. Eventually, as I turned a corner, I saw a gang of men looking up in the rafters. Following their eyesight up a support beam for about fifty feet, I spied a wee tyke sitting in the rafters waving at me and shouting "Hi Mommy." I could have died I was so mortified. I didn't know whether to claim ownership or not. Eventually, I decided I had to since that tyke had claimed me, and I said, 'Get right down. Do you hear me Mr. Ephraim Malone?' 'Yes ma'am,' he replied, and without a moment's hesitation, he shinnied on down as if he was climbing from his bed.

"I've already mentioned how stubborn Vianna was. Well, she was also impulsive, and heaven help her poor brothers. One time, Vianna was about eighteen months, two years old when we went to a tavern for a Sunday dinner. It was a quiet noontime, and the regulars were just dozing at their tables when Walter let out a blood-curdling shriek with Vianna sitting beside him with a knife in her hand. For some unknown reason, she had decided to whack Walter on the head with it and looking all the prouder for the job she had done. Needless to say, our dinner that Sunday was hurried.

"The worst was when you were all tired and picking on each other. 'Momma, David hit me.' 'Did not!' 'Did so!' On and on this bickering would

231

continue exactly when your father and I were tired and wanted only peace and quiet. How tempting it was just to reach out and whack each of you. But, we tried not to do that unless our patience was just worn to a frazzle. Generally, it was just enough for your father and me to get in the middle of your argument and separate you and tell you all to be quiet or go to your beds. But, really, you were good kids.

"We started reading to you early on. Finding books you could understand was really hard, and often all we had was the Bible. So, your father and I would find simple passages from Psalms and read them. Sarah, in particular loved the story of Ruth, which is really one of my favorites as well. Over and over we'd read your favorite stories until you actually had them memorized. Try to skip a section or line to finish the reading, and a small hand would pop up over the book and turn the page back to where it belonged. I do think, however, this early start gave each of you a thirst for reading.

"Although, while you all enjoyed reading, girls, your other subjects were less fervently pursued. 'Oh mother, why do we have to attend school or our tutor? You know we won't need any of this education. Girls can't go to college and become doctors and lawyers.' Well, you were right. They can't, but they can run plantations, businesses and in general, be intelligent contributors to family and community. So, off to school you went. Sarah in particular had to be pushed. Perhaps it was because of her sickly childhood, she didn't have the energy to go out that the other kids had.

"And our businesses prospered. William's black smithy grew from shoeing horses to fabricating all sorts of iron products. He took on large contracts for making window frames, stair risers, and even some artwork. A lot of Germans lived in Charles Town and they really liked decorative signs to advertise their businesses. As I mentioned earlier, the War prevented David from attending college, so instead he entered his father's smithy as an apprentice. William was truly proud of that day. *__Malone and Son__* was written on a large sign over the shop.

"For me, my sewing business continued to grow. After I had gotten Abby, I eventually bought another three nigrahs. Sundru was kept constantly busy teaching them. About this girl, I have always given prayers of thanks. She did not leave my employment after having finished her indenturement. Rather she stayed on until 1765 when she met her husband and then moved West. By this time, the French-Indian War was finished and the frontier was fairly safe for settlement. So, she was able to follow the path that Mr. Smith had dreamed of taking. Her path was long and arduous. Occasionally, I would get a letter from her when she had a moment from her labors. She would describe how she walked several hundred miles into the western Carolinas to build a cabin before the snows started. That first winter was really hard. They hadn't had time to get a crop in, so they had to pretty well live on what could be hunted and shot. I can only imagine that they almost starved to death. It was so close that they almost had to eat the seed crop they had brought with them. But, they did survive and laid in a crop. Eventually, they broke several hundred acres and planted a diverse crop of tobacco, wheat, and cotton. Rice and indigo could not be grown in that higher Appalachian elevation. Occasionally, they were able to trade in some furs and deerskins taken from their plantation for some cash money. Mr. Manigault would trade in them, although they never made up much of his business.

"I had thought about going West while I was at the Drayton plantation, but after hearing of Sundru's life, Charles Town was clearly the better choice. Many of the people living out there were staunch loyalists, but when the War came through there, many of them were destroyed by the violence that was generated by the armies and rebel families. I believe that Sundru survived these problems, but her life was never easy. I can only hope her children have had a better time of things.

"Meanwhile, while she did stay with me, my slaves got good training and were able to let my business keep up with demand. Only on the rare occasion did I have to depend on Sarah and Sadie to finish the basic work on dresses. Sundru was also able to tend the sale of cloth, ribbons, buttons etc. that ladies would need for altering their dresses. In short, Sundru let me tend to the business accounts and meeting other families who were looking for seamstress work.

"My business actually grew so much that I had to rent the entire building. The front rooms on street level remained a store and fitting room. The back rooms contained inventory stocks. The second floor became a sewing center where the slaves would do most of the basting and hemming of dresses. Abby eventually became another finisher with Sundru. Finally on the top floor, Sundru got an apartment of several rooms and the slaves had common quarters. A separate kitchen was erected in the back where we took our meals in common.

"Actually, business got so good that one time we took a holiday. David, you don't remember this 'cause you weren't yet born. But, maybe the other kids have told you this story. Anyway, things were a bit slow, nothing serious mind you, just a lull when your father and I looked at one another and came to the same thought. 'Let's get out of here and just have some fun.'

"So, we went off on a two-week holiday down to Savannah. My! What an experience. It was something that your grandparents in Ireland couldn't even dream of doing. They worked every day of their lives excepting Sundays when they went to church. No wonder they got old so young. But, for us, we had been struggling for years, and this was a time to play. And play we did.

"We packed some bags and you in the wagon and headed south. Savannah is about 75 miles south of Charles Town which meant about a three-day trip. The

233

weather was cool being in late September and the leaves were just turning a bit. So, we rumped and bumped along the road stopping when we were hungry or just felt like stopping. A couple nights we just slept under the wagon while the horses were tethered nearby. You kids just howled like Indians as you ran through the woods. Of course, Ephraim, you had to climb every tree you saw.

"One night, both going and coming, we were able to stop off at the Jacobson's plantation. It wasn't a big farm, but they did have some extra space where they graciously put up five total strangers. But, unlike here in the Bahamas, where most all of us are pretty well settled in, wayfarers naturally expected to stay at houses where they passed. Cities tend to be smaller and further apart from what I've heard about New England, and hotels just aren't to be found. So, hospitality opened doors to people like us.

"Actually, most of these farmers enjoyed having company. Living off in the woods as they did, they were pretty much isolated for company. Not like you know from Charles Town and here in Hope Town. Newspapers, if they get any, came through the post and you know what sort of service that is. So, as we came in, we were able to talk about the latest happenings in the outer world.

"The War ruined the Jacobsons when the rebels burned down their house and barn. So, we haven't heard from them for years.

"Anyway, about Savannah. None of you kids have seen it and more's the pity. It's smaller than Charles Town, but absolutely as gracious. In fact, more so in some respects. It was a planned city if you can imagine that! Unlike the streets in Charles Town that run higgledy-piggledy, Savannah is laid out in neat squares, just like a checkerboard. But, what is so nice are parks that are fitted in everywhere. Families can come out and meet under the cool of the oak trees while their kids are playing safely. I hate to think of the times I worried about you kids playing in the streets under the hooves of horses and wheels of wagons. I guess the good Lord was smiling on you all since you survived, but when I think of those families in Savannah, many's the time when I wished I was there. If you ever get a chance to see it, you really should and you'll see why I fell in love with the place as soon as I saw it.

"Of course, it wasn't always rosy. Southern plantation owners lived off credit because cash money was so hard to transport between debtors and creditors in America and England. So, for them, actually paying bills to people who had to live from cash transactions, was often difficult. At best, they would often settle up only after their rice crops were in. Occasionally though, and I really hated to do this because I didn't want to develop a reputation for miserliness, I just had to protect myself by going to the local Court of Common Pleas and ask for my money. Because I had insisted on keeping our businesses apart before we were married, it meant that I had to make my own pleas, which was not an easy task being a woman. For William, as a man, the task was always a lot easier when he had sue a customer. But, anyway, when someone got behind by several hundred pounds, we just didn't have any choice, and it was off to court we went.

"If only King George knew to leave well enough alone. We were all happy and proud to be British subjects. We had our liberties based on long tradition that no one else had. Certainly not the French or Spanish. Certainly better than what we got as Irishmen. The French Indian War, I guess, was supposed to have brought great riches to the Empire. At least that was what we were told as we endured it. I do know that it created an uprising with the Indians out west as they were prodded by the French to raid our settlements in the Carolinas. A bunch of young boys also got killed or wounded after they joined the army of Colonel Washington or put on the King's uniform for a couple of shillings. That didn't do them any good or anyone else for that matter.

"So, what did we get after seven years of warfare? The king could claim all of the land in America from Canada to the Gulf of Mexico and east of the Mississippi. But, what did that mean? As far as I could see, the Indians were still in charge there. We couldn't move out further than the Carolinas because of an agreement with them. The Ohio Valley was forbidden. It seemed that the Indians still wanted it even though the king was supposed to own it. But, he didn't want to upset them and so, we were forbidden the right to settle the land we had fought a war to obtain. So, again, what did we get for the war?

"Oh, yes, there were those new taxes. First came the Sugar Act. Then, came the Stamp Act, and a couple of others in between and together, they almost brought the empire down during those years. It surely did rile the Adams family up in Massachusetts, particularly that mail clerk, Samuel. He seemed even then hell-bent on creating trouble, proclaiming independence all the time. I agree that the war had created an unnecessary strain on everyone, and probably the king's coffers were empty after fighting for so long after something that never panned out. I don't like paying taxes of any kind and particularly without having any say in the matter in Parliament. I had also seen enough of taxes in Ireland and would not have wanted that experience repeated here in America. But, clearly, as someone who was dependent on British cloth for my dresses, I didn't want anything to interfere with my getting supplies on a regular basis. So, independence? From what? The king was thousands of miles away, and how was he seriously going to oppress us?

"So, that hue and cry in Massachusetts for independence just didn't make sense. Least while for me. If Massachusetts wanted to become independent, that was fine with me. They could do whatever they wanted. But, no, they had to get everyone all stirred up. People even got to the point of refusing to buy anything British, which just about ruined me. Local cloth just wasn't of the same quality or quantity and ladies just weren't buying as much. Of course, they all felt so patriotic. H'mmmph. Patriotic my eye. I sometimes wondered if the rich landowners were pushing the war so they could repudiate their debts overseas. Never could prove it, but it surely seems logical.

"And to top things off, that stupid "Tea Party" held in 1773 takes the cake. As I understand it, Parliament had actually worked things out so that prices were actually going to drop. But, oh no! That wasn't good enough. It had to be sold tax free, so a bunch of grown children painted themselves up like Indians and threw tons of tea overboard in Boston harbor. What a waste. After that, it became almost unobtainable. Coffee became the drink of patriots, which just gags me almost as much as grits. I've drunk tea since I was a wee girl and have never seen any reason to change. But, that was the idiocy of those times.

"But, the worst of it, William, your father didn't see things this way. He tended to side with the Adams family and their arguments. Of course, in our house, at that time we didn't have any fights on these issues. They started later. Generally, we grumbled, and hoped that the king would get rid of his taxes, regain his mind, and generally leave us alone. As I said, we were very happy then and our lives prospered. You children were the joy of our lives and our businesses allowed us to plan for a rich and rewarding life with you.

"To be honest, the differences at first between us weren't that strong. Essentially we tended to look upon our lives as a farmer in Pennsylvania described his life. I'll quote a bit here:

> I felt myself happy in my new situation, and where is that station which can confer a more substantial system of felicity than that of an American farmer, possessing freedom of action, freedom of thoughts, ruled by a mode of government which requires but little from us, owe nothing, but a pepper corn to my country, a small tribute to my king, with loyalty and due respect.

"As you can see, all we wanted was to be left alone and to that extent, we were both agreeable to paying a small tax to the king for his governance of this colony. But, as things developed and became more heated, things just got harder for us to agree on. But, that's another story about your father. Suffice it say that he tried hard and loved all of you kids, and that's enough for you.

"Actually, we had enough money coming in that school was to be a regular part of your lives. Together with several other families, we hired a tutor to teach you your lessons besides whatever you got out of school.. Eventually, you were all to go to college. What a dream! My parents could never dream of learning to read and

236

write while we were dreaming of college for you. Ephraim got to go to Harvard for a while and all of you learned to read, but our dreams were for more…for all of you to study.

"And while we dreamed, our lives wandered forward through many happy years. Besides the holiday I mentioned earlier, we had other times to ourselves. Sundays saw us attending church and then going off on picnics in the woods or on the beaches. You children just loved the sea beaches when it was hot. You'd strip down and just romp in the surf provided it wasn't too high. Otherwise, we'd go for long walks looking for the strange sea urchins that were brought in by the tides.

"Other times, Sam and Old Sal would come into town, and he'd let you ride in his wagon. Such adventures you had. He knew Charles Town like no one else I ever knew and he would show you all the sights. He truly loved you and I was always happy for him to take you on his local journeys. Unlike other slaves who ran away during the War for their freedom, he and Sally, his wife, never did. 'I's too old to do such things,' he'd say sadly. Fortunately, the Draytons always took fairly good care of their slaves, and Sam was always a favorite, so he knew where his best life lay for him. He and Sally certainly left a lot of kids behind at the plantation.

"Of course, it wasn't always happy. Susannah died in childbirth, which just devastated me. She was such a friend; I really haven't gotten over it to this day. You children don't remember her because we saw each other so seldom. But, what wisdom she gave to me. There never was a problem I had, but what I couldn't go to her for help. Even through letters, she was always there for me when I needed her. I have kept each of those letters as my most precious treasure after you kids.
"The worst thing was learning about Susanna's death after she was buried. Not being able to attend her funeral was so sad. I've commented on my friendship with her many times in the past, but it was a fact, she was the best friend I ever had. There wasn't anything we couldn't or didn't talk about. Even today, I miss her so much while feeling that she is still as near to me as tomorrow. I understand that Mr. Killebrew married again. Well, that's normal. It's not right to live alone like Susannah did for so many years after the death of her Tom. Besides, he needs help raising his babies. Still, I miss her, I truly miss her."

CHAPTER TWENTY-THREE

"Come here, son," ordered my mother, and I knew there was no resistance. What Ma wanted, Ma got.

"Your hair is a mess. Here, turn around and let me re-tie it."

"Yes, Ma. But what's to worry? After all, ten minutes after I'm at sea, the wind will blow it apart anyway."

"That has nothing to do with this. When you take off to college, I want you looking right."

"Yes, ma'am," turning around. Like I said, there was no arguing with Ma even if I was fifteen years old and ready to leave home.

A quiet took over, and I had a chance to look over my parents. For the first time, I think I was really seeing them.

Pops was standing there as he usually was, quietly and in the shadow. His hair was turning gray showing all of his forty-odd years. Lines were plowing furrows in his face. But, looking at his arms allowed me to see what sort of man he was.

They were fit of course, as would be expected of a blacksmith. But, they weren't huge as many believe they would be. Actually, smithys don't flail their iron. Rather, the force of their blows come through their wrists so it is their forearms that are really strong. Besides, most of their work consists of gently coaxing a shape out of the hot metal, and it's where and how hammers land that determines how well a blacksmith does his work.

But, when you looked closer at him, you could see the cost of his labors. His arms were scarred by the many slivers of hot steel and iron that fly off in every direction. The forefinger of his left hand was flattened as a result of being smashed many years ago. His face was also scarred by other flying slivers and his eyebrows looked permanently scorched from bending over a million fires. Pop's ears constantly ring in time with the rhythms of millions of hammers. He joked about this whenever he asked anyone to repeat himself as he did increasingly with the passage of time. "I've got bells in my head," he would often say with a rueful grin.

Ma, on the other hand, showed far fewer ravages of time. Of course, carrying five babies had thickened her waist, but she was still a handsome woman. Her red hair was still bright even when swept up in the bun she always wore, and she still had all of her teeth. This was truly unusual. Missing teeth was so common that most people refused to smile rather than to reveal black gaps in their faces. Her biggest consent to age were the reading glasses that perched over her nose or up over her brow. All her years of sewing had made her unable to see anything clearly within an arm length of her eyes. So, as she now tied my queue, her glasses were firmly down and focused on me.

"Now turn around and give me a hug. Your ship is about ready for everyone to board, and I know you don't want us hanging around. So, let's say our goodbyes now."

With that last command, Ma held me firmly in place for a second and then released me to everyone one else in the family. Pops came forward and offered me his hand.

"Son, you're the first person in this family to attend college, and I can't tell you how proud we are of you. When you return, you'll be a lawyer when the world will be open to you. So, while you're up in Boston, behave yourself and don't lose sight of why you're there."

"Yes sir," I mumbled. Actually, I was so anxious to get going, I really wasn't hearing anything that was being said. Going out to see Boston and meet the famous people whose names resounded throughout the colonies was a dream come true.

Next came my brothers and sisters. Giving each of them a hug was somewhat harder for me. I knew, and they knew that our lives of piling over each other like puppies in bed and crowding around the kitchen table were coming to a close. They would truly be missed.

"Avast, people. The tide's ebbing and we need to be off. All aboard who's going aboard."

With those words, people started to shuffle up the gangplank, and among them was me, off to Boston and Harvard college.

Once aboard, I leaned over the gunnels and looked for my family. They were standing alone off behind the crowds. Seeing them, I waved broadly as they did to me when they saw me. By now, the sailors had thrown of the restraining hawsers while small boats were straining to move the ship from the harbor. Slowly, it started to catch the tide. Meanwhile, other sailors were scampering topside to release the sails that would catch the morning's breezes. Eventually, enough speed was gained that steerage was possible, and the towing boats were released for them to bend their oars for other departing ships.

I was oblivious to all of this activity as I remained by the ship's side waving at my family while seeing them becoming ever smaller. Finally, I could see them turn to go home. At that moment, I truly understood that I was on my own. My life had taken a new turn and was leaving theirs.

The *Compass Rose* was a small packet of about thirty tons that plied the coastal waterways from Nova Scotia to the Caribbean. As such, it rarely left eyesight of North America. It also meant that it was constantly tossed about by the rough shoreside currents flowing over the shallow waters. It wasn't long that I began to understand why my mother hated to sail. But, that was yet to come.

Right now, I turned to find my quarters. Asking a sailor where I could find the passenger berths, I was shrugged aft by a hook of his hand. Dancing around and over the coils of rope and capstans while trying to remain erect on the heaving deck, I lurched in the direction given to me.

Eventually, I found several other people also struggling in a similar direction, and assuming they must also be confused passengers, followed them below to a dark, smelly crawl way. There, I found a sailor indicating to each person their hammock and giving them directions about their new daily lives.

"Mr. Malone, your hammock is over here. You can stow your baggage along the bulkhead here, but keep your eye on it as we're responsible for nothing down here. Meals will be topside on the deck, and you'll be called by the bells. Fortunately, this is a coaster and you'll find the water fairly clean for drinking. Bathing of course is with salt water so you probably will find it preferable to keep them short and seldom."

Little did know how stinky I would become and what a foul treat seafood really was. As it was, I found I really didn't want to eat anyway because I would only lose it overboard immediate afterwards. My stomach never, ever became a sailor even though I have been forced to sea on several occasions.

Once settled in, I immediately left the darkness that had surrounded us to get above into the sunshine and fresh air. Otherwise, I was certain my stomach would lose itself right then and there. Besides I was curious as to what sort of people my fellow passengers might be.

After a few minutes orienting myself on deck, my search for a fellow passenger was rewarded. Leaning over the side of the ship smoking his pipe was another young fellow of about twenty years of age. That was enough for me, and I went over to introduce myself.

"Excuse me, but you're a passenger to Boston?"

Turning toward me, he replied, "Well, yes. And I assume you're bound there as well?"

"That I am," I replied proudly. "I'm off to Harvard College."

"Well, a college boy, as I live and breathe. Well, welcome aboard, as I'm bound there as well."

"You are? Oh wonderful. I've never been there as this is my first year. You've been there already?"

"Yes, actually, this should be my last year, thank goodness as I want to get on with things. Anyway, stick with me, and I'll get you through the process of learning how to be a student. By the way, your name please?"

"Ephraim Malone. And yours?"

"Jeremy Wilson from Savannah," reaching out to shake hands.

"Savannah, what a lovely city. My family visited it several years ago," as I clasped his hand in mine. With that, friendship ensued that was to be strained tragically by the War. But that was all to the future. For now, we were two young men eagerly seeking the start of our lives.

"What will you be studying?" asked Jeremy.

"The law. I had thought about philosophy, but the law offered a better chance at earning a living, so in lieu of starving as a dusty professor, I settled on it. And yourself?"

Jeremy said, "Good choice and it is mine as well. But I'm not really certain I want to become one. What exactly, I can't say, but probably not the law. Besides what with the colonies becoming more sour with the king, I can't say that anything will let us plan with certainty. Who knows, maybe there'll be war."

"Oh no. War?" I had to laugh despite myself. That seemed to be so foolish. Of course, we'll remain loyal to the crown. After all, we're all Englishmen and proud of it.

241

"We'll see," replied Jeremy coolly. "Anyway, that's not for us to decide. Meanwhile, where will you be staying? We're not always going to be stuck on this bucket."

"Well, actually, I think I'll be staying with my uncle Kevin. I've never seen him and my mother has had only sporadic contact with him. But, he does sound like fun. Ma told some stories about his running from home one step of His Lordship's hunting grounds. Actually, I believe she knew other stories, but never told them to me. She only said that I should be careful when I'm around him as he had a slippery touch with the law. But, she always laughed when she said so, and I'm inclined to think that he must be a genuine rascal."

"What a wonderful fellow to have lead you around. You must introduce me to him." Jeremy's eyes were twinkling at the thought.

Thanks to our ship's several stops and need to tack before contrary winds, our way north was slow. Altogether it lasted about three weeks which gave us plenty of time to talk about every subject on the face of the earth. Of course, as is true of young lads, our concerns centered around the forces of change.

Jeremy proved to be a committed revolutionary. Not just a grumbler about the recent taxes that Parliament seemed bent on levying, but actual separation.

"You need to hear John Adams and James Otis. If you think I'm committed, wait until you hear them speak. Likewise, I can hardly wait until you read the writings of John's cousin, Samuel. He was one of the earliest revolutionaries going all the way back to the 1750's.

"1750! My god! My mother had not yet come over from Ireland, and …"

"Ireland. She must be against the king," said Jeremy. "What the English has done to the Irish is a crime. I'm a protestant, you must be Catholic, but unlike earlier waves of immigrants to Ireland, the army of Cromwell came as conquerors."

I laughed and replied, "My, this is a change. A Protestant who doesn't have a hatred of Catholics." I had to laugh in spite of myself. "I'm Catholic as you have noted, but bless me if I've ever been to a Catholic service. Charles Town doesn't have any such churches, and it's generally best not to advertise one's religion. So, it's been to Protestant churches whenever I attended service."

"So, surely, you're mother is against the king. Being oppressed for centuries and now denied her right to worship as she wishes by decree of the king's religion."

"Frankly, this is a lot that I haven't considered. But, surprisingly, my mother has never mentioned much about it. Politics never seemed to interest her, but rather just wanted to be left alone to tend her sewing business. Now, my father, on the other hand, has been following these current events with great interest, and that has occasioned a number of arguments between my parents."

"Is your father a Catholic?" asked Jeremy.

"I really don't know. As I said, they really didn't talk about such things and we all just went to church on Sundays."

But not everything became a political diatribe. Jeremy offered many funny insights about the Yankee pilgrims.

"You would never believe these Yankees. Slipping into a strange drawl, 'They are so positive about everything including their divinity. Divinity you say! But, of course, my deah sirrah. We have been anointed by God himself to create a new city of gold. And we want to ensure that everyone joins in. Either that, or we'll make you severely sorah for being so benighted. Ah stakes of fiah stand tall awaiting doubtahs.'"

In spite of myself, I couldn't wait to hear Jeremy mock these pilgrims and their turgid righteousness. And with these long conversations, our cruise slowly wended northwards until, thank God, our bouts of seasickness came to an end.

"Well, Jeremy. I have to find my uncle. His last known address was in an area called the 'Back Bay.' You wouldn't happen to know where that might be?"

"Frankly, no. This town is crazy. Every street just goes higgledy-piggledy wherever it wants. Probably they were just following the cows that grazed here. So, you'll have to ask until you find him. But, meanwhile, here's my address, and if you have problems, don't hesitate to contact me."

"And I'll be seeing you at school?" I asked.

"Without a doubt. I'll be looking for you in about a week."

With this departure, I set out to find my uncle. Amazingly enough, I almost got seasick again. This time, the ground was solid while I was still swaying to the rolling of the swells under my gratefully departed ship.

But, pressing on, and after asking many directions, I finally found the last known address of Uncle Kevin. Of course he wasn't there. It seems that he left a couple of midnights ago for failure to pay his rent. Somehow, I wasn't surprised. So, on with my search.

A couple of taverns in the vicinity led me to some tough sort of fellows who knew of Uncle Kevin. At first, they were reluctant to speak with me, but when I started telling some stories about him, they began to laugh and warm up. Eventually, with a glance around to ensure that no one could overhear his directions, he told me where I could find him.

Of course, Boston streets made these directions very confusing, but eventually after several hours of lugging my carpet bag, I finally straggled to a seedy house and knocked on the door.

"Who's there?" came a slurred voice.

"Ephraim Malone from Charles Town looking for Master Kevin Farrell." The door still did not open.

"From Charles Town, you say. And how do I know ye're telling the truth?"

"I guess 'cause I'm fifteen years old, I've just arrived from a long, ugly trip, and I'm tired after walking all over this city looking for a man I've never seen. Now, do you know Uncle Kevin or not?"

The door opened a crack and a pair of eyes looked me over for a long time. Eventually, it opened a bit further and eventually a man motioned me inside.

"So, ye're Wyanne's boy. I didn't know she had any. And how is my sister?"

"Well, sir. She sends her regards and asks for me to stay with you until such time as I can find my way around."

"Well, I guess you be her son alright. Anyone else wouldn't have been a brash as ye show y'rself to be. Take after your ma, ye does. Well, come on in and set y'rself down. Then,…ye got any money? If ye does, then we can eat."

"Yes, Ma gave me enough to get started. If you tell what's needed and where I can get it, we can eat."

"Just give me some money, and I'll take care of things."

Doubtfully, I gave him some money, but not having any choice, and being overcome with hunger, I gave him a couple of shillings.

"Good enough. Set down, make y'rself a home, and I'll be back along." With those words, he left leaving me to wonder what to do next.

Looking around in the darkening gloom of the evening hour, I could see a rough hewn table and a couple of chairs. In the corner was a clothes chest where a couple of drawers stored whatever clothing Uncle Kevin had. Here and there were a couple candle sticks where some stumps listed forlornly. A small grimy window let a few weak rays of light shine onto a narrow bed in the corner. It obviously hadn't been tightened up in a long time and the tick looked grubby at best. I wasn't sure whether I would pick up some bedbugs if I slept on it. Anyway, it was too narrow for two anyway, so perhaps sleeping on the floor would be a better choice anyway. At least I wouldn't pick up some unwanted critters. And when I think how clean my mother was wanting me to bathe weekly. Uncle Kevin obviously hadn't bathed in a long time.

Leaning back against a chair, I soon snoozed. It wasn't comfortable, but I was tired from my long walk and I didn't have much else to do. So, a nap was the thing to do.

A couple of hours had passed when I heard steps approaching the door. At the very least, the room was now pitch dark and even when Uncle Kevin opened the door, no other light appeared until he struck a flint and steel to fire a faggot of paper that was used to light a candle.

Uncle Kevin was clearly not as sober as he was a couple of hours ago. He smelled of ale and the smoke of a dram house.

"What? Ye're still here? Well, I'm damned. I would have thought that ye'd have looked around here and gone on elsewhere."

"And where might that have been, seeing as how I don't know this city. Although, I must say I really got a tour today looking for you."

"Now don't ye be smart, young man. Ye might be y'r mother's son, but I'm still y'r uncle, and I'll not be taking any guff from a pup like ye."

"Sorry, but I'm here at least for the night. I'm also hungry. Did you remember to bring anything home?"

"Of course, do ye think I'd drink it all up? I'm not one to pass up a drink, but even I gotta eat." With that, he laid out some bread and sausages. Even though they would never compare with what Ma would have gotten, they still beat anything I had been eating on board the ship. That being the case, I set to eating them like a hog going for slop.

"Whoa, pup. Don't forget I'm eating as well." With that, he shoved me aside and began to devour the rest of the snack leaving me to sit still hungry in the middle of the floor. Rather surprised too to learn how strong he was. I needed to remember that in case he got angry.

After a few minutes eating the rest of his meal, Uncle Kevin finally turned to me asking, "Well, what's been happening to y'r mother? I ain't seen her in almost twenty years."

"That makes me ask, what made you disappear when Ma was first coming to America?"

Grinning ruefully, he replied, "Well, let it just be said that just as I had to leave Ireland unexpectedly, I found it wise to leave the Draytons. I was sorry that I couldn't meet y'r mother, but stealing a man's cattle can get ye hung as fast as stealing his deer. So, I lit out. Anyway, back to y'r ma, what's been happening to her?"

Without going into a lot of details that I have already related to you dear reader, I brought Uncle Kevin up to date. Throughout this story, he remained quiet and occasionally nodded his head. Here and there in my story, he would ask a question to get some points straight in his mind. The tale lasted for about an hour leaving us both pretty tired.

"Well, thank ye, my boy. You're coming from fine stock, you know. You never knew them, but your grandpa and grandma were good people and Wyanne took after them. They all worked hard, but Wyanne took advantage of America that her parents never had a chance to do. All they could do was work themselves into an early grave. I suppose that's why I took the path I did. If I was to die early, then I wanted it coming for something that might bring an easier life. Not that I really succeeded judging from this room."

A long pause where we just stared at each other in the flickering light of the stumpy candle. Finally, he stirred to say, "I expect ye'll be needin' to find a permanent place to stay 'cause I'll probably be needing to leave shortly. It seems I still owe people money I borrowed and I don't have a farthing to repay them. Debtor's prison is not very appealing."

With this remark, Uncle Kevin turned to bed and was soon snoring off his ale. Not having else to do, I lay down on the floor and was soon asleep.

The next morning came early with an aching stiffness from sleeping on the floor. From saggy hammocks to rock-solid boards, all in one day. It was enough to keep a person awake. But, yesterday had been a long ordeal, and sleep did come surprisingly easy.

But, today was another day. Clearly, I couldn't stay here; Uncle Kevin made that clear unless I enjoyed living with a potential jail-bird. I had to find Jeremy and see what he could offer in the way of better, more permanent lodging. Besides, it was also obvious that I couldn't afford Uncle Kevin's hospitality. He came back with exactly no change from the money I had given to him. His alehouse should thank me for sponsoring him.

"Uncle Kevin, I want to thank you for putting me up for the night."

"Y're taking off, are ye?"

"Yes sir, I think it best. You've got enough problems without having to worry about me."

"Well, not that I'd worry too much, mind ye. When the time comes, I'd be lighting out for strange country where people don't know me, and the sheriff'd be grilling ye for information about me. So, I 'spect that it's best that ye be findin' y'r own place."

"Yes sir..."

"But, don't think it's not been a pleasure to be meeting with a fine, strappin' boy as y'rself. Also, to learn what became of me sis. She's done well, I believe. Certain, better than I."

Yes, I had to agree with that assessment. Looking at Uncle Kevin carefully, I could see how once he had been a rake, able to seduce girls with a wink of an eye. But, hard living was catching up with him. His hair was grizzled and oily. A layer of fat hung loosely around his waist, and his eyes were rheumy from too many pints of ale. His front teeth were missing, giving his face a vacant look. No, life hadn't been good to him.

"I'll be giving Ma your regards when I write to her next, sir."

247

"Ye do that, ye do that. And now off with ye before I talk ye out of your last farthing."

With those words, I grabbed by satchel and left. I never saw Uncle Kevin again. When the war started, it was said he enlisted in the militia in order to get a meal and a shilling. Whether he survived or not, I've never learned. Certainly, Ma never said, but I think she was saddened by what had happened to her brother. Not surprised, but saddened. He apparently had charm and ability, but never came to anything. This failure seemed to sadden Ma whenever his name arose.

But, for me, I was off, and where was Cambridge? I was still down along the wharfs where the streets were a confusing jangle of blind alleys. Still, after asking directions every few minutes, I got going in a general direction. Along the way, I managed to catch rides with wagoneers passing by.

"Where you headed, bub?"

"Cambridge, sir. Am I headed in the right direction?"

"More or less. Hop aboard and I'll take ye as far as I can."

"And how far is Cambridge?"

"Where ye headed exactly?"

"In the vicinity of Harvard College. Here's the address I'm seeking."

"Don't know that address myself, but the college is a good five, ten miles from here, so it's good ways for you to be hiking."

This conversation was repeated several times with the mileage gradually shrinking until finally I was deposited in front of a couple of buildings.

"Well, here ye are, young man. Hope ye kin find your friend. Don't have an idea where he'd be. Perhaps if ye went inside there, someone could help ye more."

"Thank you kindly sir. I'll be doing just that."

Walking into what seemed like the biggest building of the lot, I stopped an older man and asked further directions. He knew exactly where Jeremy was staying; it seems that he had lived there once himself as a student.

Getting directions and trudging off, I found the house and knocked on the door.

"Yes, what kin I be doin' fur ye?"

"My name's Ephraim Malone, and I'm looking for a permanent room and a friend of mine, Master Jeremy Wilson. I'm here to attend Harvard and we met on a ship coming here from Charles Town."

"So ye are, so ye are. Well, young man, I don't have permanent rooms, just beds with other young men like you. If that's ok, then welcome aboard. Rent is a shilling a week and meals are extra. Let me show you your berth."

"That'll be fine sir, as I'm really tired from having trudged all the way from the Boston harbor."

"Boston harbor ye say? And what's fine lad like ye'sel' be doing down in those parts. It's a rough neighborhood, it is. I know. I was shanghaied several times into long trips from the local taverns after I was drunk."

Chuckling, he went on, "But, I was a youngster in those days full of piss and vinegar and wanting to see the world. Did so too. Saw London, Constantinople, all up and down the eastern seaboard. Aye, but I'm an old beached whale now just smokin' m' pipe and letting me wife take care of me."

"And your name sir?"

"Just call me Salt. Haven't been known by anything else for years."

"Thank you, Mr. uh, Salt..."

"Nope, no Mr. Just Salt."

"Then Salt it is, and I thank you for taking me in as you have."

Leading down a dark hall, Salt stopped before a door and pounded on the door.

"Avast, Jeremy. Ye ha' a friend here. Name's Ephraim. Would ye' be knowin' him?"

249

With that bellow, a welcome face popped out from behind the door. "Ephraim, as I live and breathe! It didn't take you long to find this disreputable place."

"No, it didn't, but considering that my uncle is a horse thief, this is truly a step up."

"A horse thief you say. Why didn't he come here instead of you? It would have been more fitting company."

"Actually, he's now on his way West I believe. But he sends his regards and hopes that I'll be a suitable substitute for his esteemed company."

Salt then spoke, "Well, ye two do know one another. So, don't just stand there, Jeremy, invite this lad in 'cause he's your new bunkmate."

"Aye sir," replied Jeremy.

"Tha's a proper reply, young man, and one I don't get too often. Ye'll do well in this world provided you don't let fast women lead ye astray."

"Only the careless ones 'll do me in. Meanwhile, Salt, I'll take this youngster in and keep him under my wings.

I was now home where I would stay for the next three years.

CHAPTER TWENTY-FOUR

March 2, 1775

Dear Ma and Pa,

As you can see, I've arrived safely here in Boston. It was a long trip and one that I'd care not to take again. That damned deck never quit rocking much to the distress of my stomach. I remembered all too often you're description, Ma, of being seasick for days on end. The accommodations and food were also mirrors of what you ate. Needless to say, I would only consider taking another sea voyage if any alternative existed.

However, on a more cheery note, I met a fellow by the name of Jeremy Wilson who is also a student at Harvard. What luck! He's about twenty years old and has been studying for about three years. Anyway, he's in his last year at school and was been guiding me around this confusing city.

Before I start talking about Boston however, I want to report on Uncle Kevin. Frankly, I did find him, and stayed a night, but it wasn't a happy reunion. I don't want to go deeply into our meeting, as it would only distress you to know what has become of your brother. Suffice it to say that he has not given up his rascally ways and in fact may now be fleeing the law by heading west. So, I am doubly fortunate to have met Jeremy. Oh yes, before I forget, I must say that Uncle Kevin does send his regards and was most happy to know that your life, Ma, has been to a good end.

Boston is a strange city. The accents here are very hard to understand being very clipped and without the languor of our Carolina drawl. There have been many times when I've had to ask someone to repeat themselves until I grasp their intent. Also, the streets…well, let's just say they were planned by the cows that once roamed the lands here. They are totally without rhyme or reason. Even long-time residents here can get lost.

Actually, Harvard doesn't lie in Boston, but rather in a near-by town called Cambridge. After I left Uncle Keven, I traveled for about ten miles until I actually found the college. After three weeks a-sea, a hard night sleeping on the floor of Uncle Keven's room, and hiking to Cambridge, I was a tired young man. Again, fortunately, I found Jeremy and am now living permanently with him and several other fellows. I have a bed of sorts, the landlord, Salt is his name, provides a good meal thanks to his wife. So, I am well ensconced in my new environment.

Classes are going well. Right now, as a new student, I'm being obliged to memorize more law that I ever dreamed existed. Every day is race between memorizing the law assignments and the setting sun when my room becomes too dark to study. When the sun has fully set, then I have naught to do but eat, chat with my fellow students, and go to bed.

But beyond studies, I've had a chance to observe the temper of this city. Amongst my fellow students, there is little talk of anything but independence from the crown. Over the past several years, mobs have ransacked the city on numerous occasions, even to destroying the governor's house once. Other scenes have occasioned hanging people in effigy. The "Boston Tea Party," as their destroying a cargo of tea is known, was amazingly the least violent uprising of these movements.

One particular name has come to my attention, and that is Mr. Samuel Adams. I have read a number of his articles, or least attributed to him, and they are most virulent diatribes. I don't know why he is attended by others either. He is not a successful man by any standards. His professions are various, ranging from being a failed postman to merchant of sundry sorts. As near as I can tell, the Crown has done nothing personally against the man. Yet, I believe he truly hates the king.

He has a distant cousin named John Adams. He is a lawyer, rather successful in fact, and a graduate of Harvard. If anyone were to be rabble rouser, he would have been my choice. I say this because he is a member of the House of Representatives and perhaps the sound of political favor in his ears would cause him to seek out the rabid rabble. Yet, despite favoring independence, he has displayed a sense of propriety. In fact, several years ago, after a tragic altercation resulting in the death of several residents, (the newspapers called it a Boston Massacre), he took on the unpopular decision of defending several of the British soldiers who were involved. He effectively won the case as well, which attests to his skill as a lawyer. I haven't met this man, but if I do, I'll describe him in as much detail as I can in later letters.

Your loving son,

Ephraim

Dear Son,   April 1, 1775

Your last letter was most interesting. I can just picture your life in Boston through your words. So, please continue writing as your mother and I are most anxious to know of your new life.

You were right about not dwelling on your Uncle Kevin. Ma was most distraught about the apparent lows to which her beloved brother had fallen. She did love him deeply even after all these years and despite his betrayal of Judge Drayton's trust. I believe now she's given up all hope of seeing him and has consigned him to his own fate. May the good Lord have mercy on his soul.

We are also gratified you have fallen into good company. The Lord was truly watching over you, and may He always do so. As far as your studies are concerned, we have never worried about them; you've always been a good student. However, as you go out in the evening, be careful of your mates. Jeremy sounds like an excellent lad, but others will always be available to lead you down the pathways of sin.

Your remarks about the fever of independence is worrisome. This particularly concerns your mother as she sees no purpose in creating problems for the king. He is many thousands of miles distant while she believes that unbridled passions of the unruly mobs of democracy will overtake the measured governance of established law. I, on the other hand, have seen and lived with many people from many different colonies and generally find them to be less so. Indeed, I begin to believe that our colonies have grown so much that we are about to swamp the mother country in size and wealth. With these developments, it seems to be only right that we Americans should have the right to decide for ourselves the taxes that will be levied.

Of course, our businesses are different. As a blacksmith, people always need their horses shod and have artifacts wanting repair. Occasionally, I even have some art work to make for the German merchants. On the other hand, Ma's business has fallen off greatly with no relief in sight so long as the embargoes continue to deny the importation of the fancy silks and ribbons she needs. Homespun simply doesn't lend itself to worldly fashions and the local ladies are reveling in their new-found "plainness." So, clearly, your mother would be much happier if the clouds of war would disappear and we could restore ourselves to the good graces of the king's eye.

With love from your father,

William Malone

War and Separation

1775 - 1785

CHAPTER TWENTY-FIVE

There are events in everyone's lives, at least in mine, when everything stops with crystal clarity. This was one of those events when Jeremy burst into our room. It was about ten in the morning. I know because the sun was well above my window frame, and I had been studying Master Jenken's law course for about an hour. My bed was still a mess, and my coffee was cold. Ice cold. The room had a chill in it because it was still April and the warm spring winds hadn't yet arrived. I'll never forget that scene for as long as I live.

I didn't know it at the time, but this scene spelled the end of my family's time in America. Not that we left immediately, mind you, but the news marked the beginning of a long slide that had us leaving Charles Town and going to the Bahamas. It also marked the beginning of the dividing conflict in my family. Eventually, my father left us to go with the rebels. My mother seldom spoke of him thereafter. This was the hardest part for us children. My parents were good; they loved us; and in their own fashion, loved each other. At least they had the greatest respect for one another.

"Ephraim! Have you heard the news?" Jeremy was just beside himself with glee. He was so excited he could hardly talk.

"No, I haven't and calm yourself before you throw yourself into a fit."

"The war has started. At long last!" said Jeremy.

"War? What war? Are the French up at it again? Or the Spanish?"

"No, you ninny. The British…"

"Of course, the British, but against whom? Better yet, who are we fighting?"

I was really stunned and stammered, "What? I don't believe this. Of course, you're kidding. That's got to be it. Ha, ha. But, this isn't just funny. It's serious. The farmers at Lexington blocked a British movement to take over this entire country and drove them back to Boston. Mark my words, Ephraim, this is war, and the King has lost his colonies."

How right Jeremy was. The colonials also lost immensely in the way of treasure, land, and family. But that was yet to come. For now, I was stupefied.

"Jeremy, what are you talking about? How can there be war between the Massachusetts colony and the King? We're all subjects of the crown and Parliament. This doesn't make sense. It's like a son taking up arms against his father."

Jeremy was not listening. He was dancing so hard, he couldn't hear my questions.

"Jeremy, for God's sake, calm down and tell me what's happening. It sounds as though war has broken out between Massachusetts and the King, which doesn't make sense. Now start from the beginning as tell me as calmly as possible what you mean."

As though he were addressing a dunce in school, Jeremy recounted the events of yesterday. It seemed as though the king had been having increasing difficulty controlling the Massachusetts colony, and he was intent on using military forces to correct this situation. Certainly, I was aware of the Boston Massacre, which by the way appears to have been started by some local hooligans and where about five people were actually killed. Not that I want anyone killed, mind you, but after all...

Anyway, things had apparently been brewing for about a year. In December, 1774, a number of men from New Hampshire captured a powder magazine. Later on, some other Americans attempted to seize a fort belonging to the crown. Later on, the Army retaliated by tried to confiscate some munitions only to be turned back by an angry mob. Last night, they attempted to take a magazine at Concord .

Apparently, some locals got wind of the Army's plans and rode forth to alert the countryside. Members of the militia gathered at the Lexington meeting house to decide what needed to be done. Among the leaders there was a Captain Parker who got together about thirty-eight militiamen to oppose the advancing soldiers on the road to the magazine.

Some heated words were exchanged in which the officer in charge was reported to have said: "Lay down your arms, you damned rebels, or all are dead men." "Fire," was his next word and immediately several of the opposing militia were slain. Of course, the Army claims that the rebels yelled "fire" first. Who was right will never be known, but the fact is that for the first time, British subjects in America were firing at British troops.

From there, the firing became hotter as more militiamen joined the fray and the troops were driven back to Boston.

"And now," cried Jeremy, "the whole colony is up in arms. Even as far as Worcester, 40 miles away, patriots are answering the call."

Turning to me, Jeremy then asked: "When will the Carolinians join in? They will be sorely needed."

Stunned, I stammered, "I don't know. I'm not sure they would even know about these events now, and I'm not at all certain they'd want to join? After all, what's Massachusetts to us?"

"What's Massachusetts to us?" cried Jeremy. "Why man, don't you know that this outbreak will, no better, must include all of us. No king has the right to enslave anyone!"

"H'mmm. Ahhh! Well,...ahhh, enslaved. What do you mean? No one in Charles Town is enslaved except of course the Africans who's natural state is to be enslaved. They really don't have the intelligence to be free, so we have to think for them. But, otherwise, who is enslaved in Carolina? No one that I know of. So, I really doubt that we'll become involved."

Well, this last remark really set off an argument. I'd like to say that we had a discussion, but that would not be the truth. Jeremy just became incensed at the thought of South Carolina, or any colony for that matter, not joining immediately into the conflict. But, he couldn't seem to recognize that most of the people in the other parts of America had no knowledge or interest in other colonies. What did we have in common with Canada? Not even a common language seeing as how most of them up there spoke French. Most of the people in New England were either small farmers or merchants whereas agriculture was usually the business of large plantation owners who got their products from England.

Anyway, as far as I was concerned, my only reason for being in Boston was to study, and that's how Jeremy and I left things between us.

"One last thing though, Ephraim. I'm bound to join the militia somehow. I've got to get into this fight before it all blows over. I'd hate to say that I just sat out these exciting times in school bent over books."

"Do as you wish, but I'm staying here. I've got no reason to do else."

Dear Ma and Pa,   The 25th of May, 1775

I'm certain by now that you've heard about the shooting that occurred here in Massachusetts. My roommate, Jeremy, whose name I have mentioned in previous letters, was so excited he could hardly talk. We had a heated discussion about whether the Carolinas would be joining the fray shortly. I opined that such would not be the case within any short period of time.

He found it incomprehensible that all of the colonies wouldn't rise immediately in arms to support Massachusetts. When I asked him why they should, the question stunned him. Clearly, he assumed that we were all united in this uprising, and when I asked him what interests the Carolinians had in this local fuss, he went on about freedom and enslavement. Funny, I had always thought that freedom and liberty were what differentiated us British from the other nations such as the French or Spanish.

Since the outbreak of these hostilities, a different excitement is in the air. One can feel the tension as though more is yet to come. I'm hoping that the king's ministers take note of it and advise him of an urgent need to address their complaints.

As for me, I'm still of two minds. One side can see the justice of Americans about arbitrary taxation, and I must admit to feeling an urge to join in the adventure unfolding in front of me. But, on the other hand, my studies on the law have clearly shown me how the wonderful history of English jurisprudence has guaranteed our liberties in a way never seen since the fall of ancient Greece.

At any rate, I'm still too young to participate in these events, as attractive as they might be. So, I'm content with my books and just watching what is happening in front of my eyes. I will keep you informed of what they see.

Your loving son,

Ephraim

Dear Ephraim,   June 15, 1775

Your letter arrived just yesterday with the most disturbing news. War of any type is just not acceptable. Not between the Irish, who have reason to dislike the English, and not Americans who have enjoyed the greatest liberties under the King's rule. It just isn't acceptable.

I'm proud of how you are working your way through these turmoil's. Yes, being young, the sap of adventure runs through your veins. I remember my trip from the Old Country and the thrill of a new, unseen life lying in front of me. I also remember wondering what I was doing while hanging over the ship's railing throwing my stomach into the ocean. Adventure became quite old very quickly. Survival remained with me thereafter. I suppose that's why I have worked so hard these years...to ensure you don't have to do so. The same is entirely true with your father.

I pray that you remain steadfast in your studies. Observe, yes, above all the activities surrounding you as they are also part of your education. But, again, remain true to your studies.

Your mother

Dear Son,   June 15, 1775

I'm taking a break from my labors at the smith to write you this letter in response to yours of the 25th. First, I must tell you that your brothers and sisters are all agog about your witnessing firsthand the outbreak of this war. They are all being besieged by their school chums with questions of what is happening. Thank God, they can only ask and not experience.

Yet, I'm intrigued about the causes of the distress that plagues the people in Massachusetts. Of course, I've never been there, nor expect to, so your observations are very important to us here. As a small tradesman, I can understand their rebellion of burdensome taxes. Every time I turn around, my business is plagued with new burdens that the Crown has laid upon us. In that respect, I feel myself in league with their complaints.

Your mother is also writing a letter to you this day, and while I don't know exactly what words she will be using, I can imagine the tone. She wants nothing to do with this war. "Stupid" is the way she describes it, and frankly, she is astounded that I have any sympathy for it at all. We have had some discussions about this periodically, and generally, just agree to disagree. When nothing violent is occurring, that is indeed a gentle way of resolving issues. But, now, I'm afraid. Our opinions are being forced to the fore by these winds of war.

As of now, these winds are just zephyrs stirred up by tempests far away. But, I truly fear they will become roaring hurricanes before they are done. I truly fear them.

Please be careful, remain true to your studies, and tell us of events as they occur.

Your father

These letters pretty much spelled the differences of opinion regarding my mother and father. As time passed and the war waxed hotter, their differences would become equally more bitter. But for now, I continued to study as the months rolled by.

I saw continually less of Jeremy during these months. For all intents and purposes, he had vanished from school. When I did see him, his talk was only of war and his drills with the militia.

Canada began to appear increasingly as a threat from the north. A "Quebec Act" that had been passed the year that the Americans were using to agitate the old British settlers there. It seems that this act had granted religious tolerance to the catholic French majority and thereby cut out the established British protestants. Americans were clearly hoping the grievances of these protestants would be sufficient to make for a fourteenth colony in rebellion. Delegates of the First Continental Congress even sent 2,000 copies of a "Letter to the Inhabitants of the Province of Quebec" urging them to join forces with their southern neighbors. These words were to become followed with a drive towards Montreal in hopes of making American dreams of a fourteenth colony a reality.

On September 5, 1775 General George Washington, who had been appointed Commander in Chief of the fledgling American army, called for volunteers to go north under a Colonel Benedict Arnold. Jeremy was among the first to respond.

"Well, Ephraim, I'm off," he announced as he strode into my room wearing his militia uniform. "We'll be departing most any day now, and I wanted to say good-bye."

I was greatly saddened, but not particularly surprised. To the contrary, my surprise would have been greater had he not enlisted. Considering his enthusiasm and time spent drilling, he could have hardly done otherwise.

"Do you know when you'll be leaving? Also, who is this Benedict Arnold? Do you know anything about him as opposed to the officers who have been commanding you these last months?"

Jeremy said, "Well, personally, no. But, his reputation precedes him as having been a successful ship's captain and trader. He also participated with some honor at the Ticonderoga raid last May, so he must be a man of some bravery."

"Do you know how long you'll be gone?"

"It won't be a short trip. Montreal is a long way off, and we'll be going through the forests of Maine, which are still pretty wild. But, I expect we'll be making a short work of the war though. Once Montreal falls, Quebec will be ours and the king will be forced to admit we have overwhelming advantages. Perhaps by Christmas, the war will be settled."

"I hope so," said I doubtfully.

"Not to worry" replied Jeremy gaily, and with those words we bade each other adieu.

On September 19, Arnold's army had boarded some ships and set sail for Canada. This event was entirely lost on me as I was busy with my studies.

The months continued to flee as my studies continued to press forward into ever more abstruse issues of the law. January 1776 came and went without word from Jeremy. I heard rumors about the attack at Montreal having failed after a daring Christmas raid. After New Year's day, these rumors became ever more substantial. It appeared that numbers of American soldiers had either been killed or been captured. Arnold's personal bravery was acclaimed everywhere. He had been wounded in the leg, but continued to press his attack until nothing was left of his force.

The Continental Congress voted to send more men to Canada, but by now the realities of war were becoming clearer to even the most rabid fire-eater. People were dying, and costs were beginning to mount. Finding volunteers now became increasingly harder. Still the war dragged on into the new year...long past the optimistic guesses of Jeremy.

Even so, the war would not go away. Arnold's campaign sputtered down the New York Lake country until it reached Lake Champlain country during the summer reaching Ticonderoga by July 20. By August, the general became an admiral organizing his forces into a boat brigade that would defend the southern reaches of the lake country. By late October, rumors of huge "Battle of Valcour Island" reached our ears. There, Arnold apparently battled against superior forces and firepower to create a pyrrhic victory for the British.

Meanwhile, the British had long since left Boston following the battle on Breed's Hill, often misnamed Bunker Hill where they lost almost fifty per cent of their attacking forces. Eventually, they took the hill forcing the remaining Americans to flee, but a terrible impression had been made in the mind of their commander, General Sir William Howe. Ironically, although General Howe and his brother, Admiral Lord Richard had never lived extensively in America, their original impulses were to be peacemakers. They actually thought they had a chance to reconcile the warring parties and reunite the colonies with the crown.

Their delusions were based on a long family relationship with the New England colonies. Their older brother George was killed during the Seven Years War and Richard had overseen the erection of a statue dedicated to his fallen sibling and his heartfelt attachment to this raw land. So, very early Richard had actually entered into unsuccessful negotiations with William Franklin to secure a peace. Such were the illusions of these actors.

The ensuing battles around Boston followed by Washington's construction of fortifications convinced the Howe brothers that peace attempts were folly and the need to consolidate to stronger bastions was needed. Consequently, they left Boston on March 17, 1776 taking as many loyalists as possible with them. Certainly these people felt shock at the prospect of leaving all they had owned and loved for generations with no hope of recovery. One such fellow, John Taylor, became so distraught as to commit suicide. But, reality being what it was, they debarked rather than remain rather than face the wrath of the rebels alone.

Several months later, the colonies gathered again in Philadelphia for their now annual convention. This time however, they did not merely debate as to how they could address their grievances to the King. They crossed a line never to be retraced: independence. The dawn of July 4, 1776 brought forth a declaration of complete and open revolt from the motherland.

The speed at which these events were turning was leaving my head spinning. As a sixteen year old student devoted to studying the law for a career in Charles Town, I could hardly imagine anything more distracting. What was I to think of the future? Were the very foundations of British law to exist after this explosion? Would France or Spain see the weakness of the empire and attack? If so, then what? Would the colonies retain their newly gained unity or would they fall into internecine war? What was my personal future? Would I be swept up in a war that truly had little meaning to me? After all, what was wrong with the old regime? As Englishmen, we had liberties undreamt of in other countries? Why destroy them on the hope of a few radical hotheads?

By July, I was preparing to return home for an extended summer. Boston was virtually closed down at this time anyway, and continued studies seemed impossible until things settled down. I had written a letter to my parents telling them of my arrival schedule, and was packing a case with clothing. The next day or two would see me off on another gut-wrenching sea voyage home when Jeremy staggered into my room.

To be truthful, I didn't immediately recognize the withered scarecrow standing before me. Only his voice identified him as Jeremy Wilson, the eager rebel ready to do war against the King.

"Ephraim, I'm here."

Once again, I was stunned, and could only stammer, "My God, Jeremy, is that you?"

"Yes, such as I am."

Indeed, closer inspection showed how truly he had spoken. He had lost about two stones of weight leaving his face a gaunt skull from which protruded eyes haunted by untold grief and horror. Further inspection showed a withered left arm that would clearly never do physical work again. It hung pendulously at his side down to a hand shriveled into a claw turned into itself.

Recovering with a shock, I quickly tried to urge Jeremy to a chair before he would collapse. Without murmur, Jeremy accepted my offer of hospitality, leaned back, and shut his eyes for long seconds. It seemed as though he was viewing a kaleidoscope of events unseen by human eyes.

Finally, he stirred, and with the grin that I had known so long before, he remarked dryly, "I suspect I've changed a bit these last months."

Speechless, I could only nod my head, but that was enough for Jeremy to ask, "Have you got any food? I can't seem to get enough in me to relieve the starvation gnawing at my belly."

Of course, I scurried around to prepare a plate of bread, cheese and water. Such was all I had as a student in my room, but Jeremy ate it as though it were a feast. Finally, he pushed his plate aside and slumped back into his chair. By this time I had begun to recover my senses and attend him with care.

"Of course, you'll stay here with me for however long you need."

"That won't be long as I'm returning to Savannah where I hope to leave this damned war behind me forever."

"What ship? The Compass Rose?" I asked.

"It is that."

263

"Wonderful, 'cause I also have booking aboard that puke bucket. Now at least we can talk."

The two days before our departure were totally uneventful. I continued to pack my case, paid outstanding bills, and notified my landlord that I most likely would not be returning. The events surrounding the war made me anxious to return home to my family. Salt and his wife understood and agreed that being with family was best for anyone. Meanwhile, Jeremy just slept and ate. Occasionally, during his slumbers, he would writhe and twist his sheets while mumbling curses and shouts. The following day, he would remember nothing of his nightmares, but I suspect they were re-enactments of all that he had seen. Such is the power of the human mind to recall and replay such events in total detail.

Eventually, the dawn's morning tide ebbed out to sea, and we both stared at the receding shoreline thinking about all that had happened to us. For me, I knew my college life had closed, so soon after it had started. For Jeremy, however, his entire youth was gone with a permanent reminder of a withered arm. Whether it would match his soul was something yet to be learned.

But, Jeremy eventually started to talk.

"When we left, the weather was brisk as our ship left Boston harbor. We were bound for Maine full of hopes and anxiety for battle. We could hardly wait to get there for after all, our enlistments were only for ninety days and to come home without having whipped the British was unthinkable. Not after the cheering send-off from the local patriots. Therefore, speed was of the essence.

"The sea trip was relatively uneventful lasting only three days dropping anchor at Gardnerston, Maine on September 22. But, that was the last easy stage we were to enjoy for the next three months until getting to Quebec. My God, Ephraim, you can't imagine just how big and wild the Canadian forest is!"

"In theory, we were supposed to travel up the rivers by flat bottomed boats until reaching the St Lawrence River. In practice, it was hauling, crawling, and keeping the boats afloat. They had been built by local contractors who used green wood that refused to retain their shape properly. Consequently, they leaked and capsized causing the loss of scarce food and munitions.

"Then there was the portage across the 'Great Carrying Place' where everything had to be transferred from the Kennebec River to the Dead River. Slave labor doesn't describe the efforts that went into this ten-mile portage. The ground was muck with no bottom. Walking meant sinking up to one's hips.

"Meanwhile, the weather was turning cold as winter approached. We were not dressed at for the rain and snow driving down on us. We were constantly soaked to the bones. This, along with the water we drank out of the local lakes, we became sick to our stomachs. As our medical officer once remarked, 'No sooner had it gotten down than it was puked up by many of the poor fellows.' And if this wasn't enough, a hurricane, yes, that's right, a hurricane blew through our camp in October to virtually destroy everything.

"Food now became a serious issue. Our commander, Benedict Arnold did not try to hide the prospect of starvation with us. But, after a meeting with his officers, we all agreed to push on to Quebec City. The lure of independence still glowed brightly within us. But food was to become even worse than we could imagine. Game was not to be shot as it had been scattered by the storms. We got down to eating our candles for the fat they contained.

"Without going into detail, suffice it to say that we arrived in mid-November at Quebec City. Whether one would call us an army or a column of ragged, starved, half-crazed skeletons would be hard to say. Behind us lay the bodies of comrades who had died or for the lucky ones, those returned home because of illness. Starting with more than a thousand soldiers, we were now down to 650 survivors living in temperatures hovering at 24 degrees below zero at night.

"Upon arriving at Quebec, Colonel Arnold learned that his letter outlining his plans for attacking the city had been intercepted by the British. This almost became a crushing blow because our plans were based on a rapid attack that would surprise the garrisoned soldiers in their quarters. This was no longer possible.

"None the less, we pressed on and after a period of time gathering what local forces we could, our attack was pressed on New Year's Eve as the wind was bitingly cold. The fighting soon heated things up, and we came so close to winning. Had only the smallest of things gone our way, Canada would probably now be another state opposing the king. And it was then that I was wounded and taken prisoner."

These tales were scarcely believable, but I could no more draw myself away from Jeremy's tale than to stop breathing although it seemed at times that was exactly what might happen as I sat listening to this incredible ordeal. What would make a soldier slog on in spite of such cruel hardships?

Jeremy paused long before answering this question. Finally, he drew a sad breath and continued his tale.

"That's a good question, one that I ask myself many times. I suspect there were two reasons, and neither of them had anything to do with my flush of patriotism last year. I was too tired, sick and cold to have concern about them any more. Rather, it was because of my friends and Colonel Arnold.

"You can't imagine how close you become to your friends when enduring such suffering. Literally, you will lay your hands in the fires of hell if it means their lives. So, quitting to leave them behind in such terrible circumstances becomes unthinkable. Rather, you slog along hoping that each step will put you out of your misery.

"The other force was Colonel Arnold. As bad as things got for us, they were worse for him. We had only to survive for ourselves. He had to survive and lead for all of us, and that, By God he did! I will never see again such a man. The fire in his belly consumed him and us. He accepted all privations without murmur or complaint, but with an honest acceptance of reality. Truly, he was a magnet to whom we were drawn as a needle to the North Pole. To my dying days, I would follow him into the very gates of Hell itself.

Such were the discussions we held for almost all of the way south. Yet, there was more to be said and more that lay heavily on Jeremy's heart. Finally, about two days out from Charles Town, he started up again. This time, however, it was not recount further his sufferings; rather, it was to unload the suffering that boiled inside him.

"Would I do it again?" he asked himself. "In fact, I can't say that I would. In fact, I know I wouldn't. It was too painful. So many good men were lost for a chimera. Even in spite of Colonel Arnold's leadership, I wouldn't do it again. The price was too high.

"As I reflect back on my memories, I see things that don't make sense. The patriots of Boston urged us to go and we did. But, who were we? The officers of course were men of some means, but the soldiers were the scum of life. I was truly the only one of my company who had had an education. Where were the sons of Adams and the other firebrands?

"As I looked about in the prison, I saw the British soldiers being well fed and dressed. No freezing for them. They were scum, just like us, but the king took care of them. What was our 'government' doing for us? Nothing, and that's all. Well yes, making money of course profiteering from whatever they could buy or sell. Where's the equity in that? We left for glory and came home grateful to the king for letting us go. All we had to do was give our parole never to return to battle."

Jeremy was not to speak of these things again during all the years I was to know him. It seemed that this ship's journey was also a journey through his soul. Later, I was live through all of his experiences and understand his despair.

CHAPTER TWENTY-SIX

"Well Ma, that's really about all there is to tell."

The last several days were a whirlwind of activity. Jeremy and I left the ship to meet my family. You'd have thought I was the prodigal son returning from his lost travels. I introduced Jeremy and of course, he was also given a prodigal welcome. He was immediately invited to remain overnight until the Compass Rose left with the dawn's morning tide.

We all had a lot to say. I had to hear of all the activities here in Charles Town. It was now being heard as Charleston, which is a natural slurring of the two words. What was interesting was how it was also being spelled in that way as well.

Jeremy of course had to tell stories about his family and his adventures in Canada. Of the former, he was always happy to talk about his brothers and sisters. Pranks at school were also a source of jokes that had everyone laughing. Canada, on the other hand, was another issue. When asked, he made passing references about the campaign could have meant to the colonies that he called America now. It was strange to hear this reference. Growing up in the colonial era, we thought of ourselves as British living in various colonies. The idea of a common nation growing from this collection still seemed strange. But, further than these off-hand comments, Jeremy was not willing to go.

When the family, and especially my brothers and sisters, saw Jeremy's arm, there was a short moment of embarrassment. Jeremy felt it, but with his usual wit, joked about his broomstick setting everyone at ease. Within seconds the arm was a settled fact not to be noticed further.

My brothers and sisters all seemed to have sprouted up. And of course, they all remarked about how I had filled out. But in fact, it was true. Two years told their tale; we all were growing. Sarah was positively becoming a young woman. She wouldn't have long to wait before callers would be making their intentions known. Of course, Pa would be adding more lines to his ancient face worrying about exactly what he had wanted to do at their ages. David had joined Pa in his blacksmith shop. Since this oncoming war prevented him from following me to Harvard, he had already started working as an apprentice. Ten years of age was not too young to start learning his trade. Vienne and Walter of course were still children eager only to play games with themselves and friends.

Ma and Pa, more than us kids had really changed in the last two years. Not physically too much, but more of a spirit. Even Jeremy noted a sense of apartness and commented on it that night as we prepared for bed.

"Ephraim, it's probably none of my business, but judging from the stories you had told me of your family while we were students, it appears that something has happened. I feel a split that I can't describe better or more."

I answered this observation with a note of relief and sadness, "Then it's not my imagination. No, thank you for telling me your thoughts, 'cause it confirms what I also have been feeling."

"Any idea what's happening?"

"Over the past two years, their letters have been showing a continually stronger split over these rebellions. Pa was never as strong as you about them, but he has apparently become more convinced that rebellion is the only course of action left to the colonies."

"I'm glad he didn't follow me to Quebec," grunted Jeremy.

"Ma, on the other hand, is becoming just as convinced otherwise. She sees this war as a useless waste of young men. In fact, her last letters were raging about Pa's attitude. She just can't see how their businesses will do anything but suffer over a useless war."

"She's a smart lady, your ma."

"You've changed a lot since Quebec. If I didn't know better, I'd swear you're a Tory."

"One-armed men have the luxury of choosing or remaining silent since neither side wants cripples."

"Still, be careful what you say. Hotheads would love nothing better than hang a cripple. Healthy men can fight back."

"Still, your ma is a smart lady."

The next morning saw us taking Jeremy to the *Compass Rose* for his leg home to Savannah.

269

"Ephraim, one last word of advice. Don't join any damn fool army simply because some damn fool rabble-rouser wants you to. In fact, when you hear them ranting, look and see if they have any sons in the army. Chances are, they won't. Damn hypocrites. It's always easy to send some other son to die."

"Jeremy, I know. This is going to be a long war and people will be losing a lot. What I'm going to do in it remains to be seen. But, I'll keep you posted."

"Please do. But, now, I've got to get aboard or I'll miss my ship."

"Give my regards to your family, and I hope to be seeing them shortly. I won't be returning to Harvard, so I'll be wanting to meet everyone."

With a shaking of hands, Jeremy boarded his ship, and I returned home. Where I was not particularly anxious to go. This rift between Ma and Pa was clearly becoming permanent. So, I meandered through the town taking in the sights not seen in two years. The market was there. Fish was being hawked and slaves marketed. The grog and ale shops were still filling sailors with drink. The magnificent houses were still being built. In many ways, Charles Town hadn't changed. Yet, as I looked closer, it had. It was bigger. Stores hawked goods where none had existed before. Checking at the newspaper, articles of Massachusetts and the war filled the headlines. This issue of independence was not to go away soon.

Eventually, I knew that further dawdling was fruitless. Since I was no longer a student, I had to start thinking about my life. It was no longer to be thought of in the future tense. It was here and now. I also needed to learn how badly the split between Ma and Pa really was.

Returning home, Ma was in her shop working with a couple of her slave girls. Seeing me enter, Ma pushed her glasses up and welcomed me home with a big hug.

"I'm so glad you've arrived safely."

"Same with me. You're right, ship sailing is not fun. Fortunately, I had Jeremy to keep me company in both directions."

"He was a stroke of luck for you, Ephraim. He gave you guidance when you arrived in Boston. After all, you were hardly sixteen. He also has been an object lesson on this issue of independence. I do grieve for his arm."

"Yes, you're right on all counts. He is a true friend. I have learned so much from him. I shall miss him. But, we have promised to keep in touch."

"Absolutely, you must do that. I had a similar friend in Susannah, you've heard me mention her many times. Well, there was nothing that I couldn't talk about with her. God rest her soul; I still miss her these many years."

We passed an hour or two chatting in this manner. Much of the time we concentrated on my experiences at school.

"I still want to be a lawyer, but Harvard is out of the question now. That means I'll have to sit for someone as a clerk until I'm qualified. With the education I got there though, I don't expect I'll need too much time before I'm qualified to take a bar exam. The trick will be finding a lawyer who needs a clerk."

"Actually, Ephraim, I think I have an opportunity for you. You remember the Draytons don't you?"

"Oh yes, where you were indentured. The Judge?"

"Exactly, and here's another point. Mr. Samuel Gordon, who was the children's' tutor there, unfortunately died. He was such a fine gentleman. He taught me to read and do numbers, and I'll be forever in his debt, but the fact is, the Judge I believe is still looking for a tutor."

Ma didn't have to draw a picture for me. "Do you think I would have a chance? Teaching his children while studying the law under him? If so, then it would be an opportunity made in heaven."

"Be careful how you talk about heaven considering it took Mr. Gordon's death, but in fact, I think you have a chance. The Master has a new wife and that'll certainly bring more children on top of the ones already needing an education."

That of course, became the path I would try to take. But, I also wanted to talk to Ma about this rift Jeremy and I felt as we entered the house.

"Ma, there is another thing I think we need to discuss. At least, I need to 'cause I've been away a long time and things have gone on here that I don't really understand."

Ma was direct in her answer, "If you mean what's going on between Pa and me, then yes, certainly 'things have been going on' here. What do you want to know about it?"

This reply was faster than I had anticipated or really wanted I guess. But, once in, start swimming.

"Over the past two years, I've been seeing a stronger divide between you and Pa about this war and the issue of independence. At this point, I'm trying to decide what to do about it. So, why don't you start with your side."

"Which do you want first?"

"Independence. I think I understand your opposition to war, and after seeing what Jeremy has gone through, I believe I understand why."

"Jeremy, unfortunately has had to be an awful example of war is all about. I didn't like seeing excited boys following Colonel Washington during the Seven Years War, and I don't like seeing boys following General Washington. Most of them don't come back."

"Yeah, but about independence?"

"Independence. That word is like the apple offered to Eve. It has a luscious ring to it and seems appealing to taste. But, what does it really mean? No one knows. When there was civil war in England between Cromwell and the crown, Ireland got invaded and we've suffered ever since. So, did the war bring freedom? Not to us. We haven't seen the end of that evil either. The Irish will fight to regain their independence. They will never quit, and untold generations will suffer."

"But here in America?"

"So, you're using that term as well? Might as well 'cause that's what we're becoming like it or not."

Time passed until Ma collected her thoughts. Then she continued, "Here, the king is a long way away, and while he may be a tyrant, his reach is weak. In his place are the colonial governments and the landed gentry who generally run things in a fairly controlled manner. What about the people out west who often are just run-always one step ahead of the law. Will they be abiding people? Who knows?

I sat and waited until Ma caught her breath again.

"Finally, and your Pa's business is not as affected as mine is by all this which makes him less able to see things clearly. My business is vitally dependent on trade with the home country. That was a lesson that I learned early on and mastered well. Now, I can't do any trading. I haven't been able to buy the fancy materials ladies here want for almost a year. Parliament has passed the Prohibitory Act virtually outlawing trade with the rebellious colonies. Of course, I can still do fancy stitching and make clothing, which I do. But that's not where the profit comes from that paid for your college."

More time passed as I pondered these ideas. Ma seemed to have spent herself and had little more to say.

"But what about you and Pa? How are you living now?"

Ma was just as direct here as she had been before. "This is exactly part of the tragedy I've been talking about. Frankly, things have gotten so bad that we hardly speak to one another."0

"The younger kids must be feeling it," I sadly observed.

"Yes, they obviously feel the strain even though we try to be civil in their presence. After all, just because we personally are having this difficulty doesn't mean we should take things out on you kids. Of course, you're an adult now, and we need to talk about them. Also, and I'll always swear to this, your Pa is a fine parent. He loves you all desperately, and he works so hard to provide whatever he can to this family."

Long moments passed. Ma seemed to be closing down on herself. For the first time, I began to see signs of age. She was becoming so tired in front of my eyes as her shoulders sagged. Leaning forward, she rested her elbows on the table and cradled her forehead in her hands. Eventually, her shoulders began to shake as tears started to stream.

"This damned war. This goddamned war. I curse it. I curse the infection of independence. I curse it and all the 'patriots' leading us to ruin. I curse them for destroying a family that was enjoying it all. I curse them for ruining a marriage to a wonderful man."

I could only sit in amazement. In all my life, I had never heard my mother use a profane word. Never when a stupid slave ruined a bolt of cloth. Never when a child destroyed a piece of sewing with a spilled drink. Never when...just never. Yet here she was, taking the Lord's name against the entire world.

"Your father was such a wonderful man. He still is. To be honest, I didn't have a love affair with him. The phrase I believe is to be 'in love.' No, that wasn't the case with us. But, when I married him and when we had you babies, we were happy. We each worked hard, we created a modest business, and we had hopes for you. People really can't ask for more. But, now look. Your college days are done, and you're forced into an early manhood. David won't even have that much of an opportunity. Your father is proud to have him in his shop, but he truly wanted more. I give Pa credit for all this and now it's all gone, and I haven't any idea what will become of us and the futures of the younger kids. Goddamn this war to hell!"

By now, Ma's shoulders were heaving as her tears welled up from the depths of her soul. I just sat there and waited. Nothing more could be done except wonder. Nothing in my life could have prepared me for this tragedy.

Hours passed, and eventually, the sun set. Pa returned home from the shop, washed up, and puttered around the house. He didn't go into the kitchen as he used to do, but rather nudged the fire a second or third time. The kids came and went, giving hugs and kisses and chattering about their adventures of the day. Ma tended the evening's supper until dishes were set and the food was laid.

Dinner came and went. Both parents talked to each other as they related to the day's events and comments from us kids. But, it was clear; they did not talk about what was happening tomorrow or beyond. The spark of creation that lit their lives was gone.

Of course, our house was so small that there was no possibility of separate bedrooms for Ma and Pa. So, in their sadness, they would each go to bed at their separate times and lie in separate cocoons of loneliness and confusion.

The next days passed in a repetition of what I saw at dinner. The younger children didn't make any mention of the separation that shocked me so. Perhaps they had already accepted it as a normal part of their lives. Certainly, the civility that Ma and Pa showed one another in their presence masked the anguish that laid under their daily lives. At least, none of my brothers or sisters seemed interested in talking about it. I could only sit in amazed wonderment.

A day after Ma and I had talked I sent a letter to Judge Drayton.

Judge John Drayton, Esq.   January 3, 1777

Dear Sir,

I am writing in earnest hopes that you can provide to me an opportunity in life that your generosity provided to my mother, Wyanne (Ferrell) Malone.

Specifically, I am a former law student of Harvard College whose career has been curtailed by the tragic events of the current war. So, I am need of any opportunity that I can find or create. Specifically, I am applying for the tutoring position that was vacated by the untimely and unfortunate death of Mr. Gordon. With my education, I am well prepared to provide education to your children. Certainly, I would continue using the curriculum that Mr. Gordon had been using.

In lieu of payment for my services, I propose to sit with you studying the law and act as your law clerk. With all of the legal affairs demanding your attention, as well as attending to the business of your plantations, I know that time is of critical importance to you. My acting as your clerk would allow your attention to be concentrated on issues more important that looking up niceties of the law.

I look forward to hearing from you. Meanwhile, my mother extends her warmest regards to you and your family,

Sincerely,

Your humble servant,

Ephraim Malone

This letter was sent off with hopes for the best. In the meantime, I started working at my father's shop. Of course, I hadn't developed any skills such as had my brother, David, but I could relieve him of many clerical and bookkeeping chores while running errands for the other smiths. Altogether, it was not a bad arrangement. It also gave me time to renew contacts with my father and brother. After all, David was an adult now and he could inform me of all that had transpired during these last two years.

One particular occasion, when work was a bit slack, and Pa was with a customer, David and I had a chance to talk long enough to get past pleasantries.

"David, you know, at least I suppose you've noticed how cold things have gotten between Ma and Pa? I just can't bring myself to watch this happy family being torn apart as it is over this issue of the war."

"It's not just the war, there's more to it than that."

"Well, what then?"

"You've been gone a long time and this issue of independence, taxation, who's doing what to whom, and the hotheads in Massachusetts is really tearing the Carolinas apart. Really, as things now stand, the battles in New England and Canada aren't really affecting us too badly. Trade has been off I think, but otherwise, I can't really see any differences. Of course, Ma complains about her trade in ribbons and silk since she can't get them anymore."

"Then what? I really can't see the point of this whole hullabaloo. People were living well, and some were even getting rich. So, what's the problem?"

"The problem that I see is that people are making a problem of it, and that includes Ma and Pa. Ma hates war, doesn't want independence, likes things as they are 'cause she understands them. Pa, on the other hand, seems wound up on this issue of 'taxation without representation'. Around here, that's all he'll talk about other than business itself. Don't tell Ma this, 'cause she'll really become upset, but Pa has even said on occasion that he'd join the army as a artificer attending the shoeing and mechanics needs of an American army if one is joined here. Of course, he'd do so as a civilian paid for his services, but I think he truly believes this is a service he needs to give to this cause."

Simply put, I was astounded. "Leave his business that he's spent decades building?"

"No, he'd leave it to me while he goes off with the Army."

This was too much for me. I had to sit down and think about it. Besides, our break was ending as the men were returning to their duties. But, I knew I'd have to talk to Pa about this amazing development.

It wasn't long before I had my opportunity. Pa had taken to going to the shop on Sundays after church, probably to avoid being around Ma. So, I tagged along on the pretext of reviewing some books.

"Pa, I really got to talk to you about what's going on between you and Ma."

"What's to talk about?" he replied laconically.

"What's to talk about? What's to talk about?" I grunted. With that question, it almost was like a fist being slammed into my stomach.

"Yes, I believe you heard me. What's to talk about?"

"Well, and this is really tough for me, being a son trying to talk with a father…"

"Spit it out, son. I suspect I know where you're going."

276

"H'mmm, ah, um…Oh, to hell with it. These last two years since I left for college has seen you two tearing each other apart. The kids certainly know about it; I talked to David about it a couple of days ago. He seems to think it's about this war and cry for independence. But, is it really that? Is there something else? Pa, can you give me a clue? I know it's tearing Ma to bits, and I'm totally confused."

Pa sat down on a stool and thought long before answering. He seemed to age under the pressure of these questions. His answers were delayed by blowing his nose, rubbing his hands over his face, sighing, and finally just looking into space.

"You know, son, I love your Ma more than anything in the world. When she and I were courting, she could make me laugh just looking at her. Our rides into the woods during those Sundays where we would have picnics and tease each other would fill my head with dreams that would last through the week.

"Then when you kids came into the world, we would sit up through the night where Ma would feed you and I'd sit by in awe and wonder. We'd talk about whatever came into our heads, and mostly it was about you all. You kids were the future of the Malone family. Ma with her sewing business, and me with my smithy. We could see ourselves sending you off to college, perhaps even to England. And then, came this damned cry for independence and war."

"Then if it's a damned cry, why let it split you and Ma?"

"That, son, is what's so damnable about it. We just can't seem to get into agreement on it. At first, it didn't seem to be a big thing. We both agreed that the taxes being passed by Parliament were not right. We also agreed that as Americans, who are really bigger than England, ought to have bigger say in what is affecting us. But, somewhere along the line, we took different paths. I want to see America become free to do whatever it wants without worrying about the kind. I want to pay my taxes to have them stay home here where I get some benefit from them. Your Ma, probably 'cause her trade is with London, doesn't want to lose her business, and she sees this movement as a threat. I really don't know…it just seemed to have snuck up on us without our knowing how or why."

A long time passed as Pa continued to blow his nose, rub his face and hands, and look even further into space.

"About a month ago, just a couple of weeks before you came home, we had a real fight. More of an explosion really where we both said some really bad things about each other and to each other. It went on for hours with me going down to the Jolly Tar and Ma sitting in the corner crying. I wasn't in any condition to make things

277

better when I got home, and we started all over again. We only quit when we were too tired to continue, and we haven't talked since then."

More time passed. Finally, I asked my father about his joining an American army.

"Oh, David told you about that did he? Yeah, I have been giving it thought. Things are so bad here now, that perhaps it might be best. David can pretty well run the smithy, and you and your Ma can tend to the books until he gets some more learning. At least, the kids wouldn't be listening to us fighting."

"Is there any way you and Ma can patch things up?"

"Not unless you're smarter than I am."

I challenged him by asking, "Are you willing to try? It'll be tough, I know, 'cause probably now you've got your dander up and it'll be hard coming down from your high horse."

"Oh taking your Ma's side are you?"

Pa's explosion came like a cannon shot. I stumbled from it, saying only haltingly, "Pa … Pa. No, that's not what I meant."

"Then, what did you mean? It seems I'm always in the wrong here."

"No, no, I'm sorry. It didn't come out the way I intended."

"Then what did you intend if I might ask?"

"Ma will also have to come down from her horse as well. You know how stubborn she can be."

"Yes," laughing ruefully, "yes, I know that. I've long since given up trying to change her mind."

And so, we talked though the day until sunset. Did we accomplish anything? I don't know. But, perhaps Pa felt better for it. At least he had a chance to clear his mind. He didn't say "no" to any chance of patching things up.

Things kind of stood that way for the next several days or so. Finally, I got hold of the older kids and organized a meeting amongst ourselves. Walter was still too young so he didn't attend but rather continued playing outside.

I addressed everyone by saying, "You know, I've been living away, and have not seen what's happened to the family as you have been living through. Frankly, as I have kind of said to each of you individually, I was really shocked by what's happened. It's so bad my friend Jeremy even noticed it."

"Welcome home," replied Sarah ruefully. "It has been awful waking up in the morning not knowing whether a fight would break out. My schoolwork has really suffered."

To that end, the others nodded agreement, but also wonderment about what could be done.

"Well, I know you're wondering what's to be done. I don't have a really good idea, but I have seen lawyers in Boston try something called mediation."

"What's that?" asked David.

"Mediation is where two people with an argument meet in front of some other person and discuss their problems. This other person will try to keep things from blowing out of control and help everyone come to a workable solution. It's kind of tricky, and I'm not sure if I can make it work."

Vianna quickly piped up here, "You know how stubborn they both are. And, they'll just look at us as kids without any say in what's going on."

I replied, "Yes, you're right, Vianna. But, I have been away for a long time, and perhaps that might get me out from looking like a child. Also, we can talk about how their problems are affecting us, and do they really want *that* to happen? Make them feel bad for us."

"What have we got to lose? Let's go for it."

With that agreement, we laid out our plan based on what I had seen in Boston.

A night later, after Pa had returned from the shop, the kids gathered around me, and I asked our parents to sit in the parlor. We had something important to discuss. Clearly, this aroused their curiosity as such a request had never occurred before. Frankly, I was really nervous about making this idea work.

"Ma, Pa, we kids here have got a problem, and we need to talk to you about it."

279

"Yes?" they both whispered.

"Yes, we do have a problem, and sadly, it seems to involve you two more than anyone. It's creating heartbreak for all of us. Sarah's talked to me about her schoolwork suffering."

"Yes," Ma said, "I've noticed that of late."

Sarah interrupted here to say, "You know why? 'Cause I can't concentrate for worrying about you two."

"About us?" exclaimed Pa.

"Yes, about you two. At one time, we were a happy family, but of late, the only thing you two do is fight about freedom and war. Isn't there anything else to talk about? How about what we're doing? Don't you even care anymore?" Sarah's eyes began to get wet with tears.

Ma instantly responded by asking what Sarah was wanting. Sarah turned to her and said forcefully, "I want you to listen to Ephraim without interrupting 'cause he has something important to say. It might even help us get back together as a family."

Ma and Pa both turned their eyes to me. "Have you ever heard of a mediator?" I asked.

No, neither of them had. "Well, it's where someone acts as a go-between when two people are fighting as you two are. Don't deny it. You've been fighting like cats and dogs. In this case, I'll be the mediator with the kids listening. It's something I saw done by a lawyer when I was a school in Boston. But, the point is, you two have got to want to do it if it's going to work."

"What does it entail?" asked Pa, a bit doubtfully.

"Really, not much. It's a step-by-step process that goes like this. Each of you will have time to say what's on your mind without interruption or questions. Then the other of you will repeat back what you heard. You won't add or subtract, just repeat back. This ensures that what was said was what was heard. Then, the next day, we'll meet again to have each of you give a reaction to what was heard. This also done without interruption and is also repeated back. You will each think about what has been heard and said, and then start a discussion that will lead to agreement between you two. We don't really care what your agreement is, but for God's sake, agree to something that leads to peace and happiness for all of us."

280

There was a long, quiet pause at that point. Ma and Pa looked both heartbroken that things between them had gotten so bad and stunned that it was us kids who had to lay it in front of them. I won't recite what all was said because their respective positions have already been well described. However, they did agree, and we went through the process. Not that there weren't heated moments where I had to step in and calm things down or interpret what had been said. The process took a lot longer than was originally anticipated. On occasion, Ma and Pa had to start over from scratch. But, they did agree to one basic point, and that was to disagree on independence and war. That was a hurdle not to be overcome. Rather they promised to lay that issue aside and work toward rebuilding the warmth and teamwork that we once knew and loved.

As these events were becoming settled, I got a letter from Judge Drayton. He thought my proposal was excellent, and wanted me to come as soon as possible. I wrote in return that a few family affairs had to be settled after which he could expect me by the beginning of March.

CHAPTER TWENTY-SEVEN

It had been many years since I had last been at Drayton Hall. When I was there, it was to attend visit Susanna's grave which was not a time to gawk about. Mother was heartbroken. She was not able to attend the funeral. Carolina weather means people are buried quickly, and a letter telling of Susanna's death arrived a week later. So, we all were packed up and hustled off to the plantation. We stayed for several days while mother renewed acquaintanceships and wandered through the many paths she once followed during her days there.

Pa knew many of the people there from his visits as a young lad, but clearly Susanna's death didn't mean to him what it meant to Ma. So, he tended to stay with us and talk a bit about his experiences. He pointed out where he first met Ma when they were both indentured. Of course, he didn't go into details, but I suspected that even then he was flirting with her. Yes, I'm sure of it as he was almost a grown man at that time with normal interests in girls. Otherwise, we kids all tended to stay quiet and play amongst ourselves.

So, now as I walked up the long entryway, I was struck with the grandeur of the home. It was about noontime with the sun beaming down fully on the house. This image was far different from the mysteriously dark candles floating in the gloom of the evening. How often my mother talked of that first impression to her new life in Carolina. Along either side of the drive were the slave quarters mentioned by Ma. Little dark children were playing in front of retired elders while awaiting their parents' return from their various duties.

Walking up the grand stairs, I fully realized now how Drayton Hall became Ma's inspiration to succeed with the chances that America was giving to her. Knocking on the front door, I was greeted by a house slave.

"Yes sir?"

"Good afternoon, I'm Ephraim Malone. Perhaps you remember my mother, Wyanne Farrell. She worked here many years ago as an indentured seamstress."

A vague look of remembrance came across her face. "Oh yes, I think I recall that name. My mother would have known her I'm sure."

"And who might that have been? My mother told many stories about her years here at Drayton Hall."

"Her name was Sally, sir. But she died several months ago."

"Oh, I'm sorry. Well, anyway, I'm here to meet with the Judge. He has offered me a job teaching his children in return for letting me sit with him to study the law."

"Yes sir, please come in. Forgive my manners. I'll call for the Massah."

With that, I was escorted into the cool, dark foyer of the house and taken to a chair where I was to sit until called for by the Judge. Thinking about that, my mother always referred to him as the Master just as this slave had done. Amazing how a generation's time can change perceptions. Ma was an indentured servant while I'm a free man working and learning as would any other professional's son. So, to me the Master was the Judge and remained so for as long as I knew him.

The young slave returned saying that the Master would be seeing me now. Following her, I went into another room where a man of rather advanced age sat awaiting me. Remembering my mother's stories of him, I had expected someone bigger and more imposing, but here was just an ordinary man in his sixties sitting on a chair. To be sure, he still looked hale and vigorous, but he was still well past the normal life span of people in the humid, sickly air of the Carolina swamplands.

Even though the temperature in the house was still relatively cool, it was obvious that comfort played a big part of the Judge's life. He was without his wig and his suit clothes were unbuttoned to allow air to circulate around his body. Indeed, I was all buttoned up and was beginning to feel a bit sweaty myself. Hopefully, I could later follow the Judge's dressing habits after I had been well installed in my duties.

"So you're Ephraim are you?"

"Yes sir. I am."

"And it's a grand welcome you have here. Your mother was an amazing person whom I have long admired. Can't say the same about your Uncle Keven though."

"I once visited my uncle when I had just arrived in Boston as a student. Frankly, I can't say that I blame you. He was pretty much of a wasted rascal."

"Rascal, yes. That's the word for him. He wasn't an evil man in that he wouldn't hurt anyone. He just couldn't help taking the easy way in life. He also couldn't help trying to sell some of my livestock." Chuckling, and remembering past days, "Yes, he was a rascal. Although I wanted to hang him, I couldn't help but like him."

Moments of quiet passed as the Judge reminisced. Then, with a jerk, he sat upright, motioned to a nearby chair, and exclaimed, "But, where are my manners? You've come this long way to teach and learn. So, let's get about with things."

"Thank you, sir."

"Let me introduce you to my wife and younger children whom you'll be tutoring," With that, he gave a loud bawling cry, "Rebecca, come in here with Ann please!"

Shortly, a handsome young lady, looking just a bit more than my own age, came scurrying in with a child of about three years of age. This was truly surprising. I guess I had been expecting at least someone a bit elder to me. And teaching a baby? I could see I had my hands full.

"Yes sir, Mr. Drayton?" Looking around, she saw me with a bit of confusion on her face until recognition dawned upon her. "Oh yes, you must be Mr. Malone, our daughter's tutor?"

"Yes, ma'am, that I am." Now that did sound silly calling someone my own age, "ma'am," yet there it was. She was the mistress of the house and that she would remain.

"That's right, Rebecca. Mr. Malone is the son of Wyanne, about whom you might have heard me mention or perhaps some of the slaves. Anyway, he is here, and he'll be teaching Ann."

Meanwhile Ann was hiding behind her mother's skirt wondering who this stranger was. Kneeling down, I offered her my hand, "Hi there. Don't be afraid. I won't hurt, and I know we'll be having lots of fun together." No response. Well, that was to be expected.

"OK, Missy," the Judge said to Ann. "You'll be on your way and after I've talked to your teacher here, you can get to know him better. Meanwhile, Mr. Malone and I have things to discuss."

With that dismissal, the Mistress and Ann left, and the Judge and I were left alone. He and I then talked for an hour getting to know one another, discussing my teaching duties, and how I would be sitting for the law. Essentially, I would be teaching Ann for a short period after breakfast until she got tired or lunch. At that time, she would nap leaving me free to read the law. After nap, more lessons until late afternoon when Ann would be allowed to play. Again, I could return to my law. Periodically, when the Judge was free, he and I would discuss issues that either were coming up in court or questions I had from my readings. Sundays of course would be devoted to Sabbath.

With that, I was turned over to Mr. George Sand who would take me to my quarters and in general introduce me to the plantation and the daily activities of life. Mr. Sand was about forty-five, and in general, a taciturn man.

"So, you're Wyanne's son?"

"Yes sir."

"I didn't know her well as I had just come in upon the death of my predecessor, Mr. Bert Smith. She left shortly thereafter. It seems that she was to marry Mr. Smith and go west to start a farm. But, after Mr. Smith's untimely death, your ma left. I think he had paid off the remainder of her indentureship which allowed her to leave for Charles Town."

Well, this was a surprise. Ma had never mentioned knowing a man prior to Pa. Of course, in retrospect, she was a handsome woman and most likely a pretty girl, and there would have been no reason for her not to have known someone. After all, she did marry rather late. Her life here and with Mr. Smith would explain why.

Perhaps this revelation was the seed that caused me to gather up these family stories about her and our family.

As the days passed, I became acquainted with other people around the Hall. Many of them had something to say about my mother.

First, there was Sam. He had known Ma before anyone else from having picked her up at the ship. Now he was an old man living in the retired shade of his house tending his garden and couple of pigs. His children were now all adults working in the fields leaving him with the naked grandchildren playing with homemade toys. In a year or two, these youngsters would also be following their parents into the fields running errands such as carrying water. Heavier duties would soon follow as they got older and stronger.

Looking me over, Sam chuckled, "Yassuh, they was yo' mother. A scrawny girl if I eve' saw one. Green too from reacting to dry land after so many months at sea. She asked me mo' questions than any two people put together that I ever knew. I had thought at first it was just because America was so new. And that was true too, but she never quit asking questions. Every day was something new."

From there, I wandered over to Mr. Killibrew who also remembered Ma. After I had introduced myself and we became comfortable, he began to reminisce about times gone by. It was clearly obvious from the tears in his eyes that he was quite fond of Ma and truly loved his wife, Susannah.

"My wife, Susannah and your mother were the closest friends I ever saw. They could spend hours sitting in front of the house just talking."

"Talking? What about, sir?"

"Oh my, there was no limit what they'd talk about. Babies, funny things about the slaves, the Master's little rages, and the Mistress. Of course, the mistress then was Miz Margaret. She died of the fevers a couple of years ago. The Master kept urging her to leave for Charles Town and stay by the sea breezes, but truly, she was too weak to go. So, she died. Now, of course, you've met Miz. Rebecca."

"Yessir, that I have along with Ann."

"But anyway, back to your mother and my wife. Susannah just about died when Wyanne left for Charles Town the second time. She knew that her visits would never again happen. Thank God, your mother wrote often. Susannah would read those letters over and over."

"Mr. Sand's mentioned my mother was going west to start a plantation?"

"Oh yes, you're referring to Mr. Bert Smith, the overseer at that time. Yes, that's true. They were engaged to be married. Would have too, except for the fact that your mother was most stubborn about finishing her indentureship. It seems your brother didn't bother to do so, and your mother was determined to make good on the family name."

Laughing, I replied, "Well, it's nice to know she hasn't changed from her youth. She's still a stubborn woman."

"That she is. She was always pestering me to teach her accounting. She never stopped trying to learn."

"Yessir, that's what Sam also recollected about her."

Continuing, Mr. Killibrew's mind roamed back over the years. "She truly loved Mr. Smith. You don't mind my talking about your mother this way do you?"

"No, of course not, it simply makes her more human, more real if you will. Otherwise, she's just 'Ma.'"

"She was almost raped by a lout, William Jackson…I wonder what happened to him? Seems he went off the Charles Town. But perhaps, I'm mistaken. Anyway, if you ever see a one-eyed man, blond, perhaps on the fat side now, he's not a man to befriend. Anyway, after Mr. Smith learned of it, he immediately went off with the Judge to the Jackson's house. There was a knife fight that left William's father dead. William couldn't fight because your mother had taken out his eye while defending herself. Anyway, like most fights, Mr. Smith got cut up pretty badly and almost died. Your mother just about went mad. She went to her room and cried. The most frightful sound I ever heard. It almost raised the hair on the back of your neck…and it went on all night. Wyanne was inconsolable. Even Susannah couldn't approach her. Well, to make this story short, Mr. Smith did live and your mother decided she would marry him."

Other stories about Ma came out. Most were trivial, but they pretty well painted a picture of a determined young woman. Of course, while I gathered these stories eagerly and began to record them, life wasn't just about collecting old memories. I had a job to do as well as learn more about the law.

One last thing, Mr. Killibrew came to me to say, "Ephraim, I think your mother would want these letters. She wrote them to my wife, and they were the treasure of her life besides her family." Of course, little did I know how valuable they would be in putting this story together.

Ann was a charming toddler. She was well along with her walking and beginning to talk. As she would let a stream of words fly, her blond hair would bob to the rhythm of her cadences. My, she loved to talk. She also loved her books which was what the Judge wanted to encourage. He understood I wouldn't necessarily teach her to read directly, but he was convinced that reading was utterly important and his children were all to receive the best education he could get for them. It must have worked because they all because very cultured people as I was to see during my time there.

Normally, my lessons with Ann were focused around play. We would both be sitting on the floor surrounded with letter blocks, paper, pencils, simple books, and of course toys. We would often start the lesson with a game of "boo" in which I would put my hand over her eyes and ask, "Where's Ann?, Where's Ann?" This would always bring giggles to her followed by a shriek of delight when I would jerk my hand away and gently cry "boo." She could play that little game by the hour. I, on the other hand, could last for only a couple of minutes before wanting to do "Something Else."

"Something else" usually was series of games of setting up blocks with matching faces. The letter "A" for example could be found on any number of blocks. Ann would have to look for them. "Where's A?, Where's A?" Almost like "Where's A?" Any of these lessons were generally very short. Often they would last only five minutes before she would want to do "Something Else" which could be drawing pictures, walking in the garden or whatever struck our fancy. I was continually amazed at how much she remembered from these "Something elses?"

By noon, Ann was hungry and a bit tired. So, we'd have dinner after which she would take a nap. If the Judge was busy, I would read from his law library. If not, then we would talk about what I'd learned and try to apply them to events of the day. Sometimes, these lessons would be applied to simple cases he was trying or sometimes on issues as big as the war. In most cases, he would force me to take a position and try to defend it with logic. Many times these positions were opposite of what I personally believed. When I asked him about this, he replied I couldn't win a case unless I understood what my opposition would be doing.

"You can't understand your opposition unless you argue his case in your mind. By doing so, you learn and understand the facts and reasoning he'll be presenting. You also will uncover his weaknesses. Likewise, his strengths against your weaknesses will become manifest and you'll see where more preparation is needed on your part."

As usual, he was right.

I suppose it shouldn't be surprising, but the Judge was a real scholar of British law and especially of its history. I'll never forget one conversation we had about it and why he generally supported the American's war of independence.
We had been talking about the war's progress to date when I asked him point blank about why he had consistently supported the Adams family in Boston.

"After all, what have they in common with you? They are from a tribe of small merchants, lawyers and petty postal workers. In your case, your economic ties are with Britain. Aren't you hurting your own interests by supporting them?"

"Good question. And in point of fact, I suppose I am. Some of my landed colleagues ask me the same question. By way of a parallel historical event, they point out how we really have more in common with the Cavaliers who supported Charles I in the English Revolution."

The Judge paused a long time before continuing. He looked at the ceiling, out the window over the broad expanse of grass, the slaves going about their daily tasks, and then, back at me.

"The Cavaliers were the landed gentry under King Charles, and they despised the upstart roundheads of East Anglia with their emphasis on business and rectitude. Charles saw they were intent on making Parliament a direct threat to his ability to rule "under God" from whom he believed all authority on earth was derived. He was also a bad historian."

Waiting again to collect his thoughts, he continued by asking, "You've heard of the *Magna Carta* I'm sure?"

"Of course. What law student hasn't?"

"And what does it mean to you?"

"It was the basis of English freedoms."

"Really? You mean that?"

"Of course, King John was riding roughshod over the countryside with excessive taxes."

"And the people rose up in demand of their freedom?"

"Yes, of course."

Laughing, the Judge replied, "Well, I like your enthusiasm, but you're wrong."

"What!?"

"It's true the king was riding roughshod, but it wasn't the people who rose up against him; it was his own aristocracy, and those knights did not care a farthing about liberties for serfs and servants."

"What then?"

"Actually, they wanted their own rights to meet in Parliament, advise the king on important issues, and to have the king live within the traditional relationships that had existed for centuries. So, they wrote a contract called the *Magna Carta* that reaffirmed those relationships and the king's obligation to obey them. It had nothing at all in common with what we call our Declaration of Independence. But, it was important, and without it, the English liberties we hold so dear could not have existed today. Without it, no basis for revolt would lay before us."

"H'mm, I'll need to think about this."

"As well you should, my friend. Here's the point. The *Magna Carta* was a political contract between the king and his aristocracy in which the king agreed to obey the law."

Exploding, the Judge started pacing the floor, "Obey the law! Think about it. Before the *Magna Carta*, the king was above the law under the principle that the 'king could do no wrong.' Why? Because as an appointed vicar of a perfect God, his every action was in accordance with God's perfect law, and hence was also perfectly above any previous action. Now, even the king observed how there was something superior to his decree and that was the decree of the law. Of course, his knights jammed this concept down his throat at sword point, and they certainly didn't think of this contract in these terms, but none the less, that is what happened in principle. The king must always govern in accordance with the law whatever that may be."

Continuing, "This issue was revisited during the English Revolution. The principle of Parliament had existed for centuries and the king had chosen to ignore it in his attempt to rule by divine right. When he ran out of money, Parliament had to be recalled, and at that point, the Roundheads seized their opportunity."

"So, what does that have to do with us?"

"Simple, the Parliament is composed of representatives of the land, the king's realm, and its voice must, by common law, be heard."

"Yes," I cried excitedly, "and that's what makes us Englishmen different from the French and Spanish."

"Exactly, but as American colonists, what representation do we have in the Parliament? I'll tell you. Zero, none, nil. And this lack of legal representation to protest unjust taxes, or any taxes for that matter, places in exactly the same position as the knights facing King John in the 12th century."

"What about 'virtual representation?' Parliament, the king, and their governors say that we colonists are represented by Parliament at large without need for direct representation from here. They point to this situation existing even on the home island."

"Surely, you don't believe that pap!" scorned the Judge.

With those words, my lesson for the day was finished. I had to return to Ann who was awakening from her lunch. But, clearly I had much to think about as played through her lessons.

The days and months passed through these activities of teaching and learning. The war continued on unabated. General Washington never seems to win a battle, but yet, at the same time, he stayed in the fray like glue. He couldn't be driven from the field. Eventually, by 1779, it had become obvious to the British that they were not to conquer the rebels in New England. Not even the betrayal of Benedict Arnold was to change this fact. Consequently, a movement was afoot for a large movement under General Cornwallis into the southern theater. The logic was to leave the New Englanders alone and concentrate on the region where more sympathy for the loyalist cause was higher and where increased protection could be given to the Caribbean trade could be protected. After all, the sugar trade there was truly the center of British financial interest.

Finally, I felt prepared to challenge any exam that Court of Charles Town could give to me. Ann had grown immensely and was ready to enter a formal education program. In short, the time had arrived for me to return to my family. I was about ready to discuss this issue with the Judge, when I got a frantic letter from Ma.

Dear Son,   December 18th, 1779

Enclosed is a note from your father. I'm heartsick as this was totally unexpected. I know we had had problems concerning the war, but never in my wildest dreams could I expect this. Now, I'm totally at a loss as to what will be done now and what misfortunes will befall us next. At this point, I can only say come home at once.

Your mother

With these words, I now looked at the note that had fallen into my hands.

Dear Ma,

This is the hardest letter I've ever written, and I simply can't understand why I'm doing so. Yet, the fact of the matter is that I'm leaving to join the war. I've sat back on the sidelines for about four years now, and I can't wait anymore.

The American army is leaving Charleston now ahead of the arrival of the British. It won't be long before no one will be able to leave, and I have to make my move now.

Perhaps you may or may not know it, but for the last several years, I had been doing work for the Americans. They were a customer and it allowed me to feel like I was making some sort of contribution to the war effort. But with their departure, I was strongly urged (perhaps drafted) to join them. I will be working as a contract sutler providing all sorts of smithing and other mechanical work. Of course, this means that several of the men and a fair amount of my materials will be taken with me. How long my absence will be is unknown. Probably for as long as the war lasts. Fortunately, David is of an age now that he can take over my position as master of the smithy. This will be a heavy responsibility for someone so young, but I know he is up to the task.

Pray for me,

Your loving husband

Clearly, with my father's sudden departure, I had no choice but leave immediately. The Judge was equally surprised to hear of this news, but he gave me a letter of recommendation to the Charles Town bar and his best wishes during these heavy times.

This departure proved to be the last time any of the Malone family saw of this distinguished gentleman. As the Americans left the region, Judge Drayton's position became untenable. His well-known activities in the rebel cause made him a prime target for the British. So, he left his home for safety and while gone, died within a few months. Ultimately, the ardors of travel and illness caused by yellow fever claimed a true friend.

My arrival home was a somber event. Everyone was completely at a loss. My mother, in particular was as distraught as I had ever seen her or ever would see her.

"Ephraim, I can't tell you how badly I feel. There's a hole in my soul that will never be refilled. Your father wasn't the love of my life; Mr. Smith was. I know you know about him. You couldn't have helped not knowing about him from living with the people at Drayton Hall. But, your father was a good man, and I married him with a good heart knowing we would build a modest living, have a large family, and grow old together in this new land called America. Now it's all gone."

"Would you have Pa back if he returns from the war?"

"At this point, I can't say. On the one hand, I know he has acted with honorable intentions for the Americans. It's not as though it was for another woman or such as my brother, Kevin's departure. He was just enraptured with this drive for independence from the Crown. But, on the other hand, to leave a family struggling to survive in these hard times,...I really don't know."

"How is David doing?"

"As far as turning out the work, well enough. He has a talent for working iron, that's for sure. But, meeting people and selling work, tending to his books, etc. are beyond him. We'll all have to pitch in and help him. But, all in all, that's not the worst of things. Actually, now that the British are returning, I'll be able to get supplies from England that I know women will buy." Ruefully, "These self-righteous 'patriots.' They want the sons of other mothers going off to war, but they want to

293

keep their sons and ribbons. So, to hell with them. I'll sell them their damned ribbons."

The next several weeks were incredibly busy. I met with the Charles Town bar and took my exam. It was hard, but the Judge had prepared me well, and I passed it to become the newest lawyer in town. David and I surveyed the mess left behind by Pa and determined the sort of work we could still do and the jobs we could undertake. Lacking the men that Pa had taken with him greatly reduced our capabilities, and with all other young men gone to war, replacements could be found only from the retired ranks. But, eventually, life took on its own tempo.

The girls continued to attend school. Ma's business actually began to improve with the relaxation of the earlier embargoes. I started looking for legal work to do, and the occasional job came in.

Eventually, a letter came in from Pa. Although it was received with a sense of bitterness, it was word from someone who loved us.

Dear Family,   February 3, 1780

I expect you will probably read my words with a sense of reluctance. Considering how I left you, I wouldn't blame you if you burnt this letter without reading it. But, I have to tell you all how much I miss you and love you. Again, these words must sound false, but it's true. Every night, I go to sleep with an ache that is indescribable. But, I know what it is. It is a longing for you that doesn't go away. I know I don't have the right to do so, but please pray for me.

Army life is extremely bad. We have been living in the deep woods living off whatever can be gotten from nearby farms. We try to offer payment, but the American money is so badly debased, few will accept it. So, many times we have no alternative but to confiscate what we need followed by a forced payment.

Meanwhile, as we await food, we are often forced to eat whatever is available. On occasion that has included boiled bark. I have actually seen soups made from shoes. Such is the madness of hunger.

The camps are very dirty. The commanders try to encourage us to keep them clean, but usually without avail. Many men must have been raised in a pig sty such is their sloth and dirtiness. Consequently, I must believe that disease is the reward for such inaction. To help protect myself, I undertook a small pox vaccination. Why it works is not well understood, but basically it amounts to making a small cut and smearing the pus from an infected fellow. Of course, I broke out with a mild case of the pox, but it brought only minor discomfort and none of the scarring that a full-blown case leaves behind.

Since arriving, I have been offered a commission as a support officer that I have accepted. Running a business under these conditions is a difficult enterprise that is full of risk. Being an officer will relieve me of this problem and also provide a pension after the war.

This job doesn't bring much glory. In fact, we are somewhat regarded with disdain by the line officers. But the simple fact remains that wars cannot be conducted without the support given by men such as myself.

With these words, let me close by sending all of my love to each of you. Please forgive me for what I've done.

Your loving Pa

These were the last words we heard from him. A few weeks later, we got a letter from some officer whose name I have forgotten saying that he was stricken with Yellow Fever and died soon thereafter. The letter went on to say how proud we must all be of his sacrifice to our new country. Ma actually went outside and threw up. The younger children just cried as they realized how they would never see him again.

Of course, there was no funeral. Pa was simply buried in an unmarked grave somewhere in the Carolina woods. To this day, I never learned where he was during his last hours.

As 1780 pressed on, another event occurred that would again change my life. By now, the last of the Americans were leaving the city as the British assault on Charles Town ensued. Sarah had gone to the Market Place to get some fish and make some deliveries along the way. She hadn't been gone for more than an hour when she returned. She was truly a picture of horror as I saw her.

"My God, Sarah," I cried. "What happened? You look like you had a fight!"

Sobbing, Sarah could only nod.

"You did have a fight? Then why? How? Who?"

Sarah was not to answer these questions for many minutes. First, she had to continue crying as I held her like a child. Gradually, her weeping was heard by the other children as they were returning home from school and play.

Coming home from work, David was the first to come upon us as we sat in the back area of our house. I explained to him what I knew. He in turn shushed the other children upstairs and told Ma what happened.

"Sarah, what's happened?" Ma asked as she took my place hugging her. Eventually, Sarah calmed down enough to begin talking.

"I don't know Ma. I don't know what I ever did to that man. I don't even know who he was!"

Tensing, Ma waited a long time for Sarah to continue.

"I was returning from the market passing an open lot when they came out and dragged me back to a field. As two of them held me down, a third fellow laid on top of me and stuck his thing into me. My God, it hurts. I've never felt anything as terrible. No matter how much I squirmed, he was able to force himself. Oh Ma, will I ever feel clean again?"

"Sarah, I hate to ask this of you, but can you describe them?"

"The two who held me down were ordinary fellows. But the one who laid on me, I'll never forget. He was a little fat, greasy blond hair, and had one eye."

In substance, this was all that Sarah ever said about this incident. She would never discuss it to anyone. She also never married. Rather, she stayed at home, learned Ma's sewing trade, and rarely strayed far from home. No encouragement from anyone would ever remove the sad, haunted look in her eyes.

Meanwhile, Ma went deeper into her despair that had settled upon her since Pa's departure. Her bitterness toward the war and independence movement grew ever more foul.

Little was said to the children since they couldn't have understood what had happened anyway. As for me, I spent the next several days looking for a ghost from my mother's youth, but William Jackson was not to be found. As I searched for him, I talked to several other friends about wanting to find him. Of course, I didn't go into details, but it was clear that Jackson had done something awful to the Malone family.

Eventually, it became clear that our local search was fruitless. Further action was needed. Two generations torn by the terror of this lout was enough. Terror needed to be returned. This had nothing to do with the public law. Knowing what Mr. Smith and the Judge taught me the difference. This was private, family matter.

"Ma, I think I need to be taking a trip."

"A trip? What? Where will you be going? And for how long? And Why?"

"Let's just say that I'll be gone with some friends to take care of some untended business. The less you know at this point, perhaps the better."

Ma looked grimly, and didn't say anything other than to admonish me to "be careful." Things had gone on too far for her to push matters.

That evening, two friends, Jeffery and Mark, came by the house. Together, we walked to the blacksmith shop where we got some horses. They had been left there for temporary boarding, and no one would miss their disappearance for a few days. From there we left for the ferry across the Ashley River. We arrived just in time to catch the last trip to the other side.

From the river, we progressed up along the road past the Drayton place and several other plantations en route. In the early pre-dawn, we arrived at our destination: the Jackson house. As we rested our horses, we observed a quiet, ramshackle hut that clearly showed the effects of poor maintenance.

"Are you sure you want to go through with this?" I asked Jeffery and Mark. "This will not be like hunting doves. It might also mean you might be marked as murderers. So, think carefully before starting."

"Are you still going through with it?" asked Mark.

"Yes, this is a private, family affair that requires a strong, personal reply. The law has no business here."

"I don't know exactly what happened that has gotten you so riled, but I can imagine, and you're right, the law's got nothing to do with it.

Jeffery then asked, "If William isn't there, then what?"

"What then? There's nothing. This has been going on for about twenty years starting with my mother, and it's not going any further."

"You mean, just ride away and continue looking for him?"

"You have it half right. If William isn't here, then I'll continue looking for him. But other than the three of us, no one else leaves here alive."

"Kids too?"

"All of them. William was a kid at one time when he attacked my mother. I'm not about to leave other kids to do similar things to other people."

There was a long pause. Clearly, this possibility hadn't occurred to either of my friends.

"Kids too?"

"You heard me the first time."

"How many of them are there do you reckon?"

"I really don't know and really don't care. Only the three of us will be leaving here. One way or the other."

Finally, Jeffery came around to say, "I'll tell you what. I'll take care of any adults that come out, but I won't touch the kids. That's something I can't do."

"That's fine. Mark?"

"You're absolutely sure it's the Jacksons?"

"Yes."

Another pause.

"Then let's go."

"Got your guns primed? Torches ready?"

"Yes" both replied.

"Then let's go."

The raid itself was rather simple. Twenty minutes finished the entire task. We stacked some brush up along the house and torched it. Because of the late hour, everyone inside was asleep, and we were quiet enough not disturb them. A hound came by and nosed around, but quickly lost interest and curled up to continue sleeping. Then we threw fire on top of the roof. Slowly, the flames began to lick the dried wood of the cabin. Smoke seeped inside awakening the people inside.

"Hey Maw!" cried a young man's voice. "The house is on fire. Let's get out of here!"

The rest was simple. As they poured out the front door, the Jacksons were cut down like sheaves of grass. Mark had all of our guns and shot each person as they poured out. Meanwhile, Jeffery and I stayed by the windows. A couple of the Jackson kids crawled out, and as I had promised Jeffery, I took care of them with single slashes of my axe.

It wasn't long before the remaining one or two members of the family understood how certain death was awaiting them. Consequently, they elected to remain inside hoping we would leave before they died. That was their choice, but it had the same ending. Not a single person remained alive. It was like shooting fish in a barrel.

We turned the bodies over hoping to find William, but without luck. The remaining two in the cabin were hauled out and checked as well. While a bit scorched, they had died of smoke inhalation and heat. The fire had died down before they were unrecognizable and we were able to determine they too were not Sarah's rapist.

Finally, Mark said, "Ephraim, we've got to be going. It's almost light, and eventually someone's going to be coming by the road in front of this house. We need to be gone."

"Yes, you're right. We've done what we can here, and there's no point staying any longer."

With that, we mounted our horses and were about to ride out when I stopped by the dog. Getting down, I whistled softly to it bringing it to me. As I was patting its head, I reached behind me and found my knife. Five seconds later, the dog too was dead as blood poured from its throat.

Jeffery was astounded. "What did you do that for?," he demanded. "It was just a dog, for God's sakes."

"Remember before we came here, I said only the three of us would live to ride away? Well, I meant what I said. That included the Jackson's dog as well."

With that, we rode away.

Our ride was quiet. No one really had much to say. Of course, my friends knew what would be happening and had continued on. But, now, with the deed done, its enormity sank on them like a heavy weight. In point of fact, while we never once mentioned this night again, our friendship had dissolved that night. Perhaps, in retrospect it was too much to ask of them, and had I to do it over again, I probably would not have asked them. Not that I felt any guilt. William Jackson had attacked two women in my family, and I was determined that no Jackson would ever do that again. Even the dog.

We got home around six o'clock the following evening, and each went their separate home. Supper was waiting for me. The younger children were playing quietly or doing homework. Sarah was upstairs in bed. Ma had little to say.

"How's Sarah?"

"She's upstairs asleep. In fact, since you left, that's about all she's done. Almost like she doesn't want to wake up."

"Probably not, considering what's happened to her."

A long, quiet time passed as I finished eating. Finishing off the last of my stein of beer, I turned to Ma, as if to ask what will come next.

"Supper's done; hope it was enough."

"Yes, ma'am. It was. But,,,now what? What will happen with Sarah?"

"Frankly, I don't know. Actually, when I was sailing here to America, I was about her age, and a sailor tried to attack me. How I got away, I don't know. Then of course, there was William, but I had learned to carry a needle that took out his eye. He probably had known of Sarah and planned to do this for a long time...probably in revenge for what I had done to him." A long pause followed by a sigh. "I don't know what will become of Sarah. I guess I was more alert to the possibility of rape on shipboard where Sarah did have the slightest chance." Another pause. "I only know we can only give her our constant love."

Several minutes passed, when Ma turned to me asking, "What will become of you now?"

"What do you mean?"

"Don't be daft son. Most everyone here knows something terrible happened to Sarah, and when the Jackson family is found dead, it won't take a genius to figure out who killed them. That's why you went there wasn't it?"

"Yes."

"Did you kill him?"

"No, he wasn't there. He may have gone off with the American army. Probably did. But the rest of the family is surely dead, and one day, with luck, William will follow them to Hell."

"Anyone go with you?"

"I'd rather not say. The less you know the better."

"Sounds reasonable. But, now, what are you going to do? Where will you go? You can't stay here."

"You're right, I can't stay here. How long I can be gone, is anyone's guess. Probably several years until things calm down and people forget about the Jacksons."

Time passed as we both sat is a seeming stupor. I really hadn't thought this aspect of murdering the Jacksons through. Just killing them seemed to be enough. But now, it clearly wasn't. I needed to go someplace where I could hide and survive.

"Ma, I hate to say this, but it appears I've really gotten myself into a jam."

"Yes, that you have son. As a lawyer, you clearly have no defense legally about what you've done. You know the consequences of murder and you chose to do what you did. So, you really need to leave immediately if you don't want me to attend a hangman's party in your honor."

Surprisingly enough, Ma then continued with an idea I would have never expected from her.

"I've had some trade with the wives of British officers, and they have talked about a cavalry commander of some renown. His name is Lt Colonel Tarleton something or other. I really don't know his name for sure. But, anyway, he'll be leaving town shortly, and from I understand of him, he's not too particular about who enlists in his army. You ought to look for him tomorrow morning and enlist."

"Ma, do you know what you're saying? You've hated war all your life. Pa left you and he died. Now, you want me to join up?"

"Amazing isn't it? I have to send my son to war in order to keep him alive. Goddamn this all anyway!"

301

We talked about this until late at night going over the pros and cons of this plan. Finally, several things became clear. One, I was in real trouble and needed to stay away until the Jacksons were well forgotten. Two, I needed someplace to live where I could be supported without questions being asked. The military seemed to offer a way out. Of course, the American army was out of the question, so what was left? The British army, and Tarleton's Legion.

Finding the Legion was not too difficult. I just looked for a green uniform and asked where I could go to enlist.

"Enlist, do you want now? A gentleman such as yourself? And why'd ye be wanting to do that? The colonel don't run a lady's sewing circle."

"Let's just say, I'm tired of rebels trying to tell me what to do. I want to remain loyal to the crown, and joining up is one way to do it."

"What's this? A patriot?"

"Put it as you wish, but I'm here to kill Americans, and one in particular if I find him."

"Killing it is, you're sayin' now! That's language I understand." Standing back, and looking carefully at me in my lawyer clothing, 'talkin' is one thing, be ye able to do it? 'Cause while the colonel wants strappin' boys able to wield a sword, he don't want nobody who'll get sick at the last second."

"You'll not know until you see me will you? But, let me put it this way, I have my reasons to kill, and given a chance, that's what I'll be doing."

"Have ye got a horse or two?"

"How many do I need?"

"Two's plenty."

"That's easy enough."

"Then, let's get on with things. I'll take you to the recruiting sergeant and he'll have you in the Army by sundown."

"I have family here. Will I have time to say good-bye to them? Besides, I'll be needing to get my horses."

Eyeing me suspiciously, the soldier said, "Right you are about your horses. Tell you what. I'll follow ye home, and give you five minutes to get your things and say your good-byes."

"That'll do fine. Let's go."

And that's how, in the Year of Our Lord 1780, I came to join the Army and become a loyal soldier for His Royal Majesty, King George III.

CHAPTER TWENTY-NINE

Later on, after the War, Ma commented shortly about how she felt and what she saw of me.

"After Ephraim left, the destruction of our home was complete. William was dead for months and buried in some unknown hole. To this day, I really never understood what motivated him. What started out as a simple disagreement over the colonial rights gradually brewed into a witch's tea of argument, recrimination, and icy silence. Even after we reconciled when things became at least bearable, an unspoken divide existed. It was never mentioned, but behind the kind gestures and gentle laughs, it was always there acknowledged by the silence.

"So, this damned war destroyed a home that was once full of hope and happiness. Five children were born into it with the promise of a new land and opportunity. Two businesses once flourished only to decline into survival. Once friendly neighbors grew cross with one another. My son, Ephraim slaughtered one in its entirety because of the turmoil that permitted a foul son to roam free under the guise of a patriotic uniform.

"Ephraim himself, once the stalwart hope of the family, became twisted beyond recognition. Originally, an upstanding man dedicated to the law and its proposition of civilized rule, he turned almost overnight into a murderer of almost monstrous proportions. Of course, Sarah was unspeakably violated, and I well remember the reaction of Bert Smith when William tried to attack me, but his attack was singular and focused on one person.

"Ephraim seemed hell-bent on killing every American he can find. Ironically, when he slaughtered William's family, William himself was not there to be included among the victims. So, he escaped, and Ephraim made it his obsessed duty to search and destroy once again this haunt from my past. Let me read some lines from one of his letters. It's dated April 22, 1780 and typical of his thoughts.

Dear Ma,   April 22, 1780

I've been in Carleton's Legion for about a month now, and it's nothing like I could have imagined. This experience has shown me the heights and depths of what men can do to one another.

On the one hand, my mates are slowly accepting me. Some of them have been following the Colonel Carleton for years now and

I'm just an upstart to them. However, amongst themselves they show an intense concern and sense of caring. After all they have suffered together, they have formed a band of friendship closer than any existing between a husband and wife. When one is sick, the others will do without in order to provide help.

By contrast, as we pass through the woods, our paths have crossed the burned out homes of poor farmers. When asked what army did this foul deed, their reply is often "our neighbors," the Judsons or Smiths or what have you. One family is a Tory and the other is a Rebel and their hatred is as deep as the war itself.

I know at this point, you're wondering about me. Yes, you're right. I too am swept up in this fire. For all that William and his ilk have to done to our family, and as God is my witness, I'll bring him to justice. No matter if I go through this land like the Four Horsemen of the Apocalypse, I will hunt him down and shoot him for the dog that he is.

Brave words for someone who has done nothing but sit on the back of a poor horse these last weeks. Besides a couple of days of training so that I can recognize an officer from a sergeant and perhaps some close order drill, all we have done is chase after the American General Greene. Our travel has taken us from Charleston, through Camden, and beside some posts in Augusta and Ninety-six. Apparently, this all being done to secure British rule over the Carolinas or at least South Carolina.

Pa was right about one thing. Army life is hard. The food is bad or often non-existent. Like the Americans, we often have to extort it from the locals, although the British Sterling is more welcomed than any local currency, usually called a "Continental." Keeping clean is a problem. We've been marching so hard that little time or energy is left for hygiene. Consequently, men fall by the wayside each day as a result of their fatigues.

All this is probably distressing news to you, but it's important that I write of what I see or feel. If I didn't, I would probably lose my mind. So, as things happen, I'll send letters to you.

Your loving son,

Ephraim

"There, you can catch a glimpse of what I mean. 'The Four Horsemen of Apocalypse' indeed. What destruction did Ephraim bring to families in his mad search for a lout who probably has no idea of what he had done? As much as I dislike the Americans for what they started in their drive for independence, I begin to realize most of them are not much different from we who have remained loyal to the Crown. They have families, hopes, dreams, passions and disappointments. Most of all, they just want to be left alone. Unfortunately, these times have stirred emotions and self-righteousness to point where differences are not allowed to exist. One must choose and suffer the sad consequences of their decision. In our case, I can see how our own idyllic lives here in Charles Town have come a sad close. Eventually, we had to leave friends and fortune for a new life on a strange island for reasons that in retrospect don't really make much sense."

CHAPTER THIRTY

Lt Colonel Banastre Tarleton was just my kind of leader in those days. Sarah's rape by William Jackson and his attempted rape of my mother along with the general hostility my family continually felt from neighbors as a result of our not being rabble rousers for the colonial revolution, had slowly boiled a canker of hatred within me. I truly wanted to kill anyone who supported Washington and his ilk.

Colonel Tarleton was twenty-six years old; hardly my senior in age, but greatly my senior in rank. He had been born of a wealthy family in Liverpool and educated in Oxford. Seeing a chance to gain glory in this war, he had joined the King's Dragoon Guards early in 1775 and been engaged in a number of battles. Consequently, he had risen rapidly to his present rank and command of "Tarleton's Legion."

Our unit, formally known as "The British Legion," were dragoons or mounted infantry. Able to move quickly and consequently, we were used as scouts in the advance of the British forces. When chasing the Americans, we were often used as harassing forces against any rear guards posted by the enemy. During battles, we could make sweeping maneuvers to flank the lines of opposing infantry.

This organization was unique in how it was composed of both regular British soldiers and loyal colonials such as me. Our uniforms were also unique in their colors. As described in a London newspaper:

> The cavalry that Coll. Tarleton commands is a provincial corps, and makes rather a singular figure; for as service has been consulted more than show ... their uniforms are a light green waistcoat with skirts, with black cuffs and capes, and nothing more. Their arms consist of a saber and one pistol. The spare holster contains their bread and cheese. Thus lightly accoutered, and mounted on the swiftest horses the country produces, it is impossible for the enemy to have any notice of their approach till they actually receive the shock of their charge.

This unusual color actually led to a humorous situation, or at least it could have been had not an alert soldier noticed an unusual passage by Colonel Tarleton's counterpart: Lt Colonel Henry Lee. Known as Light Horse Harry, he was two years younger than Colonel Tarleton, but renowned for his dash and daring cavalry tactics. Eventually rising to Colonel during the war, he had outfitted his men with green waistcoats and buff pants very similar to ours.

Anyway, shortly before I enlisted in the Legion, it was playing a cat and mouse game with Lee. He had chased us back into the Carolinas until we had crossed the Haw River. Thinking ourselves secure for the evening, we made bivouac and settled in for a relaxing evening.

Meanwhile, Lee had continued pressing toward us. He must have already learned we were well settled in without realizing how close he was to us. Anyway, noting the similarity of our uniforms, he proceeded to infiltrate directly amongst us with the idea of a raid. Soldiers literally passed each other in the dead of night without anyone noticing what was happening. Fortunately, for us, a sharp-eyed solder noted some rebels in a near-by thicket and sounded the alarm.

Of course, the jig was up for a Lee and without further ado, he and his men scattered into the wilderness with no more than a few shots being sounded on either side. Of course, our anticipated evening of ease was destroyed as we mounted a secure guard while preparing for an early departure at morning's first light.

But, to give Lee his due, we all had to admit, his daring was superb and as such was a worthy enemy to whom great honor should be given. In fact, throughout the Southern campaign, he doggedly nipped at our heels. Sir, we salute you.

Just after this now funny episode, I joined the Legion and promptly started my training. Mostly it consisted of learning to distinguish officers from the enlisted soldiers, drills, and the manual of arms with our weapons. Horsemanship was not too much emphasized as we were expected to be knowledgeable about riding and caring for our animals. Any riding we did trained for was mostly riding in groups such as assembling and carrying sprints for a charge.

This training was somewhat given on the move as we were continuing the cat and mouse games I had described earlier. So, much of my training came from the other soldiers as we bedded down for the evenings or as we rode along. Mostly they were glad to provide this instruction as our sergeants were busy taking care of the many orders issued by the officers. I quickly learned by watching them that non-commissioned officers were really the backbone of the Legion. Officers gave orders, and we lower enlisted obeyed them. However, the sergeants turned vague orders into precise directions for us to follow. I can't say I really liked my sergeant because he was rather rough about doing things; but, he did get his job done.

But, mostly, life was a matter of constantly moving. Occasionally, we would have a skirmish, but mostly during these early weeks, life was just a long series of marches. Our horses, never really got much a chance to rest, and so they became rather scrawny and tired. As their condition deteriorated, we found ourselves marching afoot more and more with each passing day. Otherwise, if we were to ride them, they wouldn't be of much use to us during battle.

Generally, during this period, we headed south and east toward South Carolina which was under siege. Eventually, by mid-May, Charleston had fully surrendered to the British, and the American Colonel Abraham Buford was ordered to retreat into North Carolina. Colonel Banastre was consequently ordered to reverse direction and follow him. Of course, knowing from where Colonel Buford had left, I was more than happy to go along. I'd follow him to Hell if need be, just so long as I eventually caught up with a certain William Jackson.

Actually, I wasn't to wait for very long for satisfaction with Mr. Jackson. We had chased Colonel Buford's group to a place near Lancaster, South Carolina where we made contact with his rear guard. The date was 29 May 1780; I'll never forget it.

Colonel Buford lined his men up in a frontal rank ready to fire upon us as we rode pell mell towards him. Normally, under such conditions, the defenders wait until their opposites are within just a few yards before unleashing a tremendous volley. With infantry, such firepower is usually enough to cause the attackers to slow down or to fall back. In this case, the mass and speed of Tarleton's 270 horsemen was such that they rode through the volley, and before a second one could be unleashed, the Americans were surrounded and the slaughter began.

Colonel Buford, seeing the hopelessness of further fighting ordered a white flag of surrender to be raised. Colonel Tarleton immediately rode toward it when a shot rang out that toppled his horse. Convinced the Americans were falsely fighting under the flag, my comrades started again their slaughter that became known as "Tarleton's Quarter" among the rebels.

Here's the real story. By happenstance, I was fairly close to my commander when I saw a spark from a raised rifle. Immediately, I headed for it to protect Colonel Tarleton and as I came ever closer, I began to believe I saw my man. Yes! It was him! His greasy blond hair and weak, scarred face where my mother had scratched his eye out so many years ago were plainly visible. Nothing more was needed than to spur my horse with saber raised. Sweeping by him, William's rifle was raised as a useless shield against the blow about to rain down on him. And, in fact, it came with such force as to amputate his right hand. Sweeping past, I immediately wheeled my horse to bear down again. This time, Mr. Jackson was unprotected allowing me to slice through his bowels. He went down mortally wounded. Meanwhile, the battle ensued.

309

Seeing this, my attention turned to the rest of the battle. Who I killed is impossible to say. It was just a matter of trotting around and picking off rebels remaining upright. Others were doing to the same in their revenge for the knavery shown to our commander.

Within minutes, the engagement was done except for me. Going back to Mr. Jackson, I dismounted and knelt beside him. Amazingly enough, he was still alive with fear streaming from his one good eye.

"Hello, Mr. Jackson. And how are we today? Well I hope."

No reply.

"You probably don't recognize me since we've never met. But you certainly know what happened to your family several months ago. They're all dead aren't they? Well, cast your eye on who did it. Yes, I burnt them alive. You know why? Probably not, but do you remember a young lady twenty years ago named Wyanne Farrell at the Drayton Plantation? Of course you do. She cost you an eye. What you might not remember is my sister, Sarah, whom you raped. But, again, perhaps you do.

Slowly, a glimmer of recognition flickered across Mr. William Jackson's face. He also was wondering what would now be happening.

"Yes, that's right. You're dying, but that's not all that will be happening to you."

With that I opened his breeches and pulled out his male appendage, and with my bayonet, hacked it off.

Grabbing his mouth to force it open, I jammed his appendage into it saying, "Now turnabout is fair play isn't it?"

With that, and with his screams in my ears, I got up and walked back to my horse.

After returning to our assembly, Colonel Tarleton came over to me.

"Good work, solder. You surely saved my life."

"I was only doing my duty, sir."

"Yes, you were certainly doing that as I could see. You particularly did your duty with that one rebel. He'll never be of use to them...or to any female."

"That was my intent sir. Without going into details which the Colonel would not want to hear, please be assured he deserved all that and more."

Looking at me for some seconds, wondering what my reference was, he finally remarked, "You're an educated man aren't you?"

"Yes sir. I've studied at Harvard and am a lawyer."

"Harvard? Not Oxford, but good enough school. And a lawyer to boot! So, tell me soldier, what's your name and what are you doing here? You certainly could have gotten out of military service."

"Ephraim Malone, sir. And to put things bluntly, I'm here to kill Americans. As many as possible."

Grinning ruefully, the Colonel replied, "Well, you've certainly been doing that successfully. Your zeal is to be commended; but, does it have anything to do with that screaming lout over there?"

"That among other things sir. These damned rebels have basically ruined a good, happy family. My mother is a widow of a dead rebel father and I have a sister who was violated in a most foul manner. I started killing before I joined the Legion, and now I find it brings even more opportunities to continue."

Now, the Colonel was looking deeply into my blank eyes staring straight ahead. No life was to be seen in them as it had departed from my soul months ago.

"Yes, I believe you, and can understand what you mean," he sighed. "But, I've lost a couple of good officers lately and I need replacements. So, with your education and desire to inflict damage on these damned rebels, I can use you in a capacity greater than what you're now capable of providing."

Slapping his leg with his quirt, "Mr. Malone, you're now a lieutenant. Effective immediately. This means you're out of uniform, so upon return to camp, your rank needs to reflect this change. After that, I'll see about ensuring you get your wish to kill Americans."

Before I could reply, the Colonel turned on his heel and went to check on the rest of his men. And this was how I became an officer at the ripe age of 20 years of age.

Following this grand ceremony, we headed towards Cornwallis who was taking command of the Southern Theater of War. Recognizing this area was actually

311

more sympathetic to the king than was true in New England, he had been ordered by his superior, General Clinton, to wrap up any last vestiges of rebel resistance here and at least hold this territory.

Meanwhile, things seemed to auger well at first. We met the American general Horatio Gates at the Battle of Camden in August 1780, where Tarleton's Legion played a singular role in the victory. Exactly as he promised, I had lots of opportunities to kill Americans. In fact, Camden was proclaimed by even the Rebels to be the worst defeat endured during this long, bloody conflict.

General Gates then showed his true mettle by abandoning the field and riding like a whirlwind through night and day 180 miles until he reached a measure of safety in Hillsboro, North Carolina. It was not long before he was sacked. Too bad. With generals like him, our jobs would have been much easier.

In his place was assigned Major General Nathanial Greene. Originally, the quartermaster of the US army, he received his new orders on 5 October 1780 and finally arrived in theater on 2 December 1780. This began a long chase by General Cornwallis that ultimately led to Yorktown, Virginia.

I won't recite the various battles we fought as they really became monotonously similar. We would chase General Greene only to catch him for a sharp battle after which he would escape and retreat further north in North Carolina and then Virginia. The pace of this forced march was horrendous, yet we could never truly catch and corner the rebels. Unfortunately, one time when we did catch them Cowpens, our noses were severely blooded. General Morgan, Colonel Tarelton's opposite, displayed excellent maneuvers such that we were sucked into an envelopment of serious consequences. We were lucky to get out with our hides. But, still we continued to press on trying to catch General Greene.

By January 1781, the chase was truly on. Cornwallis committed himself and his army to follow wherever necessary to force the decisive battle he wanted. Recognizing his logistical impedimenta was slowing him down, he ordered all unneeded baggage to be destroyed. Included in this order was his own personal gear. Such was the General's passion to move faster and quicker. Of course, this meant increasing strain on the troops as they had less with which support themselves internally. Scavenging off the land became the order of the day. Yet, we followed. If the General would sacrifice himself, then we could do no less.

This attitude of the General is perhaps more important to understand than a dull recitation of the battles we went through. Suffering always exists, and we certainly did that with our forced marches, little food, and no replacement clothing. Eventually, we began to joke about being unrecognizable from our rebel opponents.

Our ability to sustain was clearly coming from the General. He was not a backslapping person. He was also not particularly handsome being rather short and round. But, soldiers' stories soon began to show what sort of a man we were following.

He had been involved in the war from its earliest days working first under General Howe during his campaign to conquer Philadelphia: first the city and then the ladies. During these days, the General did his duty while remaining apart from the frivolity of parties and soirees. His demeanor was not driven by prudery but rather a professional concentration on completing the war and an abiding faithfulness to his wife.

As the General was toiling at his duties, his wife, as are all military wives, was left behind in Suffolk, England. Her health was generally poor, and by late 1778 was in such state that he was called home to attend her. Upon arrival, his worst fears were confirmed and he resigned his commission. This decision was surprisingly not difficult to do. Through his years of observing his superiors' feckless dithering over politics and the tenacity of the rebels, he had become convinced of the war's futility. So, it was a fine officer's resignation that was tendered.

By February 1779, his wife, Jemima, the light of his heart, died. Hardly more than two months of union with her was provided to the General. Instead, all he felt was a hole in his heart with no comfort being given in England. So, with that bleakness facing him, General Cornwallis withdrew his resignation and volunteered for America again.

By contrast, we have the sordid tale of Benedict Arnold. Although he did provide valuable service to the British, he still was a traitor to the rebel cause, and as such has found neither honor nor glory with his new army.

But, these are stories of generals. From my perspective as a common soldier, valor and steadfastness and knavery on their part was of little daily importance. Of course, I joined to kill Americans, and I did that. I can't say how many I killed or maimed, but it was more than simply William Jackson. I also can say categorically that I regret none of them. They chose their lives and I mine. We met on the field of battle to see who lived or died. I lived and they died. It was as simple as that.

However, the burning anger that impelled me into the army slowly evaporated upon Jackson's death. In its place came exhaustion. Constant pursuit of an elusive enemy interspersed with sharp conflicts; loss of comrades, destruction of dumb horses incapable of controlling their destiny all added to exhaustion. This litany does not include the living conditions we endured. Jokes alone can do justice here.

313

Of course, as a newly minted officer, I did have things to distract me. First, I needed to find the best sergeant I could to teach me the skills of leadership. Following is easy. Just do what you're told. Deciding what to tell, and how to tell it, and ensure it gets done is entirely different. This was especially so when one understands how my callow youth had to order someone ten years my senior to do a distasteful or dangerous task.

One could say, "But of course you had done these things yourself, so what's the problem?" Yes, that's true, but soldiers could also ask, "Too good to do it for yourself, mate?" Combat was the exception to this observation as I had to lead them by entering first. But, cleaning a latrine is not combat. It's grimy and stinky. Officers don't do that work, so it was important I learn the fine line between being aloof and jumping into shit. My sergeants helped me here by providing a barrier between me and the man cleaning the latrine. They taught me the fine arts of organizing mass drills that would stay faint hearts from fleeing from the hail of bullets pouring down. Our battle at Lancaster against Colonel Buford proved the value of this knowledge to me, and I wanted to impart it to newcomers coming in after me. The survival of every man under me depending on this steadfastness that comes from drilling.

So, the days flowed on like a never-ending river of time. We constantly pressed generally northward until we were in Virginia. General Arnold had been making forays up there which tended to ease our burdens as he could draw off reinforcements from joining General Greene's army. En route, on 15 March 1781, we had won a bloody victory at Guilford's Courthouse when the lack of rebel steadfastness caused their lines to collapse. This victory was soon followed by a decision to abandon it. So much blood, and for what? At this point, I began to learn what had become obvious much earlier to General Cornwallis about this war. It was a conflict torn by the politics of indecision. Pointless fatigue and death were our rewards.

Our arrival in Virginia occurred in early May. But, instead of a rest, our marches and countermarches increased. Now we had to engage the French General La Fayette who also scurried around the countryside trying to avoid a pitched battle that he couldn't win. These chases led us to Williamsburg, Virginia in the heat of August weather. At this time, after a period of confusion as to whether we would remain here or have part of us transported up north, orders came down for us to retreat to a place suitable for a defensive stand with our backs to a seaport capable of receiving large ships. The place selected was Yorktown.

Frankly, after all of our marching, reposing on this peninsula was a welcome break despite the swampy climate that hosted us. Slaves were brought in to build the bulwarks and to improve the ports. Of course, soldiers had to heave weapons into place, drill, and repair equipment. It was all boring, but it provided for regular hours, a chance for regular food, and in general rest.

Of course, the enemy was well aware of what was happening, and they bent every effort to amass an army to engage us. General Washington was joined by Generals La Fayette and Rochambeau. What was worse, their forces were joined by the French navy under Admiral DeGrasse who effectively blockaded the harbor that was to be our escape valve. No British sails were to be seen anywhere. We understood they were to be coming "any day now." But, "any day" never appeared. Even the lowest private could see what was in store for us: general siege with no hope for escape.

I won't describe the battle itself because again, it is monotonous and without point. Suffice it to say that the French, from long years of siege warfare in their history directed the battle. They gradually tightened the noose until such time as their artillery were raining cannon balls upon us from point-blank range.

The siege began on October 9, 1781 and lasted until October 19 when the end became obvious. General Cornwallis, despite obvious courage in remaining exposed to enemy fire, could no longer continue to rally his forces against the prohibitive odds offered by the enemy. Finally, he was forced to send an emissary to General Washington to ask for terms of surrender. After negotiations, they were agreed to and firing ceased.

We were ordered to evacuate the barricades, march by the enemy, and lay down our arms. As we did so, our band played, "The World Turned Upside Down." Our 8,000 soldiers were herded into a prisoners' camp in the Shenandoah Valley. Ironically, as we were being marched along, we learned that British sails indeed had arrived on scene. A bit late, I would say.

Effectively, this ended my war. I spent the next several months in the camp living under the most wretched conditions imaginable. If our forced marches were awful, these were indescribable, so other than to say that death through starvation and sickness was a daily, almost hourly occasion. For the worst of my mates, it was also welcome.

Eventually, as was the custom, we were paroled on our word not to raise arms against the rebels. This was an easy promise to make with death being our alternative. So, I was released from service after almost two years of strife.

The question now was what to do. I wasn't ready to come home immediately. My emotions were too raw from the many things I had seen and experienced. So, despite the fact that my family was alone in this terrible time, I had to send the following letter.

July 22, 1782

Dear Ma,

At last, I am free...out of the army. I'm sorry I haven't written for these past six months or so, but frankly, I had been imprisoned as a result of our losing the Battle of Yorktown. After it was done, the Americans took us to a prisoner of war camp where nothing was available to us. So, this has really been my first chance to write.

First news first. I'm all right other than having lost a lot of weight. I estimate I'm down to about 14 or 15 stones which is a lot less than when I first enlisted. But, God was with me, and miraculously, I emerged without a scratch. Such hasn't been the luck of many friends.

Right now, I'm stuck up here in the northern Virginia region called the Shenandoah Valley. Stuck is really a good word for it because I have no money, no horse, and no clothes. I say "no clothes," but I'm not naked. My body is still covered with the tatters of my uniform. However, there's a more practical reason for wanting clothes.

Civilian clothes allow me to blend into the background. Even though the war is effectively over, war-fevers are still at a high pitch, and I don't need for some hothead, who probably never served a day in the war, jumping all over me for having been a Tory. On politics, the less said, the better.

I expect I'll be needing about six months to get home. Being in the condition that I'm in, with a long distance between here and Charles Town, getting home will be a slow proposition. I'll probably have to go from town to town picking up jobs as I go along to keep myself fed. Fortunately, I grew up in a blacksmith's shop, so work shouldn't be too hard to find.

I also think I'll need the time to rid myself of the many hard experiences I've endured these last years. Whether I'll be able to do so entirely will be God's choice, but I know time is needed for me to return to myself.

This letter is a mixed blessing for you. I'm alive and reasonably well, but won't be home for some time when you need me the most. But, I've never been able to be anything but honest with you, and I'm not about to start doing otherwise now.

Meanwhile, please take the love I send to you and pass it on to everyone else. I'll try to write when and where I have an opportunity.

Your son,

Ephraim

With this letter posted, my first task was to find some work once I had gotten some clothes. Of course, since I had been a prisoner of war, I received no money from the Crown, and without penny to my name, I was really in a serious state. So, in the best tradition of soldiers in need, my best action was to do a midnight requisition and then scamper quickly from town, which I promptly did.

The Shenandoah Valley is a long north-south highway that I tended to follow. Towns were reasonably close so that I could find work. Farm houses were likewise located near my route of travel which also provided some work as well places to bed down. Generally, most farmers were glad to provide at least a night's shelter and perhaps a meal. I tried to repay their hospitality by working at odd jobs, but often times none was accepted.

My biggest concern was to be non-committal about my war experience. If the subject came up, and it generally did, I indicated my service was a long way from "here." Then, I would try to coax the other person's leanings about the war. If they were rebel, I said as little as possible; if Tory, then perhaps I would open up a bit. Obviously, I didn't want to indicate a persuasion opposite that of my hosts.

Actually, I got to be pretty clever at this dodge. Once though, I met an old fellow who seemed to be rather garrulous but who actually was just trying to pry my intentions from me. Relaxing a shade too much, he guessed I was a Tory, and worse, his son had been killed in a battle with the Legion. I instantly became no friend of his, and only by the grace of God and his need to step outside the room to get his gun was I able to leap through a window and hightail it down the road. It was a long, cold, rainy night for me.

But often I actually chose to remain out of doors through the night. When the weather was warm and dry, I found comfort in lying under the trees listening to the hooting of the owls. After all the foul contact I had had with people over the past several years, I needed time to be alone where I could re-order my thoughts.

I'm not sure what my thoughts were then. They tended to ramble. When sleeping, dreams would flash in my mind. Often I was killing Jackson. Other times, I was holding a friend who had just died. Amazingly enough, I could see him as clearly as the sun at noon, but I couldn't remember his name. Occasionally, I would dream of marching endlessly from nowhere to nowhere. Perhaps that last dream reflected reality more than any of them because chasing Greene was a constant part of my life. The worst dreams resulted in my awaking in a sweat. They were so real I honestly didn't know whether I was awake from a dream or dreaming I was wakening. A few seconds were always needed to determine what was real.

As the nights passed over the weeks, these dreams became less frequent. However, to this day, there are sounds and smells that are instantly recognizable. Reactions too became so ingrained they never leave. I remember one day when I was walking under a heavy canopy of leaves. The sky was completely obscured making me unaware of gathering clouds. Only the heavy air gave any hint of a storm, and I was so engrossed in my walking I gave it no mind until a really loud clap boomed over my head. Pure reaction drove me under cover while my mind was saying, "Relax, Ephraim, it's only thunder!" My body agreed rationally, but still it was not taking chances. It only relaxed when I was safely hidden under leaves by a huge protective tree. After calming my heart down and peering out from under the leaves, I laughed at what must have looked totally ridiculous.

Recently, I smelled pepsin which is not an odor I have encountered often in the last thirty years. Without thinking about it, I wondered who died. Bodies left in the sun for more than a day begin to decay emitting a distinct pepsin odor.

But again, as I said, the horrors began to recede as the miles passed under my feet. I left Virginia and crossed deeply into the Carolinas. By now I was starting to head southeast in what I thought would be the general direction of the coast and Charles Town. Each farmer I passed would direct me to my next guidepost. As I continued to press east, the roads actually began to improve. At least they began to resemble roads instead of mere cattle trails.

As I began to arrive in South Carolina, the hills were becoming flatter and more in keeping the Piedmonts I had known early in my military career. By chance, I stopped in a farm that clearly had seen the effects of war's destruction. The barn was being repaired over charred timbers. Fence lines were still in disarray which allowed cattle to wander at will. The house was a simple log structure that had been constructed to meet problems of the day.

Stopping in, I asked if I could stay for the night. "I'll be glad to work off my keep, and from what I see here, a good hand would be helpful."

The farmer raised his tired eyes, and looked me over. "What can you do to earn your keep?"

"Actually, quite a lot. My father was a blacksmith, and I learned from him. This means I can do all sorts of mechanical work around here. It also means I can use an axe well enough to shape small timbers into fence lines. Finally, I'm not afraid of work."

"You a returning soldier going home?"

"Yessir."

"And where might that be?"

"Charles Town."

"You don't say! I lived there once before coming out here some fifteen years ago. You be the first man in a long time coming from there. Let me call my wife and let her know you're here."

"Well," I thought, "I have a place for the night."

The farmer came out with a tired wife who had clearly spent too many years working far too hard.

"Sundru, I'd like to have you meet this man. He says he's from Charles Town. What might be your name?"

"Ephraim, sir. Ma'am, it's a pleasure to make your acquaintance."

Her eyes instantly lit up. "Ephraim...and who might your parents be, young man?"

"My mother was Wyanne and my father was William...William Malone."

"Was your mother's maiden name Farrell?"

"That it was Ma'am. Did you know her?"

By now, the wife was beginning to cry. "Know her? I was present when you were born. I was Sundru Smith until I married and came out here."

Turning to her husband, she straightened up and asked sharply, "James, what are we standing here for? Now take Mr. Ephraim out back and let him have a chance to clean up. He also looks like he could use a change of clothing. You might consider burning those he has on. Then, let's come in and have dinner. Mr. Ephraim can meet the kids then as well."

I stayed here through the winter. I had not particularly hurried and the way had been long. I also was tired. Dog-tired would have been a better word for things, and I truly needed time to recover from all my exertions through the past year.

As I had indicated, there was lots of work to be done, which combined with the constant feeding I got gave me an opportunity to recover. The work distracted my mind from my dreams. The meals fed my starving body as it had forgotten how to do. My weight began to return along with my endurance for continuous work. It felt good to work.

The evenings were spent talking about the good times. Of course I had to introduce all of the children born after Sundru and James' departure. They were both interested deeply in how my brothers and sisters were doing. As the evenings wore on, I began to relax within myself and found it ever easier to talk about what had been bottled inside me for so long.

"Yes, the war was hard. It divided my family. My father joined the American army while I enlisted in the King's forces."

"That must have been terrible on your mother seeing ..."

"Yes, exactly that. Seeing her life's work being destroyed from under her feet almost killed her."

"I remember how proud she was of what all she had accomplished with her business and William's smithy. Then, when you were born, Wyanne just glowed."

"And this glow continued well into the 1770's as the children were born and their businesses continued to prosper. Clearly, both my mother and father were anticipating a gentle old age together, but such was not to come."

From there, our talks coaxed the story of my parents' divide over the war and their eventual split with Pa's joining the rebel army. From there, I talked about how I came to join the British army. Through it all was Ma's anguish over the stupidity of the war in general.

"Yes, taxes were onerous, but to fight over them? That, my ma could never understand."

In turn, Sundru and John talked about their lives. They had always been hard. Sundru's, early life of course, I had known from what my mother had told of her life. John had grown up on a hard-scrabble farm, but had loved the life. So, when he had the opportunity, he left Charles Town and headed west to stake a farm of his own. Sundru followed him.

Their lives were difficult in this western region. Simply surviving off the land was a challenge, but added to that was the constant threat from Indians. Even though they were declining in numbers as the white settlers forced them to move deeper into the forests, marauders would still go on raids. One of their children was actually kidnapped, and they had never seen her since. She presumably had since become an Indian with only vague memories of her parents.

The war, however, was even more destructive.

John explained, "We really had no truck with either side. Out here, government really don't mean much. No one came to collect taxes; elections were not held and we didn't send no one to the legislature. Although we were part of the Carolina territories, we in fact didn't belong to no one."

Sundru continued, "This being the case, we were free and wanted nothing else. However, as the war clouds built, neighbors did start becoming concerned. Some wanted to join the rebel cause and others remain with the Crown."

"Outsiders also began to come in and agitate people. These outsiders was really outlaws as far as we was concerned. Unfortunately, the effects of the war raised tempers to the boiling point and shots was fired back and forth. Raids became commonplace forcing us to defend ourselves as best we could. Sometimes we could lie successfully and convince the raiders we were on "their side." But, as you saw when you first arrived, we wasn't always successful. We lost a second daughter during this last raid."

I do believe my arrival here and spending the winter with the Adams was directed by the hand of Almighty. I often do not understand the events of life. Certainly, the attack by Jackson on my innocent sister Sarah is beyond comprehension. But, this crossing of our lives was truly a blessing.

Our long winter evenings came after rewarding days of labor spent repairing the damage done by the raiders. The remaining two children would be put to bed leaving the house quiet for a pipe and a glass of homemade whiskey. Conversation would start flowing often with funny memories. Sundru had lots of them as she recalled her early days with my mother.

"Your mother, bless her soul, was a fanatic about cleanliness. I couldn't believe she wanted me to bathe once a week. How I would grumble, and every time, she'd say, 'What was that, young lady?' And her only being a couple of years older than me! Talking to me like a mother."

In turn, I'd talk about fights we kids had amongst ourselves over what seemed to be monumental problems…such as who got the last piece of bread for breakfast.

From there, like onion skins being peeled back, we'd go into the more painful memories of our lives. Memories of Sarah and retribution, Jackson's last moments, Indians kidnapping a daughter or raiders killing another. With each retelling, a sense of release would come that brought a greater sense of peace.

Finally, Spring broke the winter's ice. March and early April were still too wet for me to start my last walk home. Besides, the spring crops needed to be laid in, and after all I had eaten during the winter, sowing a replacement was only proper. By late April, however, we all knew the time for my departure had arrived.

Sundru came to me as I was packing my last few items with a request.

"I know your Ma taught me how to read and write, but honestly, it's been too many years since I did either of them. I'm afraid to try now, and I want to send a letter home to her."

"I'm sure you could do fine," I reassured her.

"No, I'd rather you wrote it as I tell you. Having to worry about writing while thinking about what to say will only confuse me."

"Sure, I'd be glad to. Let's get some paper and a pen. I know you have some paper, and I can make a pen if need be."

In fact, I had to use an old bed sheet and make a quill pen. But, a letter is a letter, and here it is.

Dear Mis' Sundru,   3 April '83

By the grace of God, you sent one last gift to me in the form of your beloved son, Ephraim. We had just suffered the loss of our daughter, Josie, from the hands of rebel raiders while they were burning out our farm. Like you, we had not wanted any part of the war, and these zealots were determined for us to pay for it.

Needless to say, we were devastated. All of the years of labor building a home in this wilderness where the Indians tracked were destroyed in a matter of

322

minutes. Incidentally, we had lost another daughter when she was kidnapped by a roving band of Creeks. But, I could understand that in a way. We did enter their land and take it for our own purposes; so, perhaps they wanted our daughter in repayment. However, for one white man to destroy the home of another over something like politics thousands of miles away is incomprehensible. Ephraim's arrival, with his tragic tales of your family, let us know we were not alone. Others had suffered as well and perhaps worse that we did.

God also lent him to us as a fresh spirit of energy. During the winter, he and John were able to restore most of our farm to a good workable condition. Ephraim also provided us with the strength to lay in a new crop that will sustain us into the coming seasons.

Ephraim will be able to tell you more about our lives when he gets home, so I won't try to repeat them all here. Rather it is more important to tell you once again, how I have loved you through all of these years. The memory of your face will be with me always.

Your dirty little Irish girl,

Sundru

Folding this letter into my pack, I took my leave giving Sundru, John and their two children long hugs.

"Thank you all for taking me. I was truly a lost soul when I came upon your farm."

"The thanks are all ours. You were God's gift to us."

"We'll try to write letting you know I got home safely and to have my mother send her love to you."

With these words, I started down the last long road to Charles Town. The Adams remained waving until I turned the last corner when I was on my own again.

The trip home lasted for about a month, perhaps six weeks. In some respects, it wasn't much different from my earlier legs in being careful with passers-by and farmers as to which side I had fought on, finding enough work to repay meals and lodging, and so on. However, a difference strongly existed now. I wanted to go home. My impatience for being there grew with each passing day and mile.

Finally, I reached Charles Town in late May. The British had long since left. Peace had been formally declared with a preliminary treaty having been signed. How strange to see the streets once so familiar to me. So much had passed and so many months had flown by, and yet, they were past...gone. In turn, I had become a stranger. Amazingly enough, as I turned onto King Street, I wondered if I would even know my own family, or whether they would know me.

Finally, a last turn up to the door where I was born. A tremulous knock. Waiting...wondering. The door opened.

"Ephraim. You're home! May God be praised."

CHAPTER THIRTY-ONE

Here was Ma's reaction to seeing me in the doorway.

"When I saw Ephraim standing there at the door like a bum asking for a meal, I thought my knees would buckle underneath me. I grabbed him and hugged him till I thought I'd squeeze the life out of him. My next thing was to say a prayer to God for bringing him home safely. "

"Kids! Come here now! Ephraim's home!"

"Sarah and Vianna came around the door and immediately pushed me aside to give their big brother a hug. Walter, surprisingly, hung back. I suppose for someone his age, Ephraim's time away was a long time in his life."

"Well, Walter, don't just stand there, give your brother a hug, and then run off and tell David Ephraim has returned."

"With this hubbub, life immediately stopped for the day. Ephraim was not get a moment's peace until he had answered questions, hugged everyone again, and ate like a trencherman."

"Of course we all wanted to know what had happened to him during these past several years. Of funny times in the army, he had plenty of stories. His mates of all types were sources of many tales."

"Then of course, he gave me Sundru's letter. "

"'My God, she's still alive? After all of these years!' As I read her letter, I cried as I hadn't since William's departure. But, these were tears of joy. To know she was still alive was a gift from heaven.

"Of course, I wanted to know all about her, and Ephraim told me all the details as he had learned them during his winter's stay. His news about the death of their daughters again brought tears."

"Ma," Ephraim told me gently, "I think you might want to write a letter to her. I know she can still read even after all these years, and she would love to hear from you. Hearing from you will bring joy to her, and if your experience was anything like mine, it'll become a solace for you."

"With that, Ephraim told me about the long winter evenings he had spent with Sundru and John retelling stories. He still didn't account his war experiences; they were done and past never to be resurrected again. But, sharing them with the Adams brought a sense of peace to him.

"Of course, I promised to write to them, and I have kept that promise. But, it didn't bring the peace that Ephraim suggested. I could only do that by writing to Susannah.

"Along the way, Ephraim took Sarah aside to tell her that Jackson was indeed dead never to be a source of dread again. In turn, Sarah began to cry to know she was to be able live again. Unfortunately, despite knowing her ghost was dead, she never really did become the little girl she once was. Instead, she would always remain pensive and fearful of leaving the house. Occasionally, someone would come by to call on her, but she was never to marry. This has been a source of constant sorrow for me.

"One thing, even in private with me, he would never talk about was his experiences in battle. When asked, he would only reply, 'I survived which is more than I can say about many friends.' About the rebels he faced, again, 'I don't know who they were, nor did they know anything of me.'

"But, survive he did. But come through unscathed? That's another question. That first night I boiled a big tub of water for his bath and as he got in I could see his physical scars. He had a saber slash on his right calf. A raw, red welt ran along his ribs. I had missed it at first, but the top of his left ear was gone, and behind it was a hairline scar hidden by his hair.

"As I contemplated these wounds that could be seen, I wondered what scars he held within him. Certainly they were there, but other than to relate what he had told me about the Adams, I could only guess how bad they were. But as time would pass, I could see they were apparently healing. Only on occasion would he shout while asleep while reliving a deeply buried battle. But, even these events became less frequent.

"The only exception to this rule of silence was the rare time when Ephraim met with an old mate from Tarelton's Legion. Then, he would go out to a tavern and not return until late at night. He wasn't drunk, but he had clearly had had enough. Some mornings, his eyes would be red, but I knew it wasn't from his drink.

"In sum, Ephraim had come home. He was truly a man, mature in physique and stature, calm in demeanor, and one not to be trifled with. He was home and that was enough."

CHAPTER THIRTY-TWO

When you haven't seen someone for a long time, things change. They aren't the same person you remembered. This was true of Ma and the kids.

It had been about three years since I had last seen her while dashing out of town. Now, a different woman was standing before me at the door. She was clearly showing some age. It seemed only yesterday when I thought of her as being sprightly with red hair. Instead, Ma had thickened a bit. Her figure was not that of a younger woman, but rather middle-aged. Perched on her nose was a pair of glasses she wore as a permanent fixture for both near and far seeing. They were called bifocals and were an invention created by William Franklin. At least he did one good thing in his life. On top of her glasses was a frame of graying hair. The redness was almost gone now.

However, one important feature hadn't disappeared. Despite all of the trials she had endured these last ten years, it was clearly obvious Ma was as strong-willed as ever. Nothing was going to get her down. Somehow, she'd find a way to pick up pieces and carry on.

The kids were all adults now. They had all finished their formal schooling as far as each was concerned. Sarah had seemingly come back from her terrible experience, but it was only later that I recognized how deeply her scars had cut into her soul. Vianna was now twenty-one, and fully an adult working with her mother going out into the community to sell sewing services and materials. I also learned very quickly she was engaged to a certain Jacob Adams. She had met him while he was doing some carpentry work in the black smithy for David. David had matured quickly. Directing his father's business immediately after Pa had enlisted does that to a young boy. Now, he was a skilled tradesman showing the signs of his work. His hands were as hard as iron and covered with scars left by countless shards of iron and burns from sparks. Finally, there was Walter. He was currently apprenticed as a bank teller at the Farmers and Mechanics bank where Ma had first started her business. Of course, by his choosing this line of work, he could help Ma and David whenever they needed financial assistance.

The house seemed to be pretty much the same except for the disappearance of Abby.

"She disappeared shortly after the British arrived," Ma explained. "It seems they were trying to ruin the plantation owners by offering slaves their freedom if they ran away and joined them. Well, Abby and her man believed that, and ran away."

327

Here then became an example of Ma's character. "I suppose I really can't blame them for taking a chance at freedom. I remember how I was bonded to the Draytons with very little control over my destiny. Of course, I did have a contract which promised an end to my servitude. But still…I can imagine how they felt."

Continuing on, "I really don't know what became of her. As the British left, they left a lot of blackies behind where they were recaptured by their former owners. Fortunately, I have a couple of other slaves who can do a lot of basic sewing for me because business has not been entirely bad."

CHAPTER THIRTY-THREE

The rest of 1783 quickly slid by and thereafter 1784. I settled into a daily routine of practicing law while the rest of the family pretty much did what they had been doing prior to my return home.

I actually spent a fair amount of time advising former Tory families as to their rights under the new laws of South Carolina. Of course, my own past was well known amongst the community, and the rebels were less likely to hire my services.

Of particular virulence was the attitude of many so-called "patriots" who had never served in any army. They would salute the flag, spit on the name of King George, and praise George Washington. Yet, when asked what they did, generally they tended their daily business.

"But, I supported the cause with my prayers every day."

I often wondered whether God added these prayers to His Golden Book when compared to the sacrifices made by thousands of young men and wives, who with their children were camp-followers through the terrible storms of the war's years. I never had much sympathy for rebel soldiers when I was a Legionnaire, but suffering is suffering, and I don't want anyone to go through what we did.

Most of these clients had had their lands confiscated and naturally wanted them returned. Often, widows requested the legislature to provide pensions as promised by law to all whose husbands served in the American army. Among them of course was Ma.

She had started first making an application at the local offices in Charleston as it became known. "Charles Town" now smacked too much of the King, and was no longer an acceptable pronunciation.

Anyway, from all the years of living in Charleston, Ma was well known by the clerks for whose wives she had undoubtedly sewn dresses. Here is a retelling of an occasion she had with the State clerk:

"Mrs. Malone, what can I do for you?"

"I've come to apply for my husband's pension, thank you."

"H'mmm. Well, you didn't support the patriots cause much did you? I know you sold lots of merchandise to the British when they were in town."

"Well, of course I did. I had a business to run that fed me, my children, and my slaves. Would you have me do something else?"

"Of course I never did sell anything to them."

"That's easy for you to say. You never sold anything, but rather clerked behind this desk."

"Are you claiming I wasn't a patriot?"

"Mr. Phillips. I remember when you came here twenty-five years ago...about the same time I did. We were both looking for something different. You found yours here behind this desk, and I found mine in a shop. We both did what we had to do to survive and take care of our families. So, patriotism has nothing to do with my being here."

"Why then, are you here?"

"Mr. Phillips, you know as well as I do that my husband served under General Washington and died while performing honorable service. His departure created severe hardships for me and my young children. So, now I want what the law has promised."

"Mrs. Malone, I also clearly know your son, Ephraim served that horrible monster, Lt. Colonel Tarleton, and I am not at all going to provide you with the satisfaction of collecting money from our government. God Bless America Ma'am!"

"That's your final word then is it?"

"It is. And if you will excuse me..."

"Yes, I'll do that with pleasure rather than waste time on a fat man who sent the sons of other mothers to war while yours stayed safely home. Good day."

As Ma said afterwards, "This is just typical of the reactions I get lately. Actually, not lately, it's a trend brewing for a number of years. This doesn't only have to do with your being a Legionnaire. Just in general...I don't know. When I was younger, just starting out, I went to the bank, opened an account, rented this building, made contracts with customers...Just everything to do with business. Now, I don't know...It isn't the same."

I replied, "Is it just that? Or does my being a loyalist have any to do with things?"

"Well, that too. But, I just got the feeling from that fat oaf, he wouldn't have wanted to see me anyway. Then you just gave him added cause to be snotty."

Continuing on, "But, those idiots in the tax office certainly take my tax money. If I were to not pay them, they'd throw me in jail in a heartbeat. But, otherwise, they treat us as if we didn't have a brain."

Then, sitting back and laughing, "Enough of this, how was your day with the idiots?"

This question became the attitude Ma displayed as time passed by. Actually, it may have developed even before I got home, but it certainly became more pronounced as time went on.

"Ephraim, I hate to bother you, but I need your help again."

"What is it now with the idiots?"

"Oh, it isn't a big thing, but I need you to countersign a small contract I'm making with a customer. I've only been in business for years, and now this…"

"OK. Let's just get on with things. Not to worry."

"Yeah, but it's getting so a woman just can't handle property anymore. I heard of a case in North Carolina where a husband could not give back property to his wife."

And so it went on. Little things that continued to creep into our daily lives. Because I was still recognized as a lawyer, and as a man, I could intercede to get by the individual problems. But, each one tended to make Ma just a little more bitter. She'd begin reminiscing about what life was like in the "good old days."

"Can you imagine it? I came over as a girl, engaged in a bonded contract and worked through it until I had completed terms to the satisfaction of the Judge?"

And another day, "Life was so free in those days. Even when I was indentured, I felt free to look forward to my own life such as never would have been possible in the Old Country."

But, life did continue on. David continued to do fairly well. The sewing business was struggling by. The clients Ma had once had not recovered entirely from the War, and she was clearly and often reminded of what I had done.

331

Of course, Vienne's wedding to Jacob in March was simply lovely. Her wedding dress was simply stunning. All of Ma's fancy needle work was used to create a floating flower of white. Actually, it's become a tradition now for the girls in our family to wear it.

Sarah, of course was the bride's maid. I just wished she could have been a bride's matron. But, still she shunned all contact with men.

The wedding was very simple. We had it in the Presbyterian church at noon, just after Sunday morning services. The men in the shop were all there as well as Ma's slaves. Of course, they had to set up in the loft, but they had to be there. Vienne would not have heard of anything else. We also had invited the children of Susannah, but they weren't able to make the ceremony. The distance was just too far, and frankly, many of them didn't really remember us.

But, Ma wanted to invite them anyway. Maybe she was hoping she could somehow bring Susannah back. I know Ma kept every letter from her, and would often re-read them in the evenings. Often, after having done so, she'd begin remembering the days of her youth at the Drayton plantation.

The party afterward was held in the open court yard in front of the smithy. Of course, David had curried the horses and shined his best carriage for the wedding march from the church. Neighbors did stop and watch us go by, and some of them would doff their hats in recognition of proud couple. Fortunately, the weather that day was glorious. The sun came out with just enough heat for us to enjoy being outdoors.

The party continued on until fairly late at night. Punch and beer was provided for all who came. Speeches were given, and the couple was toasted at length. Of course, they were teased into giving lots of kisses to one another.

Finally, it was time for Vienne and Jacob to offer their thanks. Vienne being outspoken as opposed to Jacob's natural shyness led off.

"I just wanted to thank all of you for coming. This is the biggest day of my life. The Lord must have been smiling on me when Jacob came into my father's smithy and asked to be apprenticed to him. I came in just a couple of hours later, and saw him and thought he was the homeliest boy I had ever seen. My father didn't think much of him either. So slight of bone and muscle. Of course, David had to lord things over him because his advanced age and experience. He was all of three months older! But, he stuck with us, and now David, you're stuck with him. So what are you going to do with him?"

David just blushed, got up, and gave both of them a hug. He then led a toast.

"Here's to a wonderful couple. Actually, Jacob, Vienne told me that night you were the boy she was going to marry. So, don't believe everything she says to you other than reply 'Oh yes, ma'am.' But, really, may your lives be fulfilled with love and happiness."

Finally, it Jacob's turn.

"Well, h'mmm. I'm not sure… Is it too late to reconsider? One says I was homely and the other says I was the dream boy. What's a person to do? But, after thinking it over for all of a second, I'm more convinced than ever Vienne is the wife for me. So come here woman, and give your husband a kiss!"

Lots of clapping and hoorahs followed the speeches along with a couple of gallons of punch. Finally, Vienne and Jacob went to the loft of Ma's house. Of course, that didn't finish things with us. We waited for a decent interval when the couple would be certain to be in bed and then followed them for a chivaree.

Neighbors don't always like chivarees, so you must be certain to invite them to the party because they become very loud. Pots and pans are banged. Bells are rung. Horns are tooted, and bawdy remarks would comment on what was happening inside. Our chivarees didn't go on too long, but they have been known to go on all night depending on how much whiskey had been drunk.

The next morning though, Jacob came down a little sleepy and with a shy smile. Vienne was just as happy as if she had good sense. And that was the wedding. Ma didn't have enough money to send the young couple off to Savannah for a honeymoon, but Vienne in particular didn't seem to care. She had her man, and that was enough for her.

Shortly afterwards, Ma and I started to work on getting the pension promised to veterans of the War.

"Of course I should get it. William enlisted in the army and served until he died. Widows were entitled to them by South Carolina law in 1785.

"Yeah, Ma, but don't forget who your son served under. This will probably be held against you."

"You're right Ephraim, but unless we try, we'll get nothing."

So, in July 1785, we submitted a petition to the assembly. Amazingly enough, women here had to plead their own cases. Lawyers did not usually write them other than to transcribe what was said to them in the cases of illiterate women. Here is Ma's petition:

The 15th Day of July, in the year of our Lord, 1785

The following is a humble petition from the hand of Mrs. William Malone, born Wyanne Farrell.

This widow was married to a blacksmith who had voluntarily enlisted in the army of the American forces in 1781. He served in this capacity until his death from unknown causes in the wilderness of North Carolina. During this time, his service was entirely honorable.

The result of William's death meant a loss of needed income for the Malone family. Upon his departure into the army, his blacksmith shop fell into disrepair as only my young apprentice son remained to continue working. Of course, his skills were not the same as his master, and consequently, business suffered. Only William's income as a soldier could supplement the needs of myself and my four young children. Certainly, those were extremely difficult times.

Now, by the grace of God and the wisdom of South Carolina's legislators, relief is being offered to all widows in such dire consequences. Among them is me who still has two young children. So, it is with humble gratitude that you receive my petition and with prayers to the All Mighty you see fit to grant it.

Wyanne Malone

We waited three months until cooler Fall weather prompted the legislature to be reconvened. Meanwhile, Ma continued to fret about what all had become of her as a result of the war, changing times, and things in general. But, then a change occurred.

"Ephraim, I'm beginning to wonder if it's not time for us to leave."

"Ma, what're you talking about? What do you mean?"

"Well, as you know, a lot of loyalists left immediately with the British. I thought differently at that time. I came here as a girl, grew up, and settled. To leave seemed almost daft...But now, I'm beginning to wonder."

"I know things have been hard, but to leave?"

"Yes, as strange as it may seem. But, truthfully, things aren't the same with us. Our businesses are not going very well. I don't feel as happy personally. I can't do the things I once did as a matter of course."

A long pause followed by some sighs by both of us.

"Want some more tea, Ma?"

"Please, I can never get used to this new drink, coffee. Everyone stopped drinking tea in protest to taxes, but people have to drink something don't they? And tea is the only proper drink. This coffee is awful."

"But, moving on? As a girl, you had nothing to lose or leave. Now, we actually have a lot, not to mention the fact that Vienne is expecting a baby."

"Yes, you're right. And you know, in many ways, nothing has really changed since the war other than getting rid of the King. So, if I had joined the rebel cause, I might not have lost your father as I did, and many of the social problems we're having today would not exist."

Continuing, "But, if all this remains the same, then why did we fight? Doesn't make sense to me. All I ever wanted was to be left alone, be free to run my life as I see fit, and get on with things. Life in Charleston offered me all this, and I saw no reason for a change."

"More tea, Ma?"

"H'mmm? No, no thanks. If I have any more, I'll just have to use the thunder mug. But, I guess this is all water under the bridge. I did what I thought was right, and nothing is going to change. It'll never bring your Pa back or undo the arguments we had or the crying at night."

"But where would we go?"

"That's a good question. Britain is out of the question. I left there thirty years ago, and I'll never return."

"Nova Scotia?"

"I know lots of people who've gone there, but no, that's too cold. I remember many's the time in Ireland wakening with my breath frosting in the air. No, Nova Scotia is too cold for me."

"The Caribbean then?"

"That's really about all that's left then, isn't it? And I don't know a thing about it other than sugar comes from there."

"Ah well, let's not worry about it tonight. I'm really tired."

And so, time plodded by. We really didn't do much other than to wonder about the progress of Ma's petition. Occasionally, Ma would revisit this discussion, but again, nothing came of it. Finally, an official looking envelope was delivered to our house.

October 2, 1785

Reference: Petition for Pension submitted by Mrs. Wyanne Malone, July 15, 1785

Dear Mistress Malone;

Your petition was received and reviewed by the assembly of South Carolina, and after due deliberation by all assembled, it was decided your requests were insufficient to warrant acceptance. Therefore, in light of the above mentioned decision, no pension is not now, nor will be granted or considered for such dispensation.

With Respect,

Jonathon W. Smythe
State Assembly Recorder

Ma's response was explosive.

"Well, that cuts it. Ephraim, call the children together. I've decided what I'm going to do. I'm leaving Charleston and going to the Bahamas."

With an order like that, we knew business for the day was done. So, we all gathered in our kitchen to decide what to do next.

Ma led off, "I've had it. I've watched what has happened to our family over these past ten years, and it's not been good. I lost your father to a silly revolution that accomplished absolutely nothing. I almost lost your brother to the war. Look at his ear, and you'll know once again how close he came to meeting his Maker. Our business has been in a steady decline as once good customers now refuse to have anything to do with us because I didn't support the rebel cause. Finally, I just don't like the idiocy that greets me every day. By God, I built this business, and I'll be damned if some pompous, self-righteous twerp half my age tell me what I can or cannot do. And, the last straw has arrived in the mail. I'm leaving."

With that, she passed her letter around.

To say we were surprised is a mild understatement. Speechless is probably more like it. Perhaps because we had talked about moving through our various conversations, I was the least pulsed of anyone. Still, the suddenness of Ma's decision almost bowled me over.

Vienne was the first to speak. "Ma, what...what is happening in the assembly is awful. But to leave?"

"Young lady, if you and Jacob want to stay, that's your decision. You're married and an adult so choose for yourselves. But, to repeat, I'm leaving."

Sarah remained mute. As always, or perhaps more so, she remained passively quiet as if nothing was to touch her again. Finally, in a small voice, "I'll follow you Ma. There is nothing here for me. If I never saw Charleston again, I'd be just as happy."

"That's another reason to leave. Ephraim, if you ever did anything right, it was to rid the world of the Jacksons. I just hope they all suffered terribly as they died. Afterwards, if the Good Lord forgives them, that's His business. But, as for me, damn their eyes."

Vienne then pressed on. "Where will we be going? This isn't like moving to a new house down the street?"

"Bermuda, but don't press me further than that. I expect we'll have to travel south to Florida where the British are still in control. Once there, we'll decide what to do next. Sorry I'm so vague, but I've been thinking about moving for many months...oh I don't know, perhaps years, and now I'm leaving. God will provide, and what He will give us will be better than this."

337

Jacob then interceded, "H'mmm. I'm just married into this family, and I really don't know what to say. But, Ma, I've known since I first met you how unhappy you've been. So, I can't say you're wrong. But, honestly, Vienne and I have got to do some praying on this. Particularly now that we're expecting a baby."

"Jacob, as I said, you two are adults, and I can't say you're wrong. In fact, you'd be fools if you didn't think about this decision because I have to expect this journey will be hard. Mothers die under the best of circumstances and going on this one would be possibly the worst of circumstances."

Walter then raised his voice. "Ma, I don't want to disappoint you, but I can't go."

"Very well then."

"But, let me explain. First, I'm about finished with my apprenticeship and have made a lot of valuable contacts here that I don't want to give up. Second, whether you want to think about it or not, you need me here to represent your interests. Your business here is something of value that can be sold advantageously to support you in your new life."

"Again, as I said, you're all adults, and each of you must do what you deem best. Remember, this is my decision, and I love you all with my heart, and I will always love you with respect to the last breath in my body. That's the way I raised each of you, and expect nothing less than your honesty and love in return."

David said nothing. His business had been less affected than Ma's, and he had his entire life in front of him. So, like Jacob, he wanted time to think.

For me, it was easy. My hatred of Americans had cooled since Jackson's death, but I still didn't like them. I had seen their hypocrisy, felt their animosity and heard their whispers behind my back as long as I desired. So, Ma's decision became mine. I had thrown my lot in with the British years ago, and with them I'd stay.

Of course, putting a decision like this takes time. Ma had to finish her outstanding orders. She had made commitments to her customers, and a commitment made is a commitment kept. She had always been very firm on that point.

"My brother Kevin almost destroyed my name even before I got to America, and I had to work many years to restore our family name to its rightful place," was an adage she pounded into our heads.

We also had to decide what to take and to dispose of. Some of the latter treasures brought laughs and tears as memories flooded into our hearts. Ma also talked to other loyalists who were making similar decisions and compared lists of what would be needed. Finally, through David, we bought a stout wagon into which we loaded our goods.

Vienne and Jacob eventually decided they would be coming afterwards when the baby was born and grown enough to endure the travels. Their decision also provided the rest of us time to establish a proper home for them upon their arrival. Again, with the baby, coming to an established home was important. As a result, they did not arrive until 1788.

Likewise, David remained behind until his sister and brother-in-law were ready to travel. His smithy provided enough income for the three of them until they were ready to leave. At that point, he sold his business with Walter acting as his agent.

Walter, true to his word, and as he predicted, was sorely needed to represent our interests here in South Carolina. Ma and we started some exporting of goods from our new town which we would call Hope Town.

Our trip to Florida took about two months until we reached St. Augustine. Roads were extremely primitive as we proceeded south and often we were unable to travel further than five or ten miles in a single day.

Upon our arrival, we lodged ourselves in a local hotel until we were able to contact the local magistrate and re-establish our loyalty to the King, make contacts about settling in the Bahamas, and arrange for berthage. Again, this process took several weeks until we boarded a small bark for our final voyage.

Our lives in Hope Town are the subject of other family tales. But, for now, as Ma said, "I came here many years ago, and generally, America was good to me. I got chances my parents never got. So, let us not be bitter, but rather go towards Hope.

The End

339

Made in United States
Orlando, FL
27 April 2023